dream life

ALSO BY LAUREN MECHLING

Dream Girl

Lauren Mechling

dream
life

{delacorte press}

Copyright © 2010 by Lauren Mechling

All rights reserved. Published in the United States by Delacorte Press, an imprint of Random House Children's Books, a division of Random House, Inc., New York.

Delacorte Press is a registered trademark and the colophon is a trademark of Random House, Inc.

Visit us on the Web! www.randomhouse.com/teens

Educators and librarians, for a variety of teaching tools, visit us at www.randomhouse.com/teachers

Library of Congress Cataloging-in-Publication Data
Mechling, Lauren.
Dream life / Lauren Mechling. — 1st ed.
p. cm.
Summary: Claire Voyante's dreams lead her to investigate the New York secret society that her best friend is being initiated into, while at the same time she tries to keep her own psychic powers a secret.
ISBN 978-0-385-73523-0 (hc) — ISBN 978-0-385-90511-4 (glb) — ISBN 978-0-375-89382-7 (e-book) [1. Secret societies—Fiction. 2. Dreams—Fiction. 3. Psychic ability—Fiction. 4. Social classes—Fiction. 5. Interpersonal relations—Fiction. 6. New York (N.Y.)—Fiction. 7. Mystery and detective stories.] I. Title.
PZ7.M51269Dre 2010
[Fic]—dc22
2009012697

The text of this book is set in 12-point Joanna MT.

Book design by Angela Carlino

Printed in the United States of America

10 9 8 7 6 5 4 3 2 1

First Edition

for Rhea Jack and Una McKnight, *my* Kikis

You could say I was running behind schedule, though that would be putting an optimistic spin on it. I wasn't running anywhere at all. More like barely moving. Only one of the cash registers was manned, and when the same bubblegum song about stolen heartbeats piped through the store's loudspeakers for the second time, I still wasn't within ten people of the cashier.

I'd left my apartment with plenty of time to make it to my dinner plans, but I hadn't factored in an en-route wardrobe meltdown. Back home, my outfit—a pale blue smock dress worn over white lace tights—had seemed an inspired choice. That was before I'd started buzzing toward the subway station and replaying my conversation with Becca in my head. She'd said, "We'll be sitting in the back," hadn't she? Not "I'll," but "we'll." And considering I was Becca's only friend in NewYork, the mystery third party had to be her brother. Her very cute brother. Her very cute brother with whom I'd gone on two dates and with whom I wasn't exactly sure where I stood. I checked out my reflection in a store window and tried to see myself from Andy's point of view. And that's when it hit me. I looked like a kindergartner who harbored fantasies of joining the Ice Capades. What had I been thinking? The white tights had to go.

The H&M on lower Broadway was crawling with other girls who'd realized at the last minute they needed to trade in their lackluster Saturday-night outfits for something better. People were clawing at whatever merchandise remained on the racks. One girl was climbing onto a platform to rip a faux-fur-lined hoodie off one of the mannequins.

I was still waiting to pay for the black tights that were an exact replica of the ones I'd already tried on and rejected back home when somebody's shopping basket thwacked into my side. I turned to glare at the culprit, but a sign over by the lingerie section stole my attention.

The banner for the "P.O.S.H. Lingerie Collection" featured a picture of a soaking-wet model wearing a sailor hat and a bra printed with little boats. There was a hand-drawn flock of seagulls in the background, and to drive the nautical point home, the words PORT OUT STARBOARD HOME looped around the border.

My heartbeat picked up. I'd been on the lookout for anything remotely sailing themed for weeks, ever since I'd had that random black-and-white dream about riding the rough seas in a huge old-fashioned sailboat.

I tossed the tights into a bin of half-priced reindeer socks and zoomed to the back of the store to check out the P.O.S.H. Collection. Apart from a cute pair of porthole-printed boy shorts, I didn't see anything all that remarkable about it. I looked back up at the sign for guidance, though from this too-close spot it was just one big fluorescent glare. If I hadn't been busy tilting my head at different angles, it might not have taken me so long to notice the girl drifting by.

She was wearing a peacoat and a pair of red Ray-Bans pushed up on top of her peroxide-enhanced hair. She was tall and lanky—the ultimate anti-me—but the thing about her that struck me the most was her insanely peaceful aura. She moved through the lingerie racks with a listlessness that was completely out of place in this den of frenzy.

2

I found a rack of lacy camisoles to pretend to be interested in while keeping an eye on her. A faint smile played on her face as she detached a black eyelet corset from its plastic hanger and stuffed it in her green leather bag.

Was I seeing straight?

As if to rule out any doubt, she fingered a pair of glittery gloves and dropped them in there too.

I felt nervous on her behalf—just watching her swipe the merchandise made my palms dampen. She, on the other hand, couldn't have appeared more unconcerned. Moving slowly as a rattlesnake in the moment before its attack on an unsuspecting mouse, she circled to the other side of the display and proceeded to slip a striped camisole into her bag.

By the time she'd made off with her fourth item—a pair of plain Jane white briefs—it was clear that she didn't really care what she took, so long as it didn't have a sensor attached. No attention to color, no checking the labels to make sure she'd found the right size. If there'd been a sweat-encrusted five-year-old bandana on the racks, she probably would have snatched that too.

Her bag fully loaded, she sauntered toward the door. I still couldn't believe my eyes. She hadn't bothered to pull the zipper shut, and a swatch of striped camisole was poking out of the top. There was no indication her nerves were the slightest bit frayed as she approached the security guard.

I stalled behind a half-dressed mannequin. Dread pooled in my stomach as I waited for Miss Stickyfingers to make like a human mood ring and turn another color as she approached the exit. But she just passed the rent-a-cop and strode out onto the street, cool as they come.

That made one of us. My heart was still flapping like a butterfly wing and I had to will my breath to steady.

And to think, this was just the beginning.

{ 1 }

Don't Feed the Animals

Forty minutes later, I was sprinting along the other end of Broadway, determined to reach Becca and her not-so-mysterious companion before they finished dinner and went home without me. Without slowing down, I triple-wrapped my burgundy chenille scarf around my neck. If my crazy dreams were about to send me on another life-consuming investigation, I should probably do whatever I could to avoid coming down with strep throat.

I picked up speed when I saw the sign for West 109th Street and made a sharp right at the corner. A posse of wannabe tough guys was leaning against the side of a building, smoking cigarettes and waiting for the night to start.

"Damn!" one of them called after me, stretching the word into two syllables. "Shorty be in a hurry!"

I used to hate it when random guys called me Shorty. It wasn't exactly like I needed reminding of my Smurf-like physique. But now that Andy had begun using the term for me, it seemed endearing, and I smiled inwardly.

I'd take whatever I could get. In the month since Andy and I had started seeing each other, we hadn't actually seen that much of each other at all. Last semester had been a wild goose chase that eventually turned out to have a point to it. Somehow I'd tracked down the person whose job it was to bring down the Shuttleworth family plane—and the Shuttleworth family. At the end of the big whodunit, Andy and I had shared an amazing kiss in Riverside Park, but then he pulled back a little. My grandmother Kiki had promised me that taking things slow was perfectly normal—after all, Andy needed a little time to digest the fact that the key accomplice had been none other than his girlfriend Rye.

And, to be honest, I needed some time to come down from the whirlwind too. In the three months since Kiki had given me my magic black-and-white cameo necklace, my lifelong habit of seeing weird, random visions in my head had transformed into something much weirder. Now that I was wearing the necklace, I was having black-and-white dreams that actually led me somewhere. As long as I could figure out what the clues in my dreams were trying to tell me—no easy task, not by a long shot—I could be useful. Finally.

That Thanksgiving vacation, right after I'd proven that Rye was dangerous, was the happiest I'd ever been. And so it was disappointing that the crazy black-and-white dreams and bouts of next-day exhaustion had pretty much stopped. In the past six weeks, I'd had only a couple of weird dreams, and half-baked ones at that—more like images than actual scenes. Only Kiki and I knew about the necklace's powers. She'd figured my recent dreams, which were less action-packed than the ones I was having before, were just brain twitches and I should be grateful. "If you don't take a brief respite from the Lady Inspector shenanigans, you'll run yourself ragged," she'd said. But I begged to differ. It seemed unfair to have to let go of something that I was just starting to get good at. Or rather, I was happy to run myself ragged if it meant more fun.

Ludo's Supper Club was so trendy I almost walked by it. Old New York to the core, Becca tends to pick restaurants that have been in business since the American Revolution. As for this place, it was so new I could practically smell the construction fumes. The sidewalk spillover included a bullfrog of a bouncer and a reality television crew to document the beautiful people shivering on line. It was so not Becca, but it was also the only Ludo's in sight. I rose to my tiptoes and peered into the window.

"Looking for something?" Andy was standing in the shadows of the doorway. He was staring at me like I was something beautiful and I felt a kick in the heart.

"Hi." My voice came out scratchier than a Brillo pad. I'd almost forgotten how cute he was since the last time I'd seen him, and I was feeling jumbled up.

Between Andy's finals and our holiday obligations and the more-than-slightly-uncomfortable fact that he was my best friend's brother and neither of us had the courage to tell Becca we were hanging out in a non-G-rated context, we'd only gotten together twice in the last month: first for a walk through the Brooklyn Navy Yard and, more recently, cheeseburgers at the Ear Inn and a good-night kiss in the Washington View Village courtyard. The kiss had been perfect—that is, until Sheila Vird, my neighbor and ex–best friend and now mortal enemy, caught sight of us and took it upon herself to blast "Easy Lover" by Phil Collins out of her window.

Andy's eyes flickered over me and I felt my cheeks flush.

"So you decided to come after all," came Becca's voice. She was at Andy's side, looking every bit his kid sister with her wavy brown hair and distinctive nose. Even in the dark lighting I could make out their tans—they'd just come back from a family trip to Hawaii. She reached her arms around me and pulled me in for a hug. "I missed you, C. What a terrible way to spend a week."

Nine days, but who's counting?

"I missed you too," I told her.

"That's quite an outfit you've got there." Andy was scoping out the blinding leg wear I'd been too distracted to replace at H&M.

Just my luck.

"Ignore him," Becca said, hugging me tighter before letting go. The figgy scent of her perfume triggered forgotten memories of happy times and I was beaming as I followed her right past the line and into the restaurant. The lighting was minimal, and a DJ was spinning some sort of electro-gypsy music. There was definitely some handbook everyone but me had read—the crowd was all dressed the same, the girls in silky camisole tops and hammered gold necklaces, the guys in navy cashmere blazers with popped collars. Even Andy, whose regular uniform is jeans and a long-sleeved T-shirt, was wearing a freshly ironed button-down shirt with the sleeves rolled up.

On him, though, it looked all right.

"You've been here before?" Andy screamed over the din as Becca led us to the back of the room.

I shook my head emptily. "What is this place?"

"It was recommended by a friend of Andy's," Becca offered, stopping short to let a waitress whir by.

Andy ran his hand over his fuzzy head the way he does when he's mulling something over. "I hope they didn't give our table away. I kind of lied and said you were already here a while ago."

I looked at them both. "I'm sorry . . . I got held up with . . ."

I got held up not buying a pair of tights and following a girl around who was not buying lingerie.

I started over, "I was at this store, and there was a girl shoplifting and they wouldn't let us leave for a little while."

All true . . . well, true enough.

"Sounds like the beginning of a made-for-Lifetime movie," Becca said.

More like the start of one of my real-life thrillers.

I dug my hand under my scarf and fingered my pendant, wondering if this semester was going to be any smoother than last. I never seem to find the clues from my black-and-white dreams in my waking life in the same order that I see them in my sleep. And to make matters more confusing, even when I'm on a roll and start seeing clues all over the place, it takes me a while to figure out which ones are worth chasing and what, exactly, they're trying to tell me. Most of the time I'm running around like an untrained puppy with attention deficit disorder.

Take last semester, for instance. It had been insane. Because of my strange dreams, I was paying special attention to all sorts of random stuff, like a striped duffel bag and a colossal clock. It took me ages to realize it was all pointing me to Rye, and even when I did, it wasn't immediately clear that while she was going out with Andy, she was secretly dating Andy's archrival Otto Soyle, this pinheaded loser whose father is Becca and Andy's father's mortal enemy. Rye had been instructed to tamper with the navigational computer on Andy's family's prized plane. (Yes, a plane. The Shuttleworths are the closest thing we have to royalty in America, thanks to their centuries-old ketchup empire.)

Luckily, I unraveled my dreams just in time to avert disaster. Had the engine started up with anyone in the plane, there's no telling what would have happened. Well, there was, but I preferred not to think about it.

I can see how it might sound fun, but this special talent, or whatever you want to call it, is kind of stressful. For starters, it's distracting having to constantly be on the lookout. And not being able to tell Becca everything—about my dreams on top of the stuff about her brother—has certainly taken a toll on our friendship. Still, I wouldn't give the cameo back. If I can use my special powers to help people I care about, it's worth the awkwardness and confusion.

Like now. It was one of my strange black-and-white dreams that had led me to tail the crazy rip-off artist at H&M. But who was that girl and what did she have to do with me?

I must have been spacing out pretty hard. A redhead at a table that had more cell phones on top of it than people seated around it was flickering her eyes in vexation at me. As if able to sense my discomfort, Andy reached back for my hand.

Yum.

Our fingers were barely brushing, but it didn't matter. Sometimes all you need is the slightest contact for every cell in your body to heat up.

I pulled away right before we reached our table, which was a good thing. Becca was already sitting down, her arms crossed over her pale blue V-neck sweater. She was rolling her eyes and puffing out her cheeks like a blowfish. I realized why as I heard a teenage girl at a nearby table groaning, "When is my manager going to realize she's not my agent?"

"Probably around the same time she realizes you're a complete jackelope," Andy mumbled as he settled into his seat.

Becca laughed and she studied the menu. "This is just great. Not only is the house specialty dunderbrains," she said, tilting her head in the direction of our neighboring table, "but they don't even speak English here."

I looked at my menu and saw what she was talking about. The two options—mixed salad and individual pizzas—were offered in a language that looked vaguely Italian.

"This place was Andy's choice." Becca eyed her brother tauntingly.

"Yeah, but only because this guy I used to know in mid—"

"What are you hiding back here for?" The guy standing over us looked like he was eighteen going on thirty-five, with his floppy hair and bruise-dark under-eye circles.

Andy jerked back and put on a smile. "Hey, man, speak of the devil."

The guy must have known Becca also, because he greeted her with a kiss, then squinted at me, unable to cover up his surprise at seeing a girl like me in such esteemed company. "Oliver Verner."

"I'm Claire." Tilting my head to the side to accept Oliver's second kiss, I shot Becca a look. Even my father, a French professor whose natural reflex is to exclaim things like *"C'est magnifique!"* and *"Zut alors!"* knows when to put a lid on his Euro affectations.

Kisses obtained, Oliver popped back up. "Is this place nuts or what?"

"Quite the scene," Becca murmured, clearly unimpressed. She unfolded her napkin and let it parachute onto her lap.

While Andy and Oliver caught up, I stopped paying attention to what they were saying and gawked at the engraving on Oliver's pinkie ring. Was it an elaborate calligraphic "I" or an iguana? And hadn't I recently seen a black-and-white reptile in the middle of the night? The rest of the real world faded away as I stared at the piece of jewelry.

I know, I know, I have the attention span of a hoverfly. Welcome to my brain.

Maybe one day I'll be able to casually comb the world for

details out of the corner of my eye while keeping up with whatever situation I'm supposed to be an active participant of, but for now my dreams are still confusing enough to keep me on my toes—and out of the real-world loop.

"Claire." Becca was kicking me under the table. "Oliver's asking you something."

I slid my gaze over to Oliver and smiled cluelessly.

"What's your take?" Oliver was scoping out the room. "Pretty ridiculous, huh?"

Maybe this guy wasn't so bad after all, if he was making fun of our obnoxious environment.

"Ridiculous doesn't even begin to describe it," I said, and Oliver laughed appreciatively. "Seriously, what's the thinking behind this place? That there aren't enough pretentious pseudo nightclubs already?"

Andy shook his head and looked at me, his eyes filling with amusement. "This is Oliver's spot," he said. "He and his brother opened it last month."

And it all clicked into place. Oliver had meant *good* ridiculous. Andy had been shaking his head in disbelief at *me*.

I felt sweat pricking the back of my neck as I spluttered an apology.

"No, no, don't worry about it," Oliver said, sounding all professional. "Enjoy your meal. Later."

"Can't take you anywhere, can I?" Andy broke the silence after Oliver had loped off. His tone was playful, but I knew I'd screwed up.

"I think your friend hates me." Andy's look didn't contradict what I was saying, and I slunk deeper into my seat. "Don't mind me while I disappear."

"Sounds like a plan." Becca rose to her feet and motioned for us to join her. "Last one to the door has to come back here every night for a week."

• • •

We ended up taking a cab up to Sylvia's, a soul food restaurant in Harlem. It was the opposite of the fake restaurant we'd just visited, with many diners who fell outside of the sixteen-to-twenty age range and lighting that made it possible to actually locate your fork. The walls were covered with photographs of celebrities who'd eaten there, and there wasn't a single patron who didn't appear to be having the time of their life. It was anything but a "see and be seen" kind of place.

Becca had been there before so she took care of the ordering: fried chicken, ribs, candied yams, corn bread, and some vegetable I'd never heard of. I was intimidated by the quantity of it all, but when the chicken arrived at the table and the buttery aroma enveloped us, my stomach capacity instantly quadrupled.

"God," Becca said, gnawing her way down a sticky rib. "You have no idea how good it is to be back home."

"Yeah, I hear Hawaii's pretty tough this time of year," I deadpanned.

"You try spending Christmas there," Becca said. "There was no snow and my chocolate Santa melted."

"You ate it anyway," Andy reminded her.

Becca flicked her shiny brown hair over her shoulder. "Well, it didn't feel right," she insisted. "I hate Christmas that's not in New York."

"At least you had your Brookfield friends there," Andy said, and I felt myself raising a jealous eyebrow. Brookfield Academy is the superuptight uptown all-girls school that Becca went to until sixth grade, when her parents sent her to Houghton, the superconservative boarding school in Massachusetts she attended until some creepy stalker started following her around and her parents made her come home to Manhattan.

"I didn't realize you were still friends with Brookfield kids." I was trying my best to conceal my unease.

"I wasn't." Her eyes darted away. "But I reconnected with some of them. They actually turned out okay. Maybe we can all hang out soon."

Yeah, right. I'd read enough issues of *Teen Vogue* to know how terrifying those girls were. They all looked like ballerinas and attended enough international debutante balls to use the Hôtel de Crillon in Paris as a mailing address.

"Anyway," Becca went on, "what did you do for Christmas? Were you at the Waldorf?"

Okay, I realize it might seem a little hypocritical to hold it against the Brookfield girls that they go to five-star hotels when I have a grandmother who lives at the Waldorf-Astoria, no fleabag motel. But it's different.

Kiki isn't filthy rich, she just happens to have an amazing apartment. She's been a resident at the hotel ever since the sixties, when she was a recently retired showgirl who convinced her diplomat husband that he needed a New York pied-à-terre, lovely as Washington, D.C., was. To hear her tell it, my grandfather balked at the suite's steep price, but Kiki persuaded him that regularly staying in the red-hot center of New York would have its advantages. And did it ever. She absorbed an entire library of etiquette books and saw to it that they both got invited to every costume gala and breakfast party. She was one of the top swans of New York society, and one of the most well-known pictures of Truman Capote's infamous Black and White Ball shows Kiki chatting with Frank Sinatra and some Mexican race car driver whose claim to fame was convincing a pair of sister socialites to leave their husbands for him, at the very same time.

Nowadays Kiki barely resembles the woman who used to regularly appear in the *Vogue* society pages, but she still makes a big to-do out of having fun. When her friends aren't throwing cocktail parties and gossiping about scandals from half a century ago, they're giving me pointers and trying to cook up new scandals to gossip about.

"So?" Becca was waving her hand in front of my face. "I repeat: What did you do for Christmas?"

"Sorry." I blinked hard. "Kiki was visiting a friend in Boston, so I hung around my building and watched academics get drunk on nasty eighteenth-century cocktails."

"Come again?" Andy said.

"Ivan Fargoset, this cultural studies professor who lives on the sixth floor of my building, found a historic cocktail book at a stoop sale. He gave a demonstration on classic fermentation tactics and then he mixed the homemade booze with bits of horseradish in plastic cups."

Andy made a pained face. "Sounds edifying."

"Yeah, I learned a lot. Like don't ever accept homemade alcohol. One of the faculty wives nearly had a seizure."

Becca laughed. "And what about New Year's Eve? More partying with the professors?"

"Kiki was back by then, thank God. I hung out at her place for a bit and then I went down to Ian Kitchen's."

"Just the two of you?" Andy puckered his lips.

I paused to savor his uncharacteristic—and totally unnecessary—jealousy. Adorable as Ian Kitchen may be, he's even shorter than I am, and he carries a wheelie suitcase around with him everywhere he goes.

"A bunch of boys he knows from the comic-book store were there," I told them. "They said a few other girls were invited, but I'm not convinced they actually know any. We played some video game called Vampire Fantasy and I watched a couple of the guys practically get in a fistfight over who'd collected more blood droplets."

The second I said it, I felt embarrassed. Why hadn't I just done what any normal person would do and lied about going to some regular high school party with wine coolers and a police bust?

"Vampire Fantasy?" Andy repeated. "You should invite Becca next time. She'd kick their butts."

"You're too right," I said, eyeing Becca in relief. Prim as she might look, Becca is crazy about anything remotely horror themed. She has a collection of plastic cockroaches and a fake ID she uses exclusively to get into R-rated horror movie screenings. "You would blow their minds. And those kids could use some humble pie."

"Whatever," Becca said, handing our waiter a stack of our empty plates. "Who wants real pie?"

Darkness enveloped us when we left the restaurant. "Taxi time?" Becca asked, shivering for effect.

"Not yet," Andy said. "I hardly ever make it this far uptown. Let's walk around a little."

He guided us down Lenox Avenue and west on 125th Street. There were hardly any stars out, but the trees shimmered with hundreds of tiny seasonal white lights. Andy was looking up at all the buildings and I linked my arm through Becca's peacoat sleeve.

"Hey, B," I said, "Louis and I are thinking of taking a day trip to Philadelphia. The Chinatown bus gets there in like, two hours. What do you think?" I asked as casually as I could. I'd promised Louis Ibbits, my oldest friend in the world, I'd try to get a read on Becca, and whether she had any interest in him.

"Sounds right," Becca said neutrally. "I usually take the train."

Becca is willful in all respects, oblivion very much included.

"No." I squeezed her arm tighter. "I meant what do you think about coming with us? There's this museum full of medical curiosities, like pickled organs and flipper feet."

Before I could bug her more, Andy turned around to face

us. He looked alarmed. "Am I the only one who didn't know about this?" I realized he was pointing across the street.

I scoped out the scene, but all I could make out was New York on a typical Saturday night: couples squabbling under store awnings, buses blazing by, packs of guys searching for a party to crash.

But Becca echoed her brother's concern. "You've got to be kidding me."

"Um, anybody care to fill me in?" I peeped.

"Are you blind?" Becca raised her arm and pointed up.

What was it with me missing the most obvious thing? A few feet away stood the Apollo—the famous theater where nearly all the Motown girl groups I'm obsessed with got their start on amateur night. Just when I was about to tell them a pointless tidbit about the Ronettes, I looked up at the marquee and realized what they were freaking out about.

SHOW'S OVER. COMING SOON: SHOWTIME LOFTS. HURRY UP
WHILE UNITS ARE STILL AVAILABLE.

Andy went over to study a building permit pasted to the side of the building. "Thought so." He sounded angry. "Sink is without mercy." He turned back to meet my glassy-eyed stare. "Sinclair Landon. Ring a bell? A tiny bell?"

"Sink runs this real estate development company called Zeta Equities," Becca filled me in.

"Whenever a landmark starts to deteriorate," Andy said, "Zeta pounces on it. They say they're coming to the rescue or whatever and then, before you know it, they turn it into a cheesy condo."

"Aren't there laws against that?" I asked.

"Sure . . . and loopholes." Andy kicked at an empty cigarette pack into the street. "If a landmarked building starts to fall apart and the city doesn't have the resources to fix it, developers can make a bid. They have to promise to respect the integrity of the original structure, but their definition of 'integrity' is super loose."

I could feel myself making my oh-so-attractive confused duck expression—a house specialty. It was hard to remember that, for once, I was the normal one here. My parents tend to be too worried about making ends meet and remembering which day of the week is faculty discount night at the Associated Supermarket to teach me about multimillion dollar development deals.

"You've seen the Coney Island boardwalk, right?" Becca asked.

I nodded, remembering a bike ride Louis and I had recently taken. The Coney Island of my childhood—wonky-mirrored funhouses and Skee-Ball arcades—had been replaced with a soaring purple complex that looked like an inside-out spaceship.

"They're not doing that here, are they?" I asked.

"So it seems," Becca said.

"Can we go?" Andy came as close to snapping as I'd ever seen. "I can't deal."

"Sure," his sister said. She stepped down from the curb to hail a taxi. "I'm going to the East Side," she said. "Anyone headed that way?"

The cab had already pulled up before Andy and I had a chance to turn down her offer. That moment at the end of a night where people split up into groups based on their next destination always happens faster than I'd like.

"Enjoy your last day of freedom," Becca said as she folded into her cab.

"Wait," I said just as she was closing the door. "What are you doing tomorrow?"

It came out a little desperate, but I couldn't help it. Tonight's hang-out wasn't enough to cure me of the massive case of Becca withdrawal I'd been suffering.

"Tomorrow's bad." She sounded hesitant, and my mouth settled into a pout. Was more of an explanation too much to ask for? "But I'll see you bright and early at that place that shall not be named." She made a face at the thought of Henry Hudson High and pulled the door shut.

Even though I knew I'd see her soon enough, I still felt a pang of sadness

I turned to Andy once Becca's cab was out of sight. It occurred to me that Columbia was about ten blocks away, and I still hadn't seen his dorm. Well, that thought had already occurred to me before now. But it occurred to me that maybe we could do something about it. "Should I walk you down to campus and then—"

"I'm not headed there just yet," he said, oblivious to my implication. "I told my friend Jack I'd swing by his place. He's having a poker party."

"Oh, that's cool." Disappointment rang through my voice, and I tried to cover it up by telling him I sucked at poker. "I'm better at old-lady games, like Scrabble."

"Then we're even. I suck at Scrabble," he said in a consoling tone while flagging down a cab. "I can't spell for my life."

Andy supposedly had learning disabilities, though I'd never seen any evidence of one. I just thought he wouldn't find school so hard if he hadn't skipped first grade and if he ever bothered to study.

His poker party was in the Village, so we shared a cab downtown. We rode south along the West Side Highway in near silence, and as the fare on the meter mounted, so did my sense of discontent. Kiki always says the way to a man's heart is to "leave emotional prattle to the pages of the women's magazines and keep things light as a hazelnut soufflé," but that was impossible with this heavy feeling in my heart. And then it occurred to me: might Becca be backing off because she suspected something was going on between her brother and me. Could it be?

"Hey, Andy," I said after he'd instructed the driver to take the Fourteenth Street exit. We probably had one minute left. If that. "Did you tell . . . I mean . . . does Becca . . ."

He stroked his fuzzy head and looked at me apprehensively. "You want to have a serious talk *now*?"

"No." God, why did my voice have to crack when I lied?

"It's okay, we probably should." Andy leaned up and told the driver to pull over at the corner, near the site of his poker game, then placed his hand on my knee. I pretended not to feel anything as we locked eyes. "Look, I just don't think now is a good time to make anything official," he said. "The new semester is starting and my parents lined up a whole army of tutors to keep me on my feet. Dad says if I don't get at least a B average, he's going to make me transfer somewhere in the country. He thinks I'm running around the city too much. So, I kinda need to . . ." His eyes shifted focus from me to the middle distance. "I need to keep distractions to a minimum this semester."

Was he kidding? Only a month ago I'd saved his life and now I was demoted to a mere "distraction"?

I was so upset I wanted to jump out of the car and run.

He cleared his throat and sighed. He'd have to have been an idiot not to notice my disappointment. "That came out the wrong way." Now he was rubbing my knee. He leaned in to kiss my ear. Okay, I was feeling a little better. He caught my eye and smiled. "I just need to keep things low-key for the next little while."

I could feel my brow furrowing. "So you just want to be fr—"

"Claire, shut up." That was the first time I'd heard him say those words to me. And then he leaned in and gave me a kiss on the mouth that tasted as cool and sweet as a green apple. When he was done, he stroked my cheek, and I felt my heart give a double beat. "'Just friends' is not an option. But please, a little patience. Okay?" He skipped out of the cab and crouched down to take one last look at me before handing the driver a twenty-dollar bill and shutting the door behind him. "I'll call you soon."

My head was whirling in happy confusion the rest of the way home. I hadn't seen his dorm, but we'd had our longest kiss yet. I fingered my cameo, my smile growing like Jack's beanstalk.

It wasn't until I'd made it through the Washington View Village courtyard and onto the elevator that I started thinking about the spiel that had come before the kiss. How had I missed the part that mattered? He wanted to keep things low-key. Which was a nice way of saying he wanted to put things on ice. The kiss had just been a consolation prize that he'd thrown in at the last minute.

My stomach dropped.

We were over, and we'd hardly even got started.

Looked like Sink Landon wasn't the only strategic genius in town.

{ 2 }

Plus Ça Change

I was wearing a black-and-white elf suit, and we're not talking the Victoria's Secret "Sexy Santa" line. I was on the main floor of Macy's, ho-ho-ho-ing for the little children. Everything was fine and dandy until a girl in a wheelchair approached me and my bag of presents was suddenly empty. Her face began to crumple, but then she looked elated. I looked down at my bag and saw a Cabbage Patch Kid doll poking out.

My color-challenged dreams used to freak me out. Now I woke up feeling anything but worried. The mysterious night visions were happening again, which meant my life was about to pick up. The usual postdream grogginess overwhelmed me as I tried to sit up, but I didn't mind at all. A little exhaustion seemed a small price to pay for seeing things that nobody else can.

I pushed off my bright pink silk JE DORS, DONC JE SUIS sleep mask—a Christmas present from my parents—and looked around the room. It was a mess, with fashion magazines littering the floor and the Kiki hand-me-downs I'd hand-washed the night before draped across every available surface.

"I can't keep coming in here to wake you up." Mom was leaning against the doorjamb, looking as drowsily beautiful as ever, even in her XXL LA VIE C'EST UN SOAP OPERA T-shirt. A die-hard Francophile, Mom is a sucker for any clothing that comes from France, no matter how heinous or ungrammatical. "Vacation's over, Claire," she said.

Like that hadn't occurred to me already.

I groaned, pulled myself out of bed, and shuffled out of the room and down the hall. After a quick shower, I threw on my back-to-school outfit: jeans, a gray and white striped T-shirt, and a skinny French blue cardigan that Kiki told me her "dear friend" Oscar de la Renta had special-made for her. Kiki has a way of embroidering the truth, but when I looked in the mirror I had to hand it to her—the sweater was perfectly cut for somebody with the short arms and epic butt that my grandmother and I share. Finally, I put on my cat eyeliner and took a step back to study myself in the mirror. With my blond bob, Cheerio-shaped mouth, and freckles, I'm more Girl Scout than Gisele. The most interesting thing about the way I look is that I have one green and one hazel eye. One can only hope for future developments.

Dad was sitting cross-legged on the Moroccan rug in the living room, his face scrunched up into a tight red ball. My little brother, Henry, was next to him, studying a stopwatch through his mop of blond curls.

"Your father's trying Saffron's positive visualization exercises," Mom whispered, draping her arm around me. She was referring to Saffron Scott, the supermodel-turned-home-design personality who was the subject of Mom's latest ghostwriting project. Mom's B-list celebrity clients usually keep their relationship with Mom strictly professional, but Saffron was going through a divorce from some jerky fashion photographer, and it must have really been messing her up. She had latched on to my weirdo household with a fervor bordering on obsession—sometimes she came over when there wasn't any work for her and Mom to do at all.

"Time's up!" Henry cried out.

Mom made a little airy gasp and clenched my arm. To see her face, you would have thought she was watching the last minute of a championship basketball game. In fact, she was looking on as her French-professor husband tried to fight his writer's block. Now that a publisher had agreed to put out his book on Émile Zola, Dad had suddenly discovered how much he loved going to the gym, watching Law & Order reruns, and re-organizing the spice rack. Anything to avoid working.

"Was it a success, Gustave?" Mom couldn't contain herself.

Dad shrugged noncommittally and padded over to his computer. "Good things take time. My book is not McDonald's."

"But you like McDonald's," Henry reminded him.

Mom sighed and turned to me. "He can't keep losing days. He's driving himself crazy."

"Maybe he'll get it done if we stop paying such close attention?" I suggested.

"Yesterday he was avoiding work by watching reality television." She spat out the words like poison. "Maybe I should fiddle with the cable box and see if there's a wire to pull out."

"Good call," I said, and on my way out the door, I took one

of Dad's gym sneakers from the shoe heap and stuck it in my bag, to ward off any spontaneous stationary bicycle sessions.

It was worth a try.

When I reported to Henry Hudson High, the crowd milling outside school seemed more energized than usual. A cluster of kids was competing Mr. Universe style to see who had the heaviest backpack. A girl with butt-length corn-colored hair was pacing around, conjugating Latin verbs into a Dictaphone.

Nerd school never ceased to amaze me.

I rose to my tiptoes and searched for Becca or Ian. Instead, I got a glimpse of Sheila and her friend Ariel trying to abuse a pencil-necked guy who was playing with a handheld video game device. Sheila had no interest in video games—or, I was pretty sure, in Señor Pencil-neck—but that didn't stop her from homing in on him. If anything, it made the game all the more fun for her.

"Pleeease?" She was tossing her brassy hair for flirty effect. "Just a little lesson?"

"How 'bout a trade?" Ariel said in a fake sweet voice. "You let us play with your toy, then we'll grant one of your wishes."

A few months ago, their taunting surely would have reduced the boy to a pool of compliance. But ever since the publication of The Adventures of Evil Radish, the awesome comic book that Ian and I made about Sheila's quintet of wannabe mean girls, everybody had stopped taking them seriously. Janice and the two Laurens had found new cliques to glom on to, leaving it up to Sheila and Ariel to carry on the tradition. Or at least try to.

"That a yes?" Sheila wouldn't back down.

"Close. It's a no." The pencil-necked kid couldn't be

bothered to raise his voice—or even look up. "I'm sort of in the middle of something."

I bit down a smile. Things had come a long way since the beginning of last semester. When I'd started at Hudson, all I could think about was how much I wanted to kill Sheila and her evil friends and go back to Farmhouse, the hippie school my parents pulled me out of when I made the mistake of acing the entrance test to Hudson, New York's most prestigious public school.

That was all before I met Becca. I'd known her for only four months, but it felt longer. She was my partner in crime, my conspirator in bad puns, and the only other kid in the entire Hudson student body who didn't spend every waking hour studying. Since Becca has a photographic memory and I have a way of tuning in to my hunches during tests, our academic survival requires beautifully little work. We get to focus on "more important" things. And by more important I mean more fun.

"Excuse me!" A classmate's voice came through like a foghorn and I moved aside to let her pass and walk up the school steps. It took a few seconds to register what I should have noticed from the beginning: she had on a Santa scarf.

It seemed a little weird. And not because nobody in her right mind wears Santa clothing in January. It was a little too close to my Santa dream for comfort.

I watched the girl reach into her pocket for a ball of paper and toss it into the trash can by the school entrance. Then I counted to ten and made my way up the stairs. I took one glance behind me to make sure that nobody was watching. And then, making an effort not to breathe through my nose, I reached into the bin and snatched the girl's tossed-out paper. A quick glance down revealed what looked like the lines of a map.

Intriguing.

A sneaky feeling worked its way up my spine. I opened the building door and stepped into the hallway's soupy green light. Once I'd passed through the metal detector, I leaned against a glass trophy case and smoothed out the paper.

Only then did I realize what she'd tossed out: a Chinese takeout menu.

My insides deflated like a balloon from yesterday's party. How many false starts was I going to have to suffer through before I'd understand what this new cluster of dreams was trying to tell me?

"This is your final reminder." Assistant Principal Dr. Arnold's nasal drawl came blaring through the loudspeakers, rupturing my defeated reverie. "First period is suspended. You are all to report to your homerooms immediately."

Of course, none of the other kids flinched. I'm always the last one to know what was going on at Hudson.

When I got to homeroom, everyone was sitting up straighter than usual and paying extra-close attention to Mr. Tisardi, our beanpole of a homeroom teacher.

"In light of this year's disappointing results in early entrance college admissions," he was saying, "Hudson is requiring all of its students to submit to a trial interview."

"Like a mock college interview?" Sarah DeVeers gasped excitedly. You could say my classmates have a thing for college preparation.

"No." Mr. Tisardi shook his head. "This is for internal use. We're trying to determine whether your outside interests are adequately developed."

A creaking sound came from the back of the room, and up stood a lady whose beady eyes matched her tomato-red lipstick. She introduced herself as Ms. Dykstra and told us she worked for a team of consultants Hudson had hired. "Colleges are looking for more than participation in school clubs. I'm here to make sure you have interests that extend beyond the realm of Hudson. I'm going to be interviewing each of you to make sure you're on track."

Considering the new strange dreams I had to work out, I was pretty sure I had non-Hudson interests covered. But maybe not.

When my turn rolled around, Ms. Dykstra looked at my transcript and complimented me on my grades. "I see you're a very hardworking student," she told me.

Hardly. I just have a way of acing tests—so long as I wear my necklace, my hunches tell me what bubble to fill in. "I do my best."

"And what about your extracurricular activities?"

"I stay busy," I said, trying to keep my voice level and not let it show how proud I was of all the cool ways I filled my time.

"Busy how?"

I shrugged. "I do lots of stuff. I belong to a Sunday night Scrabble club with this group of senior citizens who live at the Waldorf-Astoria hotel. . . . Sometimes I attend academic conferences. . . . I take lots of long bike rides all over the city."

A crease formed at the corner of her mouth as she took it all in. "And does anyone supervise these excursions?"

"I'm pretty self-directed," I said, still confident that I was charming the pants off of her.

"Self-directed." She sighed. "You should know that when college admissions committees see such independence, they tend to think 'liability.' Have you considered joining any organizations that reflect your interests?" And then she started offering possibilities, like fashion design classes at Pace University or the Jewish Youth Association Sunday morning bicycle league.

What had I been thinking? Even if Hudson activities didn't carry weight, we were being judged by Hudson standards. And from what I'd seen this year, Hudson is the most regimented institution this side of West Point.

Having apparently failed my interview, I was assigned to attend the same intensive "character-building" program as practically everyone else in the school.

Joy.

That wasn't the only thing about this semester that was different. We all had new schedules, our classes meeting at different times and with different people. Every time I walked into a new class, I looked around for Becca or Ian. And every time I did that, I came up empty. The one upside was that my lunch had been bumped down to sixth period, meaning I no longer had to eat at ten-thirty in the morning. And while we're on the subject of positive developments, I did notice a cute guy in my lunch period—a Hudson first. He was wearing a cowboy shirt and reading an issue of The New Yorker. He definitely hadn't been around first semester. He was the kind of guy I would have noticed.

It wasn't until the end of the day that I saw Becca. As usual, she was floating down the hall, looking oblivious to the masses of kids who were streaming past her. Her hair was done in a French braid and she was wearing a tweed blazer with elbow patches, as if to rub in the fact that she can dress like she'd raided her grandfather's closet and still look hot.

"Becca." I rushed toward her. "Please tell me you have SHINE."

"I do?" She patted her nose with her fingertips.

"No." I pushed her hand away. "This mandatory character-building seminar. Students Having Idiotic New Experiences or whatever."

"*Interesting* New Experiences," threw in a classmate who was cruising by on roller sneakers.

Becca made a face. "They gave you that? I thought it was only for kids who never left the confines of this place."

"Apparently I'm too 'self-directed.'"

Becca laughed. "I'd take that as a badge of honor."

"It would feel like more of an honor if you got it too. It's every day for two *whole* weeks. How'd you wiggle out of it?"

She pulled sheet music out of her brown leather satchel and made an aren't-I-perfect face.

"Of course." I rolled my eyes. Being a member of the Shuttleworth family, one of Lincoln Center's most generous donors, Becca is entitled to take opera lessons from world-class masters, even if her voice is unremarkable.

"Can't your parents pull rank and get you in some NYU society?" she asked.

"Like what, Tenure Track?" I asked.

"What's that, the jogging club?"

Impressive. Were I in her shoes, it would have taken me at least five minutes to match the unfortunately named group to its actual activity.

"Yo." Ian and his wheelie suitcase have a way of creeping up out of nowhere. I was still getting used to his new look, which perfectly coincided with his recent induction into the Propeller comic-book store's exclusive group of latchkey kids. His brown hair now fell shaggily over his ears, and he wore T-shirts advertising comic books I'd never heard of, like *Dog-tropolis* or *Miracle Showerhead*. Ian gestured toward the auditorium. "You guys ready?"

"She's not in it," I said grumpily, then turned to Becca. "You want to meet up somewhere afterward?"

Her face went slack. "I'm actually supposed to hang out with some Brookfield kids."

I felt a little kick in the stomach, and when she didn't invite me along for the ride it only felt worse. "Oh."

"But maybe we'll catch up later?" she tossed out lamely.

I was too dumbfounded to respond. It was one thing when she said she'd hung out with the Brookfield girls over vacation, but that was when I wasn't around. Could she seriously be trading me in for a bunch of uptown aristocrats?

True, Becca is sort of an uptown aristocrat herself, but she's not the type to use and lose. There had to be something she wasn't telling me.

The way she was nervously tapping her green and white Oxfords into the ground confirmed my suspicion. Was our friendship going to be an eternal game of Becca hides and Claire seeks?

Becca sucked in her cheeks. "All right, let's talk later." Before I could respond, she started to walk down the hallway. After a few steps she turned around to make the universal call-me gesture.

I couldn't believe what had just happened. As Ian and I walked into the auditorium, I mentally reviewed the conversation I'd just had with Becca.

"Ian," I rasped when we'd taken our seats, "Becca was acting weird, right?"

"I don't know how girls work," he said. I could tell he didn't want to get dragged into it.

"Oh, come on. I deserve more of a reaction than that."

He mussed up his hair and thought for a moment. "I'll say this much. The only time I ever see people do the telephone hand signal is on Italian soap operas."

"Thank you." I repressed a smile.

The only thing that made less sense than the fact that Ian watched foreign soap operas was Becca's jumpy behavior.

Something was up, no question about it.

• • •

I had too much pride to keep chasing after Becca like a puppy, and apparently she had too much going on to track me down. We didn't end up hanging out until Thursday night. Henry was out at his friend Dov's house and Dad was at the library, pretending to work, so it wasn't a typical two-hour-long everybody-must-comment-on-current-events Voyante family dinner. Over mushroom and ham crêpes Becca and I helped Mom come up with horoscopes for her always-overdue "Priscilla Pluto" astrology column. I told all the Virgos to say no to compromise and keep their eyes open for exciting adventures. Becca chose a month of love and Marc Jacobs flats for her fellow Geminis.

Mom was taking notes on it all, and continued scribbling as Becca and I got up to clear the table. "Okay, but let's just say 'great shoes,'" she said. "Remember, this is for the *Planet*, not *Vogue*."

"Everybody deserves something nice," Becca argued from the kitchen.

"Everything's cleaned up," I told my mom, eager to be alone with my friend. "Can we go now?"

"Sure," she said, and I heard her mutter "Marc Jacobs" as we shot into my room.

"It looks different in here," Becca said, looking around. "It's fuller. You have more random crap than I do."

My room hadn't changed at all since the last time she'd been over, and it was kind of upsetting to hear how unfamiliar it seemed to her.

"I just have less space than you," I told her.

"Whatever." She paused to admire my BONJOUR, MADEMOISELLE Coco Chanel poster, then headed over to my fish tank and let off a squeal.

"Are you feeding them something different? They are pork-ing out like crazy!" She pointed at Margaux, who was blowing bubbles by the plastic chateau. "He's growing a potbelly."

"That's a girl," I corrected her. "And she is so not."

"If you say so, but she's a fat one," she said softly, then started snickering into the palm of her hand.

"You're messing with me!"

"Sorry." She was grinning. "I couldn't resist. You should've seen your face."

"Those are my babies." I picked my Eiffel Tower pillow off my bed and raised it overhead.

"No! Don't!" She held up a hand and pulled a half-eaten chocolate chocolate-chip cookie out of her bag. "Truce?"

The cookie was loaded with thick shards of dark chocolate and I could feel myself going weak in the taste buds.

"You can't buy your way out of everything, you know." I'd intended it as a friendly jab, but she sure didn't seem to take it that way. She just sat down on my fake polar bear rug and twisted her airplane ring, a sign that she was uncomfortable.

"Is that how you think of me?" She looked hurt.

"No, I didn't mean anything by it," I said. An awkward moment passed before she broke what remained of the cookie in two. We polished it off in no time, then started flipping through magazines, one of our favorite activities. It felt a little quieter than usual, and I was still feeling sorry about what I'd said. There was a cloud hanging over us. I got up to put on the Shirelles, hoping their energy would rub off on us.

"Hey, B," I shouted over the first notes of "Mama Said." "Do you want to come with Louis and me to the New York Documentary Film Festival on Saturday? There's this movie about this high-fashion makeup artist who's really into embalming. You know, dead bodies."

Her eyes filled with delight. "No way!" Then she hugged her knees to her chest and she looked down, clearly disappointed. "Oh no. I just remembered."

"Let me guess. You have a Brookfield thing?" This time I had to hold back the anger.

"No, I have to go to this family birthday party thing in Vermont. I'd invite you, but it's strictly family."

"That's okay," I said, trying yet again to cover my disappointment. Last semester I'd been a fixture on the Shuttleworth travel circuit. You'd think my lifesaving discovery would have earned me a permanent spot in the caravan, but who was I to think I understood anything? I shrugged, doing my best to look nonchalant. "I should stick around here anyway. Louis gets freaked out pretty easily."

"You're a good friend," she said.

Yeah, I thought. *That makes one of us.*

Inclined as I was to pout, my weekend was a typical mix of fun and lame. Louis's dad gave him tickets to the film festival party. Then, thanks to his thick tortoiseshell glasses, some publicist mistook Louis for some filmmaking prodigy and we got to spend the night in the VIP room watching everybody try to figure out who we were. The next day, my parents roped me into joining them at a concert put on by the Belle Curve, our building's resident chime ensemble. It wasn't all bad, though—Andy happened to call during the concert, and there was nobody around to tell him where I was. Oh, the mystery!

I didn't have any black-and-white dreams all weekend, a fact that I couldn't help seeing as directly linked to Becca's disappearance. She wasn't just my best friend. She was my good-luck charm. All of the clues I'd seen last semester had pointed me to things related to her—the airplane ring, her family photographs, her brother's demonic girlfriend. And now that she was fading out of the picture, so were my powers.

"What do you think?" I asked Kiki on Sunday night. We were riding the elevator up to the Starlight Roof for her Scrabble game and I'd just shared my theory with her. "I mean, I had the boat dream and the Santa dream and then Becca got sucked into her Brookfield cult and everything stopped. It's got to be related, right?"

"Sounds to me like your friend might just have a few other commitments," she said, watching the floor numbers light up overhead, "and I'd expect as much from a Shuttleworth." She stiffened her posture. "Give it some time. Patience is an attractive quality that pays off. You can't expect everything to spring from the loins fully formed."

Loins? Ick.

Leave it to Kiki to put such a poetic spin on things.

Life got a little more interesting on Wednesday. I was sitting in the back row of SHINE, drifting off to sleep during a presentation on some amateur astronomers' society we were all encouraged to join. That was when I saw Becca. Not in the flesh. In a fully formed black-and-white dream.

Even from my faraway spot, there was no mistaking who it was. Tall. Graceful. Wavy hair parted in the middle. Becca was in front of a brick wall, and I could make out the bust of a colorless head, like one on a Roman coin, in the background. And then a girl appeared on the sidelines, raising a gun at my friend. Becca's face was etched with terror. I ran toward her, but not fast enough. Everything washed out and all I could see was white smoke.

I woke up with a jolt. I'd had my share of eerie dreams before, but never anything this unsettling. Ian was doodling in his sketchbook and most of the other kids were watching the lecture as if it were some barely tolerable in-flight movie. The teacher up front must have been talking, but all I could hear was the infinite echoing of the gunshot.

The picture of Becca looking so terrified was firmly lodged in my field of vision, like a fingerprint on glass, and when the bell rang I could barely get out of my seat.

If this was what Kiki had meant about patience paying off, I was ready to erase the word from my vocabulary for good.

{ 3 }

Trouble Is My Business

"Look what the tide brought in!" Kiki was standing in her doorway, a grin curling on her face. Her cheeks were flushed and she was decked out in the red silk robe she often wears when she entertains. I peered into the background and saw all her friends clustered around the coffee table. Just my luck. I needed to get her take on the scary movie in my head, and peeling her away from a party is about as easy as keeping a Persian cat from shedding.

"I tried calling," I said by way of apology, "but your line was busy."

"Still is," Kiki muttered, ushering me inside. "Jon-Jon's on the blower with his psychic." She widened her gray eyes as far as they would go.

"His psychic?" I asked as my favorite member of Kiki's posse, Clem Zwart, came over and helped me out of my coat.

"It's all twiddle-twaddle to me." Kiki turned to me and fixed the waist of my royal blue silk Pucci dress. "Dear, do you really expect this piece to retain its integrity when you hunch? You need to carry the dress—"

"Not let the dress carry you," I completed automatically. I'd heard it a hundred times before.

"Right-o," Kiki boomed. "Now come and meet Jon-Jon, my new friend." She gestured to the other side of the room and I noticed a dapper-looking stranger who was seated on one of the paisley damask couches, the phone pressed to his ear.

Kiki has a thing where she adopts a new friend every year—she says it's "to replace the outgoing ones," though the new friends are generally out the door the fastest. Last year's acquisition, a horse trader named Jules, ended up having a tendency to fall asleep in the middle of parties.

"Actually," I said to Kiki, "I wanted to talk to you about something." I tugged on my necklace and gave her a look.

Kiki nodded understandingly and looped her arm through mine. "Well, come meet Jon-Jon first. Then there's something in my bedroom I simply must show you."

My heart thumped in gratitude and I headed to the back of the room. Edie and John Wilcox, George Jupiter, and Clem all followed us and swarmed the newcomer. He was wearing a bright blue suit and his dark hair was slickly combed back, in the manner of a maître d' at a fancy restaurant. As Kiki and I approached, he hung up the phone.

"Jon-Jon Dewars," Kiki trumpeted, "meet my granddaughter. Her name is Claire Voyante, though don't fault her for it. Her parents are too busy thinking to be thoughtful," she said indignantly. "They're of the mentally constipated persuasion."

That's Kiki's way of saying "intellectuals."

"Well I won't hold you accountable, darling." Jon-Jon's melodic Southern drawl made Scarlett O'Hara sound as if she came from New Jersey. He was eyeing me funny. "My, she is cute as a tomcat's kitten," he said to Kiki, then turned to face me. "Won't you sit down and tell me you'll marry me?"

"Jon-Jon is a *fascinating* painter," Kiki said as I eased myself into the one available patch of couch. "And he's also very spiritual."

"So I've heard," I said, biting down a smile.

"Let me see your hand," Jon-Jon said. "I bet you have a long destiny line."

"Don't worry, he won't bite," Edie assured me in her Betty Boop squeak. Kiki and Edie met back when they were both showgirls. Edie has the same black bob and fondness for miniskirts as she did then.

"He won't marry you either," Clem said. "He's already got himself a husband." Clem is just as interesting looking as Edie—but in a completely different way. He has a long white beard and he wears lots of silver jewelry, along with a permanent expression of grief. His favorite word in the English language is "melancholic."

"*Did* have a husband," Jon-Jon told me with a sigh. "We're separated."

"I'm sorry," I coughed up. Nosy as I am, I can get a little antsy when complete strangers pour their personal histories into my lap.

"Our age difference was too much to overcome," Jon-Jon purred as he studied my palm.

Kiki flashed what looked like a peace sign at me. "Two years," she mouthed.

"It's not just two years," Jon-Jon barked, dropping my hand.

"I'm talking spiritual age. My dear, I am an old soul. And David is a child." He tilted his head and stared at me. "You know, Claire, you are the spitting image of those photographs I saw of your grandmother back in the day. The only difference is—"

"Let me guess," I said. "My eyes?"

He let off a pleasant hum. "I once had a dog with different-colored eyes. That beast was such a sweetheart, always rubbing up against the wallpaper and wagging his mangy tail whenever I came around."

"So, dear," Edie interrupted, saving us from the awkwardness that was setting in. You can always count on Edie to lighten a situation. "You haven't talked about school in a little while. How is all that going?"

Or at least semi-lighten a situation.

"The usual Hudson stuff," I said with a shrug. "All the kids are stressed out and all the teachers would rather be home watching TV or whatever."

They all seemed amused, so I told them more—about the unendurable SHINE meetings, the weird identical twins who were teaching my English and history classes, the silent protest I'd unwittingly been a part of at the library the day before. "About twenty kids came into the library to oppose the proposed cuts in hours. But they were so afraid of getting into trouble, nobody said a word. They just left these little flyers on the tables."

Clem stroked his beard. "Isn't that deliciously sad?"

When everyone was done chuckling, I turned to Kiki and opened my freaky-colored eyes as wide as they would go.

"How could I forget?" she said, picking up on my desperation. "I wanted to show Claire something. I hope the rest of you will excuse us." And without further ado, we went to her room.

"Now, what was it you wanted to talk about?" She was reading my mind. I don't say that loosely—Kiki can read my mind. At least when I'm thinking something important, she can. Kiki was the one I went to when I was younger and having wacky visions. Pictures of tabby cats and oversized sun hats would lodge in my brain and then I'd usually see the same images in real life, though it never turned out to mean very much. Later on, she was the person I turned to when I started wearing the cameo and having my black-and-white dreams. Turns out the cameo amplifies your natural talents, and skips generations. When Kiki was my age, the cameo made her intuitions even clearer, and she was able to sniff out everybody's secrets.

"Well," I started slowly, "that SHINE seminar isn't as boring as I made it out to be."

"You saw something interesting in a dream?" Amazing. I hadn't even mentioned the word *dream* yet. "You have shadows under your eyes," she explained.

"I fell asleep in a session and had a dream, about Becca," I said. "She got shot."

Kiki's eyebrows drew up. "That's not a very nice thing to do to your friend."

I gasped. "It's not like I chose it."

"Not on the surface." She tilted her head.

"Come again?"

"You are hurt by her diminished attention, am I correct? Have you ever heard of the subconscious?"

"Um, I only live in the same building as a zillion psychology professors," I reminded her.

"How could I forget?" She looked like she had just swallowed a bad scallop. As far as she is concerned, the only thing Washington View Village has to recommend it is that it's in the same city as her much nicer apartment.

"So you're saying even though she's my best—" I caught myself and started over. "Even though she's one of my best friends, I *subconsciously* want her to be hurt?"

Kiki laughed. "Naturally. You're cross with her, running around with those other girls."

I leaned back on the green silk comforter, sinking deeper into the mattress. Half of me resented Kiki for bringing it up. The other half was glad to have somebody who understood what I was going through. "Maybe I'm a little annoyed, but it's not like I want her to get killed."

"Of course not." She laughed. "You need to reconnect with Becca. Why don't you call her up and invite her to tea? Do you know where they do a lovely afternoon tea?"

"Let me guess. Peacock Alley?" I said. Of all the restaurants in New York, Kiki's favorite happens to be in the hotel lobby. It also happens to be the stodgiest place on earth.

"Now, that's your magic fix," she said.

"Thanks," I told her, though to be perfectly truthful, it wasn't exactly the kind of magic I'd come looking for.

{ 4 }

Shot in the Dark

"A tea party?" Becca couldn't stop giggling when I called her that night. "I haven't had one of those since I was a kid."

"Me neither. I thought it would be . . . funny." I looked out the window and saw that nearly every apartment across the courtyard had a television on. Interesting, considering how much my professor neighbors like to go on about the medium's "brain-deadening tendencies."

"I'm down," Becca said. "Especially if I can bring my stuffed animals." She snorted. "When is it?"

I hadn't thought that far. "Friday?"

"After school?" She sounded disappointed. "I told some friends I'd go to a Summer-in-January screening at Bryant Park this Friday."

This train was heading from bummer city into the land of totally depressing, and fast.

But then the most shocking thing happened: she invited me to join them. "You and Louis should come. It's *Cat People*, my favorite movie of all time."

My heart was trampolining all over the place. Thank you, Kiki! It actually worked.

"Come, come," she pleaded. "Besides, we need to celebrate."

"We do?"

"Friday's the end of that whack-job seminar of yours. Don't you think I haven't been counting down the days."

Her comment made me feel warm all over, and I was so excited that Kiki's advice had worked, it didn't occur to me until after school on Friday, when I was fixing my hair in my locker mirror, that I was meeting her new friends, which was more than a little terrifying.

Thank goodness I'd invited Louis to tag along. Knowing he'd be there for moral support was a huge relief. He had other motives—ever since he'd met Becca at my family Thanksgiving dinner, he could barely talk about anything else. She, on the other hand, had barely brought him up. Not that I told him that small detail.

As I was leaving school, I ran into Ian. He barely said hi before launching into a spiel about someone from Global Pictures who'd come to the comic-book store to do trend forecasting, but my paranoid thoughts about Becca's friends not liking me were churning in my brain too fast to pay close attention.

"None of us is cooperating," he was saying when we got outside. The sky was tinged with purple and the after-school crowd was more boisterous than usual—we weren't the only ones celebrating the end of SHINE. My focused friend went on, "The whole point of Toro Boy is he has this one amazing power, his superstrength, and is otherwise a totally normal teenager." He was so worked up, he barely paused to take a breath. "He's supposed to live in a normal apartment building and listen to punk rock and never get girls but they've changed everything. Now they're setting it in a castle and he has a supermodel girlfriend."

"Doesn't sound very punk rock to me," I mumbled.

"I know, they're ruining everything. They've also added stupid powers like a cloak of invisibility and I bet they'll find a way to mess up his horns too."

We stopped in front of my bike, which I'd locked to a pole down the block from school. I can usually unlock it with my eyes closed, but my hands were shaking and I didn't get it until the third try.

"What's with you?" he asked.

"I'm fine . . . just . . ." Then he caught my eye and the truth came spilling out. "I'm meeting Becca's new friends. I mean, they're her old friends, but they're new to me. . . . How do I look?"

I was wearing black jeans and a cream-colored tunic that had once belonged to Kiki. I had carefully applied black eyeliner à la Brigitte Bardot.

"Fine. Is some *guy* gonna be there or something?" He scrunched up his face, clearly confused.

"No, but . . . The girls all go to Brookfield. It's the most uppity school in the city."

"I know what Brookfield is." He sounded peeved. "But so what? I mean, you go to the biggest dork school and it's not like you're the biggest dork on earth."

"It's not like I'm the biggest dork on earth? Is that supposed to be a compliment?"

Ian's face lit up with a trace of a smile. "Around these parts, sure."

• • •

I rode uptown and locked up my bike outside an Indian video store on Forty-first Street. Louis and I had planned to meet up by the sandwich shack on the edge of Bryant Park. Waiting there, I took in the park's transformation. Its new temporary movie house made it look like the world's biggest container of Jiffy Pop, with an enormous silver bubble looming over the grass.

Something sharp pressed into me from behind and I jumped back like a spooked horse.

"Why are you such a spaz?" Louis murmured. He smelled like deodorant soap and his racket case was strung at a diagonal across his navy puffy down jacket. Louis is always coming from either tennis or his shrink's office. "You're the one who told me to meet you here," he uttered.

I looked down. "So I'm a little nervous. I haven't met Becca's friends yet." Might as well get it out in the open.

"I thought I was the one who's supposed to be nervous." He pulled a CD out of his pocket and waggled it in the air.

"You made the mix!" The night before, I'd told him he needed to ramp up his efforts at getting Becca's attention. "Nothing too gushy though, right?" I checked.

"Just my favorite Barry White and Justin Timberlake love songs." Louis waited a second, then shook his auburn nest of hair in disbelief. "Give me some credit. Now are you ready to watch me work my magic?"

"You better believe it." I hip-checked him.

Inside the bubble, there were so many electric heaters I nearly forgot it was January. In one corner a band was playing swingy old-fashioned music and volunteers were coming around and handing out pizza and soda to the people who'd settled on the ground.

My green jacket must have been brighter than I'd realized;

barely a minute after we'd entered the area, Becca had spotted us and called Louis's cell phone. I know, I know, I am the only fifteen-year-old in the Western Hemisphere without one. My cheapskate parents share a shoe-box-sized cell phone that they use about once a year, combined.

Louis hung up. "She says they're by the stage," he told me.

"Then we should go there."

Louis cast me an unsure look through his tortoiseshell frames. "I guess so." He looked nervous beyond belief and I felt a ripple of uncertainty flutter through my stomach.

"We can do it," I said, more for my benefit than his, and we proceeded to try to navigate the cracks left between people's blankets.

Becca and three other girls were front and center, sprawled out on a striped sheet that was covered with junk food. From a distance, the new girls didn't look as photo-shoot-ready as I'd expected. There was a vaguely messy aspect to all of them, or maybe it was just that they had bigger, more untamed hair than I'd expected. Becca looked up and motioned for us to hurry over.

"Nice spot," I told Becca as I crouched down next to her, trying not to stare at her friends. "Very . . . um . . . VIP."

Leave it to me to sound like somebody's corny uncle.

"I know it's too close, but I forgot my glasses," she said sweetly, pushing aside a takeout container of guacamole. "Hey Louis!" she exclaimed in the cheerful tone of somebody who couldn't possibly be romantically interested.

Louis rallied a "Hey" that was probably intended to sound macho but came out defeated. He took a seat by one of the blanket's corners.

"I haven't seen this movie in so long," Becca said, and launched into a sales pitch about its epic greatness. As she detailed a scene where a terrifying hiss turns out to be nothing but the sound of an ordinary bus, I snuck a glance at the other girls. They were pretty, but more than that, they were interesting-looking, a development I was not expecting. One of them had a wavy brown hairstyle that looked straight out of a 1940s movie. Another one had a round face and long frizzy curls the color of boiled carrots. And then there was an otherworldly-looking one, with paper-white hair and skin to match. No wonder Becca was so taken with this bunch. The light-haired one caught me looking at her and smiled. "Hey, I'm Reagan." She turned to our friend in common. "Becca, you gonna introduce us or what?"

The other two warmed up after Becca rattled off our names. Diana, the redhead, asked Louis where he played tennis. Sills, the retro movie-star girl, set her sights on me and rolled over on her stomach.

Suddenly my cross-legged position felt overly formal, and I leaned closer to the ground.

"Becca said you went to Farmhouse, right?" Sills asked.

"Yeah." I was trying to contain my surprise. Becca had told them about me? I glanced over at my friend to see she was playing with a sheet of temporary skeleton tattoos and a water bottle.

"I always wanted to go there," Sills said. "It sounds much more humane than Brookfield—that's where Reagan and I go."

Unless she was messing with me, she was actually pretty nice. I just nodded as nonchalantly as I could while the pale girl made a puking gesture at the mention of her school. "Thank God I'm a senior. I'm so outta there!" She seemed nice too.

Sills ignored the interruption and went on, "My ex-boyfriend went to Farmhouse. I used to hear all about it from him."

"Really?" I looked over at Louis, our resident Farmhouse student, but he was busy investigating the inside of a bag of

SunChips. I couldn't picture somebody this polished going out with any of the eccentrics from Farmhouse, and my normally raspy voice raised a few octaves. "Who's your ex-boyfriend? Maybe Louis and I know him."

Before she could answer, though, a guy with a VOLUNTEER T-shirt came over and delivered a whole box of pizza to our blanket. As far as I could tell, everybody else in the tent was just getting slices, but then again, nobody else in the tent looked as special treatment–worthy as Becca and her friends. Becca rubbed her new skeleton tattoo in place and dug into the pizza.

I was dying to ask how they'd hooked up this four-star pizza delivery, but it was probably best to wait until we were out of earshot of our less lucky neighbors.

"You probably don't know him." Sills raised herself off the ground and helped herself to a slice. "He graduated a long time ago."

"Sills—there's no way she doesn't know him." Diana rolled her green eyes as she took a slice and passed the box to Louis.

"Wiley Martins," supplied Reagan.

Louis and I locked eyes and exchanged a silent *whoa*. Winston Martin-Schultz was Farmhouse's first and only celebrity alum. When we were in middle school, he used to sit around the hallways playing the guitar and looking like a hotter version of Bob Dylan. Nobody was that surprised when he got a record deal, though we all found his transformation into straitlaced pop star "Wiley Martins" a little baffling.

"You know, he used to be a total hippie," I told them.

"Still is," Sills said. "He's just playing the game."

"Well, he's doing a good job of it," I said, disapproval ringing in my voice. "Did you see the huge spread of him in this month's *TeenVogue*?"

"He did *Teen Vogue?*" Sills looked disgusted. "He always said he was holding out for *Rolling Stone.*"

"Yeah. Actually, I think I have it in here," I blurted out. The second I pulled the new issue out of my bag I regretted it—Sills couldn't have sounded more condescending in her pronunciation of the magazine's name, and now I was broadcasting that I was one of its faithful readers. But, much to my surprise, the quartet seized on the issue like a pack of vultures.

While they combed the magazine's pages, I checked up on my buddy Louis with a sidelong glance. Not one to give up easy, he was watching his beloved Becca, and I could tell by the way his lips were wobbling that he was racking his brain for something Becca-worthy to say. "Hey, Shuttleworth," he called out at last. "What's with the tattoo?"

She laughed. "It's temporary. Want one?"

"I was thinking of getting a real tattoo," Louis said. "Maybe a tiger, or Elvis?"

My heart panged for my friend, who was losing his cool by the second, but Becca wasn't even paying attention to him. "Yeah, cool . . . ," she said absentmindedly.

"I once saw this guy with a—" Realizing Becca wasn't listening, Louis's jaw tightened. I could tell he was about to break.

"Give her the CD," I whispered.

He gave me a desperate look, then shook his head and stood up. "I should get going. My dad just texted me to remind me I said I'd go to some recruiting dinner with him."

What a terrible liar. Louis's delivery was fine, but his excuse was pathetic. In his five years as the general manager of the New York Knicks, Louis's dad had yet to invite his son to any glitzy functions—those honors fell exclusively to Ulrika, my oldest friend's wicked stepmother.

"No!" Becca protested.

Well, what do you know? Maybe there was hope after all.

But when I looked over at Becca I saw her outburst had nothing to do with whether Louis stayed. "Sorry," she mumbled. She was visibly embarrassed. "I just know her, that's all." She was pointing at the magazine. "Annika Gitter."

"I never realized what an idiot she was," said Reagan.

I was struggling to see who they were talking about and was late to tune in to my friend's byes. I waved disappointedly to Louis, then scooted closer. The magazine was open to the regular "My Crib" feature, and it showed a girl jumping on her bed in a chartreuse tutu-style dress.

"Have you read this part yet?" Diana asked.

When I shook my head, Becca foisted the magazine in my lap. "You have to. It's so embarrassing."

I took the magazine and glanced up at Becca. I had no clue what she was talking about. By this point, I'd seen many sides of Becca, but embarrassment wasn't one of them. Her eager eyes told me to stop looking to her for clues and to check out the magazine. I didn't have to study it for long to figure out what the girls were reacting to. TeenVogue isn't known for featuring Nobel Laureates, but the girl of the month had the rest of the "My Crib" girls beat in the idiocy contest.

Apparently Annika liked to draw the number seven on everything because she thought prime numbers were "inspiring," and she kept her collection of raindrops in vintage contact lens containers. "This is great stuff," I said sarcastically. "You couldn't make this up, could you?"

"Read the bottom, about the animals," said Sills.

"'I'm an animal-rights activist and in honor of that, all the animal rugs in my room are reproductions,'" I read aloud.

"You all know that's not true," Sills said. "Her grandfather was, like, the great white hunter of Africa. He gave her all his skins."

"Priceless." Becca smirked. Then she looked around, suddenly upset. "Wait—did Louis leave for good?"

I smiled inwardly. Better late than never.

Cat People was about a lady who was convinced she was going to turn into a killer panther. I'm not sure I'd call it the greatest movie ever made, but I could definitely see why Becca liked it.

"That was awesome," I said afterward.

Becca smiled graciously, as if she had made the movie herself, and rolled up her blanket. Disappointment gripped me. I didn't want the night to be over just yet. I was finally with Becca's mysterious other friends and I still wanted to get to know them better.

One of the pizza volunteers, a man with a beard and thinning hair, came by to pick up our trash and I noticed him steal a smile at Becca.

Granted, I knew my friend was beautiful, but what a pervert.

"Do you guys want to get dessert at the Bryant Park Café?" Sills asked.

So the night wasn't over just yet. Hurray! I had to hold back from crying out "Pretty please."

"Excellent idea," Becca said. "You guys go ahead. I'm going to use the bathroom here first."

"Isn't there one in the café?" I asked, separation anxiety kicking in. "It's probably a little nicer."

But Becca was already buttoning up her coat and starting for the exit. "I really have to go," she called back at me.

Was she in a hurry to break away from us or was I imagining things?

Befuddled, I put on my coat and followed Reagan, Diana,

and Sills onto the street. Without Becca there to buffer us, I started to feel awkward. The crowd was heaving and I was pretty wrapped up in my sudden feelings of discomfort, so I was surprised when I noticed the same golden face with the crooked nose from my dream I had in the SHINE lecture. The image was affixed to a bathroom shed at the edge of the park.

No way. My breath stopped.

"Guys," I said. "I'll meet you there."

"Where are you going?" Sills eyed me in confusion.

Sometimes I wonder how much further I'd get in life if I didn't have to spend so much time making up excuses.

"I have to get my bike," I said after a tormented pause. "I'm going to bring it over to the restaurant."

I didn't stick around to hear her remind me that the restaurant was only across the park. My eyes set on the golden face, I pushed through the crowd. I was so close to something major, I could feel it in my bones.

I was almost at the bathroom shed when I noticed a girl around my age sitting on a bench outside the bathroom. She had her nose stuck in the *Daily News* but the nearest streetlamp was a good distance away and it was dark—there was no way she could be reading. Everything about her looked suspicious with a capital S—the only thing I could think was that she had to be waiting for Becca.

But why?

Without stopping to think, I pulled the shed's door open. Inside, there were two stalls and a sink area with busted-up mirrors and paper towels strewn all over the floor. More to the point, it was just like my dream: Becca was in the entryway, standing in front of a brick wall and conferring with a man wearing wire-rim glasses. I gripped the wall and watched the man hand her a pile of tin containers.

Something clicked from behind.

My heart skipped a beat. If I was seeing so many details from my dream, then that had to be somebody loading a gun.

Ice ran through my veins.

"Becca!" I screamed.

There were cries of panic as Becca and the man scurried into a corner. My heart pounding, I turned around to face the shooter.

But it wasn't a gunman. It was just the girl from outside. She was holding up a digital camera.

A blinding flash went off but by the time I could see again, she'd already run away.

I spun back around and locked eyes with Becca. Her lips were parted and her eyes had popped open as wide as silver dollars.

What the hell was going on?

"Get out of here." She sounded worried—for whose sake I couldn't tell. "Now."

{ 5 }

Under the Radar

You'd think after a head-on collision like that, I'd get some sort of explanation, but Becca just stayed in the corner of the entryway, crouching by a radiator.

"Claire, just go. . . ." I'd never seen her look this anxious. "I'll call you later tonight."

She had to be kidding me.

"I don't understand," I said sadly.

She tilted her head softly and snuck a glance at the man beside her. "It's the best I can do right now."

The man gave me a stern look. Becca's shoulders shot up in a minuscule shrug.

"Fine, see you around," I said, my hurt ringing through

55

every syllable. I clenched my fists and huffed out the door. If she wasn't prepared to explain what was happening, then there was somebody else who might shed some light on the situation.

I made my way to the edge of the park and crossed the street. There was a pay phone outside a dry cleaner and in no time I was dialing Kiki's number. I needed to share every minute detail with her. I needed to hear what to do next. I did not need her new friend to pick up and inform me that my grandmother had decided to go to Newport for the weekend. "She's catching an ice sculpture show," Jon-Jon said lazily. "I had to pass on the opportunity. I'm a Southern boy and the only ice sculpture I like is in the shape of a cube, in a glass of bourbon."

Just my luck.

I made my way around the corner and hopped on my bike. Riding down Sixth Avenue, I felt all kinds of messed up. I could barely pay attention to the traffic lights and I had to pedal extra slowly to keep from getting rubbed out by a bus.

As I pulled into the Washington View Village courtyard, I was hit by a gurgly "Yoo-hoo!"

Standing in front of me were Cheri-Lee Vird, my mom's lovable best friend, and Sheila, her rather less lovable daughter. Sheila narrowed her eyes at me.

"Hi, sweet pea!" Cheri-Lee's tone couldn't have been kinder, but I wasn't in the right frame of mind for an encounter. "You headed up to 8C?"

I shuddered. "Are Mom and Dad having one of their salons?"

Cheri-Lee nodded.

Friday nights, my apartment tends to get overrun with cigarette smoke and French professors. They'll begin by talking about serious things, like philosophy or the French national arts endowment, but the second they get blitzed on Pernod, they blast Marseillaise rap songs and try to dance like the kids in *la banlieue*. It can get kind of embarrassing.

"Guess I'll see you up there," I said, turning toward my building, but Cheri Lee reached out and stopped me.

"While we're all here, I could use your help with a *quandary* of mine." A poetry professor, Cheri-Lee thinks it's her duty to sprinkle all dialogue with interesting words.

She took a Macy's bag from her daughter and foisted a stiletto boot into my hand. "Sheila's going clubbing and she got these new shoes for the occasion."

"Mom." Sheila dragged the word out into three syllables. "It's obvious you hate them. I don't care. And besides I'm not going clubbing. I'm going to *a* club. Elle House." She raised her chin and shot me a pointed look, as if I was supposed to be jealous she was going to the "it spot" I'd read about three years ago in *W* magazine. But instead all I felt was pity—with her head held at this angle, the fake tan line along her jawline was as sharp as a paper cut.

"So, Claire, what's your professional verdict?" Cheri-Lee said. "Are these really what the kids are hobbling around in these days?" She couldn't have sounded more amused. I guessed it was her coping mechanism for having the most awful daughter on earth.

"Why are you asking *her*?" Sheila groused. "I mean, I wouldn't call Claire an expert on fashion of the twenty-first century." She pursed her lips and stared at me.

"They're perfect," I said, ignoring her dig. "And very useful. Pair them with a sword and you're invincible."

Okay, so my swipe at Sheila's secret life as a sword and sorcery fanatic was a low blow, but it did the trick. Her mouth did that turkey-gobble thing it does when she gets upset, and she grabbed the boots from her mother and trotted toward their building.

Luckily, the full extent of my cruelty was lost on Cheri-Lee, and on the elevator ride up she just told me for the hundredth time how important it was to her that her daughter and I patch things up.

Why didn't she realize that after what Sheila and I had been through, making nice wasn't in the cards?

"Sometimes people grow apart," I said. Of all people, Cheri-Lee should know that. Her husband Wendell had recently up and left her for a grad student who ate different-colored foods based on the day of the week.

"And sometimes people grow *up*," she countered, stepping off the elevator toward my apartment. I unlocked the door and was hit by a blast of Edith Piaf. Trailing behind Cheri-Lee, I slunk down the hallway and slipped into my room, where I wouldn't have to deal with anybody in my immediate family or the NYU French department.

Or so I thought.

When I opened my bedroom door, my jaw dropped. Mom and her ghostwriting client Saffron Scott were rifling through my bookshelves. Their cheeks were flushed from cocktails and their hairdos were similarly disheveled. If they weren't both unfairly beautiful, they would've looked completely mental.

"These are cute, no?" Mom picked up my new Empire State Building and Chrysler Building paperweights.

"Love, love, love!" Saffron proceeded to take a zillion digital photos.

What on earth was happening?

"Um, hi?" I cut in. "Do you guys need any assistance?"

When they realized they weren't alone, the pair turned to face me. Saffron looked a little embarrassed but Mom just smiled. "Oh, hi, dear. Saffron's working on a segment on hot teen spaces for her show," she said airily. "She was thinking of including your room."

Saffron tucked her camera in her sweater pocket. "Only if you want to," she said, training an endearing smile on me. Then she turned to Mom. "We should probably get out of her hair for now. Claire should think it over."

Though you wouldn't think it, having been an actual functioning member of the real world for the past few decades, Saffron's pretty grounded. I think she just gets silly when she's palling around with my mother.

Saffron started for the door and my mother took her time making her exit. "Do it," she mouthed to me on her way out.

I waited until the door had fully closed, then straightened my polar bear rug and put my plush ham and cheese baguette back in its rightful place. I lay down on my bed, wishing with all my might that the noise outside would die down and my phone would ring. I needed to hear from Becca. None of today made any sense. I closed my eyes and willed every molecule in my body to settle down.

Sheila was wearing star-shaped sunglasses and was tucked into the passenger seat of a vintage convertible, letting the dimpled guy to her left do the driving while she coolly took in the slate-colored scenery—rolling hills, elm trees and, weirdly, a clan of polar bears. I was running alongside and trying to hop in, offering all these presents that she kept pushing away. It wasn't until I produced a huge lollipop that she let me dive into the backseat.

Next thing I knew, my eight-year-old brother Henry was bearing down on me, handing me a message he'd written on the back of a Batman party bag.

GO TO BECCA'S AT NOUN TOMORROW.

My heart skipped.

"You're the best, Hen." I was too happy to hear from my friend to tease him for his spelling and he'd already started to scamper toward the door. "Hold up. Aren't you going to wait for your tip?" I reached under the bed and felt around for a piece of chocolate. The area under my bed doubles as a candy storage unit.

"There's none left." His face went pale when he realized what he'd effectively admitted.

I sat up. "How do you know what's under my bed?"

He hiccupped. "Charlie W. came over before."

"And you let him plunder my chocolate supply?" I could feel my face turning purple in anger. "You know you're not allowed to let your friends in here."

His eyes shifted from one corner to the next, like a Kit-Cat clock.

"Too late to think of an excuse," I said. "You're already busted. You can just pick up some refills on your next walk and we'll call it even."

Henry nodded and ripped out of there, the back of his neck as red as I'd ever seen it.

I made a mental note to kill my little brother and lay back down on my cozy comforter. I gazed at the glow-in-the-dark star stickers on the ceiling and soon my eyelids were heavy as soup cans.

Everyone at the party had on the coolest costumes. Which might explain why my dance partner wasn't Andy—or even a guy for that matter. It was a gray kangaroo, with a margarita in one paw and my oven-mitted hand in the other (I was dressed up as Julia Child). Mr. Kangaroo dipped me with the finesse nobody dressed like a minor league baseball mascot has any right to possess.

When I woke up the next morning I felt so groggy I kept looking over at my clock and then drifting off for another two minutes. Or forty-five minutes. Two dreams in one night was almost too much to handle. Eventually, I got out of bed and opened the window shade. I tried to get my French homework out of the way, but I was too hyped up about my upcoming visit to Becca to think, let alone conjugate *savoir* in the subjunctive. It was Saturday morning, anyway, so I ended up killing time reading about *Cat People* on the Internet (random trivia: the reason the panther was hardly ever visible was the movie's tiny budget) and painting Nailgrowth Miracle solution on my stubby fingernails.

When it was finally time to get ready for my rendezvous with Becca, I was feeling tired to the point of dizzy. Drawing from some perk-up advice I'd read in a fashion magazine, I massaged minty toothpaste over my neck in the shower. Then I remembered another supposedly helpful tidbit, so I dressed as brightly as possible, putting on a yellow turtleneck under a blue smock-style dress from Kiki's closet. I bundled myself up in the living room, said good-bye to my parents, and off I went.

By the time I pulled up outside Becca's town house, I was a little more awake—and a lot more annoyed. The pole I usually lock my bike to was taken by a tangerine Vespa. I sighed and started to roll my bike down the block.

"And I haven't even told you the scary stuff yet!" I looked up to see Becca was screaming at me from her bedroom window. "What's the deal? Are you leaving already?"

Fat chance.

I pointed at my bike and she waved her hand in the air, then disappeared. She must have shot down the stairs like a cheetah, because within seconds she was standing in the doorway. Looked like I wasn't the only one with sleep issues: there were dark circles under her eyes and she had on a long white flannel nightgown.

She looked like she belonged in one of the horror movies she's obsessed with. But the spooky effect was completely ruined when she smiled ear-to-ear.

"Bring the bike in," she instructed. "Nobody will slash your tires."

"You sure it's okay?" I checked. She'd never made this offer before.

Becca nodded crisply and shut the door behind me. I followed her up the marble stairs and into a room on the second floor that was crammed with state-of-the-art exercise equipment, a massage chair, and an industrial-looking margarita machine. "This is where we park all the toys that Mommy buys and never uses," Becca explained. Her statement made me grimace; the only things my mom ever buys and doesn't use are the items she decides are too expensive and returns the next day. "You can put it wherever you want," Becca said.

I was looking around when a plastic bin caught my attention. It was spilling over with gorgeous aprons, dish towels, and oven mitts, and I immediately thought of the dream I'd had where I'd been wearing an oven mitt.

Could it be . . . ?

"Mom went through a cooking phase," Becca explained, picking up on my interest. "She signed up for some intensive six-week pastry program and made a cake in the shape of Dolly Parton's head. None of us had the heart to tell her it tasted like soap."

I took one last look at the bin and decided there was probably no more to it than that. My curiosity sated, I rested my bike against a mirrored wall and followed my friend to her bedroom. As far as I could tell, we were the only people in the house, which was sort of eerie. I wasn't used to it being this empty.

"Sorry to be such a zombie," she groaned. "I just haven't slept at all."

"And why's that?"

Becca opened her mouth, then paused. "Lemme just go to the bathroom first."

I sat down in the super-soft brown leather chair by the window and glanced around. I hadn't been in Becca's room in at least a month. It was enormous, with high ceilings and dark orange walls that somehow seemed more elegant than Halloweeny. Next to her computer, the new *Teen Vogue* was open to the "My Crib" spread we'd been laughing at the day before.

"I am so not into sleep deprivation," Becca said when she came back. She fell onto the bed, propping her neck up against a huge corduroy teddy bear.

"Not sleeping is the worst," I said, trying to swat away my own dream-hangover fatigue. "But I'm not going to clear out so you can nap. You need to tell me what's up."

"Like I can ever sleep in the day." She shook her head. "You know my brain's wired funny."

Make that two of us.

She gave me a pleading look. "And we've barely hung out. I've missed you."

"You've barely even tried to see me," I challenged.

"And you think that was my choice?" Becca sucked in her cheeks and picked at what remained of her temporary skeleton tattoo.

"But who's trying to keep us apart?" I asked, genuinely perplexed.

Just then, it occurred to me that Andy might be behind this trial separation.

"Does Blue Moon mean anything to you?" Becca said.

"What's that? Like, a brand of cheese?"

"Catch." Becca tossed a sharp object at me. "Oops, sorry."

I crouched down to pick it up. It was a key chain—a blue and white oval charm with an old Christopher Columbus–style ship printed on it. A chill went down my spine. It was the same boat I'd seen in my dream—the nautical one that I'd thought had been leading me to the shoplifter girl. I could feel the hairs on the back of my neck come to attention.

I looked up at her. "What is it?"

There was a beat of hesitation. "The *Blue Moon*," she said. "It's actually Dutch, so it's called the *Blauwe Maan*. The Blue

Moons are this . . . little society of girls whose ancestors supposedly came over to these shores together."

"And you're in this secret society?" I could feel my eyes bugging out.

"Do you have to call it that? I'm telling you about it, aren't I?"

She had me there.

"Sorry. This not-entirely secret society," I said. "Is that what you've been doing all this time, when you said you were hanging out with the Brookfield girls?"

She smiled guiltily. "It wasn't a lie—most of the other members go to Brookfield." She stretched out her arms and cracked her knuckles. "All the girls' moms were members. I know you're thinking it's really stupid, but my mom was in the Moons, and so was my grandmother, and so on." She looked at me with widened eyes. "I couldn't really say no."

"I understand." I fingered my cameo under my turtleneck. I knew a thing or two about family traditions

"Anyway, I'm sorry I've been so weird. When I was tapped I didn't think it was a big deal, but the whole initiation turned out to be an elaborate process. The worst part of it was the rule that says you're not allowed to tell anyone except your family until you get your boat."

"You mean this thing?" I dangled the key chain in the air.

She nodded slowly. "Isn't it pretty? I got it last night. Or I guess it was officially this morning."

Hmm . . . anything that took place in the middle of the night was by nature intriguing. "And you're allowed to tell your friends now?"

"I'm allowed to tell you. I got . . . special clearance."

"Sounds fancy. What do the other rules say?"

"Just that you have to dress in all white and drink blood once a week." Becca watched me with mounting amusement, then laughed. "No, I'm kidding. It's all very innocent. Innocent to the point of being dorky."

"Sorry, B, but I met the other girls. Say what you will, but they are *not* dorky."

She looked up at the ceiling. "Okay, but the things we do are." Her voice rose defensively. "The whole point is doing little favors for the city, like planting community gardens or repainting the youth wing at hospitals."

"How ladylike," I muttered. "And do you throw balls too?" I felt caught between jealousy and curiosity.

She pshawed. "The group is way too obsessed with privacy to throw parties. The clubhouse is in a secret location and you're not allowed to do anything that will get you mentioned in the press."

Kiki once told me that the number-one rule of old school New York society was: "A lady only agrees to be written about on the occasion of her birth, marriage, or death." I was kind of stunned—it seemed unfathomable that anybody would actually take that kind of thing to heart.

"So," I said, breaking the silence. "Who was the guy I saw you with yesterday in the bathroom? Is he a member of the not-secret society?"

"Russell?" Becca laughed. "No, he works for the Parks Department. I was picking up the movie they showed."

She was losing me. "Come again? Your club was secretly behind the event?"

She bit down on a fingernail. "I was. The Moons weren't. The movie night is a Parks Department project. My dad heard through a contact that the print of *Cat People* they were planning on showing got lost and since we—my family, that is—have a copy . . . it made sense to call the city and offer to lend it."

"I see," I said, repressing the temptation to remark on how

she'd said "call the city" in the offhand manner most people use to talk about ordering Chinese delivery. "And why didn't you want the picture of you and that guy getting out? Because you're in a club that's publicity shy?"

"Yeah, kinda." Becca's eyes were fluttering closed. "God, how am I going to survive tonight if I'm this tired?"

"What's tonight got to do with this?"

"Nothing," she said evasively. "Anyway, back to the picture and why it can't get out. It's more about . . . my family."

My heart bumped against my chest. And not in a good way. Only a few months ago somebody had been plotting to kill her family. What could it be now?

"What about your family?" I asked.

"It's nothing that bad." She was looking at me through half-open eyes. "It's just business. The company has to shut down the ketchup plant in Queens because of some new zoning codes and now they're starting to build a new factory in the Bronx." She shifted onto her side. "I need to be careful. I can't let pictures get out that make it look like I'm all buddy-buddy with the people who run the city. People will go crazy and say there's corruption at work and we're buying favors or whatever and they could try to prevent the new factory from being built."

My mind was about to explode. This was all so much more complicated than any of the five-alarm political issues that came up in Washington View Village, like whether to invite the cranky University Provost to building parties. I picked up a rubber spider from Becca's dressing table and pulled its gummy legs up over its head.

"I'm not just protecting my family," Becca went on. "It was really stupid of me to meet him in public like that. There are thousands of New Yorkers with jobs on the line. I should have had a messenger bring it back the next day, but it was all very last minute."

"Well, were you supposed to know there'd be some psychopath with a camera following you around?"

"Actually, yes." Her words came out slowly and she tilted her head. Only now did I realize how little of the situation she'd bothered to fill me in on. I put the spider back down on the table.

"What do you mean?" I said it gently, but I was feeling as tense as a tightly wound spring.

"I'll show you." Becca got up and I followed her over to her computer. She typed in an address she seemed familiar with. Moonwatcher.net's home page had a line drawing of a girl with a telescope pointed at the night sky, and at the top were the words: "Your number-one source for Blue Moon sightings."

"Your community service club has a full-time stalker?" I asked in disbelief.

"It's not exactly the most cutting-edge site," Becca said as she flipped around from page to page. "But yeah, all eyes are on us. Some people have remarkably little to do with their time." She looked up at me and caught my horrified expression. "It's just a stupid prank that's been dragging on forever. Not that they've gotten any better about it. We moved clubhouses but I don't think they know—sometimes we walk in and out of the old building to keep them confused."

My jaw dropped: a square inch in New York City real estate is worth its size in gold.

"You kept the old building?" I asked.

"No, but it's easy to get into. A bunch of psychiatrists use it for their offices. The people behind this site wait outside and take pictures of all the high-school-aged girls going in and out."

Feeling creeped out, I looked back at the screen. There was

very little text, and as for the few pictures of the Moons, they weren't particularly revealing. And yet, they were still *there*.

"They're wrong about who's a member at least half the time," Becca said. "But it's the other half of the time that worries me."

My head clouded over as I studied the Moons' faces, as well as pictures of a few unfamiliar girls. "I'll show you who they're right about," Becca said, flipping through the pictures to point out herself, the girls I'd met the other night, a chubby-cheeked girl named Poppy, and, most surprisingly, Annika Gitter, tiger skin collector/animal rights activist extraordinaire.

"*TeenVogue* girl is one of your sorority sisters?"

"She *was*," Becca said shortly, not bothering to take offense at my calling the society a "sorority." "She was de-Mooned for violating the club's number-one rule."

"The one about having no public profile?" I asked.

She nodded and smiled. "We had to bounce her out last night. Look, there's something else you should see."

Becca leaned over the computer and started clicking around faster then before. Then she stood back up and crossed her arms. "Look familiar?"

My heart skipped a beat. It sure did. Whitewashed and hyper-magnified as the picture was, there was no mistaking those different-colored eyes and that scrunched-up nose.

"No way," I murmured.

But the real mystery wasn't how I'd ended up on the screen—it was how I'd ever got it in my head that I looked re-motely like Brigitte Bardot that afternoon.

Before I could say anything, somebody rapped on the door and flung it open.

"Beck, have you seen my Spanish textb—" Andy stopped suddenly and stared at the computer screen. "Whoa. That's pretty brutal."

I gulped and took another look at the picture. Its horribleness was growing by the second. My pores looked big enough to crawl into and, even lovelier, the fuzz on my cheeks recalled a freshly hatched chick.

Andy came closer to me for a quick comparison. He was a couple of inches away from me and staring straight at my face as if everything were normal and he and I weren't the same people who'd had that terrible conversation in the cab about how he needed his space.

I could feel my cheeks crimsoning, and I was dangerously close to screaming with frustration.

"That picture is more realistic than reality," Andy marveled.

I made myself take a deep breath before speaking. "I'm glad you find it all so fascinating."

"Sorry." He was holding back laughter. "At least you're not one of those people who only look good in photographs and are freaky in real life."

And that was that supposed to make me feel better?

"That picture doesn't do you justice," he clarified, sensing my hurt feelings. His eyes lingered on me a beat before turning back to Becca. "Let me know if you find my book, okay?"

She nodded and put her arm around my shoulders after her brother left the room. "Ignore him," she said.

If only it were that simple. Turns out that when the boy of your dreams decides to stop liking you, ignoring him is the last thing you feel like doing.

{ 6 }

Girl at Random

I left Becca to catch up on her sleep and tried my hardest to dart past Andy's room without attracting his attention. Which might have been easier to do if I weren't lugging around an enormous red bicycle.

"Claire, wait!" I looked back to see Andy poking his head out the door, motioning for me to come over. Damn it. No matter how many droplets of anger were polluting my bloodstream, I couldn't say no to that guy.

Once Andy had reeled me back, he patted a spot next to him on the couch. "Have a seat." He fixed a smile on me. "I'll behave."

"I trust you," I said, maybe somewhat bitterly, from my

spot in his doorway. In truth, it was myself I didn't trust. I was trying my hardest to forget about him. If I came in and sat down next to him I'd end up saying something stupid or staring dopily at his rosebud lips and saying nothing at all. "Actually, I have to get going."

"I'm walking out too," he said, jumping up. "Can you hold on one second? I just have to find that book. I know it's here."

"Fine," I huffed. Waiting for him in the doorway, I focused on everything in his room that wasn't Andy himself—the Columbia hoodie on the floor, the bookshelf of dog-eared paperbacks, the wall that was covered with children's crayon drawings of ghosts and skyscrapers.

"Why are you being like that?" came his voice.

My gaze shot back to Andy as he dug his arm deep into the couch. "I don't want you to be upset," he said.

Then don't be so cold to me.

Before I could think better of it, my eyes were drawn to his lips. His perfect lips. His perfect lips, which I wanted to kiss. I was screwed.

"Everyone can look weird in pictures," he said.

Oh right, that was what he was talking about.

"It could be worse," he went on. "You could have to go to tutoring every stupid waking hour."

I looked down and sighed. Part of me felt sorry for Andy. But only a small part. I was also mad at him. If he just spent a little less time wandering around the city and a little more time at school, he wouldn't be suffering like this. And while we were on the subject, he wouldn't have an excuse to avoid me.

"Looks like we're in business." He plucked his Spanish book out from a crack between his couch cushions. "I wish I wasn't running late, we could get lunch or something."

Still unsmiling, he stepped closer and looked at me straight in the eyes. His mouth did that trembly thing it does before he grins. Without saying a word, he wrapped my burgundy chenille scarf around and around my neck until there wasn't any scarf left to wrap.

"Much better," he said.

I'm not proud, but my heart cracked like an egg.

We walked downstairs and I stalled outside the house, waiting for him to put his gloves on.

"Anyway," Andy said. "I heard what happened at the park."

I gave him a double take. "How'd you—"

"Family privileges, I guess." He shrugged. "Plus her big mouth. Of all the members of our family, I'm the only one who wouldn't kill her for her little mistake. You have no idea what a lucky thing it is that the picture was of you and not Becca. If our parents ever found out how careless she'd been . . ." He puffed out his cheeks. "You know my sister. Sometimes she doesn't think things through."

Andy is only two years older than Becca, but he was talking like he had his kid sister beat by a century.

"She seems to know what she's doing," I told him.

"Sure, in some ways. But she had no idea how close she came to messing things up. I mean, not until it was stupidly late. And now that she's in the Moons"—he paused to raise his eyebrows proudly—"she has to be extra careful."

I felt a stab of disbelief.

"Wait—how do you know about the Moons? And how do you know I know about them?"

He grinned. "She was nervous about telling you."

Everything in my head went slightly foggy.

"And you know everything about the Moons?"

"A little." He smiled, little crinkles forming at the corners of his eyes. "It's kind of messed up. My grandmother was insistent that Becca join, but she doesn't get it. In her day there wasn't even a rival club, let alone an Internet."

Weird. Becca hadn't said anything about a rival club. Could they be the merry pranksters behind Moonwatcher.net?

"If you ask me," Andy went on, "it's a high price to pay for belonging to some ring of socialites. She's lucky she has you to keep her out of trouble."

Was he on to something or was he just being nice to make up for his earlier gaffe?

"I just went to the bathroom," I replied nervously. Kiki had told me I wasn't to let anybody know about my strange dreams.

"Whatever, you still did my sister a huge favor. Good looking out. Or as the Spanish say . . ." He opened his textbook and consulted a couple of pages. "*Gracias para ir al baño.*"

"That was beautiful." I rolled my eyes.

His gaze lingered on me and church bells started to peal in the background. I turned away, embarrassed by the yummy sugarplum feeling that was spreading through me.

"What's wrong?" he asked.

"Nothing," I lied, "I just wanted to see where the bells were coming from."

"Christ, it's one already! My tutor is going to kill me."

"I'm not keeping you here," I told him, irritated.

"You kind of are." He made sure to glance up at Becca's window first, then leaned in and gave me a speedy peck on the lips. It would have been nice if it had lasted long enough for me to realize what was happening. "Don't be a stranger, okay?" he said.

Watching him charge toward Fifth Avenue, I could feel myself lighting up inside, and I also felt slightly ashamed. Why was he so sure I'd wait around for whatever rare moments he happened to feel like kissing me? And why was he so worried about keeping his tutor waiting around for five stupid minutes when I'd been right here for ages?

By the time I got home, I was done trying to decipher Andy's mixed messages. I knew I had to stop with the wishful thinking and be realistic: by this point, he was probably just stringing me along in case he ever started to like me again.

I poured myself an Orangina and went straight to my computer. First, I checked my e-mail, and found a message from Andy that just asked if I was more scared of heights or snakes. I didn't bother responding to his random question—Kiki always says the thing men like less than clingy women is those who don't put up a chase. Besides, I had more urgent things to deal with.

Moonwatcher.net was easy to find, and Becca hadn't been kidding when she said that the site wasn't cutting edge. The majority of the pages were labeled "Under Construction" or "Check Back Soon" and the ones that did have pictures weren't much to write home about either. Excluding the glamour shot of yours truly, all the other images of teenage girls appeared to have been taken with cell phones from very far away, and it was hard to tell the real members apart from the children of divorce who were headed to their therapist's office. I would have been hard-pressed to identify Becca if it weren't for her trademark brown leather satchel.

Feeling let down, I stood up to put on the Primettes, the girl group most of the members of the Supremes started out in when they were still little kids. I can always count on them to sing me out of a funk.

My hip must have banged into the computer when I'd got up to reach for my iPod, because when I looked back at the screen, a new picture was up. Like so much of my life, I hit the jackpot by total accident.

It's January, which means it's New Moon season. We proudly present you with a guide to the newest inductees. Please be understanding of the lack of detail—we're still gathering information on the new crop. Watch this space.

Annika Gitter (Gitter, Lowell & Harrison—Attorneys at Law)
"Least Likely Moon"
–Loud as a trumpet.
–Annika puts in an appearance at every party, often with her frenemy Cosi de la Goya.
–Don't expect anything she says to make sense— we hear she's no Einstein.

Diana Stoeffels (Stoeffels Realty Development)
"Horsey Moon"
–A die-hard animal lover, Diana has been spotted talking to squirrels and birds in Central Park.
–Keeps her thoroughbred Blue Thunder in a Cold Springs stable.
–Rumored to be a nudist.

Reagan Hendricks (GDB Global Media)
"Pale Moon"
–Has the blondest hair in New York—and it's supposedly natural.
–A senior at Brookfield Academy, she's the oldest Moon, and is headed to Dartmouth next year.
–Throws infamous house parties (her parents are *always* in L.A.).
–Only eats sugar-based products.

Poppy Williamson (Red Apple Bank)
"Man on the Moon"
–Don't let her baby face fool you—Poppy has gone out with every boy north of Canal Street . . . all for less than a week (it's rumored she's never gone farther than a kiss).
–Taller than most professional basketball players (some of whom she's dated).
–Used to study at New York City Ballet, hence her impeccable posture.

Samantha "Sills" Dressler (Dressler Life Insurance)
"Loner Moon"
–Armed with a bone-dry wit and Veronica Lake hairdo, Sills doesn't get the pack mentality.
–BFF with her dad, Jackson.
–Used to date Wiley Martins.
–Still might date Wiley Martins?

Rebecca Shuttleworth (Soul Sauce fortune)
"Scary Moon"
–Die-hard horror movie aficionado.
–Studies opera at Lincoln Center.
–The most enigmatic New Moon, Becca takes after her kooky mother and doesn't care about social customs. Attended zero galas last year and hangs out with Clara, a random girl from Henry Hudson High. Nobody knows anything about her.

There were also write-ups on a bunch of girls whose names I didn't recognize, but I didn't bother with the false leads. I was too keyed up, and, yes, a little hurt from the lame mention I'd scored. But I could either sit there licking my wounds or I could do some snooping of my own.

Not surprisingly, my Google search of Annika Gitter, Miss

Teen Vogue, was incredibly fruitful. She was pictured on countless society Web sites, often accompanied by a girl who had a thing for wearing her dresses backward—I could only assume this was the famous frenemy "Cosi."

The other five girls were a different story. There were only a handful of pictures of them, which was interesting considering how many parties their ridiculously connected families must get invited to on a daily basis. Reagan, the ghostly one with the media mogul parents, was last photographed at a movie opening when she was twelve. There were two pictures of Sills—one taking a walk with her dad, the other wearing a grungy knit hat and trying to have a secret brunch with my former classmate, Wiley Martins. The supposedly boy-crazy Poppy Williamson was captured leading a jazz dance class at a public school in the South Bronx. Becca was looking off to the side in a Young Friends of Lincoln Center Christmas party shot. And on the Web site for Miller's Saddlery store, there were a few shots of redhead Diana "Horsey Moon" Stoeffels, rocking an outfit that was appropriate for the English countryside circa 1896. And yet, she still looked crazy good. If I ever dared to don a riding cap, the horse would take one look at me and gallop away.

The thing that really did my head in, though, was the realization that I'd been so clueless all this time. I'd always taken it for granted that Becca's social life was limited to her family and me, and that her reason for maintaining a low profile was that she wasn't interested in rubbing her good fortune in everyone's faces. How had I never stopped to consider that she belonged to a world that mandated keeping under the radar?

I'd grown up shuttling between my immediate family's pseudo-bohemia and Kiki's world of former playboys and showgirls, where nothing could be too fabulous or loud. The concept of an upper echelon where people's entire lives were to be conducted in secret was too alien to even begin to understand.

I chewed the end of a pencil as I stared at the screen. My dreams seemed to be pointing me to the club. But was it my cameo's way of keeping Becca and me from drifting apart, or was something bigger going on?

Last thing I did was check the Blue Moons' official Web site. It was password protected, so I didn't get far, and the main page provided precious little information. The tagline said its "volunteers" had been "making New York a better place since 1743" and featured a group photograph that looked like it had been taken around the same time (okay, the 1980s). A group of girls with puffy, Princess Diana–like hairdos were clustered around a young girl in a wheelchair. It gave an East Seventy-third Street address, which was probably now the psychiatrists' office. There was no club e-mail or phone number, and no pictures that had been taken anytime since the invention of roll-on deodorant.

"Claire." Mom's voice scared me. I turned around to see her sinewy body leaning in the doorway. Her face bore a trace of embarrassment. "I just made some *langue du chat* cookies and discovered after they started baking that Henry had left his Shrinky Dinks in the oven."

"Uh-huh?" I said. Not that Mom ever notices anything, but I minimized the screen, just in case.

"I can't tell if the cookies taste like burned plastic or if the room just smells that way," Mom went on, utterly clueless. "Can you spare your professional opinion?"

"Okay, one sec." As I was getting up, something made me open the window again, and what I saw this time made me fall right back in my seat.

The little girl in the wheelchair was holding on to a butt-ugly Cabbage Patch doll. Just like in my Santa dream.

"Claire?" Mom almost sounded worried.

"Coming," I said, squinting at the photograph until it was nothing but pixels and dust. It made zero sense, but there had to be more where that came from. And there had to be more going with this club than I understood.

It was kind of scary, but it sure beat a life of pretty gardens and Shrinky Dinks.

{ 7 }

Flight of the Swann

The French writer Marcel Proust was born in the middle of July, though not a single one of my parents' regular Proust birthday parties has ever taken place in the summer, or even in the same month. Dad tries to sell the scattershot nature of the tradition as an "homage" to Proust's book *In Search of Lost Time*, but I don't buy it. My space cadet parents just like to fill the apartment with madeleine cookies and their crazy-pants friends whenever the mood strikes.

All this to say, while Becca must have been running around with her secret socialites, Henry and I spent Saturday evening helping our parents get ready for the fifth annual Proust party—and by "helping" them I mean we were doing the work while Dad graded papers and Mom locked herself away in the bathroom, applying Eau d'Hadrian lotion or whatever it is she does to get in the French mood.

Every now and again, she'd drift out into the living area in various stages of makeup to say how "*magnifique*" the place looked. And even though he was chained to his wheelie desk, Dad was also in unusually good spirits. When I put one of my favorite CDs on the stereo, he cried out, "The *Zoup-reams!*" and raised his stubby thumbs ceiling-ward.

After a little while, Henry's friend from downstairs, Rio Dershowitz, came by.

"You ready?" he asked my brother.

"We're working on a secret project," Henry said by way of explanation. Rio was impatiently jiggling in place. "We'll be back."

"All three of us," I heard Rio say as he and my brother disappeared into the hallway, their footsteps followed by peals of mad scientist laughter.

I felt a pang of depression. How was it that the only semi-normal member of my family was also the only one who had nothing better to do on a Saturday night than put out paper cocktail napkins for my parents' friends? And how was it that instead of feeling bitter, I was grateful for any distractions from my own nonlife? Becca had her mysterious secret society plan and Louis had told me he was spending the night manning the waterless urinal booth at Farmhouse's sustainability fair. I continued to spruce up the place and tried not to take it personally when Diana Ross sang about being trapped in a world that's a distorted reality.

"Bravo!" Dad exclaimed after I propped the last remaining prop—a Proust postcard—over one of Mom's Versailles snow globes. "Now *vas-y*. Go and be fifteen."

Like the thought hadn't occurred to me.

For once, I was relieved to see Mom poking her head out the bathroom door and smiling sheepishly my way.

"Claire, I still need to finish my column and send it off. What can I do to convince you to look after the crudités? Everything's in the fridge and—"

"It's okay, I'll figure it out," I said, trying to project a little annoyance and not give away the pathetic fact that I was happy to have a task. In truth, if she'd asked me to unclog the toilet with my bare hands, I would have jumped at the option—anything to keep my mind off the Blue Moons and how I wasn't one of them.

After I'd reorganized the platter of raw vegetables for the fifth time, there was nothing left to do but wait for the party to start. I lay down on the couch and let my eyelids flutter closed, the sounds of my household filtering in from all corners. There was Mom humming in the bathroom. And there was Dad muttering "Imbécile!" at some less-than-brilliant student's paper.

I was wearing a cat mask and scaling the wall of a grit-colored building. I effortlessly hoisted myself onto the roof, slunk across the surface, and slid all the way down the dove-gray chimney. Midway through my descent, a gray pair of hands reached out and pulled me into a secret compartment and someone started kissing me. Andy's lips felt more rubbery than usual and when I pulled back and looked closer I saw why: my secret lover was none other than a rubber chicken.

"Wake up or you're going to get baked, couch potato."

Henry and Rio were standing over me, both sporting eyeliner mustaches. Henry's blond curls were flopping over his eyes and he was holding the cardboard robot HAPPY BIRTHDAY sign he'd gotten at his eight-and-a-half birthday party. Thanks to a vigorous application of Wite-Out, the two-foot-tall robot now had a bow tie, heavy undereye circles, and a droopy mustache just like Proust's. Above him were the words HAPPY 108½ BIRTHDAY.

Feeling way too sleepy to contend with a couple of hyperactive eight-year-olds, I wiped sleep from my eyes and slowly came up to a seated position. Rio passed me a copy of Proust's *Swann's Way* and pointed to the author photo on the back. "You see?"

"One and the same," I said, glancing between the guy in the picture and the transformed robot. "Nice job."

"We're not done yet," Henry said. I could feel a grin curling on my face as Rio drew a line above my lip. Who knew the path to a better mood was to let a couple of eight-year-olds graffiti your face?

I got up to check out my pencil mustache in the mirrored Renault ad, then placed the Proust Robot over it. Then the three of us planted ourselves on the couch, where we patiently waited for the guests to arrive and marvel at Henry and Rio's wit.

But when our parents' friends started to trickle in, they just walked past the robot of honor and headed straight for the table, where they stuffed their mouths with Mom's cooking and tried to say clever things about Proust.

It was only a matter of minutes before conversation turned to French department gossip—namely, how Rudolphe Clavet had plagiarized his paper on the extermination of the Huguenots.

Party on, dudes.

"I think I'm done," I mumbled to my brother.

"Me too." He got up and motioned for his sidekick to follow. "We have a project on the twelfth floor."

Before I could ask what he was talking about, somebody tapped me from behind.

I put on my best face and turned around, ready to assist a newcomer who was looking for the wine stash.

The girl standing there was dressed in standard-issue French department garb—head-to-toe black. She had a hood over her head and she was holding a lit candlestick in front of her for the ultimate Left Bank effect.

"Red's by the window, white's in the fridge," I monotoned.

"I'm actually not thirsty."

I gasped. A loose red tendril fell over her cheek. This girl was no friend of my parents. It was Diana "Horsey Moon" Stoeffels, and gathered behind her were the other girls dressed in identically creepy getups. There was no sight I would've been happier to behold. Becca hadn't forgotten about me after all!

Poppy, the one Blue Moon I'd never seen before, was easy to pick out of the lineup—she was about six feet tall, and her yardstick-straight posture only accentuated her height. On the far end, Becca was biting down her lip the way she does when she's trying to tamp down her excitement. Looked like I wasn't the only one who was feeling good about things.

"No way!" I cried happily, my exhaustion letting up for the first time since Henry and Rio had crashed my sleep party. "How did you guys get in here?"

Diana brought a finger to her lips and handed me a small box. "Open it."

The box was made of blue stone and it contained a tiny ivory sculpture of a boat, just like the one on Becca's key chain.

One of the other girls—Sills, I think—stepped forward. "Blue Moon," she said. "Do you accept?"

"Sure," I rushed to respond, as if they were going to take away the gift if I didn't accept it within a nanosecond. I was still in shock from the whole Moon invasion as I tried to pry the boat out of the box, but it was stuck to the bottom, like the ceramic frog inside of Henry's Kermit surprise mug.

"I can't get it out," I said, frustrated.

Becca reached out for the box and grinned. "Not the *boat*, silly girl. Do you accept the whole thing?"

"The box?" I squinted at her.

"No." Becca rolled her brown eyes. "The . . . Moons. Do you accept our invitation?"

I was suddenly wide awake. Was it possible I'd fallen asleep on the couch and was having another crazy dream? Come to think of it, with all the candlelight, everything in the apartment did look black and white.

So I pinched myself hard. And again. Nothing changed, though—all the girls were still standing there, staring at me.

Next thing I knew, Becca and Reagan were holding on to my elbows and pulling me to my feet.

"The boat isn't yours just yet." Becca took back the box. "First you have to go through our initiation process."

"That is, if you live through it," Reagan tittered.

"*Attends*, Claire!" my dad called out.

Oh right. My parents. My stomach dropped like an anchor.

What was I going to say when they asked what was going on? *Oh, nothing, just letting a quintet of New York princesses abduct me and take me to places unknown. If you need to reach me, you can check out their Web site. It doesn't have the address or phone number of their secret clubhouse, though there's a hot Cabbage Patch doll.*

But to my eternal relief, Dad's curiosity didn't extend beyond the party's purposes. He showed no signs of registering the alien invasion—he must have mistaken my visitors for weirdly dressed grad students. "We've run out of lemon. Can you bring some back, *poupée*?"

"You got it!" Reagan answered for me, and pulled me into the hallway just before the door shut.

As we waited for the elevator to arrive, everyone was looking a little bashful. At first I thought it was because of my hallway's ugly multicolored walls, but then Becca pressed something wet into my palm.

I felt a rush of embarrassment as I realized what she was looking at. I wiped away my mustache and stuffed the dirty cotton pad in the garbage chute. Becca threw me a nod of approval.

"Here," Sills said, handing me the green Courrèges jacket she'd grabbed from its hook by the door. I was flattered that she'd recognized it as mine.

I finished zipping as we filed into the elevator. The fluorescent lights didn't exactly jibe with the sacred mood the girls were trying to project, and it didn't help matters when we got down to the lobby and Stanley, the night doorman, started freaking out about the candlesticks. "When I told you to put your fire hazards out, I didn't mean when you got around to it!"

I shot him an apologetic glance, but the troupe just kept going. Just as well, though. No sooner had they burst through the doors and into the winter night than the wind snuffed out their candles.

Sills led us around the corner, to La Guardia Place, where a van was waiting for us. It had seen better days—or more like better decades. I was so distracted checking out the shark-sized dent on its side that it took me a few seconds to realize what the lettering said: AIRPORT EXPRESS.

Becca hadn't mentioned where the clubhouse was. Could it possibly be out of state?

"Wait." I turned to Becca, more confused than ever. "I don't even have a toothbr—"

"I wouldn't get too excited," she said dismissively. "This and 'Mama's Plumbing' were the vans the rental agency had that would fit us all. We're not going to the airport. There are two more inductees after you."

I felt a rush of confusion. "What two—"

"You'll see soon enough," she said brusquely, and before I could say anything else, she pushed me forward. "We've decided to be a little more inclusive."

Still feeling dizzy, I crawled through the open door and found a seat in the back. Becca climbed in next to me. "You're okay with this, right?" she whispered.

I nodded, trying not to let on just how pathetically okay with it I was.

In the row ahead of us, Reagan reached into her pocket and pulled out a fistful of Mon Cheri and Bacci chocolates.

"What else do you have in there?" Becca called ahead, then glanced at me. "Reagan's always loaded up with the most random stuff. I don't think I've ever seen her use the same lipstick twice."

I bit down a smile. Feeling like this much of an insider wasn't something I was used to.

Reagan turned around and shrugged as she fed herself a Bacci. "It's unsanitary not to refresh your makeup regularly."

"Whatever." Becca rolled her dark eyes.

The van's driver gunned the engine and started toward Bleecker Street. I was checking out the nightclubs' MARDI GRAS MONDAYS and 2 4 1 LADIEZ NITE signs when my vision went out.

And it had nothing to do with my strange dreams.

Somebody had slipped a silky blindfold over my head and I didn't like it one bit.

"What are you doing?" I sat up straight. I was totally disoriented. And a little embarrassed for how scared it was starting to make me.

"Just relax." Becca's voice was calm. "We've all gone through this and lived to tell."

The words were probably intended to take the edge off, but

they had the reverse effect. I'd seen enough after-school television to be wary of secret societies.

"We'll explain everything soon enough," she promised. "Once we get back to the clubhouse."

Then I heard some papers rustling and the girls broke out into a chant. Apart from the couple of mentions of *Blauwe Maan* that flew by, it sounded like complete and utter gibberish, and a few giggles leaked through—it was a good thing their foremothers weren't around to hear their rendition of the song.

Being blindfolded, it was hard to keep track of time or judge distance, so I had no idea how long it was or how far we went before we stopped for a couple of pickups. The first newcomer kept quiet and the second one had a California valley girl voice and kept asking what was going on. I felt like an old hand already, which made as much sense as somebody gloating over having been born two minutes before her twin.

At last, the van came to a halt, and I was led by my hand through a doorway and down a staircase. The air was warm and smelled of mothballs and pine needles. I stumbled after the last step, not realizing I'd reached the bottom of the stairs.

"Ready or not . . . ," Becca said as she pulled off my blindfold. "Ta-da."

Given how fancy the club's members were, it was shocking how austere the clubhouse was. A collection of mops and dustbins was stashed in the corner, and furnishings were limited to a hanging iron candelabra and a semicircle of wooden chairs with exceptionally tall backs. High-ceilinged and narrow, the room's walls were bare but for a stained-glass window whose panel depicted a glorious blue ship. And it smelled dank, like cold stone covered in moss.

"This is the inner sanctum," said Poppy, the tall girl the Moonwatcher.net Webmasters had nicknamed "Man on the

Moon." I was surprised by her gap teeth and her build—she was bordering on stocky. As I watched her pull three seats out for the newbies, I thought about how bizarre it was that out of the group, she was considered the boy magnet.

"By 'inner sanctum' she means the basement," Becca said, stealing an amused look at me.

Easing into my seat, I checked out the other inductees. One of them was staring at me. Her baggy clothing and brown bob made her look a bit like a mushroom. I couldn't get eye contact from the other one, who was the picture of punky-chic, with her tight black jeans and rainbow-colored hair. I could only imagine what I looked like, with my blond bedhead and trace of a Proust mustache.

The only thing any of us had in common was we were equally as un-Moon as it got.

Poppy cleared her throat. "Now I know each of you has a friend in the Blue Moons, and you've all been briefed on what the group does, correct?" She didn't wait for any of us to answer. "Today's your lucky day. Our society has chosen to open up to a few girls without preexisting ties."

I took that as a nice way of saying girls without gobs of money. It was a little embarrassing, her putting it out there like that.

The mushroom girl sounded skeptical. "Is this some sort of affirmative action thing?"

"If you want to call it that," said Diana "Horsey Moon." "But to be honest, it's more for our benefit than yours."

"We all agreed this place could use some livening up," said Becca. "And you all have some pretty big talents." She looked at me dead-on.

Crap. Unless she was referring to my exceptional command of girl group music trivia, Becca *had* to be on to my flair for seeing more than meets the eye. But how could she? I'd never said anything to her about my dreams, and she hadn't so much as hinted at suspecting anything before. I squirmed in my seat and looked away, focusing on a patch of moonlight that was streaming through the window onto the cold concrete floor.

"What talents?" the punky newcomer asked.

Reagan stepped forward and brushed back her pale hair. "Sig here is a computer dynamo who will be running the CIA before we know it."

"Google," the mushroomy girl spoke up. "Better pay scale and killer cafeteria."

Poppy gave a gap-toothed smile. "Of course. And Hallie is a master of all things edible."

The punky girl smiled modestly and looked down at her pink Converse shoes. "Well, most things. I don't cook red meat. Or anything genetically modified."

"Thanks for the clarification." Becca looked at her impatiently. "And my friend Claire . . ." There was a torturous pause and I could feel my heart beating against my chest. What was she going to say? Even if she had a hunch about my supernatural talents, she couldn't just out me here. Was she going to tell them that I was good at taking standardized tests and hiding chocolate under my bed?

"Claire is an expert in etiquette and entertaining," Becca said at last. "Plus she saves my life approximately every other day."

She said it in an offhand tone that suggested I regularly lent her pens and told her when she had food in her teeth, but I knew that she was talking about the photo in the park and last semester's averted plane crash. I felt bashful, relieved, and still no closer to knowing whether she had so much as an inkling about my special talents.

I nervously fingered my cameo necklace and tucked it under my shirt, as if that would keep my secret safe.

Sills stepped forward and pulled off her black hood to reveal her Jessica Rabbit curls. I wasn't sure what was more mysterious—how she styled them to look that good or why anything that good-looking had ever gone out of fashion in the first place. "The initiation process is three months long," she said. "If you make it to the end you go from being Half Moons to Blue Moons. Good luck."

I felt myself rising to the challenge. If there was one thing I wanted, it was to belong.

"We have some pretty big plans this year," Sills went on. "And we need your help."

"Do we have to pay dues?" Sig sounded dubious. "Because I'm flat broke."

Kiki would have had a fit over the inappropriateness of her introducing the subject of money, but I was glad she had the courage to bring it up.

"Me too," added Hallie.

"Me three," I murmured bashfully. Sorry, Kiki, but you've been outnumbered.

Sills shook her head and smiled. "You don't have to do anything but share your skills with us. And clear next weekend for initiation. We need you." Her tone was soft, and it didn't sound like we were being completely used.

"And no more kidnappings?" Hallie raised a skeptical eyebrow, and I noticed that she had a thin ring through it.

Becca held back a smile and turned to face her sisters. "No more kidnappings."

Too bad. Looking back, this whole adventure had been kind of fun.

"Allow me." Diana stepped forward and came to stand over Hallie. "Are you in?" she asked her.

"Sure."

Diana looked at Sig. "And you?"

"Okay."

"Me too," I jumped in, slightly ahead of turn.

"Finally, a little enthusiasm." Diana's green eyes burned appreciatively.

And thus one and a half moons were born.

{ 8 }

Talent Show

The week leading up to the Blue Moon inauguration, I was so riled up I could barely focus on anything as attention-draining as homework or conversation. Eating, sleeping, and regular deodorant application weren't happening all that much either.

I was desperate to know what Blue Moon adventure was coming next, but Becca was staying mum. Between making preparations for the upcoming weekend and her typically busy roster of family obligations, she was hard to track down and sweet-talk into giving away any secrets. Apart from the Gramercy Park address where I was to show up at eight o'clock on Friday night, the only thing she would share was that I was to bring one of Kiki's old etiquette books. "It can be an old one she never uses, it's more symbolic than anything," she said after school on Wednesday—one of our few encounters that week. I was walking her to the subway stop she uses for her weekly voice lesson at Lincoln Center. "But whatever you do, don't tell her about any of this, okay?"

My stomach emptied out a little—lying to Kiki is just not in the cards. I knew Becca well enough to understand that when she started acting cagey about something, there was probably more to the story than she was letting on. And if she was going to be needing my help, I had to keep my grand-mother up to speed. I'd barely had my cameo for four months, and Kiki was the closest thing to a user's manual I had.

Soon as Becca had headed into the station, I dug in my pocket for change and made a beeline for the Buddhist chapel across the street (of course, one of the three remaining pay phones in New York would be directly outside a silent medita-tion center).

"I need your help," I said when Kiki picked up.

"Is that how girls are greeting their grandmothers by tele-phone these days?" she asked sarcastically.

"Sorry," I said, digging my feet into the ground. "How are you, my dear beautiful grandmother?"

"So kind of you to ask. Very well. And how is life treating you these days?"

"Tremendous," I said, using one of Kiki's favorite words. "I was wondering if you were free for dinner tonight."

"You've taken up cooking?" I could tell she was making fun of me.

"Actually, I thought we could do it uptown."

Like she ever came south of Fourteenth Street. Why was she putting me through this?

"And by 'uptown' you mean my place?" She chuckled.

"Would that I could, love, but Jon-Jon was kind enough to invite me to a dinner party at his gallery owner's house tonight." Her voice dropped to a whisper. "And I was kind enough to accept. I tell you, I'm ready for him and his lover boy to kiss and make up. This slumber party is getting rather tiresome."

Either Kiki was lonelier than she'd been letting on, or her houseguest was deaf. If there is one thing Kiki can do, it's drop a hint like a grenade.

"Why don't you tell him that thing you like to say about how visits should be—"

"Like an angel's stay. Short and bright," she filled in for me. "Don't think I haven't."

"Then why don't you tell him that I got in a huge fight with my parents and I need to crash on your couch?"

"No, no, I have everything figured out. Speaking of plans, shall we do dinner tomorrow?"

"Okay," I said, "but just you and me, right?"

It would be pointless if Jon-Jon elbowed his way into the mix.

Kiki laughed and told me to meet her at the 21 Club the following night. "I'll have them reserve a table for two."

I couldn't have been more excited, and not just because I needed Kiki's advice. The place she'd suggested, a toy box of a restaurant, has been one of my favorite New York spots as long as I can remember. When I showed up, the room was still decorated with bright red-and-white-checkered tablecloths and old-fashioned model planes dangling from the ceilings. Looked like Kiki was eager too—she was already seated at a corner table, working on a martini. She was wearing a cream-colored suit and a smear of coral lipstick, and her pale blue stilettos were peeking out from underneath the table.

"There's nothing like a houseguest to remind you of the joy of being alone," she said when I joined her.

I froze in place, not sure what she was saying.

"You want me to come back later?" I asked her.

"No, no, I'm enjoying some time away from Jon-Jon. You don't count." She motioned to a nearby waiter. "Being with you is like being with another version of myself. A pubescent version." The waiter was one inch away, helping me out of my coat, and my cheeks flared. "I didn't mean anything biological by that. Just that you're very much a young lady."

She instructed me to sit down, and I obeyed. "Speaking of Jon-Jon, how was your dinner last night?" I asked.

"Oh, can we save the chitchat for later? I'm guessing you want to talk about something that has to do with your you-know-what." She eyed my cameo.

"Sort of." I shifted in my seat. "It actually has to do with— Becca's in a secret society. And I was tapped to join."

"Is this the Blue Moons?"

I was so surprised I nearly fell out of my chair.

"Darling, that might be a lovely sight for your dentist, but some people here are trying to eat."

I willed my mouth closed and stared at her, shocked.

"I wouldn't look so startled," she said dismissively, and took a contented pull of her martini. "Some things are just in the air."

Would it really hurt her to drop the codespeak every now and again?

I picked up a roll and pulled off a bite-sized piece—one of Kiki's rules: don't bite into a roll—before spreading any butter. "Well then, I must have been breathing something else all this time. How'd you even know about the Moons?"

"Must you sound so woebegone?" Kiki's gray eyes gleamed

like mother-of-pearl and it hit me that she was proud. "They have some of the swellest parties—at least, they did in my day. Care to tell me how this all came about?" She almost sounded jealous, not a tone I was used to hearing in her voice.

"Sure," I said, and proceeded to tell her about the movie in the park and being kidnapped from my parents' Proust party.

"And you missed their singing? A shame that," she said without a shred of conviction. "And instead you had to be handpicked by one of the most elegant and exclusive societies in New York."

"I don't think its my elegance they're after," I said, and making sure to check that all the other diners were sufficiently engrossed in their conversations, I told her about the dream with the Cabbage Patch doll. "There has to be a—"

"Hamburger?" A white-haired waiter had popped up out of nowhere and filled in my sentence.

"Well, isn't this perfect!" Kiki looked on brightly while he delivered the plates she must have ordered before I'd shown up—creamy chicken hash for her, a "21 burger" for me. For decades, the burgers had cost twenty-one dollars, and now the price had been jacked up even more. Mom would have been mortified.

"A cameo connection?" Kiki finished off my previous statement as the waiter stepped away.

Nodding, I twisted the cap off the Soul Sauce bottle. Kiki gets hysterical whenever I use a knife to dislodge ketchup, so I turned the bottle upside down and came to terms with the fact that nothing was going to dribble out of it for years. "Someone's been stalking the Blue Moons and putting their pictures all over the Internet," I said. "For now it just seems like another bitchy blog, but if all these Moon girls' families are as big as everyone says and they all have their own enemies . . .

something could go very wrong." Now that I was saying it out loud, the idea of danger seemed to grow from a dim possibility into an absolute certainty. "They must need me for something serious. It could be like last time."

Kiki put her fork down. "That would be something. But I wouldn't let your imagination run ahead of reality. It would be a shame to mistake an opportunity to have a very pleasant social life for Murder Mystery Hour." She signaled to somebody behind me for another drink. "So how did Becca pull this off, anyway? Isn't the group exclusively for the descendents of its founding members?"

I felt a pinprick of offense.

"There are three new people, and they told us they're bringing us in for our supposed talents. They say mine is that I know about entertaining and etiquette."

"Do they?" She threw a disapproving look my way, and when I saw what she was trying to say I yanked my elbows off the tablecloth.

Kiki smiled forgivingly. "They may not have taught you this at L'Ecole Voyante, but sometimes people use one thing to mean something else. If I'm simply not in the mood to go to Mrs. Rockefeller's party, I might call her up and say I ate a disagreeable oyster. And if Becca wants her best friend to be in her club, she might have to come up with a reason that seems legitimate even if it's a stretch."

I knew she could be helpful.

"What's that supposed to mean?"

"Just that I wouldn't say etiquette is your strongest suit."

Or maybe "helpful" wasn't the word. More like "hurtful."

"So they do want me for something else?" I asked, hope lining my voice.

"Maybe she wants you on hand for the simple pleasure of

having you around." Her face fell. "Oh dear." I looked down to see a small pool of ketchup was spreading across the tablecloth. Kiki motioned for a waiter to come over to the table. "I'm terribly sorry to trouble you," she said, "but would you please take care of this little bloodbath?"

She eyed me sharply and gave an impatient sigh.

The next night, slipping out of my apartment proved even easier than I'd expected. Atypically, there was no salon after dinner. Dad was curled up on the couch reading and Mom and Saffron were supposedly working on a chapter of Saffron's book.

"By the way, I'm going to Becca's country house for the weekend," I said in the innocent voice I'd practiced earlier.

I knew it was late notice, but better late than early, in which case they could ask me questions for days leading up to the departure. Besides, I knew they'd be fine with my going away. They loved that I had a friend from Hudson—it alleviated their guilt about pulling me out of my old school—and they doubleloved that she had a cute older brother. Weird fact #54 about French parents: nothing, but nothing, thrills them more than the prospect of teenage romance.

"Where is the house?" Dad asked.

My throat clenched—I hadn't prepared for an interrogation. "What house? Oh, the country house?"

Dad looked at me like I was crazy and nodded.

"Upstate?" I squeaked, and everyone seemed to approve.

"Will Andy be there?" Mom asked, turning to give Saffron a suggestive smile.

"I don't know." My cheeks burning, I had to remind myself it wasn't a lie. Andy hadn't exactly been updating me on his whereabouts.

Dad waved his paperback copy of *Getting Things Done* in the air. "Our *poupée* is having *une petite aventure!*" he exclaimed.

Maybe, but not the kind he thought.

I bounded toward my room and put on the flirtiest outfit that came to hand—a blue crêpe de chine dress, cream-colored wedge boots, thick black tights, and an extra coat of lip gloss. I packed a suitcase with a weekend's worth of clothes, and at the last minute I remembered Becca's instructions and grabbed my trusty 1959 edition of *Poise, Polish, and Pluck: Helpful Hints for the Teenage Girl.*

"And Claire," Mom called on my way out. "Don't forget to let Saffron know when you want to do that shoot of your room. She has to reserve the lighting guys in advance."

Ugh. Just my luck that Mom was scatterbrained about everything but that.

The address Becca gave us turned out to be a run-down deli. Star Foods Emporium's window displayed a faded Newport Lights poster and a handwritten sign for a mysterious-sounding "$1.99 San Francisco Chicken Patty."

The sky was pitch-black, and the only other people on the street were Sig and Hallie. Sig was wearing a dark, shapeless down coat that came to her knees and Hallie had on a heart-patterned ski parka. It would have made anybody else resemble an overgrown second grader, but Hallie still managed to look punk rock in it. It might have had to do with her multibuckled boots.

"Do you think this is some sort of test?" I asked them, resting my suitcase on the ground.

"What do you mean?" Sig asked.

"You know," I said. "We buy the chicken patty and there's a key under the bun."

"Nasty," Hallie said. "I don't do processed meats."

Just then, a ghost appeared at the deli door. It took me a second to realize it was Reagan "Pale Moon." She motioned for us to come inside and helped herself to a bag of Swedish Fish from the candy display. "This is Stinko," she said, indicating the guy with the neck tattoos behind the counter. "He knows to let you through whenever you come."

"Let us through?" I repeated. "Is that a code for selling us beer or something?"

Stinko laughed and Reagan slipped behind a curtain in the back of the deli.

My confusion was increasing.

"What's going on?" I asked. "Are you putting us to work here?"

"Just come and see for yourself" was Reagan's response. "Right this way, ladies."

The other newbies and I exchanged curious glances as we followed her up a musty staircase that spat us out into what must have been the coolest room I'd ever had the pleasure of being spat out into. If their stunned expressions were anything to go by, the other newbies were equally impressed. All the Full Moons were seated on a couple of couches, wearing house-proud grins.

"The clubhouse is hidden inside that grungy deli?" I exclaimed. The last time, I'd been blindfolded when I'd come and gone.

"Behind it, but yes, same idea," Reagan answered.

"This is the main room," Poppy added. "You guys were in the basement before."

Covering three of the deep violet walls were hundreds of framed photographs and oil paintings of what I assumed were former Blue Moons. The fourth was devoted to bookshelves crammed with all manner of junk—wigged mannequin heads, vases of cabbage roses, a stuffed owl. And if that wasn't awesome enough, there was a black-and-white photo booth where the bookshelf ended. The rest of the room was sparse by comparison, with a few shabby-chic couches and dark green reading chairs on a bare wooden planked floor, all safely tucked away under a vaulted ceiling.

Reagan motioned to the unoccupied diamond-print couch, and the three of us obeyed her gesture. As I settled into my spot, Becca smiled and wiggled her pinky at me. I grinned back, happy to see her too.

"Welcome, ladies." Poppy, the club's resident Amazon, squared her shoulders and drew a line through a piece of paper on her clipboard. "So I see you guys made it through the door policy."

"Our secret entrance is pretty hot, right?" Sills raised her eyebrow. "So far nobody's figured it out."

"The club moved in here about ten years ago," Becca explained. "Though the Moons never got around to sending out change-of-address cards."

"This building used to be a private club for actors," Diana said, pointing to a stained-glass panel propped against the bottom of the wall. It had the ancient comedy and tragedy masks and some Latin words. "We replaced that window with one that means more to us."

So that explained the stained window with the ship I'd admired in the basement the last time.

Poppy consulted her clipboard and, in the spirit of a psycho summer camp counselor, rambled off the house rules. "Number one you already know: Moons must enter and exit the clubhouse through Star Foods Emporium. Number two, publicity is to be shunned." She raised her head and gave us an appraising look and seemed satisfied. No doubt she was determining that unwanted publicity wasn't going to be our problem—*Teen Vogue* wasn't about to come knocking down any of our doors.

Thanks.

"Number three, there is to be no canoodling with celebrities." She paused to glance at Sills, who looked down and pushed a couple of well-defined waves over her left eye.

"Number four," continued Poppy, "Moons must refrain from wearing clothing with visible designer labels."

Not a problem in my books. Kiki says brand names aren't to be worn like tattoos. Poppy went on, "Five, no males in the clubhouse."

"Except Linus here," Diana said, pointing to a window seat, where a slender black cat was licking one of his hind legs clean.

Poppy didn't dignify Diana with a response. "Six, Half Moons are to keep their distance from the Moonery on Sunday nights. Any violations of any kind will result in de-Mooning."

Okay, I got it. All Moons are not created equal.

"Any questions?" Poppy looked up at us with the dour expression of an old woman peering over her reading glasses.

Only a million questions. But I stayed quiet.

"Um," Sig said, "this building we're in, it's the Moonery?"

"Oh yeah, that's what we call it. Anything else?"

When there were no more questions, Poppy passed out our initiation contracts—thick black envelopes sealed with black wax. Silence settled over the room as we opened them and signed the enclosed black cards in silvery ink. Who knew stationery could get so goth?

"Good," Poppy said, interrupting the somber mood with a bright smile. "Now Sills is going to take you on the grand tour."

Though I'm not sure "grand" was the right word. Quaint as it was, the clubhouse turned out to be smaller than most single-family town houses—which might explain why there were only five members. It was fine for the Moons' spare-time hangout purposes, but only a family of elves could have lived in it comfortably. I wondered how its previous tenant, the theater club, had operated within it. In addition to the room with the bookshelf and couches, the first floor had a small game room and kitchen. The second floor contained a tidy office and a bathroom that was literally just that—a space devoted to a magnificent claw-foot bathtub. A deep lemony smell hung in the air, and the floor was scattered with half-used candles and an impressive stash of bath salts, gels, and scrubs. Sills bent over to pluck a towel off the floor. "It used to be the drama library, but Gummy insisted on putting this in."

"Gumby?" Hallie asked incredulously.

"Gummy Salzman," Becca piped up, entering the bathroom. "She was a Moon during the big brouhaha, and when she died she left us a pile of money and a plan for the new clubhouse. And a few stipulations that we'll get to." She smiled mysteriously.

Things were getting more interesting by the minute.

We clopped downstairs and waited by a back doorway while Sills put on a blue wig and a Richard Nixon mask and cased the courtyard. "Just to be safe."

I glanced at the others to make sure I wasn't the only one who thought this was taking a turn for the mildly crazy. Hallie caught my eye and we started giggling nervously.

"She loves this part," Becca whispered to me. "She's an actress at heart."

Sills returned a few minutes later and pushed the Nixon mask up on top of her head. The beauty of her features came as a shock. Her eyes were the color of sea glass and her mouth was shaped like a Valentine's Day card—a perfect heart. Her beauty was so extreme I didn't even feel jealous. I just wanted to keep staring forever.

"We're good to go," she announced, oblivious to my thoughts. "Nobody's outside. It's safe." She gestured for us to follow her through the door and we obeyed, careful not to make too much noise.

The clubhouse occupied an alley that was hidden from public view by the messy vines and brambles twisting around the gates on either side. The courtyard was charming in a munchkiny way, filled with tiny trees and snow-covered cast-iron furniture. It was as different as could be from Washington View Village's litter-strewn courtyard. My parents would kill to have a place like this to come out and read in. They might even be willing to go along with the dead Republican president masks.

A *tap-tap* startled me, and I looked up to see an owlish man behind a window. My heart stopped when I saw he was waving at Sills.

"Crap," I muttered.

Sills laughed and waved back to him. "Oh, he's not a problem. Mr. Dimitrius is always there. He invented a self-cleaning toaster oven twenty years ago and hasn't had any reason to leave his house since."

"That's intense," Hallie muttered, narrowing her kohl-lined eyes. Her eyebrow ring glinted in the moonlight.

"He's harmless," Sills said. "He never crosses to our side, never asks any questions. Anyway, take a look at our building. It's hard to tell apart from the others in the alley, except for the—"

"Star-shaped white stone on the top?" Sig hazarded a guess.

"Impressive," Sills said. "Do the rest of you see it? Look up, on the right-hand side, close to the edge of the building."

I craned my neck to follow her gaze until I saw it, fastened onto the stone by the second floor. It wasn't particularly small or large and it didn't call attention to itself. It looked as if it belonged there, like a birthmark.

When we came back in, the fireplace was lit up and crackling like something out of a Christmas movie. It was the picture of coziness, and even though my heart had been pounding just moments before, I was suddenly in the mood for a nap.

"You guys ready for history hour?" Poppy asked us before we'd settled back in to our seats. "Diana's prepared a little paper on the club's background. Don't worry, it won't be like school."

She turned to her fellow Moon, who was consulting a paper. "Blue Moons from 1741 through the present," Diana read in a voice drained of vitality. She reminded me of how nervous Dad gets when he gives one of his lectures at academic conferences.

I felt restless at first—I'd already heard a bit about the Moons' formation from Becca. New York's early settlers, yadda yadda. I snapped to attention when Diana got up to 1965, and it wasn't only because that was Kiki's golden era.

"Here's where the drama starts. Some members wanted certain reforms." Diana smiled shakily.

My curiosity-ometer immediately shot up and hit the roof. "What kind of reforms?"

"They wanted to allow guys in the clubhouse," Becca told me. "Which would be fine, I guess, on the face of it."

"And on the not-face of it?" I pressed.

"Well, that's not what the Moons are *really* about."

"What *are* they about?" Sig's voice was lined with annoyance.

"*We*," Diana corrected her. "*We're* about taking care of the city. And it can be hard to do what needs to be done when there are dudes making a mess of things."

"Not that we don't like guys," Poppy put in. "I have a boyfriend and so does Diana, but there's a time for everything."

Especially if you're waiting around for Andy Shuttleworth, I thought with a sinking heart. Then you have nothing but time.

Diana returned to her paper, interrupting my thoughts. "April 1965, a few dissidents left and started the Ladies League."

Reagan poured the remaining contents of her candy bag into her mouth. "Which couldn't be a more inappropriate name for them."

"Why's that?" I urged them along, ready for some dirt.

"Ladies don't multiply like rats." Becca's lip curled. "They have something like a hundred and twenty-seven members."

"And when they're not busy posting stupid things about us on Moonwatcher.net," Diana said, "they're running one of the city's cheesier institutions."

Did she just say Moonwatcher.net? The online stalkers who were driving Becca crazy and had outed my need for a professional facial? So my suspicion had been correct. They *were* connected to the rival club after all.

"You know who those people are?" I was quick to ask.

Becca gave me a tender look. "We're not a hundred percent certain."

"Only, like, ninety-nine percent," Sills added. "It *has* to be them. We just don't have any proof."

Becca sighed. "They hired some branding expert and now they call themselves the Elle House."

I gasped and blurted out, "That hell house place? That's the club Sheila just joined!"

"Who's that?" Poppy raised her left eyebrow.

"Just the biggest creep on earth," I told her, cringing at the mental image of Sheila setting her narrowed eyes on me.

"I like that, 'hell house.'" Becca snickered, then made a woeful shrug. "They'll take anyone."

"So long as that *anyone*'ll pony up these days," Diana added.

"You can feel free to explain what you're talking about any day now," muttered Sig. I was grateful for this interjection—I had no idea what was going on either.

"The group did this stupid renovation that they didn't think through," Poppy filled in. "And now they're in big trouble." She made the cash-money sign with her thumb and forefinger.

"What do you mean?" Hallie asked. "How much?"

"Whatever it is, it's too much," Becca said. "Rumor has it they're hurting so bad they tried to pay the Domino's delivery guy with a half-empty bottle of tequila left over from a party."

"That's terrible," I said, and I couldn't help being reminded of how Sheila's favorite prank in middle school involved ordering ten super-stuffed pizzas to be delivered to our bossiest neighbors' apartments.

Becca's eyes flashed in amusement. "Now they're selling these partial memberships where you're allowed to go for a few hours on Tuesdays and Sundays or something stupid."

"Don't forget the reality television show," Reagan added, catching my eye. "They're making this show about themselves that they think they'll be able to sell to cable."

Sheila must have been excited. Maybe she wasn't the most popular girl at Hudson anymore, but here was her big chance to be a reality television star.

"But the main thing," Poppy said, "is in addition to supporting the local fake tan industry and getting identical blond highlights, everyone in the club—members new and old—is supposed to get dirt on us. Or at least who they assume the Moons are."

I felt a rush of dread.

"Why would they do that?" asked Hallie.

Diana shrugged. "It's just an old rivalry thing. They know our anonymity is important to us. So they know exactly how to drive us crazy."

"We do our best to keep 'em guessing," said Sills.

"Bit of a losing battle," moaned Becca. "We've been out-numbered something like fifty to one."

Was I to take this to mean we newbies had been invited for more reasons than the pleasure of our company?

"And would that have anything to do with why you invited us?" Sig asked. "You've practically doubled your numbers."

She was a smart cookie, that Sig.

A smile spread across Becca's face. "Never hurts to have more moving targets if you're the target. Plus, we wanted to mix it up a little bit—we were craving new company. Put your coats on," she told us, and let the other old-timers know we'd be back in an hour or so.

Ten minutes later, when we were racing up Park Avenue in a cab, I still had no idea what was happening. Becca was giving the driver directions from the passenger seat and we newbies were relegated to the back.

"Is it just me, or are you totally confused?" Hallie asked me.

"At least we don't have blindfolds on this time," I said, gaz-ing out the window at the swooshing nighttime traffic.

"Can you pull over here and wait a minute?" Becca asked the driver as we breezed past East Fortieth Street and ap-proached the old Pan Am Building. Then she turned and soberly instructed us, "Get out and look around."

We stepped onto the sidewalk. There was a stillness to the

night—not a soul in sight, not even any interesting garbage blowing about.

"I don't get—" I started to say.

And then I saw it: embedded in the wall at eye level (well, dwarf eye level) was a tile the size of a sugar cube. It had a Blue Moon ship on it.

Something sparked inside me.

"Nice work," I muttered. "Is this how fancy people make graffiti art?"

"More like the opposite." Becca's eyes were gleaming. "We broke in one night and cleaned up all the graffiti on the observation deck. And then we had a midnight dinner up there."

"Are you serious?" Hallie asked. "What did you guys have?"

Would she ever give this foodie thing a rest?

"The tile is how we sign off on our work." Becca ignored Hallie's question and ushered us all back into the cab to continue the tour.

The rest of the ships were easy to find. The Morgan Library? Check. The Armory building? Check. Central Park's angel fountain? There it was, just under the second tier.

"All the fish had died and nobody was going to do anything about it." Becca made a sad face then watched me, waiting for a reaction. She knew I'd be thinking about Didier and Margaux.

"I read something in the *Daily News* about the fountains' miraculous fish restoration, how they all started multiplying," Hallie said in wonderment. "But I thought it was supposed to be some scientific mystery?"

Becca suppressed a grin and dug her hands in her pockets. "You have no idea how hard it is pulling off these projects without getting caught. Sometimes we host charity tea parties and don't even show up ourselves, to throw them off. Now that we kicked Annika out, we wouldn't be surprised if she joins Elle House and spills the beans, but so far they haven't been able to keep up with us."

I was starting to get what was going on.

"How can you keep her from saying anything?" I asked.

"We can't," Becca replied. "But we can try to stay one step ahead. This year's main event is going to be extra tricky. The Elles are dying to get some real dirt on us, and our big project is a little crazier than usual." Her eyes narrowed and her teeth glinted in the dark. "We might need your help."

I couldn't have been less surprised. Or, more important, thrilled.

{ 9 }

Stargazer

When we got back from our midnight tour, I had no idea what was in store for me. The Moonery's main room was empty except for Diana, who was curled up under a plush red blanket on one of the sofas, dead to the world.

She twitched and opened her eyes. "There you are," she said groggily. "I'm supposed to give you your directions." Something under the blanket moved. Linus the cat shot out and raced across the floor.

"There are more adventures?" I asked, suddenly feeling a little tired—and, for once, not from dreams.

The sleepy redhead got up with a yawn and told us we were to make ourselves at home.

"The rest of us will be upstairs getting some work final-ized," Becca said. "You guys just get to know the place. And each other."

Now I was starting to feel like a lab rat in one of my par-ents' professor friends' sleep-deprivation studies.

"What work?" Sig asked, voicing the very question I was wondering about.

Diana had already trudged most of the way up the stairs, the blanket loosely wrapped around her waist. "Boring stuff. Don't worry about it."

The other newbies and I were left to look at each other in confusion. I was feeling kind of crummy, like a kid sister left out of the good stuff.

"Guess we have to throw ourselves a house party," dead-panned Sig.

"There are worse houses to party in," Hallie reasoned.

"Let's raid the fridge," Sig suggested.

There wasn't much in the black-and-white-checker-tiled kitchen, and we helped ourselves to the only things on hand: a box of graham crackers and a deli-bought provolone and tomato sub somebody must have forgotten about.

Once I had food in my stomach, I wasn't feeling so tired anymore. "Let's explore the rest of the place," I said.

"Good call," Sig mumbled, still stuffing the remainder of the sandwich into her mouth.

Free of high-tech contraptions or even modern heating, the clubhouse was charming in a knocked-up, vaguely dusty way. The library's walls were lined with old maps of New York. The shelves contained an epic out-of-print book collection, and in the corner of the room were eight fastidiously rolled-up sleep-ing bags.

Sig and Hallie settled on the couch in the library, where

they watched a ridiculous highway massacre movie involving a clown. I'd already seen it at Becca's, and I decided to test the bubble bath facilities. And, I'll fess up, see what I could overhear.

When I trooped upstairs I could hear muffled conversation behind the office's closed door. If only I had X-ray vision instead of indecipherable dreams!

I took off my cameo and drew the water. When it stopped running, the sounds from the office grew louder. I tiptoed over to the wall and pressed my ear against it, though I still couldn't make out a syllable. Feeling helpless, I returned to the tub and leaned back and closed my eyes.

I was on the stage at Radio City Music Hall. The lights were blinding and all I could see were my fellow showgirls, though they weren't exactly girls. The chorus line consisted of leggy number ones, their endless limbs moving in perfect synchronization. It was a math professor's fantasy.

When I woke up, I sat bolt upright in the water. I had no idea what time it was, but the water had cooled to room temperature. It was pitch-black outside the pocket window and the night was clear enough to see a few stars. A thump through the wall told me the girls were still in the office overseeing their mysterious project.

Freshly dried off and coated in lemon-rosemary oils, I went back downstairs and joined Sig and Hallie in the library. The movie hour had ended, and Hallie was engrossed in a mix tape on an old Walkman she'd dug up. Sig's personal bliss appeared in the form of an Atari console.

I grabbed a book I'd already read from the library and settled on a reading chair, hoping to distract myself from feeling left out of the good stuff that was happening behind a tightly closed door. Thank goodness for Agatha Christie. Three chapters into her classic *The A.B.C. Murders,* my dire frustration had given way to resignation. Just in time for the girls' return. "Meeting adjourned," Becca declared, settling onto the arm of my chair. I looked up, searching her face for any clues, but she wasn't giving anything away.

The rest of my stay there was actually pretty mellow. Saturday afternoon, we took a field trip to see a show of Salvador Dalí's weird melty painting at the Museum of Modern Art. At one point I saw Professor Glanford from my building and hid behind a gallery wall—my parents thought I was upstate, after all. Later that night, we goofed around, watching TV and enjoying the s'mores station Hallie rigged up. Sunday morning, we feasted on egg and cheese sandwiches from the deli and all painted our toenails the same cotton-candy pink, though not because of some cultish ritual—it was the only color in the house.

By the end of my stay, I wasn't feeling left out anymore, but I still hadn't forgotten about Friday's little emergency meeting in the clubhouse office. When I got home late on Sunday afternoon, between aborted attempts to do my math problem set and come up with a nonpathetic reply to Andy's latest random e-mail question ("Have you ever had a White Castle burger?"), I couldn't resist doing a little more digging.

Elle House's official Web site—a separate entity from the so-called anonymous Moonwatcher.net—was nothing if not pretentious. A free-floating cube rotated over a hot pink background to reveal pictures of the club's "white room," which was a space filled with white couches and chairs. There was also a picture of the "spice room," just like the previous room, but with red walls and tasseled pillows galore, and the rooftop "splash lounge," which, as far as I could tell, was a small swimming pool that was under repair.

Luckily, not much had changed over on Moonwatcher.net. The only new picture showed Poppy and Reagan in Grand Central Terminal, wearing belted coats and craning their necks up to look at the main concourse ceiling's amazing mural of the sky. The caption underneath read: HEADS UP, SPACE CADETS. WE'VE GOT YOUR NUMBER.

Not so fast.

After school on Tuesday afternoon, Becca surprised me by fishing me out of the crowd and bringing me to a fancy restaurant on Clinton Street. From the doorway I made out pale pink tulips sprouting from fixtures on the walls. An enormous brown paper bag of freshly delivered bread was waiting on the bar and only a few of the tables were set.

"B, it doesn't look like they're open yet," I said.

"Of course they aren't, it's barely four o'clock." She headed for a table in the back, underneath a collage of yellow stars and a lion head. I locked eyes with the animal, and momentarily flipped through my roster of dreams, searching for lions or any stars. Or even anything from *The Wizard of Oz.*

Zilch.

Becca took off her coat to reveal the latest installment in her lifelong series of fabulous outfits: holey jeans, a gossamer-thin baby blue T-shirt, and a coral velvet blazer with matte gold buttons.

I took a seat in what must have been the squishiest chair my butt has ever squished into and looked up to see Hallie appear from a doorway in the back, bearing a breadbasket and looking infinitely less punky than usual. She wore a white uniform and her striped mane was tucked back into a bun that looked almost monochromatic.

"This is Hallie's parents' place," Becca said under her

breath. "I cleared it with her already, I just needed somewhere quiet to talk to you."

I had no idea why she needed to make such an undercover production out of talking to me but at least this much was making sense: Hallie's credentials as a foodie hadn't come out of thin air. She was a full-fledged restaurantista.

"On the house." Hallie delivered the basket and stepped away.

"Thank you!" Becca called after her, then ripped off a piece of rosemary focaccia. "Oh my God is it good!" she exclaimed.

The bread smelled delicious, like pine trees and spun sugar.

"Have some." She slid the basket my way.

"It is amazing," I conceded after a bite, "but please say you didn't bring me to this secret location to talk about bread."

She giggled and ran her hand through her hair. "Okay, you got me there. I wanted to fill you in on—"

"Whatever secret activity you guys were doing upstairs all weekend?" I jumped in.

"All weekend?" She laughed. "You mean when we were gone for, like, two hours?"

My eyes darted away in embarrassment. "It felt longer than that."

She looked at me apologetically. "Sorry—the timing was just really bad. Anyway, we're organizing a fund-raiser on Saturday. It's at the Oyster Bar in Grand Central. It should be fun." She tried to force a convincing expression and I felt queasy.

"I thought you said you didn't do debutante parties and stuff?"

"We don't. We're going to be lurking in the shadows—in our formal dresses." She blushed. "Reagan's mom is on the board of Hope and Anchor, this New York water protection group . . ." She paused while a waiter delivered a plate of chili-dusted French fries to our table. "It's a fund-raiser for her cause. Supposedly."

My eyes widened. "Supposedly?"

"No, it *is* a fund-raiser for the cause. But that's not our real priority. We have another restoration project in the works. You know how the Elles saw some of us in the concourse, right?"

"Yeah, I saw the picture." For once, I felt on top of things.

Becca shook her head. "Those girls are on our trail, and we needed to come up with a decoy . . . to distract them from the real Grand Central project. So we invented this party. On the invitation we're mixing some of our names with some names you won't recognize. So I need to ask you for a favor."

"You want to use my name?" If there's one thing I'm good for it's a name nobody's heard of.

"Thanks, but your name is hardly inconspicuous," she said with a twinkle in her eye. "That's not what I'm asking you for, anyway." She took a sip of water, the ice cubes clinking against her glass. "Last week, some idiots on a company softball league decided to play catch in Grand Central while they were waiting for their train. They cracked the opal on the face of the clock on the information booth and now the city wants to replace it with a nasty digital one."

I imagined a giant Seiko watch in the middle of the train station's lobby. It made me wince.

"So you're going to fix it before they get a chance to do that?" I checked.

"It can't be fixed," she said. "That's the problem. But we did some research and found out that when the clock was made, there were two copies. The duplicate's at a private club in Amsterdam." Her eyes went dreamy. "Well, it was."

I felt myself blink hard. "Did Helle House take it?"

"No." Her cheeks flushed. "We bought it. What's the point

of a club having a trust fund if you're not going to put it to use?" She fed herself another French fry and wiped her hands on her napkin. "We replaced it last night."

"And nobody noticed?" I asked incredulously.

"I hope not. There's a secret passageway connecting the information booth on the lower level to the main one. We got in with a couple of muscular engineers at the break of dawn the other morning and . . . voilà."

"Seriously?" It seemed implausible. "It's completely done?"

"Almost. Sills got distracted and forgot to stick on the Blue Moon tile. But we'll get around to that."

"Is that what you need my help with?"

"Sort of." Becca looked at me fondly. "I don't want the Elles to find out about any of it. They still don't know about half the stuff we do." She looked up, as if worried that a spy might be at one of the empty neighboring tables.

"Well, here's a piece of advice," I said. "Don't have a party at the scene of the crime. It will only call attention to what you did."

"That's where you're wrong," she said, sliding closer to me. "We're dressing up the party so it looks like the main event. The fund-raiser is going to be as big a blowout as any and everyone will be too distracted to notice the *real* main event."

"Oh, that *is* kind of smart," I allowed.

Why had I underestimated Becca even for a moment?

"Only if it works." She sounded insecure. "Your services will be very much needed. You and Sig and Hallie have to do whatever you can to make sure that the merry pranksters who crash—and Lord knows they will—have a good time."

"You want us to make sure the Elles are *happy*?" I asked in disbelief. What was I, hired help?

"How else do you propose we keep them from getting up

in our business?" She brought her water to her lips and took a small sip to conceal her widening grin. "Oh, and one more thing. You'll be talking to Kiki in the next little while, right?"

"Probably," I said nonchalantly. "Why?"

"If she has a couple of party tips to spare, that would be great. Believe it or not, the last time I threw a party it was for my tenth birthday."

"So you totally know what you're doing," I said. "What's wrong with goodie bags full of unicorn stickers and Laffy Taffy?"

"And a Fudgie the Whale ice cream cake?" she added.

We broke into laughter, and for the first time that day I started to feel entirely comfortable around Becca, in a way that had nothing to do with the restaurant's ultracushioned chairs.

Saturday night was deep winter at its most beautiful. The air was razor-sharp and icicles were growing on the tree branches.

I showed up at Grand Central Terminal at the appointed hour and found Sig and Hallie sitting on the concourse's marble staircase, their coats in a heap by Hallie's hip. They looked incredible.

"Holy hottie!" Sig cried out when I shimmied out of my coat.

"Wow," Hallie seconded. "I barely recognized you."

I rolled my eyes and muttered a slightly offended thanks, but the truth was I hardly recognized them either. Hallie was looking like a punk princess in an asymmetrical silvery strapless dress with a huge silk gardenia on the front. And Sig was obscenely stunning in a little black sequined number. If anyone was ever going to write a fairy tale about a mushroom that turned into a fox, they already had their illustration done for them.

Kiki had picked out what I was wearing—a black satin dress by Adolfo, trimmed with black-and-white feathers, paired with a black satin band I was to wear on my forehead. It matched the dress, but that was beside the point. The hair band was going to play a pivotal role in the plan Sig, Hallie, and I had worked out beforehand.

Excitement raced through me and I allowed myself a quick glance around the lobby. The "old" clock above the information booth looked as distinguished as ever. I overheard a man remark on how the clock hadn't been working all week and his companion assured him the time was correct. Throngs of train passengers milled beneath the monument, but there were no girls with fake tans and stilettos to speak of—not yet, anyway.

"All right," I said to the others, anticipation swooshing through my stomach. "You ready to rock?"

The girls nodded and we were too excited to say anything else as we crossed the concourse and descended the stairs to the lower level.

Downstairs, the party was in full swing, with a turnout of at least a couple hundred. Some people were dancing, and the rest were chatting animatedly while craning their necks to check out everybody else. Scattered throughout the crowd, the Blue Moons were decked out in formal dresses that fit them too perfectly to have come from any rack. They'd taken Kiki's cardinal party rule—"Make guests wear plastic fruit headpieces or serve dinner upside down; anything so long as it's different"—to heart. The theme they'd chosen was Ancient Egypt, and the Oyster Bar restaurant looked like a set from *Cleopatra*, with golden snakes on the tables and men in pharaoh costumes making the rounds with martini glasses full of the amber-colored "Ankh-tini" concoction that Hallie had created in the Moonery's kitchen.

"Proceed with caution," a familiar voice said when I accepted one from a tray. "Word is they used curry powder."

There went my heart. And it didn't get any easier when I turned around and my eyes met Andy's.

"Thanks for the warning," I said, placing my drink back on the tray. "I think I'll stick with curried chicken."

Andy smiled and looked me up and down. "You cleaned up nice, Shorty."

"There you are," Becca cut in just as I was about to melt. She was wearing a white dress with elbow-length sleeves. Louis was at her side, wearing a gray suit and looking more debonair than Cary Grant.

"Louis?" I said, trying to cover my surprise at how dapper he looked. "Wow . . ."

"Yeah, yeah, yeah." I could tell he was embarrassed. "I tried to rent a mummy costume but someone beat me to it at the last minute."

Becca moved in. "How's it going so far? See anything interesting?"

The way she said it made me feel like I was in trouble for not working harder.

"Not yet, but I just got here," I offered as an excuse, and nervously touched my cameo. "I'm just going to, um, get a Coke."

"One of the waiters will bring you one," Andy said, and I had to pretend not to hear him as I cut free.

"I'll walk you part of the way," Becca said. "I have to go to the bathroom." I saw Louis's face fall.

We broke free of the guys and I lost Becca to some old acquaintance of hers ten steps later. I was left to float around and look for Elle House infiltrators, all the while making small talk with anyone I bumped into. As Kiki had told me, "All you need to get by in conversation is 'How do you do?' and 'Is that so?' People are brilliant at yammering on about themselves."

The party crasher–spotting was harder than I'd been expecting. I kept my eyes peeled for fake tans, but there were hundreds of guests, many of whom had decided that tonight's

Egyptian-themed bash was the perfect occasion for bronzer and gold body makeup. The only things I learned were (a) that some people get freaked out when an absolute stranger walks up to them at a party and introduces herself and (b) that Andy likes to make funny faces at girls spending massive amounts of time walking up to complete strangers at parties and introducing themselves.

A hundred introductions later, the only people who stood out were Louis and Reagan. They were both leaning against the edge of the lunch counter, staring mournfully at the dance floor, not exchanging a single word.

"Is gloomy the new black?" I asked as I joined them.

Reagan sighed and ran a hand through her snow-white hair. "I'll be fine."

And that's when I realized she was anything but fine. I cut a look at Louis but he didn't pick up on it.

"What happened?" I asked in a softer voice.

She scrunched her eyes closed. "I just can't believe my mother didn't come to her own frigging fund-raiser."

Pain was burning though her cheeks. I racked my brain for the correct response.

"Maybe it's for the best," I said, leaning against the spot next to her. "The party's doing fine. And you can let loose, without her here."

She pursed her lips. "That's not the point. She promised she'd come and make a speech on behalf of the foundation."

I lowered my voice to a whisper. "Ray, as far as I can tell, the foundation isn't really the point of this shindig."

My words had little effect. "I can't get her to pay attention to anything but His Royal Highness. She just grooms him and chases him around all day."

"Her dog?" I ventured, remembering all the rich ladies

I've seen near Becca's house treating their Pekingese like little princes.

"Close." She almost laughed. "Her husband." She eyed me with a mixture of amusement and dolefulness. "H.R.H. His initials. My dad was named Harold Unger Hendricks, but he read some self-help book for executives that said that initials were important and he didn't want to go by H.U.H., so he changed his middle name to Reagan when I was little."

"He chose the name Reagan out of the blue?" I squinted.

"He's a big Republican. He wanted to pass it off as a family name, which is pretty rich considering how little he—or anybody I live with—cares about family."

I shifted closer to her. "So now he's H.R.H. Like some kind of royalty?"

"Exactly. And he acts like it too. We used to be close but these days the only thing he ever asks me about is when a college will take me off its waiting list."

Her face flickered with sadness and I felt a renewed surge of compassion.

I started thinking of how some years ago something changed between my dad and me and I had to ask him to stop flipping me upside down and tickling me to death. "Dad stuff can be hard," I offered.

But she was too deep down her own hole of self-pity to have heard a word of what I said. "Sills and her dad go out to dinner every Wednesday, just the two of them. I can't even imagine what my dad and I would talk about. . . . Though maybe if I'd gotten into one of those A-list schools he'd find me more interesting."

I felt guilty even for thinking about my own dad. Tickle attacks aside, he was pretty great, always ready to talk or look the other way if I was doing something Mom wouldn't approve of.

Reagan drifted away and I turned to Louis watching Becca

dance with Andy and looking devastated. I leaned in and watched along with him, the two of us longing for half of the same whole. Finally I said, "You know your competition's her brother, right?"

He looked startled. "*That's* the famous Andy?"

I felt a zing of affection for Louis. "You have so much to learn, my child." Louis heaved a sigh of relief. "Want to get some fresh air?"

He shook his head. "It's, like, negative seventy degrees outside."

"C'mon," I said, tugging him along.

When we'd exited the restaurant and come into the main dining concourse, I saw something that made me stop in my tracks. The newspaper recycling bin across the way featured an ad for a discount airline on the side. It had a picture of a kangaroo drinking a margarita. Just like the kangaroo in that party dream from once upon a time. And something was moving behind the bin!

My cameo necklace warmed up against my skin, like a mug of tea on a cozy fall night. Weird. This was a first.

Without even thinking twice, I sprinted toward the bin.

"Yo, Lemonhead." Louis was out of breath when he'd caught up with me. "Why didn't you tell me to bring my sneakers?"

I wanted to kiss the ground, except I had to keep my composure in front of the three girls crouching behind the bin. Even if they hadn't been decked out in spiky heels and fiddling with digital cameras, I would've known they were Elles. After all, who happened to be among them but—

"Sheila!" I cried out, my voice oozing with fake friendliness.

"What are *you* doing here?" she snapped. Louis was looking at me like I'd just gone completely crazy.

"I was just about to ask you the same thing," I said

brightly—after all, Kiki always said *kill them with kindness.* "My friend Becca's helping put on this party and she invited me."

"Hey, Sheila," Louis mumbled in mild surprise. "Did you go on vacation or something. You look really . . ." It suddenly clicked that she was covered in instant tan, and he trailed off.

"I've just been spending a lot of time outdoors," Sheila huffed.

"Anyway," I said, trying my hardest not to laugh. "You know my friend Becca, right? She's here with some friends. I should introduce you to them."

Who knew I had so much phony charm bottled up in me? Before the girls could protest, I had met Sheila's pals Jasmine and Violet and was leading them all into the Oyster Bar. Playing dumber than a light-up yo-yo, I presented Sheila and her friends to Becca and Poppy, then took off my hair band and waved it in the air—the secret "Got 'em!" signal Hallie and Sig and I had worked out.

A couple of waiters came rushing over, their arms weighted down with dessert trays. Going along with the script we'd planned the night before, one of the waiters whispered something to Becca.

"I can't believe it," she announced to us in her best faux-distraught tone. I could tell Sheila and her friends were buying into Becca's "problem"—they were watching Becca with visible fascination, not used to seeing their prey this close. Becca went on, "Some of the waiters got drunk and we don't have enough people to pass out the desserts."

"No worries!" I told her. "We'll do it!"

"Oh that's so nice of you!" Becca's voice was dripping with fake gratitude, and she turned to Sheila and the gang. "Really? You don't mind?"

Violet was inching away. "I have no upper-body strength."

"Me neither," chirped Jasmine.

"Oh, they're really light," the caterer said. "Just cookies."

"You guys are so great to volunteer to help," Becca said artfully, sparkles flooding her eyes. "I really appreciate it."

When she said the last bit, she looked straight at me and I couldn't help lighting up on the inside.

The caterer led the trio and me into the kitchen, and next thing the Helle Housers knew, they were far too busy standing in for waiters to sniff around and notice if anything interesting was happening upstairs. While I handed out mini Linzer tortes, I could only assume Sills was sitting at the base of the information booth a level above, pretending to wait for her friend's train to come while secretly gluing the Blue Moon tile in place, per the plan. Just when my tray emptied, Andy came up from behind with a replacement—and a secret squeeze on the small of my back.

I was suddenly wearing a coat of goose bumps. I jerked my neck in shock.

"Steady there," he whispered. "You don't want to go dropping everything all over the floor."

Thanks for the tip. I counted to three and focused on regaining my composure, then continued to play caterer. If the Helle Housers got any pictures from the next fifteen minutes, they had to have been of the insides of their purses. The crowd was voracious, and the head chef made sure to bring over refills whenever any of our tray's supplies were running low. When Sills and Poppy, dressed up like a suburban train passenger with her bottle of water and leather weekend bag, came back to the party looking pleased, I knew we were in good shape. I glanced at Becca, who flashed me a wink across the room.

After the Helle Housers and I were relieved of our trays, I wanted to find Andy, but first I had the burning urge to nip upstairs and check out Sills's work.

I threw my catering smock onto a counter and raced out of

the kitchen and through the party room. Going upstairs was a little risky, but if I ran into anyone I'd just say I'd eaten something with onion and needed to get gum at the newsstand.

When I made it into the lobby, people were looking at me as if I were the strangest thing they'd ever seen, and I had to tell myself it was because I was overdressed, not because they could read my thoughts. I neared the center of the hall and saw that the clock above the information booth appeared pristine as could be. And down at the base of the booth, a few inches off the floor, was a Blue Moon tile. My eyes darted around among the stragglers in the lobby who couldn't possibly have any idea what had happened and I was filled with a sense of satisfaction. Knowing about somebody else's secret is one thing, but playing a part in one is infinitely better.

"Do we need to get you a watch?" I looked behind and saw Andy was inches away. He reached out to gently stroke my bare wrist.

"Did you come all the way up here to tease me?" I shot him a flirty look, then glanced away nervously.

"*All the way?* It's not that far. And well worth the walk up a flight of stairs."

I felt a pat of butter melt in my stomach.

He cocked his head ever so slightly. "I want to show you something cool."

Without waiting for me to agree, he grabbed my hand and led me all the way up the marble stairs that Hallie and Sig had been perched on earlier that night, and we settled onto the floor of the balcony above. This high up, all the station's sounds melted into one mellifluous echo, and the concourse spread out like a magic carpet.

"What do you think, Voyante?"

"It's pretty great from up here," I said, my fingers trembling.

And it would be greater if you'd kiss me, I held back from saying.

"Want to see something better? Look up." Andy pointed at the ceiling.

I leaned back and craned my neck. "Wow," I said dizzily. "The stars feel brighter up here."

He placed his hand on the ground directly behind me and my spine tingled. "Do you notice anything else strange?"

I turned to look at him. "The fact that you're not blowing me off for once?"

As I was saying it I felt brave, but the second I was done talking fear started karate chopping in my chest.

He scowled. "I hate to break it to you, but not all of your conspiracy theories hold water. Look up again." He waited a moment. "See that? It's all painted backward."

"It is?" I studied the order of the stars and tried to flip them over in my head. I was surprised that this was the first time I'd noticed—or even heard about this.

He scooted closer. "Some people say it was done that way to make us feel like we're looking down on the sky from the other side. There's also another, less popular, theory."

"What? That the painter had dyslexia?" I joked.

"Bingo."

What was wrong with me, making wisecracks about learning disorders in front of their poster child?

But Andy didn't seem to mind. "That's the theory I'm rooting for. Think about it: if he could create the entire universe, maybe I'll be able to get a B average. And, you know, start focusing on other things."

His implication was so obvious it hurt.

I sighed and looked away. "Keep me posted."

"Like I wouldn't." He pressed his forehead against my neck, barely missing my cameo.

"Claire?" he said. And then he kissed me, right there under the stars.

All the sound around me drained away and I saw pale pink cherry blossoms explode in my head.

It felt good—too good to get used to.

{ 10 }

The Other Kind of Salon

The next morning, I woke up to a lumpy gray sky. It was the kind of weather that casts its sleepy spell on everything, and I was no exception. Too tired to move, I lay in bed concentrating not on my memories of the party, but on the gray world I'd gone to when I'd closed my eyes the night before.

I was standing at the head of the operating table, and the patient was covered with a drab-colored sheet. Just as the head nurse handed me the tray with my instruments, the lightbulb hanging overhead went out, and I proceeded to snip and stitch in the dark. When I was done performing my operation, all the nurses clapped and raised martini glasses. Then the patient turned to me and I saw that he wasn't a man—he was a snake.

"She moves!" I rubbed my eyes and looked across the room at Dad. "Becca's on the line."

I took the phone and cleared my throat. "Hola." My voice was huskier than usual, which must have been a function of my sleepiness.

"Sorry to wake you," Becca said. "But it's too good not to. You near a computer?"

"Say no more." I stretched and got out of my cozy spot under the covers. I was on Moonwatcher.net in no time. The site's latest photo showed Reagan looking glum as Poppy sauntered past, her arm linked through a guy's.

"'Blue Moon scandal alert,'" I read aloud. "'All hell broke loose last night when Poppy "Man on the Moon" Williamson and Reagan "Pale Moon" Hendricks showed up at the Hope and Anchor fund-raiser wearing the same dress. *Quele horroir!*'"

"They didn't even get that part right, did they?" Becca asked.

"Not if it's supposed to be French."

Becca snorted. "So it's official: they got everything wrong. The only thing their dresses had in common is they were black. Poppy's was Zac Posen and Reagan's was some Italian designer. Not to mention Poppy's had only one strap."

"You going to write in and ask for a correction?" I asked.

"Considering that's the only thing they got out of the night, I'm going to let it lie." She paused. "Anyway, I wanted to thank you for finding those merry pranksters last night. You did great."

Happiness rang through me. It wasn't so much that I wanted credit for the night before as that I wanted to know Becca held me in high esteem. She wasn't going to drop me after all.

"Oh, whatever." I tried to play it off. "Thank whoever invented fake tans. Those dolts were easy to spot."

Becca laughed giddily, then changed the subject. "So what are you up to today?"

"Why?" I could hardly wait to hear what she had in mind.

"If you want, Louis was going to take me to this taco joint he discovered, down in Sunset Heights."

"You mean Sunset Park?" I asked, mildly annoyed to hear that they'd made plans without me.

"You know it?" She sounded surprised.

Know it? Um, I'd only been the one to introduce Louis to my favorite chocolate chicken tacos. "I think he's mentioned it," I said coolly, refraining from telling her that I deserved the credit.

He so owed me one.

"He's lending me a bike," she said. "I haven't been on one since I was using training wheels. Why don't you come with us?"

It was a tough call. Becca was able to sniff out my matchmaker motives from a mile away—and they always sent her running. If I said yes, Louis would kill me for crashing his two-person party. If I said no, she'd bail. I needed a good excuse.

"I wish I could, but I just remembered," I said, stuffing my chewed-up nails in my mouth. I had about two seconds to think of an excuse. Make that one second.

"What?" Becca was practically huffing with impatience.

And at that very moment, salvation walked in through my bedroom door. Henry was clutching *The Big Book of Bugs* and wearing Dad's new terry cloth workout band to keep his mess of blond curls from flopping onto his face.

"Henry and I have a date to get his hair cut," I told her.

"We do?" Henry's stupefied tone made my stomach tighten. Becca was going to know I was lying.

But instead she just laughed. "Henry goes to that culty curly hair salon? I didn't know they took kids."

And then it crystallized: she'd misheard Henry's "we do" for Ouidoo, the "curly girl" place I kept coming across on my fashion magazine binges.

"Why wouldn't they?" I had no choice but to play along. She'd never know if I just took him to Cheap Cuts instead of paying two hundred dollars for Ouidoo's signature "no shampoo" (they didn't believe in the chemicals) and "no snip" (they used a hedge clipper–like instrument that was supposed to be easier on the follicle than regular scissors).

"Reagan has an appointment there today too," Becca told me.

"She does?" I replied nervously. "But her hair isn't even curly."

"It is before she blow-dries it straight," Becca said. "Maybe Louis and I will come by and say hi."

Way to talk your way into a corner, Claire. Now we *had* to go there or Reagan would rat us out.

"Yeah, you should," I said unconvincingly, and looked over at Henry. His little belly was popping through his T-shirt and he was dragging his finger across the top of my fish tank.

That boy had "two-hundred-dollar salon" written all over him.

You've got to love the Internet. Turned out Ouidoo's had a "curly child" discount that was affordable enough to quash Mom and Dad's financial worries.

"It'll be good for us to have some quality brother-sister time," I told them.

Mom rubbed her eyes. "And what may I ask is so wrong with the quality of your time together at Cheap Cuts?"

"Nothing," I said sweetly. "They're just closed on Sundays."

I felt like high-fiving myself.

As we were on our way out, I noticed a thick envelope with Kiki's signature pink trim calling out to me from the mail pile on the sideboard. "Hang on, Hen," I said, gliding over to the envelope. The surprise was that it was addressed to both Henry and me. Kiki usually acts as if I live alone. I ripped it open.

KIKI MERRIMAN
REQUESTS THAT
CLAIRE AND HENRY VOYANTE

SAVE THE DATE OF SATURDAY THE SECOND OF MARCH
FOR A BIRTHDAY CELEBRATION ABOARD A
MURDER MYSTERY TRAIN
EXACT DETAILS TO FOLLOW

I double-checked the pile to see if any identical cards had come for the rest of the Voyantes.

Amazing. Leave it to Kiki not to invite her daughter or son-in-law to her birthday party. Not wanting to start trouble, I quickly stuffed the card in the back pocket of my jeans and rejoined my brother at the door.

"Wanna hear a joke?" he asked me. "What kind of haircut is popular with bees?"

I pushed the hair out of his face and studied his blue eyes. He was dying to get to the punch line.

"I don't know," I lied.

"A buzz cut!" He spread his arms like wings and took off for the elevator.

An hour later, Henry was off having his scalp smothered with a kelp-protein mask, and I was ensconced in a velvety lounge chair, contentedly working on my second complimentary Mexican spiced hot chocolate and flipping through the latest *Elle*. So what if I didn't fit in with the salon's bizarrely ringleted populace? This place was made for me.

I was midway through a test that would tell me what my "beauty look" revealed about my taste in men when a woman came over and introduced herself as Henry's assistant rinse technician. "The mask was remarkably successful," she said in a tone befitting a cancer ward nurse. "Come and see for yourself."

Upstairs, Henry was chilling out in a swivel chair, reading his *Big Book of Bugs* while a woman with silver corkscrew curls daubed his head with paper towels. "It's their patented no-frizz technique," he told me when he met my eye in the mirror.

I took a seat next to him. "I'll have to try it at home."

The silver-haired woman bristled. "It doesn't work on people with hair like yours."

I felt a twinge of hurt and was relieved when Ravi, Henry's main stylist, bungee jumped onto the scene and started groping Henry's locks. He launched into a story about the wedding he'd just come back from a few nights ago, not seeming to notice—or care—that Henry was reading his book and that he was an eight-year-old boy. "I'm not allowed to name names . . . a real star-studded affair . . . the cliffs of Scotland are so misty this time of year . . ."

Ravi was so consumed with his tales of fabulousness, he was having trouble focusing on the job at hand. In the time it took me to finish my magazine, he'd barely made his way through a quarter of Henry's hair.

Boredom was starting to weigh on me. "I'm going to go down to the first floor and get a magazine refill," I announced, springing out of my chair. There'd have to be *something* to distract myself with below.

Weirdly, when I got downstairs, the lobby's once-heaping pile of glossies had depleted to practically nothing. I lifted the one remaining title—an old *Organic Living* with this scintillating headline: *The Grain Drain Explained*—and let it drop back down.

"*Psst,*" came a voice.

I looked up to see a familiar face surrounded by an unfamiliar crown of Pre-Raphaelite curls. "Reagan?" I squawked. "I barely recognized you."

"Yeah, I got my mom's hair." A shadow passed over her face. "At least she gave me that." Clearly embarrassed by her self-pity, she started rambling on about her hair and how hard it was to care for. "It has a mind of its own. If I go to sleep with it wet I wake up looking like one of those bonsai sculptures." She still looked sad and I could tell she wasn't done thinking about her mother's hands-off approach to parenting.

I felt a rush of sympathy. "I like the way your hair looks now," I told her. "Honestly."

"Whatever." She cast me a skeptical look. "Anyway, I have a treat for you." She pulled me behind a palm tree and opened her salon smock. She'd taken the whole stack of magazines.

"You greedy little devil!" I cried, and a vicarious thrill shot through me as I grabbed the first one to come to hand—Nylon's new music issue. "And to think I almost bought this!"

She cast her eyes at the receptionist, who was trying to pretend she wasn't staring at the palm tree we were hiding behind. "I should probably get back to my station," she said, retying her belt.

"No worries," I said, feeling bad for my lack of subtlety about her magazine hoarding as I watched her walk away. "And hey, your secret's safe with me."

She turned around and stared at me in annoyance.

"Your hair," I clarified, making a curly corkscrew gesture and glancing over at the receptionist to make sure she was watching. "Not a word."

{ 11 }

How I Joined the Green Party

Tuesday night, a drunk couple decided the Washington View Village courtyard was the perfect location for their enactment of World War III. I got to hear every last detail about the man's unwillingness to take his girlfriend's phone calls at work and the woman's insistence on flirting with the FreshDirect guy. I slept horribly, even worse than usual, and I was in such a daze the next day at school that I'd worked through most of my lunch before I clued in to the fact that I was sitting at the same table as the cute dark-haired guy with the Western style shirts.

I must have been staring at him, because he jerked his hand in the air and grinned.

"I'm Alex," he said, scooting into the spot directly across

from me. He sounded slightly stuffed up, as if he was recovering from a cold. "Mind if I—wait, did I just kick you?"

He was so much goofier than his cool-guy image had led me to believe.

"I don't think so," I said, bringing my Orangina to my mouth. His manic energy was making me smile.

"Must've been somebody else, then." He looked down the table and called out, "Apologies to any and all injured parties." Then he turned back to face me. "I have disproportionately long legs. And a short wingspan. See?" He raised his arms over his head, then grinned. "Sorry for the information overload."

Okay, he was nicer *and* spazzier than I would have figured.

"No, not at all." I smiled again. "I'm all for information."

"No other way to be."

He reminded me of an adorable dog, with his slightly overgrown and wet-looking features. I took another bite of leftover duck confit and watched as he produced a mini box of Rice Krispies from his bag and emptied it into a paper bowl. The kid was eating cereal for lunch. You had to respect that.

"Are you new here?" I asked.

He nodded in response. "You know," he said, watching me from under raised brows, "we've seen each other like, a thousand times before."

I couldn't believe it. He'd actually *noticed* me?

"You sure about that?" I faked disbelief. He was free to spill as much as he wanted, but that didn't mean full disclosure had to be my game.

"You live in Washington Square Village, right?" I did a double take, and he answered my question before I could ask it. "I don't, but my friend does," he said. "Bash Ferris." He raised an eyebrow questioningly.

I chewed the name over for a minute. "I know most of the kids in my complex, but I don't think—"

"No, no, he's an older friend. A professor. Sebastian Ferris."

My stomach churned.

"Oh, him." I downed the rest of my Orangina in one gulp. Professor Ferris was a misanthropic film scholar who got his kicks out of approaching professors' kids to ask our opinions on obscure old movies there was no chance we'd ever heard of, much less seen. "I think he lives in building three." I didn't know what else to say.

A dimple formed in his cheek. "I can tell you think it's weird. I was raised to hang out with people of all ages."

"Not that weird," I said, thinking of my Waldorf posse. "I actually have a group of friends in their seventies. They're cool. A lot less wound up than most people our age." I looked around the room to confirm my claim. One table over, the Game Theory Club was having its weekly lunch-hour debate, and a kid at our table was using the cafeteria's scratchy napkins to make chemistry flashcards.

Almost as good as scientific proof.

"Exactly." He slurped from his spoon. "Anyway, Bash is amazing. He and my mom used to go out, like, fifty years ago, so I'm sort of like the son he never had. Also I'm planning on becoming a filmmaker. That helps."

I held back my smile. Aspiring filmmakers—or artists of any kind—were few and far between at Hudson. The school tended toward facts, not creativity.

"So that's what it takes to get on his good side!" I exclaimed. He gave me a questioning look and I admitted that I wasn't Professor Farris's favorite kid. "We got off to a rocky start," I began. "When I was little, he'd ask me what I thought of Disney movies and snort at my answers. There's not much crossover in our tastes."

"How so?" He leaned closer.

"I'm more into cheesy murder mysteries than Croatian new wave or whatever."

"You have Bash all wrong. He just got me hooked on Hitchcock."

I smiled. I love Hitchcock.

"No way. I just watched *Frenzy* last week," I added quickly, over the ringing bell.

"Suspense. Nice." He balled up his napkin, stuffed it in his empty milk container, and stood up. "Until next time?"

Strangely, I realized that I could only hope so.

I gazed at the table, studying the milk puddles he'd left in his wake. So the kid was a mess, but there was no denying it. He was pretty cool, and not just by Hudson standards.

There's one downside to having unnervingly trustworthy best friends: when they start hanging out with each other, you can be sure neither of them is going to fill you in on the juicy details.

Or even the boring ones.

Becca's and my schedules this semester couldn't have been worse for running into each other at school, and most days her afternoons were more tightly packed than the first lady's. Thanks to her and Louis's shared tight-lipped style, all I knew about their Sunday bike ride was that it was "fine" (his word) and "good" (hers).

Louis waited until Thursday morning when I was getting ready to leave for school to call and bring it up. "Hey, did Becca say anything about our ride?"

"Well . . ." I was tapping Didier and Margaux's breakfast flakes into their tank. "Just a minute-by-minute play-by-play. Is it all true?" Cruel, but how else was I going to get any dirt?

"You are such a bad actress. And nothing happened." He

sounded slightly disappointed. "Look, I kind of told her you and I were going riding today, and I think she's joining us. Can you just, you know, play along?"

"You mean pretend we had plans for today?" I couldn't conceal my annoyance.

"Exactly."

"Lou, aren't you forgetting something?" I paused to relish the absurdity of it all. "We already *do*. We're supposed to go to Stuyvesant Town and play bocce." My friend let out a pained "d'oh" noise and I reminded him he should be pleased. "At least it'll be easy for me to get into character."

When Becca and I came out of school at the end of the day, Louis was already across the street, diligently waiting for us on his bike. He had on a camel-hair coat and a green cashmere scarf. I felt a tug of jealousy—Louis was submitting to a whole-sale makeover for Becca, whereas all I'd heard from Andy was a lame e-mail where he griped about his heavy homework load and asked me if I preferred Manhattan or New England clam chowder. If there was one thing Andy was still good for, it was random questions.

"Hey, Becca," Louis said, as if I didn't exist.

If I weren't so fascinated by their lopsided dynamic, I would have killed him.

"Hi." She leaned in to kiss him on the cheek, an act, I no-ticed, she executed with the nonchalance of somebody who couldn't possibly reciprocate his feelings. Even though she was wearing a cashmere coat and ballet slippers made of fragile sil-ver leather and ribbons that came up to her knees, she radiated an impossibly casual energy. "Have you been waiting long? I was at the nurse's office."

I perked up, remembering the nurses from my dream.

"What's the matter?" I asked, sounding a little too worried.

"Nothing," Becca said. "I just needed a Band-Aid. I got an ugly paper cut." She wiggled her bandaged index finger and smiled impishly. "I know, I'm a baby."

I decided to dismiss the coincidence.

"And what are those, baby shoes?" Louis asked, looking down at Becca's feet. "She can't wear those, can she?" His first words to me.

"My mom called me 'tinfoil toes' this morning." Becca pouted. "You don't like them either?"

"That's not the point," I responded. "Those ribbons have 'accident' written all over them. They're going to get caught in the spokes and—"

"Things could get very Isadora Duncan." Louis was trying to sound cool but there was nothing mellow about the way his eyes were sweeping Becca from behind his tortoiseshell frames. She raised her chin and gave him a challenging look.

Oh, would they just kiss already!

"You know," now Louis was mumbling, "the dancer who wore the long scarf in the convertible and—"

"I think every girl who has ever worn a long scarf knows what happened to Isadora Duncan," she told him. Her cell phone chimed from inside her bag, but she ignored it. "I actually always thought it was a beautiful story."

"Yeah," I said, "nothing says beautiful like having your head snap off."

"Or your foot," Louis added, giving Becca's left slipper a playful tap. I could feel the electricity from where I was standing.

We finally persuaded Becca to go back inside and get her gym shoes.

As Becca scampered back up the steps to school, I turned to

Louis with an impressed grin. "Wow, she must really like you. Nothing comes between that girl and her fancy footwear."

"Nah, I think she just really likes bik—" His face dropped like a stone and I turned around to see Becca sailing back down the steps. She was still wearing her dancing shoes and her face was lined with a distraught expression.

She rushed over our way. "I can't," she said, slightly out of breath.

"There's no shame in wearing sneakers in public," I told her. "Millions of people do it every day." I gestured down at Louis's red Converse high-tops.

"It's not . . ." She bit her lip and looked away. Something sad was happening in her eyes. "I just got a message and . . . my voice coach needs me to come up and do something. I'm sorry. You guys are still going to Stuy Town, right?"

When had he filled her in on the details of our itinerary? Was he calling her during the middle of the day from school?

"That was the plan," I told her. "But if you want us to ride uptown with—"

"No. I'm so late I'm just going to get a cab." A frown was worrying her pretty features. "I'll come next time. And I'll remember to dress appropriately. Promise."

Without Becca, the tone of our afternoon dampened. Louis was obviously preoccupied with her flakiness, which he was taking as personally as possible. He was zoning out, and every conversation I tried to start with him felt like a long distance telephone call.

And there was another bummer to deal with. Stuyvesant Town's once-cozy warren of brick apartment buildings and community playgrounds was now slicker than a wet iguana. I vaguely remembered how a realtor had paid a princely sum for the land a few years ago, and suddenly the middle-class apartment complex had been converted into a whole new world. See-through pink terraces wrapped around the buildings at strange angles and the homey old park benches had been replaced with latex pods, also in pink.

The main attraction, the city's last public bocce courts, had been replaced by a chartreuse mini-golf course. So instead of playing bocce, a superfun game where you roll balls around in the dirt, all there was to do was watch a yuppie gab on his cell phone while he practiced his putting skills.

Not surprisingly, Zeta Equities flags were planted everywhere. Sink Landon must have been having a field day. First the Apollo—now this. Andy would have a heart attack.

"This isn't as much fun as I'd hoped," I told Louis after we'd been sitting on adjoining pods for an uncomfortably long stretch.

"You're telling me." He popped a peanut in his mouth and tossed the shell at a trash can. It missed. "Hey, Lemon, do you think if I took, like, an opera appreciation class I'd have a better chance with your pal?"

I felt a surge of warmth.

"Maybe." I kicked the ground. "Though, Becca's not being here is not what I was talking about."

"I was trying to ignore the obvious." Louis cracked open another peanut. "Ever hear of a coping mechanism?"

I bit back a smile. Louis has been going to a shrink since before he could talk, and has a habit of lacing his conversations with psychobabble.

"What's shrink-talk for 'Let's get out of here'?" I asked.

Louis smiled. "Why do you ask that?"

"Are you kidding? Because what they did to this place is totally depr—"

"No, no, it was a joke. 'Why do you ask that?' is my shrink's catchphrase." Louis got up and took a final glance at the pink putting "green." He shook his head and hopped back on his bike. "Man, oh man."

We rode out the First Avenue exit and tootled around Alphabet City, a once-punk neighborhood now known for its designer tea lounges and overpriced consignment shops. The sky was a dusky blue and the streets felt less crowded than usual, but just as we were passing Tompkins Square Park, a black SUV with a NY 11111 license plate blasted up from behind, shattering any semblance of tranquillity. It started up a siren and ran a red light, and people were sticking their heads out of nearby shops to see what the noise was all about.

My palms broke into a sweat. The vehicle had my number all over it. Or, to be more specific, all over its license plate. Okay, so the number ones weren't dancing on a stage, but it was still too close to the Rockettes dream I'd had that weekend at the Moonery to ignore.

"Let's follow it!" I shrieked over the earsplitting noise.

"Aren't we a little old for cops and robbers?" Louis replied.

"It'll be fun!"

Louis waved his arms in protest and screamed something about my needing a life, but the sirens drowned most of it out. Next thing I knew, we were hot on the car's trail.

Adrenaline pumping, I followed it up First Avenue, and down a street in the East Twenties that was closed off to traffic.

"No bike traffic either!" A policeman made a circling gesture with his finger. "Turn around!"

I hopped off my bike and motioned for Louis to do the same. "We're pedestrians, Officer," I said, walking my bike forward.

The police officer looked profoundly peeved, but just then

an old lady came at him with a thousand questions about the commotion.

"Hurry!" I cried, and led Louis through the barricades. He shot me an unwilling look.

Up ahead, the car had pulled over and I realized where we were. The people getting out were approaching the same alleyway I was used to accessing by the back door of the Moonery. My heart palpitated. Something told me this delegation wasn't going to visit Mr. Dimitrius, the self-cleaning-toaster-oven guru.

Louis was slowing down. "You saw who's up there in that delegation, right? They're going to suspect we're trying to assassinate him or something if we keep following him around."

"What are you taking about?" I kept going toward the phalanx of suits, trying to cover up my anxiety. "After what I told that cop, if we don't keep walking it'll look weird. Besides, don't you want to see what the deal is?"

"This isn't the same thing as playing Spy versus Spy in Washington View Towers." Louis looked at me like I'd lost half my brain, and I wished I could either tell him the truth or come up with a good lie. "You go, I'm staying put." I could tell he meant it.

"Whatever you want." My nervousness came out as bitchiness, but I didn't stop to apologize. I kept gripping my handlebars and walking ahead until I'd rammed my front tire into a stately-looking man's leg. That was when I noticed who got to ride around in such a rudely behaved car. The tall, broad-shouldered man who'd climbed out of the vehicle was our mayor.

I was struck by how unreal he looked. He was like a wax statue of himself. "Just give me a second while I catch up with the girls," Mayor Irving said to an aide.

The girls? I couldn't help gaping. What girls?

"Young lady!" a security man boomed at me. "No autographs today. Move along!"

The mayor turned to look at me, and a flicker of recognition crossed his face. I couldn't believe it. Did Mayor Irving know who I was? And did this mean he knew I was a Blue Moon?

Holy Honolulu. "Don't worry about her." The mayor pushed off the security man who was about to pin me to the sidewalk. "Least we can do for somebody who's doing her part to keep the city green. If only more New Yorkers would get into biking." He was speaking loud enough for everyone in the neighborhood to hear and he chuckled in the nervous, sleazy manner unique to politicians and game show hosts.

"Every little bit helps," I managed to say, patting my bike. And in that stolen moment I looked up through the trees and down the row of houses. At the end of the alley, next to the Moonery's white star marking, I could see Becca standing in the window, staring straight at me. A look of horror registered on her face and she pulled the curtain shut.

Must've been a very private voice lesson she had going on.

{ 12 }

Sight for an Eyesore

"**N**ow what?" Louis asked when I caught up with him at the end of the street. "You wanna try to run over the president?"

"That'll have to wait for another day. I'm actually supposed to be home for dinner," I said. Remembering the one food Louis hated, I added, "Mom made her special cassoulet."

"That's the nasty bean thing?"

"Sure is," I said, my thoughts drifting to the Moonery. Something major was going on in there, and my heart sank. I couldn't have been more uninvited. I had to shake free of Louis and see what was going on. "You down?"

"Nah." Louis wrinkled his nose. "Bon appétit."

I rode down Second Avenue for a few blocks to throw him

off, then turned right back around. The whole mayoral entourage was still there when I returned and I locked my bike to the No Parking signpost outside Star Foods Emporium.

Stinko was in his usual spot behind the counter while *The Simpsons* played on a snowy television behind him. When he saw me he started frantically waving his arms around. "Not tonight! It's closed!"

"What are you talking about? I just saw Becca in—"

"I'm under strict orders."

Way to add insult to injury.

"Fine, then I'll wait outside." I was feeling more determined by the second, but generally speaking, I didn't think it was a great idea to get on the bad side of anybody with half as much neck tattoo art as Stinko.

"In the cold?" Stinko looked at me, then let off a sigh and got up to drag a spare stool behind the counter. "You don't have to do that."

He made me a tomato and cheese sandwich and we watched the rest of *The Simpsons*, then *Access Hollywood*.

At the end of the show, during a segment on a supposedly famous travel writer who'd developed a sudden fear of flying, Stinko was too transfixed to notice the curtain in the back move and three girls trickle out into the shop.

Diana was the first to emerge, her red curls flashing by as she flew out the door. "Bye, Stinko!" An instant later Reagan made a beeline for the candy section. She ripped open a pack of Sour Patch Kids and stuffed half its contents in her mouth. "I was so dizzy I could barely think," she said by way of greeting. Neither of them noticed I was there.

Becca, who was hanging back by a shelf of ramen noodles, must've had some sixth sense. "Hi, Claire," she said coolly.

"Do we have to wait till the closing credits or can I come up now?" I asked her.

Becca took her bun out of its clip, a surefire signal she was stalling. The *Access* theme jingle started to play and she murmured, "Follow me," jerking her head toward the back of the deli.

We trooped upstairs in silence. She hung my coat up for me and had me wait in the game room while she made a pot of tea. She came back a few minutes later and closed the doors behind her.

An ominous mood hung over us—the lights were low and steam was rising from the dragon-shaped teapot. She handed me a cup and finally spoke. "You have some explaining to do, young lady."

Was she kidding?

"Excuse me?" I said. "You want me to explain why I made up a story about having to go to my voice coach when I actually had a secret rendezvous with the mayor? Oh wait—sorry. That's not me, it's *you*."

Becca's eyes smiled as she raised her teacup to her mouth. "I didn't say I don't have some explaining of my own. But you were supposed to be in Stuy Town."

Now I was getting peeved. Was she my best friend or my personal keeper?

"Yeah, I *was* there." Becca looked at me like I was feeding her lies by the spoonful. "B, I know you're just getting the hang of bikes, but there's something you should probably know about them: they have a way of moving around. Fast."

"Whatever—you know you're not supposed to go prowling around the alley."

I squinted in fury.

"I wasn't in the alley. I was on the street, like any person has the right to be, when I saw Mayor Irving. And I'm not even going to ask what you were doing breaking the no-boys rule. I just want to know what he was doing here. Is he, like, having a secret affair with Sills?"

"Please." Becca smiled and put her cup down. "The explanation is a whole lot less fun."

"I'll be the judge of that."

My verdict ten minutes later: she was half right. The answer was pretty crazy, but not as fun as I'd hoped.

Until now, I'd never really stopped to think about where the Moons got the ideas for their projects, but I would have been smart to. They didn't just pull them out of thin air. They had a very special consultant.

"The mayor comes up here and tells you what to do?" I was stunned.

"He doesn't tell us what to do," she protested. "He comes to us with suggestions. And it's up to us what, if any, projects we want to invest our time and . . ." Too uncomfortable to finish with the obvious word, she hugged her knees and twisted to the side.

"It's okay," I told her her. "I've heard the word 'money' before."

"Well, it's our families' money, which makes things a little weirder," she said, still facing away.

"Why doesn't he just deal directly with your parents?"

She snorted. "Think, Claire."

"I don't get it."

"It's pretty simple. Our parents leave us to take care of things and they turn a blind eye. It's safer they don't know what's going on. Otherwise something might—it might come out by accident that they had a hand in sprucing up the park or whatever."

"And if it did?" I could feel my nose scrunching up.

"Are you kidding? If people knew how closely our families were working with City Hall, there'd be riots in the street. You know how cynical people are. Everyone would say our parents were buying the mayor off so their business deals would get approved."

"What deals?" I said skeptically, still digging.

"Like my parents' new ketchup factory and Reagan's dad's bid to buy the *New York Post*."

"Oh." At least there was *something* I already knew about. "And that's not what's happening?"

She steadied her breath and met my eye. "Not at all. This"—she motioned to our surroundings—"it's a way of doing good things with no strings attached."

"And haven't you ever worried that if the mayor kept showing up here, people might wonder what lies behind Star Foods Emporium?"

Becca shrugged. "Mayor Irving is known to be involved in the Gramercy Park Neighborhood Association. Their office is two doors down from the deli."

"Wow, you have it all covered." I looked around the room, as if the older Shuttleworths might be crouching in the shadows. "So how involved exactly are your parents in the Moons?"

"In pocketbook only. They just make contributions to the Pookie Trust."

My head wasn't processing things as fast as I'd like.

"To *what*?" I said.

"'Pookie' was what Gummy Salzman's husband called her. Her will stipulated that a trust be set up to fund interesting anonymous projects. They've become a little more ambitious over the years. Most of what we do now is work with the mayor on things he doesn't want to be so public about."

I glanced across the room, my eyes settling on the oil painting of Gummy Salzman. Her features were thick and her skin was tinged yellow. The best-looking thing about her was her deeply knowing eyes. "Okay," I said, "but why doesn't he just *be* public about them?"

"Lots of reasons," Becca said. "Some of the projects, like fixing a park fountain or cleaning up the zoo, wouldn't be a favorite of taxpayers when we have serious things like murders and failing public schools to deal with. And sometimes there are heavy issues the mayor doesn't want to come out and scare the public with."

My heart beat a little faster. "Like?"

Becca smiled tightly. "Say there's a confidential report that says there's a risk that the city's water supply will be contaminated. The mayor can either make it public and watch all eight million New Yorkers freak out and, like, die of dehydration, or he can install the recommended new filter and let people go ahead with their regular lives."

"You're saying ignorance is bliss?"

"Sometimes."

I licked my lips, taking in her explanation. "So the water, is that hypothetical situation the one you're working on?"

"That was last year."

"Wow. And now you're on to . . ." I looked at her, waiting.

Becca clasped her hands together. "Say there's a secret report that says the Brooklyn Bridge isn't so, um, safe."

I could tell by the way she was twisting her airplane ring that she wasn't speaking hypothetically. "Are you serious?" I exclaimed, my heart in my throat. "There's about to be a terrorist attack?"

Becca cradled her knees and rocked back and forth. "No, nothing that James Bond–y. The bridge's central cable is losing its strength and the only way to keep it is to reinforce it with a platinum lining. But platinum is rarer than gold. And crazy expensive."

My ears perked up at this. A dedicated supporter of the TSE cashmere and Christian Louboutin shoe empires, I'd never heard Becca declare anything to be too costly. "How crazy expensive?"

"More crazy expensive than I'd care to say." She looked

embarrassed. "Long story short, the city can't afford it—they'd rather shut down the bridge for a while and replace the weak cable with a new one altogether."

"And what's so bad about that?" I asked. "Safety first, right?"

"If any of the bridge's cables are replaced, then the bridge loses its landmark status."

I still didn't see what the big deal was.

"So what? Since when were you into status?" I said.

She shook her head. "You don't get it. The current landmark status prohibits people from building anything near the bridge that is taller than a couple of stories. And if that goes out the window, real-estate developers will be able to do whatever they want with all the waterfront property."

"Oh." I was starting to catch her drift. "And more ugly developments is not something we would want, is it?"

"The developments' hideousness is the least of it. They'd be so big they'd cover up most views of the bridge. You'd hardly be able to see it with all the minicities people want to build near the bases."

I was stunned. "But the Brooklyn Bridge is one of New York's—"

"Most important landmarks. Second to only the Statue of Liberty. I know, I know. But when it was built it wasn't supposed to last this long. And landmark laws are stupid like that.

"So far this is all hush-hush." She raised an eyebrow and drew in a breath. "There's a public inspection scheduled for early April. If it fails, there's no question, they'll replace the cables with the superdurable plastic they're using on new bridges all over the country. And that will be the end of the Brooklyn Bridge as we know it."

"Can't your parents donate the platinum that the city needs?" I asked.

Becca shook her head. "They don't like to draw attention to themselves. Especially when they're in the process of building a huge factory that needs the mayor's approval every step of the way. But there's another option."

"Lemme guess," I said, starting to get the hang of it. "The Moons are installing the platinum cable the bridge needs?" She smiled encouragingly. "And you're planning a party on the bridge that will cover up the real work you're doing on the bridge? Just like you did at Grand Central?"

"Good work, Voyante." She smiled warmly. "It's actually a movie shoot, not a party. Sills wrote this awesome script, it's basically a remake of the bridge scene in the Alfred Hitchcock movie *Vertigo*. The mayor gave us a permit to close off the bridge for one night. During the shoot we're going to have engineers pretending to be actors climb up the weak cable and secretly line it with platinum. At least, that was the plan."

"*Was* the plan?"

Just then, Sills's voice shot through the room. "Becca, we need you upstairs now." She sounded as serious as I'd ever heard.

"I'm coming," Becca yelled back.

The floorboard creaked as Sills retreated.

Becca took one last sip of tea and got up. From her spot above, she studied me—a challenging look in her eye.

"What's going on?" I whispered. "Tell me."

"We ran into a bit of a roadblock. That's why I was called up here today." A resigned intake of breath. "I wasn't supposed to invite the Half Moons, but it's kind of late for that. Do you—are you—"

"Up for it?" I finished off for her.

She nodded hesitantly.

"Why not?" I said as coolly as I could manage, but my palms were as hot as turbine engines.

• • •

"I told her everything," Becca said when she stepped into the office upstairs. I'd never been inside the room before, and I couldn't help gawking. It reminded me of the pictures I'd seen of fashion designers' studios, its walls papered over with maps and postcards and dramatic doodles. The furniture was as colorful as if it had been selected by a child—there were strawberry Art Deco armchairs, a yellow see-through desk, and a peacock blue loveseat with a curlicue frame.

Sills was seated behind the desk and Poppy was in the background, facing the window. A dark mood hung over the room. "Claire might be useful," Becca said.

"I'd say it's a little late for useful," said Sills. "We already got ourselves good and screwed."

"Well, what's going on?"

"I don't think it's your business," Sills said to me. "No offense."

I grimaced. I knew as well as anyone else that the only times people say "no offense" are when offense should be taken.

Becca turned to her. "We're in so deep we don't have time to keep up appearances. We can kick our new members out or fill them in and enlist their help."

"And I see you've gone ahead and made an executive decision." I tensed at Sills's words.

"She's as trustworthy as they come," Becca promised.

"She'd better be." Sills eyed me pointedly.

"I don't get it," Poppy said, distractedly running her fingers along the window's wrought-iron grill. "Nobody could've snuck through."

Confusion warbled through me. "Wait—someone broke in?"

"I thought she told you everything." Sills rotated the computer screen to show me Moonwatcher.net's latest post. The words "Bridge to Paradise" were written above a photograph of Sills and Poppy walking over the Brooklyn Bridge, their heads tilted skyward.

I just stared, not sure how to respond. "The Helle Housers know?" I said at last.

"Hard to tell." Becca sighed. "If only that were the extent of the problem." She opened a drawer and took out a pink iPod. "You're going to love this."

"Thanks," I said awkwardly as she passed it to me. "Is this a hand-me-down or something?"

"Hardly," Becca said. "Now put on 'What's Going On.' It's by Marvin Gaye."

"Thanks," I snapped. "I thought it was Mozart."

"Just press play." Becca looked at me seriously.

While Sills got up to make sure the door was shut, I did as told and stuck the buds in my ears. "I don't hear anything."

"That's because there's nothing to hear," Becca said. "Now look at the screen."

I held up the machine for inspection. The words "Vertigo Girl" blazed across the pink machine's display window.

"It's not an audio file," Diana told me. "You can use MP3 players to save any kind of file."

"I know you can," I said, my gravelly voice breaking in defensiveness. "My mom keeps transcripts of her interviews on hers."

"It's Sills's script," Becca said. "Turn the dial and you'll see the rest."

"It's just a first draft." Sills sounded embarrassed. "I was going to revise it."

I scrolled down and studied the document. In under a minute, I'd come across directions for a two-minute-long "silent study of the rain," a scene of rhyming dialogue, and one where a woman named "Vertigo Girl" dances with a Bosc pear. It was starting to make sense why Sills was so self-conscious.

"Wow." I cleared my throat and tried to think of something diplomatic to say. "Looks artistic."

Becca flopped onto the couch and patted a spot next to her. "Go to scene three. It's the bridge scene."

I dialed down according to her instructions.

> SAMURAI SAM
> What's with the blindfold?

> VERTIGO GIRL
> (breathlessly)
> You know I hate being this high up.

> SAMURAI SAM
> Just look at me. It won't be scary, I promise.

> 11:18 p.m. power outage in districts 22, 23, 23b, 24, & 31 Downtown Manhattan and Lower Brooklyn. (Irving OK'd)
> 11:32 p.m. Power restored.

> Vertigo Girl pulls off the mask and locks eyes with Sam. He touches her nose with the tip of his pinky. She succumbs to his classic seduction maneuver and they kiss passionately.

I wanted to laugh. "The nose tickle is a classic seduction maneuver according to whom?"

"Screw the nose tickle." Becca gave me a worried look. "We had the script loaded onto two iPods, one for us and one for the mayor, and that's it. We adjusted the iPods' transmission capacities so there's no way of anyone uploading it onto anything. It's secure in the little pink machine."

"But we didn't take something else into account," Sills said.

"What's that?" I asked.

"Theft," Sills replied dryly.

Poppy folded her arms. "When Sills got here this morning, the other one had been replaced with a decoy."

"Exhibit A." Sills held up a pink iPod that was in a drawer. "It's a dummy. Someone broke in and made off with the original."

"Well, you still have a copy," I offered feebly. "You can make your movie."

"Think for a second," Poppy said in an exasperated tone. "There's a copy out there that links us to the mayor. They can take it to the press and out us."

My heart lurched. "Do you think someone's doing that?"

"Not yet." Becca shook her head. "The script barely means anything on its own. It's practically a doodle. But if we were to go through with the plan and there really was a power outage while we shot on the bridge, the script would be very revealing. Our cover would be completely blown. Look for yourself."

I glanced back down at the script. Maybe the nose tickle was more powerful than I'd given it credit for. It had distracted me from the fact that the most important part was right before my eyes—the call for the power outage complete with the "Irving OK'd" in clear typeface.

Deadly stuff, for the Moons and the mayor.

"This is terrible," I said.

"More than you realize," Poppy said in a clipped tone.

Sills stepped in. "We have another file on the iPod with a laundry list of ten possible future projects."

"Nine," Poppy corrected her. "The nine things the city needs the most. And unless we get that iPod back, those nine things are off limits."

"So," said Becca, "if we do decide to fix anything else, it's going to be . . ."

"Totally lame?" I said.

Sills nodded. "Maybe not 'totally,' but it certainly won't be all that substantial. Unless something out of the blue hit New York that isn't on the list."

"Like a hurricane," said Poppy.

"Or Bigfoot came to town," added Becca

"Shut up." Poppy play-slapped her. "This is serious."

I braided my fingers together and stretched out my arms, thinking everything over as fast as I could.

"Are there any signs that somebody broke into the clubhouse?"

Becca shook her head no.

"Could it be a Half Moon?" I said, still in shock from the idea.

Sills was tugging at her movie star hair. "No. You're the most clued-in of the bunch, and you didn't have the slightest idea about any of this."

I tried not to feel the sting. "It's got to be the Helle House girls, right?" I said, looking up to a quintet of halfhearted nods. "But they don't know where the clubhouse is, do they?"

"We didn't think so," offered Becca.

"The thing that trips me up," said Sills, "is if they did know where we were, why do they bother posting a photographer outside the fake Moonery twenty-four/seven?"

The cogs in my head were churning. "Unless . . . could somebody in the club have done it?" The accusation hung in the air and I couldn't look anyone in the eye.

Poppy stared at me like I was crazy. "Of course it's the Helle Housers. Why would anybody who's involved want to risk a leak—oh my God . . ." Her face twisted into a horrified expression. "What about Annika?"

"The airhead you kicked out for being in *Teen Vogue?*" I asked. "Now, *that* would make so much more sense!"

Becca's face fell into her palms. "*We're* the airheads. She handed in her key, but she probably had it copied."

"Wouldn't Stinko have seen her come in?" I asked.

"Not if she came during the four a.m. airing of *The Simpsons,*" Poppy answered.

"What a clever little monkey," Sills murmured, sounding sad enough to make all my previous anger at her evaporate.

I started pacing around the room. "Okay, say you're right and she did swap the iPods for revenge, why don't you just rewrite the script and go ahead with the plan?"

"Think again, Claire." Poppy came over to take the iPod from me. "Even if we change some of the details, if we go through with the shoot, there'd still be hard evidence linking the power outage to a close tie between us to the mayor. And our families would be dragged through the coals for having daughters with all that clout."

"In other words," said Sills, "it would be the end of the Moons as we know it. We'd have to go back to being a stupid socialite club."

"Did you tell her about the new cable's consequences?" Sills asked Becca.

"Vaguely." Becca inhaled and looked my way. "There's a developer who has his eye on the waterfront area. He has his pet project all figured out. It's called Bridge Towers. It's pretty gnarly."

Poppy pulled a manila folder out of a drawer and passed it to me. "See for yourself."

. I opened it up to find some newspaper clippings and computer-generated plans for the two proposed minicities, one at either end of the bridge. It looked like a cheap video game brought to life, with its neon color scheme and fluorescent signs affixed to the sides of every building. Then I looked at the *New York Post* story. The headline said *Sink Swims* and my gaze fixed on this sentence: "'My motto is simple: "Ask and ye shall not receive. Do and ye shall prosper,'" Mr. Landon told the *Post* over lunch at Silty's Steakhouse, the Midtown restaurant that doubles as his office."

"Sinclair Landon?" I cried. "The one behind the new Stuy Town and the lofts at the Apollo Theater?"

Sills looked impressed. "His plan for this dream development of his keeps getting struck down, but given everything that's going to happen, he's in luck."

"The complexes are going to be totally disgusting." Diana smiled oddly.

"So depressing," said Poppy. "We either let the mystery burglar scare us into inaction and Sink and the rest of the sleazebag developers do whatever damage they want to the city. Or we go ahead with our plan and risk whoever stole the iPod showing it to the media and exposing our connection to City Hall. And then we'll be paralyzed forever."

"Talk about bad publicity," Becca said, pulling her shawl tighter around her shoulders.

Nobody said another word as the situation sank in. And not just the Moons' situation. My situation. At the rate things were going, Becca was bound to be permanently worried and distracted. Hanging out like we used to, just her and me, was going to become as rare as a lunar eclipse.

Unless.

"One question." My voice cut through the silence like a blade. "What if I was able to get the iPod back?"

Poppy looked at me with renewed interest. "You know where it is?"

"Not at the moment," I said. "But what if I found it?"

Poppy's frown told me she wasn't going to hold out hope.

Becca, though, knew me better than that. She turned to me and lifted an eyebrow. "You think there's a stone for you to turn?"

I took a moment to consider. "Maybe one or two."

"Be my guest." She looked impressed, as did the rest of the girls.

If only I knew where to start.

{ 13 }

Hot Spaces, Hot Air

Thrashing about in bed that night, it struck me I might have oversold my abilities. Who was I to think I could find the iPod in time? Sure, I had a pretty good sense of who the culprit was and I could count on having a few more black-and-white dreams, but whether I'd be having them soon enough or they'd be leading me to the Moons' enemy was open to question.

The following morning, Kiki didn't seem to appreciate opening her door for somebody who wasn't wearing a uniform and wheeling in her coffee and buttered toast. And I wasn't in the best of spirits either. Even though Becca was home, more than twenty blocks away, I couldn't shake the paranoid feeling that she could hear every word I was saying.

Worse, when I was done briefing my grandmother on the Moons' history of covert operations they'd worked on with City Hall, she had the nerve to laugh in my face. "Stop the presses! The Blue Moon Society isn't just a grooming ground for feckless socialites." Kiki rolled her eyes.

"What don't you already know?" I muttered, feeling foolish.

"Duckling . . . I knew Gummy Salzman. She was a lovely woman, but . . . I don't think I'd be alone in saying I think clothes and cocktails weren't her strong suit. Still, she was deeply intelligent. Given her fondness for the club, there was never any question something substantial was afoot."

"Well, now nothing's afoot. The latest plan just got spoiled." I leaned by the window and tugged at her red and yellow curtain's silky tassel.

"I wouldn't start planning a funeral." Kiki gazed at me and her expression warmed. "Calm down, these things have a way of sorting themselves out."

"How can you be so sure?" I walked over to Kiki's bar and started fidgeting with her crystal coasters and decanters. "Time is running out."

"You get used to it," she said. "But I find as long as you maintain a youthful disposition and have a few interesting conversational tidbits, you'll never be at a loss for admirers."

"I'm not talking about *aging*," I said, feeling dual stabs of amusement and frustration. "The city has this plan to take down a cable from the Brooklyn Bridge within months and replace it with a spanking-new reproduction. And then the laws will make it legal for developers to decorate the bridge with their ugly architecture. This developer Sink Landon plans on building a disgusting minicity at either base of the bridge. Imagine a complex of spaceships made out of stucco and scrap metal."

Kiki looked startled. "If only good taste were half as

contagious as the common cold. Can Becca and her sidekicks repair the bridge?"

Averting her gaze, I let her in on the missing movie script, and how it could be the undoing of all of the Moons' deeds from this point on. "At least the deeds that really matter. If I don't find the iPod, the girls won't be able to go ahead with their plan. And the Brooklyn Bridge as we know it will be gone."

"A grim possibility, that," Kiki muttered.

"I know. And on top of that, Becca's a total mess. If this doesn't get cleared up I'm—" I cut myself off, realizing that my deepest fears had nothing to do with altruism.

"Going to be in need of a new bosom buddy," Kiki offered as she wandered over to the window. "No, we don't want that."

I came up from behind to join her. The Park Avenue traffic was flowing below us like electric ribbons, and farther downtown, the Brooklyn Bridge stretched over the East River, looking majestic in the morning's pale light.

"Will you look at that?" She gave a full-bodied sigh. "And you say it might be mucked up."

"Hard to imagine, isn't it?"

Without turning to look at me, she gave my bottom a thwack. "Hop to it, kiddo."

The solution came the next day during music appreciation, in the middle of a fascinating lesson on a time line of Beethoven's symphonies (our teacher, Mr. Cezpka, believed that getting kids to memorize dates was a more effective musical education than actually playing music for them). As soon as school let out, I found Becca and got her to cough up Annika Gitter's phone number, then rode up to Kiki's and unveiled my plan to sneak into the naughty iPod-stealer's house.

"I don't think she'd have much reason to let some tenth

grader she's never heard of tramp through her bedroom," I said, "but what if Saffron Scott, the queen of all home design, came calling?"

Kiki nodded slowly. "I like the way you think."

"Care to fill me in?" Clem asked cluelessly from the couch. "If this Annika girl is such a bumblebrain, why are you so interested in visiting her?"

"She's doing her mother's client a favor," Kiki helped me out as she handed me the phone. "Never hurts to have an IOU in the bank with Priscilla Voyante."

I thanked Kiki with a quick nod and dialed the number Becca had given me.

As I'd hoped, Annika's wariness gave way to excitement when she heard me say I was a unit producer for *Style with Saffron Scott*.

"We saw the spread in *Teen Vogue*," I said, deepening my already-husky voice. "We're so impressed with your, um . . . visual voice."

Kiki grinned and used a coaster to fan her face.

"Are you serious?" Annika gurgled. "Saffron Scott is, like, my idol!"

"Well, let's just say the feeling is pretty mutual."

Next, I called home and asked Mom for Saffron, who was predictably right by her side. "Remember the 'My Crib' pictures I was showing you the other day? You wouldn't be interested in filming in her place instead of mine?"

I heard Saffron glug her water. "You *know* that girl?" She sounded startled, which I didn't take as a compliment.

"She's a friend of a friend," I said. "The only thing is, the girl has security issues, so I promised her I'd come as a producer."

"Even better," Saffron said jubilantly. "You can be my teen-speak translator."

"You'll have better luck understanding Swahili," I heard my mom say in the background.

When it was all settled, Kiki found me an outfit to wear for my day as a fake producer—a pale yellow ruched satin cocktail dress that she promised would make me look a generation older. "Now why don't you get an early start on your job? Produce us a couple of martinis, why don't you?"

Clem chuckled and ran his hand through his long white beard.

"Where is Jon-Jon, anyway?" I asked when I brought two martinis with extra olives over on a vintage Planters peanuts tray that showed Mr. and Mrs. Peanut in the throes of peanut love, strolling down the beach in 1940s swimwear.

"Your grandmother hasn't boasted of her anti-houseguest-infestation ploy?" Clem asked.

"She's hinted at some plan." I glanced at Kiki. "What's the latest?"

"Let's just say he'll be at the theater for quite some time," Kiki said.

"You got him a ticket to the Ring Cycle or something?" I asked.

"Even better." Kiki grinned. "I've commissioned him to design the sets for my birthday party."

"The *sets*? I thought you were renting one of those murder-mystery express trains."

"Turns out they don't have those anymore," she told me in a pouty tone. "Security concerns about people running amok with pistols and whatnot."

"The world's a different place after nine-eleven." Clem gave his silver skull ring a mournful twist.

"Be that as it may," Kiki continued, "I've rented a performance space on West Forty-seventh Street and I asked Jon-Jon to paint the scenery. Clem will be setting up some of his disco blobs."

In the seventies, after he left Andy Warhol's Factory, Clem got into interior decorating. His original disco blobs—more organically shaped than the typical disco ball—were a huge hit with the Studio 54 set and financed his luxurious lifestyle of lying around and getting wistful about everything under the sun.

"And you, my dear," Kiki elbowed me in the rib cage, "will be helping out with the casting."

My look must have told her it was the first I'd heard of it.

"Filling out a room isn't exactly a cinch when most of your friends have departed," she said dryly.

"All the more reason to invite my parents." I tossed her a pleading look.

"I'll see if I can find any more invitations." She sounded mildly put out.

"Good. And if you want I can invite the Moons."

She frowned. "Becca can come. But maybe another occasion would be better for the whole lot of them. I was hoping you could bring some extra men to round things out—Louis and that culinary boy you mention from time to time."

Culinary boy? It took me a second to realize who she was talking about. "Ian Kitchen?"

Kiki wagged her head affirmatively. "And I don't need to tell you to bring Andy."

Just when I was starting to get excited, she had to remind me of the Andy situation. I felt my face drop.

"You might need to drag him by the ears," I grumbled.

"He's still stuck in the library?"

I shrugged. "No idea. He hasn't called since he kissed me, and that was a week ago. He must be over me."

"Impossible! He *adores* you."

I sighed. "Trust me, he just likes playing with me. Practically the only time I hear from him is when he sends me random e-mails complaining about his homework and asking if I like seltzer or pickled beets or whatever."

"Pickles, you say?" Clem sounded interested. "Could he be trying to figure out if you're pregnant?"

Kiki glared at him before turning to me. "Do you really need him to slobber all over you like some ruffian? Bring him to my party."

"I'm telling you," I said, "he won't come. He'll say he's got too much schoolwork."

"Well, isn't it lucky that Andre Rabinowitz is on the guest list?" Clem piped in.

"Who?" I said.

Kiki's eyes twinkled. "My old friend has taken the post as Columbia's dean of students. By the sound of things, your pal certainly could stand to rub shoulders with Andre. So enough of this flapdoodle about his not coming." She reached for the newspaper in front of her and started to shake it section by section. "Now, where did I put my *TV Guide*?"

Whatever they say about trick lighting and airbrushing and special angles making a place look more palatial than it is in real life—it's just not true.

Annika Gitter's corner of her family's West Village town house was every bit the plane hangar that it appeared to be in the *TeenVogue* spread. Even with all the vintage trunks and animal skins and tropical trees, there was still ample space to host the White House Christmas party.

"God, this is just perfect," Saffron was saying as she swooped through the room, taking in every insane detail, the camera and sound guys trailing her. "These lights are to *die* for." Her voice rang loud.

I'd modeled my outfit after the so-called busiest production designer in New York, who had been the subject of a recent Style Network special, and thrown rain boots and a huge beige scarf over Kiki's dress. And remembering an article in *Allure* about how wearing too much makeup makes you look ten years older, I'd slathered on a half bottle of Mom's Silly Putty–like La Mer foundation—for once there was a bright side to Mom's Voyante-family-bankrupting quest to be French.

"It's so funny you guys called," Annika chirped while I conducted our "presegment interview" (my invention). We were sitting on the edge of her bed, which she'd told me was draped in vintage Finnish fabrics.

"I'm actually thinking about starting a design show of my own, and it's so educational to see how it actually works," she said, moving a tower of enamel bracelets from one arm to the other. "My dad says I should just go ahead and do it, but it kind of gets in the way of my other plan. Did I tell you I want to be a contemporary American actress?"

"You seem more like the medieval Chinese actress type," I wanted to say, but I just smiled and kept looking around for anything I'd seen in my dreams.

"I totally think it's the right move for me. I'd actually love to talk to Saffron about how she juggles all her careers. I remember how there was one month a few years ago when she was on the cover of Italian *Vogue* and American *Glamour*! Isn't that crazy?"

"The craziest." I nodded. This was getting more bizarre by the second.

Interviewing Annika was as easy as napping in the sun. The only thing I was having trouble with was figuring out whether she was putting on an act. If she was really this daffy, I doubted she could have engineered a break-in at the Moonery. But if she *was* pretending, I wouldn't put Scriptgate past her.

And then, just as Saffron was telling us that the B roll was shot and it was time for Annika to get into place, I saw something that made my heart thump. Hanging above her bed between a vintage poster for *The Man Who Knew Too Much* and *Psycho* was one for *Vertigo*. As in, the movie Vertigo Girl was named after.

"Annika," I said, focusing on my notepad. "Can you tell me about those Hitchcock posters?"

"Huh? Those old movie posters?" she said, a bit too quickly for my comfort. "My dad got them at some art fair in London."

"Are you a Hitchcock fan?"

She laughed nervously. "It's okay. I liked *Men in Black* better."

Was she playing me? Did she really think I was talking about the Will Smith movie *Hitch*?

"Right," I said, and I couldn't resist adding: "I wouldn't have taken you for a . . . *Vertigo* girl."

The second I mentioned Sills's screenplay by name, my throat constricted. When I drummed up the courage to meet her eye, she was looking as untroubled as a child being handed an ice cream cone.

Her guilt was becoming less likely by the second, and I let off a disappointed sigh.

"Okay, ladies!" Saffron called our way. "We're ready for you!"

"One sec!" Annika reapplied her lipstick, then shot across the room like a demented cat.

"That includes producers!" Saffron added.

"I'm coming!" I got up, too distracted by my thoughts to see what I was needed for. In the space of five minutes, the girl vamping it up for the camera had said some pretty stupid things, mixed up Alfred Hitchcock the person for *Hitch* the movie, and failed to register the loaded meaning of the words "vertigo girl."

That settled it. Annika Gitter was capable of many things, but breaking into the Moonery and making off with a copy of Sills's script wasn't one of them.

{ 14 }

Devil in the Details

As if being big as a liner ship and in possession of six bath-rooms weren't selling points enough, Annika's Jane Street town house also happened to be half a block away from Clementine Records, the best music store this side of Paris. Normally I would have stopped to flip through the shop's collection of six-ties rarities, but by the time we wrapped up the shoot, dusk was settling in and I could picture the girls skulking about the clubhouse, snacking on candy and waiting for my update.

Much as it pained me, I allowed myself only a passing glance at the beautiful Petula Clark LP in the window and raced up to the Fourteenth Street subway station. Half an hour later, when I burst into the Moonery's office, all of the girls were lying on the floor and flipping through magazines, as if stranded at an airport. And it looked like the Moons had decided to bring at least one of the other Half Moons up to speed—Hallie was in the mix, sharing the blue loveseat with Poppy.

"Hey, Reagan." Diana brought her nose closer to whatever she was reading. "Here's a recipe for sticky toffee coconut trifle. How good does that sound?"

"I can go down and make rice pudding," Hallie offered.

"All we have is cat food," Becca told her. "Besides, Claire will be here any—" She stopped short when she noticed that I was leaning against the doorway. "She's here!"

When the rest of the girls turned my way, I saw their faces were full of hope, and I was instantly overcome with a sinking feeling. None of them even made fun of my crazy makeup or outfit.

Becca sat up and patted a spot on the rug next to her. "So, how'd it go?"

I didn't answer until I'd sat down and got a whiff of Becca's figgy perfume. "It was fine," I said reluctantly, "but I don't think she did it."

Their expressions went flat and all sound drained away except for a *clack-clack*. Only now did I see that Sig was behind the computer. Something told me she wasn't working on a term paper.

Diana watched me stare at Sig. "We'll explain in a sec," she provided. "But tell us why it's not her."

My eyes cut over to Becca, whose arms were folded around her knees. "First, I'm pretty convinced that she doesn't have what you'd need to operate that iPod."

"What's that?" Reagan sounded confused.

"A double-digit IQ."

My joke earned only one laugh, and I rapidly unzipped my

jacket pocket. "It wasn't just that," I said, extracting a Polaroid I'd stolen from the shoot. I slid it over to Becca. "See, she has Hitchcock posters over her bed," I said, and proceeded to tell everyone how Annika had reacted when I'd said the magic words. "There's no way she would have been so mellow if she knew 'Vertigo Girl' meant anything. I'm not saying she would have had a heart attack, but she didn't even twitch."

Diana let off a low whistle. "Crap."

"I'll say," Reagan added.

"So enemy number one just fell off the list." This was Becca.

"Which would be fine if we had an enemy number two," said Diana.

"It doesn't have to be such a gloom-and-doom show in here." Poppy was trying to affect a bright tone. "We can cross Annika's name off the list. That's a step in the right direction."

"What list?" Diana sounded peeved.

Poppy groaned. "It's got to be one of the Helle Housers. We just have to figure out which one."

"Which one of the remaining two hundred and twenty-something morons," murmured Sills.

"Well, whoever did it has to be remotely smart," Poppy said, "or else she would have put it up on the Internet already for some immediate gratification. We just have to figure out which one of those girls knows enough to hold her cards close to her vest."

"Her vest?" Diana asked incredulously. "I always thought the expression was 'close to your chest.'"

The silence that ensued must have embarrassed Diana; she got up to get a snack.

While we waited for Sig to fiddle around on the computer, Becca was kind enough to inform me that our resident tech genius was examining the computer's keystroke history. Apparently there was a way to call up a record of every key that had ever been tapped. "Maybe the burglar decided to check her e-mail when she was here." Becca glanced up and shrugged.

"You think that the intruder would've risked getting caught and wasted any time checking her e-mail?" I said.

"Actually, you'd be surprised," Sig told me. "A few months ago there was this big-time hacker who got caught at the Internet café he was using because he had the brilliant idea to download every Cat Power song from the iTunes store in the middle of his heist."

Becca smiled and got up to knead Sig's shoulders.

A few minutes later, Diana returned with a dish of what looked like mint ice cream and jelly, and Sig's clicking was slowing down.

"Hurry up." Poppy looked at her watch. "This Purple City party only goes until ten."

I felt my signature confused duck expression bloom across my face. Was I doomed to never fully understand what was going on?

"Purple City?" I repeated. "The skateboard shop?"

Poppy nodded and I looked at her with newfound approval. Purple City is a skateboard store in my neighborhood. It officially specializes in limited-edition sweatshirts, but its real selling point is the adorable skater boys who use the shop as a clubhouse. I'd lived only three blocks away from it my entire life and none of the guys there had ever deigned to talk to me.

"How do you know those guys?" I asked.

"I don't," Poppy said with a smile. "I'm piggybacking on Sig."

I glanced at the girl behind the computer. "You're friends with those guys?" I could tell I wasn't doing a very good job concealing my surprise that our resident geek was chummy with some of New York's most intimidating guys.

"Kinda." She was still concentrating on the computer.

"Turns out her boyfriend's a pro skater." The mischievous twinkle in Reagan's eye told me I wasn't the only one who hadn't been expecting to learn this tidbit about Sig. "Rafer Campos."

"Sex god on wheels," sighed Poppy.

Sig bit down a smile, then scrunched her nose. "There's no record from Wednesday morning," she announced, bringing everybody back to the trouble at hand. "It says the last time anybody used the computer was Tuesday night."

"You sure?" Sills asked.

Sig nodded. "She probably has a BlackBerry."

"You sure the perp's a *she*?" I asked.

"Just a guess," Becca said. "It's hard to imagine a guy taking the time to put everything away so nicely. He would've just run off with it and left the drawers open."

"Territorial marking's classic male behavior." Diana patted Linus on his head, and I half expected him to pee on the spot.

"Hold up!" Sig sounded excited. Never had she seemed so in her element.

"Whatcha got, wizard?" Hallie asked.

"This didn't take any wizardry. I just went to the wonderful World Wide Web. Elle House's recently updated home page, to be precise." She pointed to the screen. "Have a look."

Becca leaned in and read aloud. "'Next Sunday. Film study night in the white library. Organic cocktails, popcorn, and a recently released treasure.'" She straightened her back and looked up at me. "Looks like Little Miss Sticky-Fingers might not be so patient after all. Coming to a clubhouse near you: the grand unveiling of the looted goods."

I stared at Becca for a few seconds. "Okay, I see what you're thinking. But for all we know they could be showing the new remastered *Valley of the Dolls* DVD or whatever."

I didn't want Becca to get ahead of herself.

Becca scowled. "Then why wouldn't they just say what movie they were showing?"

"It says 'Details to follow,'" Diana read from the screen. "We'll just have to check back."

"I can hardly wait," Becca groaned, and I glanced around at all the faces in the room, each more spooked than the last.

It looked like the old saying had got it right: the devil *was* in those details.

Our meeting adjourned, we all went downstairs and snaked out through the deli. Night had fallen and the air was laced with frost. Quietly, everyone peeled off in different directions, leaving me with the feeling Sig wasn't the only one who had a date lined up. It all made me feel like a bit of a loser. A loser who couldn't help missing Andy.

"Now what?" Becca asked. "Wanna sleep over at my place?"

My stomach clenched up. Of course I wanted one-on-one time with Becca, but there were other considerations to be made. I was, after all, still dressed up like a freak. And even though Andy officially lived in a dorm at Columbia, I wouldn't have been surprised to learn he was camping out at home tonight. He was always at home.

"I don't know if I can," I said.

"C'mon, I promise we don't have to talk about this stuff." She looked up at the Moonery's ivy-covered facade. "And nobody's there. It would be a waste of an empty house."

She said it nonchalantly but I had to wonder if she knew my real reason for not wanting to come over.

"You sure?" I said. "You wouldn't rather . . ."

"What?" Becca was quick to jump in. "Go to some midnight meeting of the Hudson Science League?" She pulled her cell phone out of her bag and handed it over. "Call your parents now so they don't worry."

On the cab ride up, Becca was bubbling over with a new-found exuberance. She was laughing and making fun of her dad's diet. Some people might have found her sudden change in attitude bizarre, but I was supremely happy to be hanging out with the old, Moon-free Becca.

"Now he grazes instead of eating big meals, but I'm convinced he's actually eating more than before," she said.

"Not to state the obvious," I said, "but it doesn't sound like he wants to be on a diet."

"Of course he doesn't. My mom put him up to it. She said if he doesn't fit into his normal pants by Valentine's Day she's taking Andy out for dinner instead."

My heart sank.

"She should have a word with my mom," I was quick to respond. I would die if she could tell that hearing that Andy might spend Valentine's Day with his mother made me jealous.

"Are you kidding?" She glanced my way. "Your mom's a stick."

"No, not for her. You know how they say French women don't get fat?" Becca's silhouette nodded. "French men do. Especially when they're dealing with writer's block. Seriously, you'd think my dad's expecting Mom's ratatouille to write the book for him."

Becca laughed and told the driver where to pull over. I looked up at the building's windows and exhaled a sigh of relief. None of the lights was on.

Phew.

I got out of the cab first and waited by the door for Becca to work the locks. "Ignore the mess," Becca said as we entered the house, which was as un-messy as a meditation room at a five-star spa. "Dad set up the place so his favorite songs come on when he walks into the room." Only then did I see a few holes in the walls, with nests of telephone wires poking out. "It's the stupidest idea, but he wouldn't let us talk him out of it. Andy's already ordered, like, a hundred earplugs online."

My knees felt slightly shaky at the sound of Andy's name.

"So what'll it be, C?" she asked once we'd settled into the media room. She was holding up two DVDs: the original *Dawn of the Dead* and some Swedish movie about witchcraft in the Middle Ages. "Zombies or witches?"

"Got anything with cute high school girls?" came a voice from the doorway. The lights turned on and Andy's green eyes met my gaze.

Great. Why couldn't he have magically appeared the day before, when I'd been wearing my cool indigo Givenchy dress and my face hadn't been spackled over with old lady makeup? Of course, he looked as put-together as ever, with a dark herringbone coat open to reveal a Columbia T-shirt.

"Don't you have homework or something to do?" Becca asked him, perfectly embodying the role of snarky kid sister. The role of snarky kid sister's not-so-cool sidekick fell to me.

"Nope," he said, taking off his coat and falling into the spot next to me on the couch. His shin brushed against mine and he paused to smile at me before moving his leg away. I felt my cheeks blaze red. How could I have ever thought I was remotely interested in that spazzy guy from lunch period? "I could settle for *The Pink Panther*," he said, redirecting his attention at Becca. "Peter Sellers, not Steve Martin, that is."

Becca cleared her throat impatiently. "Fine. I'll decide, then."

The Swedish movie was better than expected. At least I think it was—it was hard to concentrate with Andy sitting so close by. When I turned to make a funny face at him during a scene where Satan took a bubble bath, I realized he was fast asleep.

Disappointment went up in me like a plume of smoke.

"Hey, B." I pointed at her brother.

"Duck," she whispered to me, then lobbed a pillow at him.

He blinked and rubbed his head. "Are you demented?"

"It's called a throw pillow," she said in a fake-sweet tone. "Don't blame me."

He looked at her in disbelief. "I'll remember that next time I get a kickstand."

"Or a punchbowl." Becca was having fun with this dorky game.

"Hey." I suddenly remembered. "Kiki's having a murder-mystery birthday party." I proceeded to tell them everything I knew about it: the date, the Jon-Jon situation, and a sampling of the guest list. For Andy's sake I made sure to throw in that Dr. Rabinowitz would be there. "Now's your chance to see what your dean's like when he's tipsy and has fake blood dribbling down his chin."

I looked at him hopefully.

"It sounds insane," Becca said. "I'm so there."

"Excellent. And you?" I was waiting for Andy.

He twisted up his lip and ran his hands over his jeans. "It's kind of hard to make advance plans right now."

I looked down at the ground, trying to hide my sadness.

"God," Becca said to her brother. "You have such issues."

There was something deeply wrong about the silence that followed. Every second seemed to stretch into a minute, until I couldn't take it anymore.

My tear ducts were going haywire.

"I'm going to the bathroom." I shot up like an alfalfa sprout. "Anyone need a Q-tip or anything?"

Lame, I know, but it's not exactly easy to come up with a smooth cover-up when you're in the middle of an emotional breakdown.

I sat on the lip of the bathtub and flipped through an old issue of *BusinessWeek*. Maybe enough exposure to boring charts and graphs would numb my feelings. When that didn't work, I got up and leaned into the mirror. Looking hard at my eyes, I tried to hypnotize myself into believing that whatever his so-called issues were, they didn't have to do with me or my crazy-lady outfit.

If only self-delusion were my strong suit.

I finally pulled myself together, but when I went back to the media room, Andy was gone.

"I'm not even going to ask what took you so long in there," Becca said. "Let's go upstairs. Your suite awaits."

There was a consolation, if a small one: at the Shuttleworth house, overnight guests weren't tossed an L.L.Bean sleeping bag and old airplane pillow. They were treated to a king-sized bed and a bedside table that was, without fail, equipped with a pitcher of lemon water and a vase of fresh flowers.

We stopped at the kitchen for cookies, then trudged all the way up to the fourth floor. Becca opened the door and flung herself on top of the red and white duvet when we got to the guest room. "Pj's are in the second drawer. There should be new toothbrushes in the bathroom medicine cabinet."

I washed up and when I went back in to crawl under the covers, Becca was on the other side of the lead-heavy duvet, resting her head on her elbow. "So I'll say good night," she said, "but there's something I wanted to talk to you about first."

My stomach churned—my least favorite words in the English language are "we need to talk." And I was pretty sure this had to do with Andy.

"Bring it on," I said, my voice cracking like crazy.

"Well, last night my family went to dinner at Quilty's and we ran into your friend Louis."

"Louis?" I hardly recognized the name.

"Yeah." Her cheeks flushed. "He was acting kind of strange. He doesn't have a girl—"

"A girlfriend?" I jumped in, and she nodded sheepishly. "How could he? He's too busy waiting for a certain somebody to wake up and smell the mix CDs."

How could Becca, the smartest person I knew, be so dumb?

"Really?" She searched my face. "I mean, I sort of got the sense he liked me, but that was a while ago. And then last night he was all grumpy and I thought he was mad at—"

"Was he with his stepmother?"

"I don't know. Some weird woman."

"A spider lady with a severe case of blond hair extensions?" I waited for Becca to nod. "Yeah, she has that effect on him. Last time I went to an Ibbits family dinner, Louis and his father didn't say a word and I was stuck talking to Ulrika about what color grouting she wanted to use on the bathroom floor— beige or bone. She has a way of killing the mood."

Becca laughed uneasily. "You tell Louis I said anything and I'll kill you."

"I won't. Pinky swear." I pulled the sheet down to show her I meant it. "You guys are perfect for each other."

"Don't get ahead of yourself." She twisted her airplane ring nervously. "There's nothing going on."

"Yet."

She was squirming, and I was savoring every second of it.

"Shut up," she said.

"You know you love it." A beat. "Mrs. Ibbits."

"Any more and I'm gonna punchbowl you."

"If you keep up the dork routine, you're never getting married."

In the morning sunlight poured into the room and Becca was on top of the red and white covers still in her jeans and red flats, the steady rise and fall of her shoulders telegraphing her deep sleep. We'd stayed up talking for a while, and we must have passed out at some point.

The only sounds were the birds outside and Becca's wispy breathing. I hadn't felt this relaxed in ages. Just then synthesizer music ripped through the room, giving my friend a rude awakening. Then vocals kicked in, and the chorus of "Born in the U.S.A." was going strong.

Becca flipped over, her face striped with pillow wrinkles. "What did I tell you? Dad's so-called smart house is the stupidest thing ever."

"It's for me!" Andy screamed from downstairs. "The doorbell wires must've got messed up!"

"Yeah!" Becca shot back. "So did my sleep!"

Curiosity raged through me—what was Andy still doing here, and more important, who was coming by to pick him up?

Becca shambled over to the window, dragging her limbs to play up her exhaustion.

I got out of bed and casually joined her, pressing my nose against the window like a little kid at the back of a school bus. If only I were a little kid, and I still thought boys were gross. Instead, all my worst fears were confirmed. Andy was with a girl who had gorgeous long brown hair and one of those supermodel bodies that inspires the people blessed with them to lie and make up stories about getting teased for being "too gangly."

Before I knew what was happening, Becca was rapping on the windowpane.

"Becca!" I hissed. "What are you doing?"

"If he's going to cut in on my sleep like this, he deserves a little abuse."

I ducked, but not in time. Andy spun around and caught my eye—though he probably couldn't see that I was tearing up. We were four stories above and besides, Becca was stealing the spotlight, applauding like a cartoon version of an opera fanatic and screaming "Bravo!"

When my friend finally stopped, she stomped back to the bed. "He totally ruined my morning."

Mine too.

{ 15 }

Night of the Herbal Verbal

Discounting out-and-out breaking and entering, there were two ways to get into the Helle House and see what their Sunday night "film study session" was all about. One option was to buy a two-hundred-dollar starter membership, though that would entail donating two hundred dollars too many to their cheesy cause and supporting their online stalking operation. The other was to get invited.

If only it were as simple as that.

The solution came to me in English class on Friday, in the middle of a pop quiz on *The Grapes of Wrath*. If nothing else, Henry Hudson, the most boring academic institution on the planet, was turning out to be a good setting for personal problem solving.

The multiple-choice question I'd been working on ("Who stars in the movie adaptation of the book? a. Tom Cruise b. Steve McQueen c. Tom Hanks d. Henry Fonda) turned out to be constructive—and not only because I had a new contender for Most Idiotic Exam at Hudson. The word "star" sparked the memory of the dream I'd had where Sheila was sitting in the convertible and I'd given her a lollipop to get in the vehicle. A bolt of inspiration struck hard. I had to feed my way into her heart!

Lucky for me, the Washington View Village's resident tea and poetry society, Herbal Verbal, was due to take place in the Sunrise Room on Saturday night. Luckier for me, my family's favorite poetess, Cheri-Lee Vird, was a founding member. And that made Sheila Vird a founding audience member. Her mom always dragged her along, and she could always be counted on to be in the back row, hiding a giant scowl behind an oversized chai tea.

Cheri-Lee sounded excited when I called her to invite her and her daughter to a post-poetry dinner. "I'm making Indian," I was sure to tell her. I knew these were magic words to her ears—when she was in her early twenties, Cheri-Lee spent a "life-altering" month at an ashram.

"Are you?" she warbled. "Well, well, who am I to stand in the way of your nurturing instinct?"

"To be honest," I said, gearing up to be anything but, "the thing I really want to nurture is my friendship with Sheila."

Who knew words could actually taste bad?

Cheri-Lee gasped. "I can't quite believe my ears. Care to repeat that?"

And so I did, painfully. We detectives sure deserved a raise.

The next morning, Henry and I were walking down Houston Street, heading for Whole Foods. "What if I swallow it?"

Henry spun my way and pushed the tip of his tongue against his very loose tooth. It was embedded in pulpy gum.

"Then you'll have an incisor in your stomach," I said coolly. "Good for digestion."

"No way!" Henry looked thrilled, then caught himself in his moment of gullibility. "Ha, ha. You are such a comedian."

"That's what you get for trying to gross me out. C'mon."

The Walk signal came on and I removed my grip from his shoulder and pushed him along.

When we reached the market, a brief scan of the crowd told me Henry and I were probably the only people within a one-mile radius who didn't have eco-friendly THIS IS NOT A PLASTIC BAG sacks smugly slung over our shoulders. I wondered if it counted as environmentally responsible to buy new bags in different colors to match the season.

My list consisted of one thing only: something I could pretend to have cooked. Henry and I made our way toward the prepared foods section, stopping along the way to taste any and all free samples on offer.

My mouth was full with a new line of olive oil flavored gelato when a sign dangling from the ceiling caught my attention. It showed a picture of two chickens locked in embrace and over it were the words CHOCOLATE TASTING SATURDAY AFTERNOON AISLE 8.

I'd already had that dream about kissing a chicken—was there any way this was a coincidence? Though even if it was, there was chocolate involved so I had no choice.

Henry and I reached the Promised Land in no time. There was a small crowd forming and I understood what the chickens on the sign had been all about: the boutique-chocolate brand was called Kissing Chickens and the chocolates were egg shaped.

"That's from Venezuela," a woman said when I stepped into

the tiny spot between two freebie-loaders and helped myself to a sample. Still chewing, I looked up to see a plump woman whose apron identified her as a "Cocoa Technician." She went on, "I find it tastes rather grassy. What are your impressions?"

Uh . . . that it's free chocolate. And therefore it's good?

Normally I would've backed off, but Henry was freeloading up a storm, and it would have been downright cruel to put an end to his euphoria. "It has a satisfying counterpoint," I told her, trying out one of the few foodie terms I could remember hearing Hallie use.

"Interesting observation." The woman frowned. "Let's see what you think of the Kenyan. It's subtler." She handed me another chocolate oval. "For its flavor to reach its potential, you have to let it melt slowly on your tongue."

Weird, but I could dig it. At least I wouldn't have to talk to her while it dissolved.

I took it, eager for another trip to chocolate heaven, and just as I'd placed it on my tongue, who should come rolling by but Sills and Reagan, both looking head-turningly cool in their tweed fedoras and belted overcoats.

"You don't understand," Sills was saying, "it's the second-most prestigious film festival in Miami."

"I didn't know there were any film festivals in Miami." Reagan stopped in her tracks. "Look!"

I went bright red, but it turned out she wasn't talking about me. In fact, I was pretty sure they didn't even see yours truly.

"Sugar!" Reagan cried.

Granted, I was stuck in a crowd, but something told me if I weren't so small and unassuming, my fellow Moons would have noticed me. Sills gave the chocolate display an unimpressed once-over and kept going. And Reagan barely touched down for ten seconds, just long enough to grab a fat handful of free chocolates, but not long enough for any of the "Cocoa Technicians" to bum-rush her and subject her to a hundred questions.

Talk about the story of my life. Here I was, letting a stranger quiz me for hours, while people like Reagan breezed around, helping themselves to anything they wanted.

When the woman asked for my verdict, all I could say was: "I'm dumbstruck."

"I thought you'd like it," she replied, and went on to tell me about the one-day-only baker's dozen special. "Will you be paying cash or charge?"

Cheri-Lee came over directly after the poetry reading that night. After banging into the apartment, she made her presence known with a customarily dramatic announcement. "What are those heavenly spices? Sheila, will you get a whiff of that?"

Crap!

I wasn't even dressed yet and I hadn't gotten around to setting the table.

Running out of the kitchen, I burst into the living area to turn on the sitar CD Hallie had lent me for the occasion. I cranked up the volume and startled Dad, who'd drifted off to sleep while waiting at his wheelie desk for my hostessing debut.

"Get any good work done tonight, Gus?" Mom laughed and planted a kiss on his bald spot.

"I . . . I was just sorting out a structural problem." He sat up quickly.

Leaving the two of them to fawn over each other, I went over to Cheri-Lee and Sheila and tried to butter them up. "Can I get you a drink or take your coat?"

It came out too fast and I ran my hands over my bob, hoping my hair didn't look as crazed as I suspected it might.

"One thing at a time," Cheri-Lee chuckled, slipping out of

her poncho. "This was such a *fab* idea, Claire. Though I'm sorry you couldn't come to the event. Laird Humbleward, that media studies professor in our building, did a positively *transporting* recitation on solitude in the Himalayas."

I cast a look at Sheila. If there was one thing we could bond over, it was her mother's nuttiness. But she just pulled her black coat tight around her body and stared coldly across the room. "We eating soon?" she asked. "I have to be somewhere in a little bit."

Something told me it was going to be a harder night than I'd bargained for.

My parents knew I couldn't cook but were willing to support what Mom called my baby step toward reconciliation with Sheila and promised to stay mum about the meal's not-so-homemade provenance. Mom threw together a salad and Henry helped me set the table. The meal got off to a fine enough start, if you were willing to overlook the fact that I forgot to put out water glasses or thoroughly heat the frozen nan bread and that Sheila was too busy sending text messages under the table to eat, drink, or speak to me.

My chances of getting an invite to Helle House were sinking by the minute. How had it failed to occur to me that you could only count on Kiki's golden rule of reciprocity ("invitations beget invitations") if both people have the barest sense of manners?

Even Cheri-Lee, usually blind to her daughter's horribleness, was growing agitated. She kept trying to bring Sheila into the conversation, and when she leaned across the table to scoop seconds onto her plate, I saw her pluck the phone out of her daughter's lap.

"What are you doing?" Sheila growled.

"Just trying to get you into the spirit of things. Did you

taste the saag paneer? It reminds me exactly of my days in Bombay!"

"Mom, nobody says 'Bombay' anymore. It's Mumbai."

"Oh, Sheepee." Cheri-Lee sounded unhurt. "Who raised you to see the world so literally? Now why don't you tell Claire that hilarious story you were telling me this afternoon?"

No way. Sheila was capable of telling a funny story?

"Which one?" Sheila groaned.

"The one about how you found out that your English teacher writes those horrible teen novels on the side." Cheri-Lee turned to smile at me. "You know, the books where all the kids shoplift Gucci purses and have intimate parties."

"Inuit parties?" Henry chimed in with a hopeful look on his face.

I could barely suppress a smirk but Sheila's face was set straight as a Sunday school teacher's. "And?" she said in a tone to match. "You just told the whole story."

Awkward glances all around, I tried to think fast.

"Sheila," I started, "I feel bad, holding you up like this. We can just hang out another time if you want."

Like, um, tomorrow night. At your stupid clubhouse.

"Sure." She retrieved her phone from her mother's pocket and brushed it off. "Another night would be better. I'm supposed to be somewhere else." She eyed me icily, and I half suspected she knew I was a Moon.

"Are you going to the Hudson Debate Club party?" I asked.

My provocation worked: Sheila reeled at the suggestion with a horrified "A ziff!" It took me a few seconds to realize she was saying "As if."

"She's going to that club," Cheri-Lee supplied. "Or should I say cult?"

Actually, you could say stalking and burglary concern.

"The club you were talking about before?" I was lacing my voice with all the admiration and envy I could stomach. "That place sounded so cool."

Cheri-Lee took the bait. "Say, Sheila, why don't you bring Claire by sometime?"

Man, this was too easy.

"I think Claire already has a friend in a club." Sheila shot me a nasty glare.

Fat chance I was going to fess up about Becca's identity as a Blue Moon.

"Don't I know it," I said, trying to infuse my voice with a sad sack quality. "Louis has belonged to the Racquet Club forever and I barely ever get to go. They're weird about guests."

Sheila threw me a dirty look.

"Sheila has guest privileges," Cheri-Lee piped in. "And you haven't used them yet, have you?"

Bingo.

Sheila's mouth was quivering like Jell-O on a turbulent plane ride, but I was ahead of her. "Really? That would be amazing. Maybe sometime next week. Oh shoot—"Then I tried to imagine awful things, Didier and Margaux's tank being drained, Henry getting eaten by a wild boar, Andy kissing that leggy girl I'd seen outside his window.

"What's the matter, Claire?" Dad sounded worried. My Method acting was working wonders.

"I just remembered I have a . . ."

Think quick, Claire.

And then I saw one of my grandmother's pink-lined note cards in a heap on the sideboard. "I told Kiki I'd help set up her mystery-murder thingie next week, so I'm going to be busy pretty much every day starting Monday."

"Another week, then," Sheila was all too happy to add.

"What a drag," Mom said dejectedly. "This was starting to sound like a great plan." I swear, Sheila and I could blow up each other's apartments and our moms would still want us to be friends.

"Hold up, you two." Cheri-Lee was looking especially proud. "What about tomorrow? It is only Saturday."

I forced a chuckle and brought my hand to my forehead. "God, I'm totally losing my mind, aren't I? Tomorrow would work."

"That would be sweet," Dad said. "Old friends."

I was going to gag.

"Fab," Cheri-Lee agreed. "Why don't you two just check in tomorrow and finalize the plan?"

Sheila gave us both a black look.

"Aw, Sheepee," her mom said. "It's just a one-time thing. Nobody's saying you have to make a weekly tradition out of it." She looked over at my parents, obviously embarrassed about her daughter's subhuman behavior.

"Fine." Sheila slumped back in her seat. "You know, there are rules and regulations. Like, there's a smart dress code. I wouldn't wear one of your hand-me-downs."

It took no small amount of willpower to resist the urge to tell her that Kiki's old wardrobe was museum-worthy. "I'll see what I can dig up," I told her.

And I meant it in more ways than one.

{ 16 }

Roll Out the White Carpet

My bladder was about to explode and I raced to the putty-colored door with a *WC* sign. There was no answer when I knocked, but when I flung it open, a girl wearing a long black dress was stooped over the stone bowl sink, scrubbing her hands. I left and tried the next door down the hallway, but the same girl was at the same sink, still washing her hands. By the third time I thought I'd found an empty room only to barge in on her, I knew I was in trouble—and not because I was annoying her. I needed relief like never before, and there was no toilet in sight.

Thank God for my Le Coq Sportif alarm clock's annoying crowing—my bathroom dream had nearly caused me to wet my bed. I had to get up early. I didn't put it past my slithery neighbor to slip out for the day and turn off her cell phone. I pulled my sleep mask up my forehead and dialed Sheila's home number before I got out of bed.

"Do you know how early it is?" Sheila asked when she took the phone from her mom.

"Sorry," I said. "Just wanted to make sure we're still on for tonight!" I was trying to inject some sweetness into my husky voice.

"Tonight," Sheila repeated, "yeah, I wanted to talk to you about that . . . I think we're going to have to resched." Cheri-Lee had to be standing by—instead of out-and-out telling me I was not welcome, Sheila was trying to wiggle out of our plans in a more subtle way. "The club's having this event and I sort of volunteered to help out. It might be awkward, with you not knowing anyone else."

"That's not a problem," I said, steamrolling over her excuse. "I'll just bring a friend."

My suggestion earned a groan, but I pretended not to notice and asked what time we should show up.

"I don't even know the details yet," she hissed. "It's barely eight fifteen in the morning."

"Are you serious?" I faked alarm. "I'm supposed to meet Ian for breakfast." It wasn't a total lie—we had lunch plans. "I gotta hurry or he's going to kill me. We'll just swing by at seven, and if it's too early we'll help you set up, okay?"

I must have been getting good at pushing her buttons; all that came out of her was a strange noise, like a dragon being strangled.

Who knew it was such a beautiful sound?

At school on Friday, Ian had told me he wanted to hang out over the weekend. His suggestion had caught me off guard. Weirder still, not only did he insist on picking me up at the

Washington View Village gate at eleven-thirty on Sunday morning, but he showed up without his signature wheelie suitcase.

"Forget something?" I asked, eyeing the empty space by his left foot.

"It's the weekend. Light load," he said with a shrug. "What do you think of that sushi restaurant on La Guardia Place? Wanna go there?"

I shook my head. "You try having pet fish and eating the stuff. How do you feel about new agey joints with surprisingly yummy appetizers?"

"Show me the way." He followed me through Washington Square Park with no complaints.

Ian fit right in at Uki's Organic, with his scrawny physique and Bugs Bunny T-shirt that had a picture of a cockroach with bunny ears.

"So what's up?" I dragged a pita chip through spicy hummus while we waited for the rest of our meal.

"You know, the usual survival tactics. Drawing. Guitar Hero. Cheetos. Repeat." He put his napkin on his lap. "Oh—I started plotting out a graphic novel, *Dirt High*. It's going to be about a school where half the population is actually dead. The first scene is going to have the school bus picking all the kids up at the cemetery."

"Sounds killer," I said, and I meant it. "But what's up with *this*? If I remember correctly, you don't love to do the whole 'hobnobbing in public' thing. Your phrase."

His smile conveyed a twinge of embarrassment. "Okay, there is something I wanted to ask. But can it wait until the food gets here?"

Wow—there really was an agenda.

"Why not?" Thankfully, the waitress was right behind him with our plates, so I knew I wouldn't die from curiosity.

He took a token bite of his sweet and sour brown rice pilaf, then got to work. "So remember I told you about the Toro Boy movie?"

"Of course. The movie adaptation where Toro Boy gets diamond horns and a supermodel girlfriend?" I took a forkful of artichoke dip.

"Good memory you've got there." He paused. "The other day, Rick Evans, the Toro Boy creator, came into the shop and confirmed our worst fears. The Global Media movie people sent him a copy of the script and it's even worse than we imagined." He went on to detail the changes. "No more diamond horns, and guess what they're replacing them with."

"What, antlers?"

"I wish. A Lamborghini with horns painted on it."

"Ew, sounds like something one of Britney Spears's husbands would drive," I said. "Why doesn't this Rick guy call the producers?"

"Like he didn't try." Ian's eyes bulged out. "He sold the rights, like, fifty years ago, when he was in his twenties and willing to give everything away for a month's rent. The same thing happened to the Superman creator." He shook his head. "I'm not sure you understand what a big deal this is, but Rick Evans is the Picasso of the comic-book world."

"I thought that was you," I said, licking my finger clean of black olive paste.

"Seriously, he's the godfather. The Diana Ross and the Agatha Christie and whoever the editor of French *Vogue*—"

"No, no, I get it." It was embarrassing hearing my interests lumped together in one breath. Was I really that easy to typecast? "So what do you want from me?" I waved a fried tofu stick at him.

"Well . . ." He coughed. "We Propellerheads are all funnylooking dudes." Another cough. "And you, my dear, are not."

I felt myself make my confused duck face. "Thanks?"

He went on to tell me about a protest they were planning outside of Global Media. "It's going to be totally peaceful. We're just going to hold up some picket signs and hand out mini-comic pamphlets. Why are you narrowing your eyes at me?"

I realized that I must have been sleepier than I'd realized and forced my eyes wide open. "So you want me to help out?" I asked.

He nodded. "We're asking all the females we know to come, in case there's any media. Not to objectify you or anything, but nobody's going to care if it's just a bunch of comic dorks."

Flattering as it was to be asked to be a poster girl, I'd signed the Moon contract that said media was to be shunned. But that rule was meant to keep us from posing for things like "It Girl" spreads in fashion magazines, not help out our favorite people's good causes, right?

"I'm an almost-yes," I told him. "Let me think it over a little more."

"Please?"

I pointed at Ian's nearly untouched plate. "Eat up. It's going to get cold."

"*Going to?*" He sounded amused. "How do you think it was when it got here?"

Unable to bring any of the Full Moons as my date to Helle House for obvious reasons, I ended up inviting Hallie to accompany me on my iPod-finding mission.

"This is so fun, I feel like we're in a Pink Panther movie," Hallie said on our walk from the Twenty-third Street subway station to the clubhouse. "I put on a disguise and everything."

"That right?" I stole a long glance at her. She was as all-over-the-place-looking as ever, despite her attempts to disguise herself. Her lips were painted an iridescent purple and her multicolored hair was piled up in a bun that resembled a bird's nest. She was going to stick out like a nudist uncle at a family reunion.

Then again, I didn't look that different from my usual self, either, in my knee-length red Givenchy cocktail dress and black cat eyeliner. My hair was in a bob that I'd only had enough time to dry halfway.

"Looks like our job just started," Hallie said, pointing across the street. A cluster of girls in spiky heels and oversized handbags was tottering in the same general direction as us. They were definitely Helle Housers—one of them was holding up a digital video recorder, probably getting footage for the homemade reality television show Poppy had told us about.

As we approached the clubhouse door, Hallie and I went over the plan—or rather, the lack of one—for the millionth time.

"We just have to act natural and make sure we don't get kicked out before the film lecture starts," I told her. "So no opening drawers or interrogating members about their pink iPod."

"But what if one of them has a really cool one?" she asked, waiting for me to look peeved. "I'm kidding! You really need to chill out. I promise, I'm not an idiot."

"Sorry," I said. "I'm just a little nervous."

"And I'm a walking oasis of calm," she said sarcastically.

We got buzzed into the nondescript door at the club's address and walked up to the second-floor entrance with mounting apprehension. I was dreading the moment when the hostess told me Sheila hadn't left my name at the door and sent me packing. It was a pleasant surprise, then, to discover there was no formal reception area. Just a doughy-faced woman manning a collapsible coat rack.

We handed over our coats and set off on a self-guided tour. Walking through the club was a bit like braving a snowstorm. Apart from the "spice room," every couch, rug, wall, and table was blinding white. When we reached the edge of the "chill lounge" Hallie bit down a laugh. I turned to give her a warning look. "Sorry, I just saw that girl say she's upping her membership level so she can stay past nine o'clock," she said, pointing to someone in the distance.

"Come again?"

"That's how they do it here," she reminded me. "You pay for your perks. Junior-level members can only spend a few hours a week here."

"Yeah, yeah—that's old news. What do mean you saw her say that?"

"I grew up in noisy restaurants." She smiled. "I read lips."

"For real?" I was incredulous.

"Trick of the trade."

This was too weird.

"Your hair's on fire," I mouthed, still skeptical.

She narrowed her eyes at me and patted her messy bun. "Don't joke about that. With all the products I put in it, we'd all go up in flames."

This was too crazy. I racked my brain for any unflattering things I might have said about Hallie when she was in the same room. I was pretty sure I was safe, but still, it was freaky.

I was feeling a little dizzy, and let her lead me across the club. As expected, there were nongirl people everywhere, though I wouldn't go so far as to call them "guys." They all seemed bloodless, with their overly styled hair and clenched jaws. One of them was concentrating on wiping down his leather shoes with a handkerchief while a girl sat on the arm of his white chair. Another was fixing the knot of his cashmere scarf in one of the clubhouse's many mirrors.

At some point a British-sounding voice came over the loudspeaker. "The film study event will be starting shortly. Please flow into the library."

Flow? This place was reaching new heights of ridiculousness by the minute.

Once in the library, we leaned against a wall that had been painted to look like a bookshelf. I glanced around, as if the iPod would be filed away between a fake edition of *Lolita* and *To Kill a Mockingbird*.

"How long have you been here?" Sheila materialized, surprised to see me. Her tone was no less spiky than the tip of her stiletto boot, which was jutting into my calf.

"Just a little while." I jumped back and motioned to Hallie, introducing the two of them.

Sheila ignored my friend and narrowed her eyes at me. "You know, it's customary to announce yourself when you show up to someone else's club. You really shouldn't be wandering around unsupervised."

Unsupervised? Since when was Sheila my babysitter?

"Guys, pay attention." A nearby club member jabbed me and directed us to the front of the room, where a Barbie lookalike was teetering on a faux-leather white cube, addressing the crowd. Was she about to raise the curtain on the stolen iPod?

"I know how extra-cool an event like tonight's is for all you movie buffs," she said. "I'm pleased to introduce filmmaker Orly Matthews, who happens to be an Elle alum." She paused for a smattering of applause, and Hallie and I exchanged confused expressions. The girl went on, "Orly will make a few remarks and then she'll stick around for cocktail hour to answer all your burning questions."

"Good," I murmured to Hallie. "I have a few of those."

The lights dimmed and Orly Matthews stepped to the front of the room to introduce the movie. My heart sunk when she said she was here to promote a documentary she'd made about growing up rich called *Daddy's Little Girl*.

Could this event have nothing to do with *Vertigo Girl*, but instead a stupid socialite's so-called filmic autobiography? No way.

Or yes way. Orly's movie cut between shots of the Matthews family vacation properties and confessional style interviews where Orly stared at the camera and philosophized about "asset management" and the "burden of privilege."

"This can't be happening," I whispered to Hallie.

"I know," she said. "Talk about two hundred thumbs down."

The movie was horrible, without a trace of a pink iPod, and left me feeling utterly dejected. Our fact-finding mission was a total bust. As soon as the lights came back on, I got up and told my host we had to jet. "You know how Kiki gets if I miss her Sunday-night Scrabble party."

Sheila's lip curled and she accepted a drink from a girl who'd come around with a tray. "I'm not sure 'jet' is the right word to use when you're talking about going to visit an old lady, but whatevs."

"I guess we can't all be part of the real jet set," I retorted.

Sensing my sarcasm, Sheila opened her mouth in indignation, but before she could spit any venom, one of her new sisters glided over and took her by the arm. "You have to meet Hanson. He's got an amazing stock portfolio and he's recently single."

Sheila shot me a wicked parting glance as the two whipped around and went off in search of the young investor. Everything to do with Sheila was so polluted, I felt like taking a shower then and there.

I also felt stupid and frustrated beyond belief. The iPod was as within my reach as eternal youth.

Elbowing my way through the crowd, my mind was spinning

and everything was a blur of mirrors and cocktails and ash blond hair. Then I saw something that made me feel a little better.

In the corner of the room, a sandy-blond girl was on a phone call. Nothing remarkable there, except for this little tidbit: she was wearing a gold bracelet that coiled around her wrist and ended with a big snake head. A head that looked remarkably like the one in my dream.

I was more awake than I had been in ages.

Bull's-eye! I mean—snake's-eye! Whatever-eye!

I grabbed Hallie and pulled her aside. "See the girl on the phone?" I gasped, moving around to stand between her and my friend. "Do me a favor. Pretend you're talking to me and tell me what she's saying." Hallie looked at me like she wasn't sure she wanted to play along. I had to come up with a cover for my strange talents. "I just," I started, "I got a weird vibe from her. I think she's on to us." I took two drinks off a tray and passed one to Hallie. "Pretend you're having fun."

Hallie took a sip and her eyes bugged.

"It's gross, I know," I said. "Just pretend to drink it."

"It's not that." Her face fell. "It's what she said."

I was overcome with a weird sense of dread mixed with joy.

Hallie went on, "She just said some Moons crashed the party and it's safe."

"She said they have the iPod?" I whispered.

"She didn't say 'iPod.' Shh . . ." Hallie was trying to concentrate. "She said that Al Capone's taking care of it."

My head rippled with confusion. Al Capone was the original Scarface, the toughest gangster of them all. I'd heard about him a couple of years ago, when Kiki and her posse had gone to his estate auction at Christie's auction house. Edie had tried to buy a plate of bulletproof glass from his Cadillac, but was outbid by the pro wrestler Captain Smackdown.

But who my age ever talked about a dead gangster?

"Al Capone?" I said. "Must be some kind of code. But this means they have the iPod, right?"

"She might," Hallie said matter-of-factly. "All she said was 'it.'"

"And that 'it's' safe. What else can she be talking about?" I was overcome with glee. "But how did she know we're Moons if none of the other hundreds of people said anything about it?"

"Can we do this puzzle piecing outside?" She tugged me by the elbow. "She's headed our way. And I don't have to be able to read lips to tell that she's not so pleased to see us."

{ 17 }

All Scrambled Up

Hallie and I wasted no time rushing onto the street. We jumped in a cab and hightailed it to the Moonery to report what we'd overheard. Or, to be technical about it, *overseen*. When we got to the Moonery, Stinko was too entranced by an episode of *Family Guy* to acknowledge us. We rushed past the curtain and up the stairway. The place was empty except for Diana, who was passed out on the couch, tendrils of red hair falling onto her face.

"Diana!" I shouted. "It's totally them!"

The Moonery's resident napper sat up slowly and squinted into the light. She was wearing a camisole that appeared to be exclusively made of Saran Wrap and strategically placed embroidery. Trying not to stare, I told her what we'd seen at Helle House.

"They have the iPod?" she drawled in a voice thick with sleep.

"Well, we're pretty sure," I said. "The girl on the phone recognized us as Moons and she definitely had something she was hiding from us. What else could it be?"

"Jeez," she said slowly. "So we were right. I'll set up a brainstorming meeting."

I looked over at Hallie for support. How could Diana be acting so blasé?

"Shouldn't we call Becca and the rest now?" I was practically panting.

"We'll talk tomorrow," Diana assured me. "I won't be able to get through to them now. They all went to a nine o'clock screening of *Terror High Three*." She must have been able to sense how let down I was feeling. "Becca's idea," she added, as if that was going to make me feel any better.

I left the Moonery and got home a little after ten. Mom was the only one up. Her laptop was burning bright on the kitchen table, which I took to mean she still hadn't finished her "Priscilla Pluto" horoscope column, which is due every Monday morning.

"Virgo," she said, by way of greeting. I could tell she needed help. And as luck would have it, I'd been thinking about a particular Virgo's future on the elevator ride up.

"You know what you want and you know how to get it," I said. "Don't skimp on sleep. A week of hard work awaits you."

"Okay, good." Mom was typing it all down. "You want some quiche? There's leftovers."

"I'm okay," I told her. "I'm too tired."

"As long as you're not on a diet. You need your energy."

"Don't I know it," I murmured.

When I slid into my room, I put on "Needle in a Haystack"

by the Velvelettes and lay on top of my covers, feeling slightly woozy and munching on some dark chocolate. I was going over the events of the night and wondering whether I'd blown my chance at ever getting into Helle House again. Next, I moved over to my computer to check up on Moonwatcher.net.

Somewhat surprisingly, they still didn't have any photos of Hallie and me, just a shot of some gorgeous Asian girl they must have mistaken for a Moon and a shot of Becca wearing Andy's herringbone coat and stocking up on tennis magazines from a newspaper stand in Midtown. It made me happy to see how serious her interest in Louis was. Normally, Becca and sports don't see eye to eye.

Next up was the Elle House Web site, its blog already updated. "Elle House hosted the Chelsea premiere of *Daddy's Little Girl* by award-winning filmmaker Orly Matthews!!! Over cocktails, members shmoozed with the babe who made the film, Daddy's little girl herself. Hundreds of cinema enthusiasts came, and we all agreed with the *Village Voice* critic who called the movie 'sumptuous.'"

Without really thinking about it, I ran a Google search on "Orly Matthews" and "*Village Voice.*" What the review actually said was "Matthews includes sumptuous footage of her parents' villas in her otherwise brainless film." Looked like the *Village Voice* had been rewritten by the village idiots.

But the glimmer of amusement I felt faded away when I remembered I still had to figure out a way to get the iPod back.

I clicked on my e-mail account, and when I was logged in, I could barely believe my eyes.

You know what they say about a watched pot never boiling? Ditto for a watched in-box. In the wake of the early-morning girl outside the window incident, I must have checked my account fifty times, never to find any word from Andy. And now, the second I'd stopped thinking about seeing him with the stupid girl with the swizzle stick legs, an e-mail from him was waiting.

I took a deep breath and tugged on my cameo necklace, as if that was going to change the nature of what he'd written. Then I clicked OPEN.

> hey, hope the cult hasn't sucked you in too deep. ive been going all kinds of nuts with midterms. But I have a zillion questions for you, like have you ever got stuck on an elevator with a pharmaceutical representative and do you like ginger ice cream and did you know you look exactly like this australian chick on that reality show cruise or lose? anyway, hope to see you around. your old friend misses his shorty —a

The nerve! It was like he couldn't figure out how to go about letting me know it was over—compare me to a cheesy reality television contestant or use the F-word that ends in "end"—so he'd decided to go with them both.

Bastard.

I lay back and racked my brain for a revenge plan. These things usually take a while, but it hit me over the head like a frying pan.

I couldn't wait for tomorrow's lunch period to get to work.

At the end of English class the next day, I couldn't get out of there fast enough. In the bathroom, I freshened my eyeliner, glossed my lips, and pinned my hair into a high crest for a vaguely rockabilly effect. Mr. Cowboy Shirts, eat your heart out.

Alex was easy to spot in the back of the cafeteria. I sat down across from him and he glanced up from his *New Yorker* long enough to throw me a friendly nod. I felt a nervous flutter and I wasn't sure if it was because of what I was about to do or because I'd forgotten how cute he was. Maybe it was a little of both.

"You know David Lynch, the *Twin Peaks* director?" he asked. "He practices transcendental meditation. Twice a day for twenty minutes, swears by it."

He gobbled the remains of his cereal, then took off his watch and passed it to me. "Tell me when the time's up, okay? I'm going to try it."

"You're going to meditate right *now*?"

This was throwing a wrench in my plan.

"Why not?" Even with his eyes closed, his face was too expressive to convey serenity. His fleshy, slightly uneven lips were twitching and when he wiped his nose with the back of his hand, I knew there was no way he was getting any meditating done. I kicked him under the table. "Alex, I need to ask you something."

"Hold on. I think I'm getting somewhere good."

"You're still in the Hudson cafeteria," I informed him. "But I'm about to invite you somewhere good."

His dark eyes opened, gleaming curiously for more.

"You're such a faker." Steeling myself for my big Move Over, Andy plan, I outlined the setup for Kiki's party.

"Murder mystery, sounds interesting." He tipped his head forward, like he was hard of hearing. "But I'm confused. Are you asking me because you know how well I get along with adults or because you want me to be your date?"

I felt my cheeks crimson and searched his face for the right answer, but all I got was an open-ended stare. "I don't know," I wavered, mustering whatever courage I had to spare. "A little of both?"

Silence followed.

"So, you want in?" I asked.

"Yeah, let's do it." He lowered his lids again and his look

turned a little dreamy. I thought I could detect a faint "om" sail out of his wet lips.

I, on the other hand, had no need for meditation techniques. My plan had worked. Nothing on earth could have made me feel any calmer.

Ian found me by my locker at the end of the day, emptying my bag of all the textbooks I wasn't going to need that night.

"You're wearing a skirt," he informed me.

"It's actually a dress." I looked down to make double sure. Yup, the black studded Yves Saint Laurent number I'd put on that morning hadn't dissolved.

"Whatever," he said. "It's perfect."

Ian is aware of many things, but fashion isn't one of them. "You feeling okay?" I asked.

"I should be asking you the same thing," he said. "You didn't forget the protest's today, did you?"

Today?

Suddenly peeved, I bit down on my lip. "How could I forget something that you never told me in the first place?"

"Oh, it's today." He waited a beat. "You're coming, right?"

"Ian—" I started.

He cocked his head gently. "Oh, c'mon. When's the last time I asked you to do me a favor?" I turned it over in my head: no. The other Moons would kill me if I ended up in a newspaper, even if it was for a good cause—but I knew New York had more important things for reporters to be covering than a bunch of kids disputing the plotline of their favorite superhero. And I doubted the photographers for Moonwatcher.net would have any reason to be there. "Fine," I said. "But you owe me."

Ian grinned and took my bag. "You have no idea how hard this is going to rock. You're going to be the girliest poster child ever."

Me, the girliest anything? But when we arrived at Global Media's Park Avenue headquarters, I noted I was more feminine in this crowd than a pink cream puff. The guys in the picket line were marching in a skinny oval outside the building's revolving doors chanting, *"Hey hey, ho ho! Your diamond-studded Toro's got to go!"*

My ears went sweaty at the realization of how noticeable I'd be in this setting, and when they saw me, the twenty-or-so Propeller regulars burst into applause. "Front of the pack, lady!" one of them screamed, and soon they were all at it, shouting *"Front of the pack! No turning back!"*

A couple of businessmen walking out of the building stopped to gawk. I looked at Ian and felt my palms go clammy. I knew the chances were slim, but what if someone *did* come by to take a photograph and I ended up in a newspaper? I couldn't afford to get kicked out of the Moons, and especially not now.

"Ian, do I have to?" My voice was warbling. "I don't like being front and center. It makes me self-conscious."

"Oh, come on, you look fabulous, dahlink," he said in a silly Russian accent. "Besides, it's just a couple more minutes. Look." He pointed out the fleet of black town cars that were warming their engines by the building entrance. "They're just personal drivers waiting for all the bigwigs, and it's already after five. When they go home, so do we."

"And what happens when the bigwigs come out?"

"We just hand them our plea letter. It's a comic I helped make. It'll be over before you know it, I promise."

I glanced around to make sure there was no press on the premises, then begrudgingly accepted a beautifully drawn GLOBAL MEDIA, WHAT DID TORO BOY EVER DO TO YOU? sign from a kid I recognized from Ian's New Year's Eve video game bash. From my spot at the front of the herd, I could see the Waldorf-Astoria's

Art Deco roof in the not-too-far-off distance. Thank God Kiki didn't believe in going anywhere by foot.

"What should I do?" I asked Ian.

"Just hold up the sign and look like you're really unhappy," some guy directed me.

"That won't be so hard," I grumbled.

But as the sunlight faded, so did my self-consciousness. For the most part, nobody was stopping to pay attention to us, and some of the chants the kids had come up with were so goofy I had to have fun with them, like "Diamonds are a Toro Boy's worst friend!" and "Stop the global war on Toro."

Before long I had joined in. When we got to "No bull! All Toro!" I was giving it my all, like the fourth member of the Ronettes I've always wanted to be.

I was actually getting a little too into it—so into it I didn't notice the way the other guys had died down just as a trio of businessmen came out of the building. "Now's our chance!" Ian was jumping up and down. "Stevie!"

Stevie Marconi, a Propeller regular who's so tall his pants barely come past his knees, ran up to the businessmen who were exiting the building. "Free of charge," he said, trying to pass out the *Save Toro Boy* comic brochures. The businessmen tried to ignore him, though it was evident from their tensed jaws that he was getting on their nerves.

The rest of us had stopped to stare, though probably not at the same thing. All the guys were rooting for Stevie, feverishly emitting whoo-hoos and tossing out lines like "Diamonds are for never!" and "May the force be with you!" Meanwhile, I had discovered something far more interesting: the HRH monogram on the briefcase of one of the businessmen.

No way.

I'd been so busy worrying about press, this beyond-obvious

tidbit had failed to occur to me: the CEO of Global Media, Mr. H.R.H., was Harold Reagan Hendricks, Reagan's dad.

I held my breath steady.

"Watch it!" said a kid who was winding his arm up like a pitcher.

"What the hell are you doing?" Ian screamed at him, but the egg was already spinning through the air, heading toward Stevie and the suits. My heart lurched and I just stood there, watching it all unfold, knowing things were going to turn out badly but not sure what I could do before—

Splat!

Mr. Hendricks's shoulder was covered in yellow gunk. And his face was red with rage. A team of hulking men jumped out of the town cars and charged our way.

"Everybody run!" somebody behind me screamed.

My thoughts scrambling, I started to sprint. The sound of scuffling feet behind me was growing louder by the second.

Compared to the others, I was as good as a cripple. Who was I kidding? I didn't have a fighting chance.

Just as Ian and the rest of the kids ripped around the corner, a hand went for my shoulder with a viselike grip. "Hold up, Missy," I looked up to see a security guard bearing down on me. His face reminded me of raw meat and he had the breath to match. "You're not going anywhere."

{ 18 }

Manhattan Murder Mystery

I was shivering in my gray one-piece bathing suit. I hustled to the edge of the diving board and took the plunge. The pool felt deliciously warm. When I looked down I saw that my legs had morphed into a mermaid tail, and there were long sections of silver hair streaming out of my bathing cap.

As my weird dreams go, it was a good one—even oddly relaxing. Then again, a hostage situation would have been soothing the night after my misadventures at Global Media. Most of the protestors were too fast for the thugs of the Global security detail, but Rick Pinkwhaler, Frank Xu, and I hadn't been so lucky. The only good thing to come from our experience with being nabbed by security was that I now knew how to torture people to the breaking point: stick them in a windowless room with a thirty-second clip from the cartoon "Dingo Berries" on constant loop, pull them out to repeatedly ask the same question about who threw the egg even if they couldn't answer on previous attempts, and make them wait three hours before delivering the verdict.

In the end, they let me go, but that didn't mean I wasn't left with a serious case of post-traumatic stress disorder. I was going to kill Ian.

A day later, I still felt worn out. I made my way into the Moonery late in the afternoon. I pinched my cheeks before opening the door to the office. I hadn't talked to anyone in twenty-four hours and was feeling out of it.

As though I wasn't nervous enough about running into H.R.H.'s daughter, Reagan greeted me with, "If it isn't the star of the antiglobalization movement."

I hung back in the doorway, speechless. The guards had taken our names, but how did she know? I thought one of her issues with her dad was that he never told her anything.

"It's on YouTube," Becca provided. She wiggled an eyebrow and got up to turn around the monitor, which was set to a video called "Verrueckter Kampf vor Globalmedia!"

"It means 'Trouble Outside Global Media,'" Sills translated. "Some German tourist is keeping a blog of his New York adventures."

My mind was spinning—how on earth had they uncovered the most random thing on the Internet, and so fast? And did it count as the kind of press that was going to get me kicked out of the Moons? My stomach started to churn as I prepared myself for the worst.

I looked out the window.

It was growing darker and the leaves in the courtyard

appeared two-dimensional. "Nice work," Reagan said. Her voice was sweet and she was giving me her megawatt smile. "I Google him all the time, but never have I come across anything this interesting. Thanks for the entertainment. Egg-cellent stuff." She pulled a new tube of lipstick out of her bag and proceeded to remove the plastic seal.

"N-no problem." I dug my hands in my pockets, stunned by her reaction. How could she be so detached? "To be honest, it wasn't my idea. I can't really take any of the credit."

"Oh, I think you can." Her voice was frayed and the volume was increasing with each word. The other girls were looking around the room in supreme discomfort, and Hallie started to thumb through the magazine she'd been balancing on her lap.

I couldn't make a sound, let alone think of anything to say, as Reagan threw on her coat and scarf and stomped toward the door. When she was inches away from me, I noticed that her nose was red and puffy.

How could I be so dense? She was completely furious with me.

My gaze fell to the floor, as if a magic salve would be there on the rug.

"Ray, I swear . . . I had no idea it was your dad."

She glared at me. "Then how'd you know it was him, just now?"

Self-consciously, I drew back my shoulders. "I'm not following."

"Has anybody said anything about my dad since you got here?" she challenged.

"I—I—" I stammered. "I mean, I figured it out eventually. I knew he worked there, but I didn't put it all together until—"

"Too late," she finished off my sentence, and turned to address the rest of the room. "Have a fantastic meeting," she said with a sneer. "I'm going to go home to say good-bye to my parents." She fixed her steely gaze on me. "You've inspired Dad to spend the next few weeks working out of the L.A. office, and Mom's tagging along so she can protect him from egg-pelting insaniacs when she's not blowing off steam on Rodeo Drive or wherever." With that, she bolted.

I felt my cheeks burn and scanned the others' faces. "I really didn't know . . . ," I started to say.

"Don't get too worked up about it," Becca said in a soothing tone. "Reagan's parents bring out the worst in her. They pay more attention to their orchid collection."

"That's not true," said Diana. "They care about her inability to get into college too."

"Ouch," muttered Sills.

"She'll come around." Becca came over to rub my back comfortingly. "And you're putting your riot girl days behind you, understand?"

"Yeah," I promised. I felt so grateful for Becca's protection. I slumped against the wall and listened to the sound of Reagan's footsteps fade to nothing.

"Good." Poppy smiled brightly and made a spot for me by the window seat. "Now what's this about your findings at Helle House? You say they're our culprit?"

"I'm pretty sure."

Nobody said anything, but Sills gave me a look that said we could do better than pretty sure.

In the meantime Kiki was planning her "Murder on the Showgirl Express" birthday blowout, for which she was assigning guests costumes. She was playing the grand dame of the musical revue, and my invitation had come with a role for my date: "dapper oilman."

The following night, when I walked into the Has Bean, the coffee shop where Alex had suggested we meet, I saw that my date's interpretation of 1950s tycoon wasn't what I'd been picturing—he was wearing a tight purple zoot suit, his hair slicked back with what must have been an entire tub of Vaseline.

Alex downed the remains of his coffee and rose to his feet. "That's quite a getup," he said.

"Thanks?" I said unsurely and turned toward the door, I glanced in the coffee shop's mock-Victorian mirror and caught sight of myself in a curly black wig, peacock feather hat, and one of Kiki's old costumes from her days as a Coney Island Follies showgirl. It had looked glamorous at home, but now I wasn't so sure.

We made our way outside. The setting sun was casting long shadows on the street, and Alex didn't look half as cute as I remembered. I tried to paste his normal hair back on his head with my imagination. There was no way Andy would have played the part of "dapper oilman" in a suit the color of a grape jelly bean.

"So remind me what's supposed to happen at this murder-mystery party," Alex said. "Is someone going to get killed or something?"

"No, somebody supposedly already did," I told him. "When we get there we're all going to get a mock-newspaper report of the murder along with four clues. Kiki wants us to approach each other and ask 'Where were you at the time of the crime?' and stuff like that. Then they'll announce the murderer at the end of the night."

"I still don't completely get it," Alex said. "How do you win?"

"It's not a win thing." I was starting to get peeved. "It's just

Kiki's idea of fun, having all her friends dress up and ask each other silly questions."

"If you say so," he said. We were silent the rest of the walk to the industrial warehouse where the party was being held.

A muttonchopped man in a conductor's uniform stepped out the door and blew a whistle in our faces. "All aboard!"

I didn't realize who it was until I saw the telltale skull ring. "Clem?"

"It's Conductor Flannagan tonight. Tickets, please!" He fed our invitations into a hole puncher and handed them back to us along with a fake-newspaper clipping and four clues. "See you inside."

I was still marveling at Clem's new facial hair as we wended our way through the backstage corridor. It was crammed with plastic plants and fake brick walls left over from an old production.

The second we stepped through the Showgirl Express door, I was instantly overcome with guilt for having ever sided against Jon-Jon. This was the coolest party I'd ever seen. He hadn't merely decorated the theater to look like an old train— he'd practically built a whole train, complete with separate cars and wide windows and *chugga-chugga* sound effects.

Everybody had followed Kiki's orders and showed up in the most outrageous costumes—or, in my parents' case, outrageously grim burlap sacks. I quickly scanned the place for Becca, who was nowhere to be seen, then watched in admiration as a gangster in a pin-striped suit sidled up to a sixty-something showgirl and told her, "I know two things when I see them, Dollface, talent and trouble. And I think I'm seeing double."

Alex's eyes were getting shiny. "This is amazing."

"Told you so," I said proudly.

Jon-Jon had filled the party with theme-appropriate snacks: magnifying glass–shaped sugar cookies, mini blood sausages, and a mound of pâté in the shape of a revolver. I took two crystal glasses of blood orange juice from the bar, but when I turned around to hand my date his drink, he was no longer on hand.

I found him a few minutes later in the first class car, talking to an older woman who was wearing what looked like an Oriental carpet around her head. She had an expression of distress, and when she saw me coming over, she seemed to heave in relief.

"Claire," Alex said, "this is Fran Haze, the filmmaker. I saw her do a Q and A at Film Forum last year. How does your grandmother know her?" He was practically panting.

"How does she know anyone?" I shrugged and smiled in Fran's direction. I could tell she wanted to go back to playing murder mystery. "So, where were you at the time of the murder?" I asked her.

"Hold up, hold up." Alex passed a small white rectangle Fran's way. "I'm studying film, and if you're ever looking for somebody to mentor, or even just want to shoot the breeze, don't hesitate to call me."

I cringed at his obliviousness.

"Thank you," she said warily. "I think I'm going to breeze thataway." She gestured vaguely across the car. "I see some . . . people I know."

"Sorry if that was weird," Alex said. I was so embarrassed for him, I didn't know what to say. "I just find adults so much easier to talk to than people our age. Sometimes I wonder if I'm an old man trapped in a fifteen-year-old's body."

He chuckled lightly and, much to my horror, turned and proceeded to buttonhole more of Kiki's friends. It wasn't long before he was greasing palms with a jazz pianist, an exiled Iranian cinematographer, and Andre Rabinowitz, the famous Columbia dean.

I could only take so much, and ended up settling on a velvet bench in the Way Station, wondering why I'd ever invited somebody whose idea of a good time was to pass out his business card—even though he didn't have a business. Pushing thoughts of Alex to the back of my head, I concentrated on the dance floor. Past the old showgirls and mobsters, my "vagabond" parents were dancing cheek to cheek. I wondered if the burlap was chafing their skin.

Off in the corner, I saw a young man with a WIMBLEDON #1 trophy hanging around his neck and his date, whose sign said METROPOLITAN OPERA DIVA, swinging each other around. Louis and Becca were pretending to be making fun of the old-fashioned moves, doing everything bigger and deeper than everyone else, but I could read between the lines: they couldn't contain their happiness. Everything inside me went sunny.

"Well, isn't this cute?" came a familiar voice.

I snapped out of my reverie to see the birthday girl hovering above me. She was decked out in a blue sequined frock and holding a plate of miniature hamburgers.

"I know," I told Kiki, looking over in time to see Louis guide Becca into a dip. "They're finally succumbing to their destiny!"

"Not them. This tomfoolery." Kiki waved Alex's card an inch away from my nose. "This buffoon claims he knows you."

"Oh yeah," I croaked. "That's Alex. He's here as the dapper oilman."

"But that role was created for Andy, was it not?"

I sucked in a deep breath. "I had to find an understudy."

Kiki shook her head gravely.

"And what about that culinary fellow?"

"Ian Kitchen?" I cast a guilty look down at my shoes. I hadn't taken any of his calls since the flying egg incident. "He couldn't make it."

She humphed. "We'll take this up later. For now, I want you to go and tell your friend to cease and desist immediately. My parties are not networking opportunities for anybody, much less youngsters with crass manners." She turned around and started to interrogate a man in a military uniform about his whereabouts on the night in question. Becca caught my eye and waved enthusiastically at me. I returned the gesture and then, my head hanging low from Kiki's scolding, shuffled out of the Way Station and searched the other cars for the offender I'd unleashed on the party.

"Looking for your ticket or something?" somebody asked me in the smoking car.

Even though he was shrouded in a cloud of smoke, I knew who it was in a heartbeat.

He'd come!

"Andy?" My voice was shot through with joy.

We locked eyes, and it took every bit of self-control not to wrap my arms around him and kiss him until the party shut down.

"What are you doing in the smoking car?" he asked, staring at me as if in a trance.

"Um, what are you doing at Kiki's party *at all*?" I narrowed my eyes, in an effort to seem angry with him, but something about the way he smiled told me I just looked like a little kid who was still learning how to wink.

He extended his arm. He was holding a blue box with a red ribbon. "For Kiki," he said.

"That was nice of you." I accepted the gift, concentrating

hard on not making any skin-to-skin contact. But he was the one to touch the small of my back. "Not bad. You should wear crazy costumes more often. Very becoming." His hand lingered for a little rub, and a warm sensation spread through my body. "So as you can probably guess, there's another reason I came. I wanted to explain something. About before, when—"

"Hey, babe," came a sinus-congested voice. Before Andy could say anything more, Alex had wiggled into the space next to me. Andy wasted no time lifting his hand from my back and stepping away from me.

"Andy!" I said quickly. "This is—"

"Alex." He slipped him a card.

"Wow, I don't know that many guys our age with business cards." Andy flashed Alex the universal you-are-a-raving-lunatic smile, then threw in a conciliatory, "Nice touch."

"You can get them for free on the Internet," Alex provided. "The Web site's on the back."

Andy's gaze traveled to where Alex was resting his hand. On my waist. His face fell like a broken elevator and I let off a skittish squeak. "Do you want a drink or anything?" I offered desperately.

"Nah, not tonight." Andy looked devastated. "I didn't . . . I . . . I gotta go. Good luck to you . . . both."

And with that, he bolted into a cloud of smoke.

Desperation burbled up inside of me and I pushed Alex's hand away. I had to track Andy down.

I ran off and scanned every car high and low, and threaded through the dance floor too many times to count.

"Watch it, lady!" Becca apprehended me when I was passing her and Louis. "You gonna dance with us or what?"

"In a minute," I told them, and kept going, moving through all of the cars.

When hope was lost, there was only one place I wanted to be.

Alone in a toilet stall, I buried my wet face in my palms and tried to comfort myself by thinking of all the terrible things that hadn't happened. I hadn't spilled my drink on anyone. I hadn't vomited on national television. Henry hadn't come down with a terminal illness.

But none of that really helped. And when I got out of the stall and checked myself out in the mirror, I saw the night was even worse than I'd realized. And no, I'm not talking about the mascara tracks running down my face.

The real problem was about eight inches to the south.

My cameo necklace was gone.

{ 19 }

Hide and Go Seek

When I was done crying and ready to face society again, I found Alex sitting by himself in the library car, shoveling murder by chocolate cake into his mouth. His shoulders were slumped, and when he caught sight of me, his eyes filled with more concern than I'd ever thought to give him credit for.

"Everything all right?" he asked.

Just great. I lost my chance with Andy. And my magic cameo.

"I'm sorry," I said, pointing to my tummy. "I think I ate a funny oyster. We should probably go."

His deep inhale said he knew something else was up, but he just asked if we should find Kiki to say good night. Convenient that his manners were appearing *now*.

"No point in disturbing her," I said, nodding toward the bunk bed of the sleeper car where Kiki and Edie were posing for a man who was taking pictures with an antique flashbulb camera. "Besides, I'm seeing her first thing tomorrow."

"You guys sure make a lot of plans," he marveled.

To be honest, we hadn't made an actual plan, but of course I'd be going over there ASAP. It wasn't like I could call the theater space's lost and found department and file a report for a lost superpower. The only person who could help me find my cameo and get my hands on that cursed pink iPod was Kiki. I didn't have a second to waste.

Alex laid his plate on a side table and I placed Andy's gift box next to it, confident it would eventually make its way to Kiki.

It occurred to me that I should probably tell Becca I was taking off, but I knew she'd freak out and insist that I stay. It wasn't a scene I was feeling strong enough for, so I gave myself permission to take what Kiki calls a "French leave."

Outside, the sky was dark as ink and the wind was whipping off the Hudson River. While Alex tried to hail a cab, I huddled under an entranceway and hugged my stomachache, which wasn't feeling so fake anymore.

Alex didn't seem as mad or flustered about leaving early as I'd feared. "That was really cool," he said, sliding into the taxi after me. "I think I made some good connections."

Good thing, I thought, because he wasn't going to be hanging out with me anytime soon.

When I got home and caught my cameo-free reflection in the Renault car mirror, the full awfulness of the situation hit me. I was so shattered the thought of sneaking one of Mom's leftover steamed chocolate cakes out of the refrigerator left me cold. All I wanted was to retreat to my tiny bedroom and lick my wounds in private.

I'd left my computer on and there was an e-mail from Ian.

For the hundredth time I'm super sorry. For what it's worth, that businessman guy is considering legal action against us and none of us are allowed to hang out in the store if we're not being 'useful,' whatever that means. Write back and save me from drawing infinite teardrops.

I knew he was half kidding, but he sounded worse than ever, and I knew I should send him a note to cheer him up.

Instead, I ended up cruising around Moonwatcher.net. They hadn't put up anything too outrageous, just a "State of Affairs" feature that linked the Moons to the guys they were supposedly seeing on the sly.

Sills's picture was shown next to Wiley Martins. Diana was linked to a James Dean–type kid in a tight white T-shirt, Reagan to a child-actor-turned-heartthrob who was starring in her dad's latest blockbuster, and Poppy with a trio of skateboarders. They were trying to link Becca to Alonzo Ladin, a junior voice coach at Lincoln Center who'd been wearing a kabbalah bracelet and ladies' platform shoes the time we'd met.

I heard a rustling and turned around to see Henry creeping into my room. Still in little boy panhandler character, his face was coated in charcoal.

"Hey." I clicked the window on the screen shut—but not fast enough.

"Why's Becca on a dating site?" he asked.

I whipped back around. "How do you know about dating sites?"

"Charlie W.'s dad does it," he said. "He lets us pick dates for him."

"You're kidding, right?"

"No," he said matter-of-factly, and proceeded to sit on the edge of my bed and reach under it for a box of Mon Cheri chocolates. "He says he's made so many mistakes in his life, we're probably better judges."

"I'm sure Charlie W.'s mom would love to hear that." It slipped out before I could stop myself.

"A lot of people are on it," Henry went on. "Jori, our music teacher, is there, and so are a bunch of other kids' parents." He popped a candy in his mouth. "Trust me, it's not a big deal."

I was puzzled—was it possible that Henry was becoming cooler than his impossibly with-it older sister?

I held out my hand for a serving of chocolate. "So who ended up being the murderer anyway?"

"Some guy named Don Juan."

"Impossible," I said without pausing to think. "I saw the entire guest list and there was nobody called—" I perked up when I realized what he was trying to say. "You mean Jon-Jon?"

"Yeah. They had a judge and a trial. His punishment was house-sitting an empty mansion in Sag Harbor for a month."

I could feel myself beaming. So Kiki'd solved the old unwanted houseguest bugaboo. I could only hope she'd be half as useful with my own problems.

I spent that night tossing and turning under the covers, touching the part of my neck where my cameo should have been and anxiously peering out the window, waiting for the next day to start. At last, the crescent moon started to melt into the sky, and not much later an apricot hue spread along the horizon.

I got up and threw on a comfortable outfit of jeans, a

boatneck sweater, and a huge fringed scarf. In the elevator down, I looked up in the corner mirror to double-check that my naked neck was covered.

Traffic was light and I biked up to Kiki's in no time. "Room service," I called out as I knocked on her door. I'd brought a liter of Coke and a bag of almond croissants—her favorites.

Her gray eye squinted through the peephole. When she opened the door she looked worse for the wear, and it didn't help that her face fell to her ankles. "Oh dear. What's the trouble?"

"I was just bringing you some break—"

"Like fun you were! I wasn't born yesterday?"

"Okay," I said. "There's something I need to talk about."

The front room was crammed with gifts and leftover party goodies—magnifying glasses, water guns, and an unused pin-the-mustache-on-the-inspector game. I could see Andy's present was on a side table, the ribbon untied.

After complying with Kiki's request to empty the croissants into a silver basket, I drifted over to the blue box and couldn't resist pulling off the lid for a peek. Inside was an amazing pair of Art Deco hair combs with parrot engravings. Andy'd got it perfect—no surprise there.

Jon-Jon was sleeping on the couch, his huge stomach rising and falling like a metronome.

"It's his last night here," she whispered as she started for her room.

"I heard," I whispered as I followed her. "Henry told me about your eviction plan. Very cunning."

"You make it sound like a bad thing. I prefer 'resourceful.'" She closed the door to her bedroom and pulled out a chair from her dressing table. I sat on the bed, tightening my scarf around my neck's empty spot. "Now what has gotten into you?"

And so I told her. Or tried to. My voice was catching, and I had to focus on a mental image of New York with a buried Brooklyn Bridge to coax the truth out. "Last night, I . . . well, somehow I . . ."

"You lost your necklace." Her tone was plain as Wonder Bread.

I reached up to feel if my scarf had somehow untwisted to reveal my bare collarbone. Negative.

"It turned up?" I asked in shock.

She shook her head and put down her pastry. "No."

"Were you able to read my mind?"

"I just knew this would happen," she said slowly.

"How?" I balked.

"Did you bring that churlish child to my party? And did I tell you to follow your heart or not?"

My head was spinning and I lay on her rumpled covers. "Is this some kind of sick punishment of yours?"

She chuckled. "You give me more credit than is due. It's not up to me."

"So it's a rule of the weirdo universe? If I disobey you, the necklace falls off?"

"No." She folded her hands together. "If you disobey your heart, your powers go limp. You got your signals crossed. Now you need to uncross them." She raised her tawny eyebrow meaningfully. "You follow?"

My head felt heavy as I nodded. If I wanted to find my necklace and dream my way back into the Moons' good graces and save the purity of the Brooklyn Bridge, all I had to do was get Andy back.

Which would be about as easy as creating no-calorie fudge. And world peace. In the space of thirty minutes.

My expression must have given away how doubtful I was feeling.

"Oh, calm down," she told me, "there's very little in this world that can't be undone."

"Okay, but you're forgetting something. Andy hates me. I can't get him back."

"Oh yes you can."

"What am I supposed to do? Tell him that if he doesn't go out with me I won't be able to find my magic necklace and I won't have any more dreams and Sink Landon will have his day and New York will cease to be the city we know and love?"

She rolled her eyes. "When have I *ever* recommended full disclosure? Just say what needs to be said."

I rolled over onto my stomach and found myself eye level with a pair of tweezers and a hand mirror on her bedside table. Kiki's eyebrows had stopped growing decades ago, but she still kept a close eye on them. "And what would that be?"

"That bringing that date was an abysmal mistake and that you adore him and only him. And be sure to remind him that he was the one not to snatch up our invitation in the first place." She stretched out her doughy arms. "And for heaven's sake, leave out the mystical bits. They're about as sexy as cheap eau de toilette." She lumbered over to her walk-in closet and flicked on the light. "Now let's find you some turtlenecks."

"Which *are* sexy?" I asked incredulously.

"No, but at least they'll cover up your unadorned neck. A sad sight, that."

I stuck around Kiki's for another hour or so, long enough to go over our favorite moments from the party and to get a little more encouragement on the Andy front. "It behooves you to act fast," she said as she saw me to the door. "There are only so many Shuttleworth boys to go around."

"Are you two talking about that mysterious tall boy who stopped by the shindig last night?" Jon-Jon's voice, thick with sleep, surprised me.

"Who else?" Kiki said.

Her guest sat up and nodded. "If I were you, I'd be on that like a duck on a june bug."

Way to get your point across, weirdo.

"He's right. Don't stand there like a flagpole." Kiki shooed me away. "Be yourself. But a little bit better."

Ouch.

By the time I rolled my bike out of the hotel manager's office and into Park Avenue traffic, I was so pumped up about getting things back in order that I neglected to think about one niggling detail: the rest of the world doesn't check in with my schedule before making its own plans.

This annoying truth didn't make itself apparent until I reached a pay phone on Fifty-first Street (I didn't want to call Andy from the Waldorf in case he recognized the number and didn't pick up). The nervous rush I'd felt when he immediately answered gave way to irritation when I realized it was just his voice mail. "Hey," came his unhurried voice. "I've gone into hiding for the next little while, but I'll be sure to call you when I'm back."

The street sounds around me faded out and I couldn't hear anything until the recording came on to tell me to hang up and try again.

As inconvenient as it is having a secret thing with your best friend's older brother, the situation does have some things to recommend it. For instance, you can ride your bike over to your friend's place when you need to do a little romantic sleuthing and she won't necessarily know you're there to sniff out her brother's whereabouts. The ride from the Waldorf to Becca's is usually fifteen minutes, but I made it in half the time—must've been all that extra energy now that I wasn't busy having energy-depleting dreams. A housekeeper answered the door and led me up to Becca's bedroom. "I should've called, but I was just riding by . . ."

Becca was curled up on her sofa, wearing her tortoiseshell glasses and enjoying a trashy vampire book.

"Who would expect *you* to call?" she said without looking up. "You couldn't even be bothered to say good-bye last night."

Crap.

I couldn't handle all this trouble, especially without my necklace to get me out of it.

"I . . . I didn't want to interrupt you," I lied. "You and Louis looked like you were having so much fun."

"We were having fun waiting for you to dance with us," she corrected me. "It was a little annoying when we realized you'd jetted."

"I thought it would be weird if I got in the way," I said. "Don't be angry with me."

"I'm not angry. I'm just saying, don't ever think about leaving another party without saying bye again. Especially a party where I only know two other people."

"Okay," I said. "I'm sorry."

"I guess I accept. Now hold on and let me finish this chapter, 'kay?"

"Of course." I paced around the room and let Becca power through to the end. Watching her turn the page for the fourth time in under a minute, it occurred to me that she must have inherited all the reading skills that had skipped her older brother, who had once confided in me he was lucky if he made it through twenty pages in an hour.

"You really like that junk?" I asked her when she finally dog-eared a page.

She looked at me dead-on. "The Vampire Institute trilogy is no ordinary junk, thank you very much. It's junk at its most brilliantly toxic."

We exchanged smiles and I took a seat at her desk chair, trying to figure out how to uncover where her brother had run off to without being too obvious about it.

"Based on your freaked-out expression," she said before I could come up with anything, "I take it you checked your e-mail this morning."

"No, why?"

A new alertness filled her brown eyes. "We weren't the only ones to play dress-up last night. Sills and Reagan decided to put on a couple of wigs and crash a party at Helle House to poke around and get the iPod back."

My breath quickened.

"Did they find it?"

"No, but they got found out. And it got ugly."

I made a worried frown. "Did they get hurt?"

She scoffed. "C, we're talking about West Chelsea, not the Wild West. But they got booted out and now there's tightened security. There's an advisory on the Web site, saying no more visitors and no new members."

"What does this mean for . . ." I could barely speak. "Everything else?"

"It means we're a hundred percent certain that they have the iPod, but game over . . . unless you have any bright ideas for getting in and finding it."

I sighed. Better luck next piece of lost jewelry.

"Didn't think so." She smiled sadly. "So looks like everything is going to proceed as feared. The bridge gets tested next week and it's revealed a cable is loose, everyone freaks out, the city announces they're replacing the cable, the greatest landmark this side of the pyramids loses any protection, the waterfront becomes the living embodiment of Sink Landon's freak-vision, and the rest of us go back to our normal lives until we figure out a new project—though nothing from the list that got away." I wanted to smack myself for all the time I'd wasted sweating over the Andy situation. Everything she was talking about was a zillion times more important. Becca went on, "I heard the sidewalk outside of Penn Station is all covered with gum. That could be fun for us, a clean-up day." Her tone was as bitter as wilted arugula and she returned to her book and began to read aloud from it. "'Clover took him by the shoulders and smelled his manly, feverish aroma . . .'" I bit down on my lip, doing the math. The iPod was in Helle House. And nobody could get in. But there had to be a way.

"By the way," I broke the silence, "Kiki wanted me to thank Andy for the combs he brought her last night. He around?"

She shook her head. "Dad had some business in Orlando and he tagged along."

"What's up?" I couldn't help being extra nosy. "Is Soul Sauce asking to be Mickey Mouse's official ketchup?"

"It already is," she said bashfully. "They went to some conference for the plastics industry. Sounded boring to me, but Andy talked his way onto the plane this morning. He seemed eager to get out of town."

And away from me, no doubt. My heart folded in on itself.

But I was also relieved to have Andy's exact whereabouts. Armed with this new bit of knowledge, I felt my worries fade a bit, and talked my friend into going for a walk.

When we got outside, the sky was clear and it was warmer out than it had been all week; Becca had untied her white scarf and pulled back the finger flaps of her mittens by the time we'd reached her corner.

The area closest to the entrance to Central Park was mobbed, but it cleared up when we trekked a little farther north and found an abandoned outcrop. This section of the park was shielded on all sides by elm trees. The shiny skyscrapers looming in the distance looked like silver French fries, and I realized I hadn't eaten in a little while.

Becca let off a heavy sigh as she fell back against the rock wall. "You know, I owe you a thank-you."

"For what, the fresh air?"

"I guess you could call it that. . . . Louis is different from most guys. He's really . . . sane."

Considering Louis spends more time on his shrink's couch than a workaholic in his office cubicle, "sane" wasn't the first word I'd pick, but I decided to let it slide. Who was I to squelch her happiness? I leaned into the spot next to her and watched a squirrel try to pick up a discarded Milky Way wrapper with its paws. "So you two really hit it off?"

She didn't say anything at first. "I'm not sure what I'm supposed to do in this situation. He's your other best friend. You must think the whole thing is gross."

"No, the idea of *me* and Louis is gross. Louis and anybody who makes him happy makes me happy. And if you're happy in the bargain I'm even happier."

Well, she was half right. I would be happy in the bargain if they would just make a little more time in their happy lives for me.

"Okay," she said. "You'd better be telling the truth. After the party we went on a long walk through Hell's Kitchen, then up to the Upper West Side."

The Upper West Side? Interesting.

"That's where Louis lives," I couldn't help saying.

"No, it wasn't like *that*. We sat on a bench on one of the

traffic islands along Broadway. There was this guy on the other bench who was listening to the Knicks game on his AM radio. Louis told me about his father issues, and how much he hates the Knicks," she said, easing into her role as storyteller. "We were goofing around and pretending to get really into the game, like the crazy fans who paint their faces and bet their life savings on the World Series."

"Um . . . I think that's baseball."

"You know what I mean." She was trying to open up to me in a way that was unusual for her.

"Sorry," I said. "Go on."

"Anyway, the Knicks were behind two points and all of a sudden there was this amazing pass that came out of nowhere and . . ."

"Louis made a pass out of nowhere?" I offered.

Becca looked down.

"He totally did!"

She smiled slyly. "Considering we'd been hanging out all night, I wouldn't call it nowhere. But yeah, the kid came through."

She pulled herself off the rock and started walking down a dirt path. "And what about you and your date?"

I groaned and watched her flounce ahead. I guessed Alex hadn't passed her his card.

"What, things didn't work out between Claire Voyante and Alex the social networker?" Apparently I'd guessed wrong. Becca's singsongy tone made me shudder.

"Don't tell me he gave you his business card last night," I said, catching up to her side.

Becca laughed. "Not last night, but he's in my chem class."

"He is? You should've warned me!"

I was so embarrassed.

"Is that right?" She turned to face me. "And remind me, how was I to know when you never mentioned him to me?"

"I—I didn't?"

"Nope." Still walking, she slowed down and her eyes filled with sadness. "It's weird, sometimes it feels like I know you inside and out, and then other times it's like you're keeping everything a secret from me." She was looking at me in a way that indicated she wasn't just talking about Alex—she suspected other things too, things about my weird talents and my relationship with her brother. "You know what I mean, right?"

"Uh-huh." I nodded my head heavily, wondering how much I was reading into what Becca was saying, and trying to calculate how different life would be if Becca was in on my secret powers and nonlove life.

"Just tell me next time, okay?" she said.

And that was when it occurred to me that not coming clean wasn't a choice anymore. Becca didn't just expect total honesty—she deserved it. More to the point, we deserved it. All this time I'd been doing my best to keep different parts of my life separate, I hadn't realized what a heavy price there'd been to pay. Becca and I had been drifting apart this semester, and maybe the Moons and Louis weren't entirely to blame.

I breathed in so deep my shoulders practically hit my earlobes. And then, awkward as it was, I started to tell her about everything that had happened—and, more distressingly, everything that hadn't happened—between her brother and me.

It was hard, but I had to do it. I'd already lost my necklace. I couldn't afford to lose anything more.

I tightened my fists and detailed the ups and downs of my secret history with Andy, watching Becca's eyes go deep with understanding. I was being as honest as I possibly could—the only place I drew the line was at the necklace.

She listened intently and didn't say anything until I mentioned seeing him out the window with his new girlfriend, at which point she howled with laughter.

"Sorry," I bristled, "but I'm afraid I don't see the humor here."

Becca smiled up at the sky. "That's Carla. His tutor."

I watched her with suspicion. "His tutor? That's all?"

"No, there's plenty more to her. . . . She's like, thirty-five, an out-of-work actress, and a mother of two."

I could barely formulate any words.

She slung her arm around me. "There's only one thing you need more than a beat-down."

"What's that?" I asked warily.

"Contact lenses."

{ 20 }

Yummy Mummy

As the F train screeched into the Broadway-Lafayette station, the conductor came on the loudspeaker with an authoritative, "Attention, all passengers, will you please make way for the naked young lady to step off the train?" All heads turned my way. And that was when I realized I was stark naked, except for my yellow and blue striped Lacoste socks.

Quelle bummer.

With nothing adorning my neck, my dreams had turned into the stuff of your typical tenth grader's subconscious. Thinking you've left the house naked is nothing compared to being me and realizing you've done so in primary colors. As far as I'm concerned, my color dreams are pointless.

It rained on Monday, and it continued to do so for the next few days, which couldn't have felt more appropriate. The Moons had all but disbanded, Andy wasn't due back in the city until Thursday night, and Becca and Louis were off in la-la land, meeting up every afternoon for hang-out sessions that lasted well into the evening. Stuck with piles of energy that I didn't know what to do with, I ended up spending a good portion of Tuesday night reading Agatha Christie and a back issue of *Elle* on the stationary bike in our building's exercise room. When I got to the magazine's advice column, I could have kicked myself for not reading it sooner—the agony aunt advised a girl who was getting mixed signals from a guy she'd hooked up with to be patient and let him reach out at his own speed.

Whole lot of good that did me now.

When I got back upstairs and called Louis, he took an hour to call me back. He was so distracted that when I asked if he wanted to hang out soon, he answered, "Not much. What's up with you?"

"Can you at least pay attention?" I was losing my cool. Louis was allowed to be as lovesick as he wanted, but did it really have to coincide with the time when Becca and Andy were both pulling away from me? "Why don't you call me when you get your brain back?" It came out like a punch, not that he noticed.

"'Kay," he said, "I'll call you soon. We should get coffee or something."

"Great," I said sarcastically. The only thing I like less than the taste of coffee is "getting coffee" as a social ritual, at least if you're under the age of sixty.

The only person who wanted to get together was Ian, and I wasn't ready to forgive him for dragging me into Reagan's bad graces just yet.

With weather this pissy, biking was out of the question, and the idea of going down to the Brooklyn Bridge for one of my last chances at a nostalgic glimpse of the landmark I knew and loved was as appealing as walking barefoot along a path of thumbtacks. I wish I could say I took advantage of the sudden opening in my schedule by learning how to make my own podcasts or helping Dad organize the annotations for his (almost-finished!) book, but the most productive thing I got up to entailed gazing out of my rain-streaked bedroom window and spying on Professor Ferris, whose apartment was across the courtyard. Turned out Alex's favorite film professor liked to feast on back-to-back episodes of The Real Housewives of Dubai when he thought nobody was looking.

Confrontation not being my strong suit, I did everything I could to avoid running into my current trio of least favorite people at school the next morning. In homeroom, I blocked out Sheila by keeping my eyes closed through Assistant Principal Arnold's daily announcements, and I spent lunch period far away from Alex in the back corner of the library, sneaking bites of my tarragon chicken baguette sandwich while flipping through Hudson's outdated reference books. And the rest of the time, I dragged through the hallways with the hood of my vintage toggle raincoat pulled tight over my head, praying Ian wouldn't see me.

Which might explain how my attempt to quietly slip through the after-school crowd and out of the building was interrupted not by an across-the-lobby wave or even an in-your-face hello, but a full-on tackle. For a split second, I was sure the person clinging to my back was Alex, dying to know what had happened to the girl he was calling "babe" only days earlier, but then I saw the dove-gray calfskin boot swinging around my side.

There was only one person who would show up to Hudson in shoes like that, and in this weather no less.

"You're not fooling anyone with that hangdog stance," Becca said when I shook free of her. "You're calling attention to yourself. If you really want to fade out the world, make like a queen bee and hold your head high."

"Easy for you to say," I replied. "When some of us look up we're still a foot shorter than the rest of the world."

"Whatever. It's all about attitude." Heeding her own advice, she swiftly turned and cut through the crowd of kids milling around outside of the building. "Now stay with me," she said over her shoulder. "Reagan texted to say there's a meeting at the Moonery today at four-thirty and I should make sure to bring you."

My throat clenched as I thought of what awaited at Reagan's hands. Was I going to have to personally drag her dad back to New York to earn her forgiveness?

"Oh good, a fresh hell on the horizon."

"Relax, C," Becca said, still threading through the group. "Ray and I went to sushi last night and I talked some sense into her. She's ready to turn the page."

"And what book would that be?" I was on guard.

"Claire, listen, here's your chance to make amends. She's open to it—she just got off the Dartmouth waiting list."

"She did?" I stopped mid-step. "That's fantastic!"

"For you it is, that's for sure. . . . Speaking of kids getting lucky, watch." She stopped near a kid with what appeared to be an unintentional fauxhawk.

"My productivity all boils down to two words," he was saying. "Vitamin. E."

"That's one word," one of his friends corrected him. "E is just a particle."

I turned back to Becca. "Sorry, but I don't get it," I said, but then I saw her gaze was set elsewhere. I followed it and witnessed a couple getting cozy against the side of a parked Cadillac. I had to squint to make sure I was seeing straight.

No way.

Alex and Sheila were the cuddlers. And they were one beret short of starring in one of Mom and Dad's *L'Amour Toujours!* posters.

"What the . . . Do you think this is some attempt to make me jealous?"

"I wouldn't flatter yourself," Becca said in an undertone. "It's nothing to do with you. He just came up to her and asked if she lived in the professor complex. It's been one magical moment ever since."

This was getting surreal—not only was Alex hot for Sheila Vird, the worst person on the planet, but he was using Washington View Village as his opening gambit. "Give me a second to process this," I muttered as we walked away. "I can't believe I live in the pickup line he's using with Sheila."

Becca pulled her leather bag up her shoulder and cast me a bemused look. "What I can't believe is that you fell for that pickup line, and not too long ago."

She had me there.

On the subway ride up to the Moonery, the energy between us was freer and looser than it had been in ages. We earned more than one irritated glance as we debated which of the four foot ailments featured on the Zopi Podiatry Institute's advertisement we'd rather come down with. A doo-wop group started singing "Little Darlin'" directly to us, and we clapped and shoulder-danced in our seats. By the time we got back on the street, we were in one of those hotheaded moods where everything seems hilarious, and the sight of a scrawny man wearing a THE PARTY STARTS HERE sweatshirt sent us into the craziest fit of giggles.

But the party came to a crashing halt when we walked through the door of Star Foods Emporium and into the clubhouse. The Moonery's office had become a veritable funeral parlor, all pallid faces and naked walls. Everyone's posture had caved in since the last time I'd seen them, and the bulletin boards were sadly barren of the Brooklyn Bridge photos and the Sink Landon–related newspaper clippings and photographs. For some reason, all the girls were holding index cards and markers.

"Did we miss an early spring cleaning or something?" I asked, trying to get at least a smile out of my question. But nobody responded and I had to rephrase it. "Where are all the pictures?"

"We took them down." Sills smiled in name only.

"I can see that, thanks. . . . But why?"

The pit in my stomach told me the answer couldn't be good.

Reagan made a loud sigh. "We've lost any glimmer of hope."

"Besides," said Diana, "we'll be able to see the real Bridge Towers project out the window soon enough."

My heart fell and I cursed myself for not having superglued my necklace in place.

"We're voting on a new club project," Hallie filled me in. "Time to move on."

How could they move on when I was so close to coming through? Well, at least I was close to getting close. I just had to finagle my way into Andy's good graces and then into Helle House.

Necklace or no necklace, I had to keep at it.

Sure, the cameo had given me a leg up. But left to my own devices, was I entirely useless or just handicapped? Fine, *severely* handicapped. Still, it was worth a try.

"You can't pull the plug!" I squealed.

"You heard what happened at Helle House, right?" Reagan asked me.

"Yeah, you guys got caught wearing your disguises and they kicked you out. So what?" I was sounding as motivational as my cuckoo phys ed teacher Coach Blendack.

Reagan looked at me like I was an idiot. "So, we can't get into Helle House anymore."

"Not as guests . . . but that doesn't mean we can't send in uniformed maids or UPS work—" I brought my hand up to where my necklace used to sit and tapped my fingers against bare skin.

"Claire," Poppy cut me off. "*Nobody* can get in there. They've locked down the place. Look." She passed me a BlackBerry that was opened to the Elle Club's homepage.

Emergency advisory: Due to an unexpected legal matter, we have frozen all operations. Members are advised to find other parties to crash for the time being. Unfortunately we cannot offer refunds. Due to high traffic volume, please allow us 30 days to respond to your e-mail. Cross your fingers and C U Soon X O X—The board

I felt the old confused duck expression take over my face. "I don't understand. . . ."

"Word on the street is they got busted serving booze to minors," Diana said.

"Maybe, but I don't completely buy it," said Sills. "I mean—that place is one big liquor cabinet, and has been for decades, and they've never had any trouble in the past. Maybe for some reason they called the cops on themselves."

"Not a bad idea," threw in Reagan. "If Helle House is shut down, we can't get the iPod back."

"My money says they want us to go ahead with the movie shoot so they can bust out the iPod and expose us," said Diana.

"I can just see the newspaper headlines," Poppy said. "*Politicians' Preppy Plot.*"

"What about *High School Friends in High Places?*" asked Hallie.

Becca grimaced. "I can't even imagine what my dad would do if any of this got leaked."

"Me neither," said Sills.

I looked around at all the girls' faces. They were so worried about what a leak's implications for their families would be, they were missing the point: if the Blue Moons weren't able to continue operating, the bridge as we knew it would be gone.

"We've just got to lay low," demurred Diana.

"Or step it up." My voice was overpowering and I cleared my throat. "We can still figure out a way to get into Helle—"

"No point," Poppy interrupted. "The inspection's too soon and there's no chance we're going to get the iPod back. We spoke to the mayor and we called off the whole *Vertigo Girl* plan. No movie on the bridge."

"You don't even want to *try?*" I whimpered.

Reagan crossed her arms and chewed on a corner of her index card. "There's a world of difference between trying when you have a fighting chance and trying when you don't. If there's one thing I learned from my dad, it's that there's no use beating a dead horse."

Diana bridled at the expression. "Do you have to put it that way?"

"But the horse *isn't* dead," I squawked, too upset to take our resident equestrian's objections into account.

"Sorry," Sills said, "but it is. It's deader than dead can be. There's no way to get into their clubhouse, and even if there were, we're not even sure the iPod is still in there. It could be anywhere." She gave me a heavy-lidded stare. "So you tell me, what's left to do?"

Give it a shot, and all the while do everything you can to get the necklace back and have a crazy dream and find the iPod before it's too late. Duh.

But before I could say anything, Sills answered her own question. "We have two options. Get so depressed we can't move . . . or move on."

"Are you kidding?" I exclaimed. "You're going to walk away?"

"We're not total losers." Poppy sounded offended. "We've just come up with a change in plan."

"We've been talking about ways to refocus our energies, little jobs that will keep the momentum going." Diana was starting to sound like an aerobics instructor.

I turned to Becca. "Did *you* know we were giving up like that?"

She didn't need to answer. Her apologetic look said it all.

Reagan handed index cards and huge glitter SEX AND THE CITY: THE BUS TOUR pens to Becca and me.

"Did you actually buy these?" Becca asked incredulously, staring at the glittery pink high heel on the end of her pen.

"Yeah right," Reagan scowled. "They were just randomly lying around my house. Now why don't you stop insulting my writing instruments and come up with a couple of suggestions for quick interim projects? Mayor Irving said he needs the next week to focus on getting through the bridge inspection. Everyone's going to go crazy, but once the reaction calms down, he'll come to us with some ideas for other things we can help out with."

Could this be any more depressing?

"Chin up," Sills told me. "There'll be something else."

Dubious, I bit down on my pen's glittery Dolce & Gabbana bra. As big a place as New York is, how many problems can exist at any given time that rate up there with the fate of the Brooklyn Bridge—or whatever else was on that list on the iPod? Mayor Irving would probably come to the girls asking for help with something lame like planting flowers around the city's dingier streets.

"Just think of a quick project," Reagan told us. "Something to tide us over for now."

Becca was scribbling away, but I could barely even make a scratch of my own.

It wasn't for lack of ideas. Just ones that I could share.

Reagan was the one to read the proposals from the index cards. It was fairly obvious who'd come up with what (only Poppy or Sig could claim the proposal to repaint the skateboarding ramp down by Police Plaza, and Diana had to be the brain behind the plan to spruce up the city's stables in Van Cortlandt Park).

"And this is supposed to make us feel better?" Becca asked. "It's only going to remind us what a disaster this whole thing has become."

"Well, what do you propose?" Reagan asked. "That we throw stones at Helle House?"

"That could work." Becca tugged at her hair as she thought. "We need to think of a solution."

"What about a mental health night?" Poppy suggested. "Nothing but guilty pleasures all around. Maybe it'll loosen us up and give us some inspiration."

I was nervous about losing any more time, but it wasn't like I knew what to do with my time, just that I needed it. Everyone else seemed to love Poppy's suggestion.

For Diana, a mental health night meant taking a bath and reading *The Black Stallion* for the twentieth time. For Sig and Poppy it entailed going to a video game arcade in Times Square. And the rest of the girls, reluctant Reagan included, decided to watch the first season of *America's Next Top Model* on DVD. I would have happily joined them, but Becca had another kind of binge up her sleeve. And she insisted on my coming along.

"What about Louis?" I jabbed.

"You're prettier."

"You're so superficial," I praised her.

"It's still before six, right?" she double-checked when our cab pulled up outside of the International House of Pancakes in downtown Brooklyn. By the doorway, a man had set up a fake Louis Vuitton handbag stall. "Andy says their early-bird special is not to be missed."

I'd never taken Andy for a bargain hunter, but when we crossed the threshold, it all clicked. The scene was yet another postcard from "Only in New York," with brown-suited nine-to-fivers somberly reading the *New York Post* in front of heaping pancake platters.

When we took our seats we couldn't decide on what to order, so we ended up picking the two dishes with the silliest names—the "Rooty Tooty Fresh 'n Fruity" and something called "Buns Away." While we waited, Becca fiddled with her cell phone and tried to contain a smile.

"I know what you're doing," I said.

Her mouth twitched. "Is that right?"

She was such a bad secret keeper it was adorable.

"Give me a little credit." I took a sip from my water glass

and pressed an ice cube against the back of my teeth. "Please tell him I send my regards. And Henry wants his copy of *The Great Brain* back."

She tilted her head. "Who are you talking about?"

I smiled obnoxiously. "Your lover boy."

"Thought so." A look of relief washed over her face and she glanced back down at her phone, leaving me to read the depressing Calorie Counter affixed to the wall.

Finally, a couple of waitresses came over carrying our milk shakes and skyscraper-high plates of carbohydrates. I wasted no time unplugging a trio of paper umbrellas from a stack of pancakes and popping a bite into my mouth.

And then I nearly choked.

Looking over a pile of sweets, it dawned on me there had been a switch of Shuttleworths. Andy was seated directly across from me, his dimple shining like a diamond.

Becca was standing over the table, struggling not to let her smile get too wide. My heart began to palpitate.

"I—I thought you were in Orlando?" I spluttered.

"He texted to tell me his flight just got in, so I told him to swing by," Becca said from above, pausing to shoot me a meaningful glance. "You guys have some major fessing up to do."

My heart bounced giddily.

"Now, if you will excuse me, I'm done with this place." Becca plucked a strawberry off one of the plates. "See you later, suckers!"

"So what's this fascinating-sounding confession of yours Becca was promising me?" Andy's sharp tone was offset by the soft way his green eyes were fixed on me.

"I think she may have got a little ahead of herself," I said. "I don't have anything that horrible to lay at your feet." I cast him a nervous glance.

"Why don't you let me be the judge of that?"

You got your signals crossed. Now you need to uncross them. Kiki's words were fresh in my mind.

I drew in a breath. "The guy you saw me with at Kiki's——"

Andy gave a little head shake. "This story is horrible already."

"Excuse me?"

"If you're talking about that social climber who had his hands all over you, I'm not sure I can think of a single thing about him that isn't horrible."

"But I didn't do anything horrible," I squealed. "I didn't do anything at all. He was just an extra."

He eyed me with a mixture of disbelief and bemusement. "What are you, Martin Scorsese?"

"Will you shut up and listen?" My words came out sharper than I'd intended, and he looked startled. "Sorry. I brought him because the person I wanted to come with me was acting kind of horrible himself. And when I saw him . . . when I saw you," I clarified, my cheeks burning, "with that cute girl . . ."

"What cute girl?"

"It doesn't matter," I said. "Becca explained it was actually your thirty-five-year-old tutor."

Andy's jaw dropped. "You thought I was with Carla?"

I smiled in a way that I hoped would lighten the situation, but he only laughed awkwardly. "Is that all Becca told you?"

"Wait—there's more?"

There was a long silence, and I felt sick as I watched him drown a pancake in syrup. "You *are* hooking up with your tutor?"

He pshawed. "She's actually thirty-six, and our two-and-a-half-year age difference is enough, thank you very much." He helped himself to a bite of pancake. "I didn't want to go to Kiki's party because—" He stopped abruptly, like he'd said too much already. "Because Dean Rabinowitz was going to be there."

"So?"

"He's not my dean."

"I'm totally lost."

He squeezed his eyes tight. "Look . . . I'm not at Columbia this semester. I flunked three of my finals and they're making me finish the year at City College." He shifted in his seat and looked away. "That's why I've been so obsessed with passing my midterms, so I can prove that I can 'apply myself.' My advisor and I made a deal, that if I can do well this semester, I can come back to Columbia. Dean R. signed off on it." He waited a beat. "Make sense?"

I was so stunned I could barely make a sound.

"And I didn't want you to find out." His voice was cracking.

Man, he was cute. And man, was I a paranoid freak. How had I managed to misinterpret *everything*?

"Why were you afraid?" I asked. "What were you afraid I was going to do?"

"It's not about what you'd *do*. I just didn't want you to know. You have no idea how embarrassing this whole thing is."

"I don't care," I said. "I mean, of course I care that it bothers you. But I don't care if your grades slipped."

He waited a second before smiling softly. "I'm not quite sure 'slipped' covers flunking *three* classes out of four. I just thought you'd think I was a fool for messing up."

"I don't care, I don't care, I don't care." I said it like a magic spell.

"What if I kissed you?" He paused. "Would you care about that?"

"No," I blurted, my head buzzing. "I mean yes. I mean, please . . ."

I wanted a kiss so badly I could barely remember how to finish off the sentence, let alone what the question had been.

He leaned in as far as he could and I reached over to meet him halfway, over a pile of pancakes. Strangely, the skin by my collarbone warmed up, as if the necklace hadn't gone anywhere.

Maybe things weren't so hopeless after all.

{ 21 }

The End of Anonymous

When our waitress dropped off our check, I saw she'd written *Thanx guys!!* and added two smiley faces—one wearing a top hat, the other a mound of squiggles that resembled Whitney Houston's "How Will I Know"–era hairdo.

"Am I the only person who feels uncomfortable when people draw things on the check?" I asked.

Andy folded his brow in befuddlement as he examined it. "They're not bad drawings."

"That's not the point," I said. "She shouldn't have to try so hard. She's working hard enough as it is and . . . it just makes me feel funny, that's all." I trailed off and waited while Andy slung his duffel bag over his shoulder. He looked even cuter than usual with his tan and a freckly nose.

"No, I think I get it," he told me when we got outside. "I have random things that make me feel a little sad too."

I eyed him suspiciously. "Like what?"

"Lots of stuff . . ."

Traffic was backed up all the way to the Brooklyn Bridge and the sky was glittering with stars.

He flagged down a cab and opened the door for me. "Disney World, for one."

I laughed as he scooted in next to me.

"Your trip wasn't good?"

"It was okay when I was hanging out with my grandparents on the golf links, but then I thought it would do me some good to check out the Magic Kingdom."

"The magic was gone?" I asked.

"You could say that. So were the kids." He took my hand and kept talking.

Stay cool, Claire.

"It was mostly fully grown people posing for their wedding pictures with Goofy and Minnie. It was creepy. Please tell me your parents didn't go to Euro Disney for their honeymoon."

I assured him he was safe. "Didn't I tell you they eloped in some chapel in Niagara Falls and Kiki has never forgiven them?"

Andy laughed. "Of course." Our car shot up to the top of the bridge, then stalled by a snarl of traffic. The driver was muttering about how he should have known better than to take a rush-hour fare to Manhattan and Andy was tossing him a steady supply of "Sorry, mans."

We were on top of the Brooklyn Bridge, which, given what I knew about the weak cable, probably would have felt a little more frightening if I weren't sitting next to Andy and letting him play with my fingers. The city spread out before us like a feast and I was wishing I could freeze the moment and make it last ten years.

Andy and I started talking about some old detective book he'd read in Florida that he thought I'd like and I was reminded of how easy talking to him could be. He made me feel heard and he made me laugh. Next thing I knew the car was pulling up outside the Waldorf. Andy leaned in to kiss me, and I heard cars honking.

"Let's go!" the driver said. "This isn't a motel on wheels."

"Tell Kiki I said hi," Andy called as I hopped out.

"She'll be happy to hear it," I told him.

As for how happy, you have no idea.

I rushed toward the hotel door and was feeling so floaty I almost forgot to respond to the bellhop's "Evening, Claire." In the elevator, I tried to pull myself together, fixing my hair and taking in a deep, bracing breath.

"Well, there you are," Kiki said when I appeared at the door. She sounded vaguely peeved, as if I was showing up late for something.

"Did we have a date?" I asked, and walked over to the couch. I straightened my back and neatly folded my hands in my lap. I needed her help getting my necklace back, and I didn't want to waste any time being lectured about how nobody wants to spend time around a "Slumpy Susie."

"No, I just had a feeling you'd be passing by." Kiki poured herself a refill from her silver martini shaker and tottered over to her favorite spot on the couch, by the I DON'T REPEAT GOSSIP SO SIT CLOSE needlepoint pillow. "You must be tired, dear."

"What makes you say that?" I sat up straight as a lamppost.

"Oh, all that groveling and making your case with the young Mr. Shuttleworth."

I felt my face go cranberry. "Do you have a spy following me around or something?"

"Nothing so glamorous! Just a custodian." She paused to savor my confusion. "He called to say this little trinket turned up during the post-party cleanup." She pulled my cameo necklace out of her pocket and dangled it under the lamp's glow. The onyx background appeared unscratched and the ivory profile was white as fresh snow.

"Can I see it?" I was practically foaming at the mouth.

"Of course you may. Now I hope you'll keep a better eye on it." A heavy pause. "And on your beau."

"You bet I will."

"That's my girl." She fastened the necklace back in its rightful place and I felt as if I'd had a two-hour-long massage.

When I got home that night, I went straight to bed—blue jeans and eyeliner and everything. I was so psyched to get back to my dream life I didn't even remember to turn out the lights until I was already under the covers.

"Henry!" I yelled out, and he came pattering into my room in no time, wearing his ASTERIX ET LES VIKINGS T-shirt over a pair of canary yellow Farmhouse School sweatpants I'd long since outgrown.

We worked out a trade: a flick of the light switch in exchange for a slightly deformed Lindt truffle I'd bought half-off at Bleecker Gourmet. "If you give Didier and Margaux a pinch of fish food, I'll toss in the remainder of an obscenely sized Mickey Mouse sugar cookie," I said, remembering the oh-so-romantic plastic-wrapped dessert Andy had unloaded on me in the cab.

"Deal."

A bunch of old-school gangsters were seated around a bright white table, smoking cigars and laughing heartily. I was wearing a slinky black turtleneck dress and coming around with a tray of gray cocktails. When I got to the man at the head of the table I saw that he was hiding something in his lap: an art magazine with his own portrait on the cover. And then, as if that wasn't weird enough, he winked at me—from the page.

Okay, I got it: he was a gangster, just like Al Capone, the dead gangster who was supposedly watching over the iPod. He was trying to tell me something about where it was hidden.

But why couldn't he just tell me, then? And I'm sorry, but the fact that he wasn't a real person was no excuse.

Feeling exhausted—blissfully exhausted, that is—I secretly chugged from Mom's J'♥ PARIS coffee cup before leaving for school, and turned the dream over and over in my head all day long. What was most frustrating was the fact that there were parts of it I understood—the snow-white table was obviously straight out of Helle House Decor 101, and the gangsters had to be stand-ins for the lovely ladies who ran the show there. But for the love of dark chocolate, why was the guy in the portrait winking at me? Was it a taunt? A come-on? Was I supposed to be on the lookout for people with blinking problems?

My brain felt as fuzzy as unbrushed teeth, and Hudson's never-ending background noise of chalk marks and atonal teachers wasn't helping matters. I needed silence. I needed space.

In other words, I needed some quality time with my Schwinn bicycle.

If only it were so easy.

When school let out, Becca cornered me by the bike stand to tell me there was a listening party for Wiley Martins's new album. "It's called *My Secret Girlfriend* and the cover art apparently has a girl who's the spitting image of Sills," she told me with a lively look of the eye. "It's at Global Media and Reagan said she can get us all in. You down?"

I'd had enough of Global Media, hadn't I? "I wish I could," I told her, "but I have this thing I have to do . . . for Kiki."

She pursed her lips and blew her bangs out of her eyes. "What if I said Andy might come by?"

I looked down. "I'd say you were exploiting your family connections."

"Isn't that what they're there for?" She smiled barefacedly.

And at that moment it occurred to me that family connections could blur your vision to the point of blindness. Even though the girls were upset about losing the opportunity to carry off their big plan, it was painfully clear their hearts were no longer in it. Their parents' reputations were at stake, and that overrode the issue at hand, as if opportunities to keep the city's crown jewels intact came around every other Tuesday. The task of making everything better fell to me.

"Well, say you'll come to the after party. It's at this converted pickle store in the Lower East Side."

I hopped on my bike and kicked off. "Sounds weird, but possible. I'll call you later." And then I gave her that ridiculous telephone hand signal she'd made the first day back to school.

My plan was to go up to the Seventy-ninth Street Boat Basin, which Louis had been telling me about for months on end. When I need to think things through, there's nothing like a bath or a quiet moment by the river.

I turned down Delancey Street and waited at a red light by the Bowery when a bus growled up from behind, engulfing me in the most obnoxious cloud of exhaust.

And then there it was. An ad for Christie's auction house was on the side of the bus. And what was shown on the ad but a picture of a pair of eyes—one open and one shut. I was being winked at.

Bells went off in my head louder than at the end of a boxing round.

Christie's. The auction house that had the Al "Scarface" Capone estate auction that Kiki and her friends all went to a couple of years ago. My dream about the winking gangster. What if this was a clue about where the girls were hiding the iPod? Could it have to do with something from the Al Capone estate?

Wouldn't hurt to check. And thanks to the miracle of public records, I could probably find out.

I raced home and barely said hi to my parents as I ran into my room and booted up my computer. When my Internet browser came up, I typed in: "Christie's Capone auction."

Lo and behold: the centerpiece of the auction had indeed been the original Scarface's cigar box.

A cigar—just like the one the gangster in my dream had been smoking!

I read a press report confirming an anonymous bidder's purchase of the original Scarface's silver cigar box, "one of the most important historical relics of our time."

There was no way things were neatly falling into place for absolutely no reason. Unless my hunches were totally wrong, the iPod was hiding out in Al Capone's cigar box. Weirdest of all, the price it fetched was one hundred thousand dollars. An inconceivable sum for a bunch of girls who couldn't even pay their pizza bills.

And that was when it dawned on me. What if the Helle Housers weren't clued in to the Moons' relationship with Mayor Irving? There'd been so many people at Helle House's film night event, who was to say they were all actual members? What if the girl we'd seen on the phone at Helle House was a lowly visitor, or a member who happened to be in cahoots with the *real* culprit?

Had to be.

But I was getting ahead of myself. That real culprit took

anonymity pretty seriously. He or she was truly impossible to pin down—there were hundreds of articles about the auction, but nary a trace on who'd bought the box.

Talk about close but no cigar.

I'd gotten as far as I could on my own. I needed help—and fast.

Next thing I knew, I was locking my bike outside Global Media's headquarters. I made my way to the reception booth and tried to bop my head in a shaggy way that a music journalist might, and mumbled something about the "listening party."

The security guy scrunched his face at me and I prayed he didn't recognize me from my egg-pelting episode. "Who you with?"

"Um . . . Orbspot." I bopped my head some more. "It's a blog."

"What isn't?" He rolled his eyes and shooed me through to the elevator bank.

I made my way to a conference room on the forty-fifth floor. Sig was listening to a pair of headphones and didn't seem to notice I was there.

I pulled back her headphone and she looked startled to see me. "You got a second?" I asked.

She cast me an expression that told me she knew something major was up. "Sure."

We slipped out and walked to the women's room at the end of the hall. It was brightly lit and empty, but for the muffled sounds of sobbing coming from one of the stalls. We exchanged awkward looks as I passed her the printout from the Christie's Web site. She looked at me, dumbfounded. "Al Capone's cigar box . . . ?"

"You know how that girl at Helle House said that Al Capone was looking after it? I think that's where the iPod is stashed away," I said. Realizing I would sound crazy if I said I'd had a dream about a gangster cigar party, I added, "Everything else of Capone's that was sold at the auction was destroyed in a fire."

She looked at me skeptically, and I embellished the lie, "I read an article about it on the *New York Times* Web site." I went on, "Though I'm not sure it belongs to the Helle Housers. If you'll look at the cigar box's price tag you'll—"

"See there's real money behind it," she said, finishing my thought. She narrowed her eyes like a cowboy in an old Western.

"The auction house has records in an online database, but it's user restricted." I pointed to the URL on the top of the page. "You think you can hack in there and see who bought the cigar box?"

She folded the paper in quarters and stuck it in her back pocket. "Must you make this so easy?"

{ 22 }

To Catch a Sugar Fiend

As I walked through the lobby of Global Media's headquarters, thunder boomed. But when I looked outside, I saw that the sky was still blue and there wasn't a drop of rain. It took me a second to realize that the sound was coming from a video monitor over my head. The actor in the *Toro Boy* promo was prettier than Miss Venezuela, with bone-white teeth and a swath of dark, shiny hair. Ian was going to need a familiar shoulder to cry on when he found out about this. It was time to make my amends.

I was downtown twenty minutes later. Lucky for me, Ian is a creature of habit. I found him in his usual spot in the back of Propeller Comics—only this time, he wasn't curled up on the ratty tan couch and reading yet another comic book he wasn't going to pay for.

The space was now doubling as an art school of sorts. Ian's couch had been usurped by four little kids who had notebooks in their laps, their legs dangling nowhere close to the carpet. Ian was standing next to a huge drawing pad on an easel, his enormous army coat accentuating his tiny physique.

"Angry is the easiest!" he was saying as he drew a stick figure. "All you have to do is make their arms go up the air. Like this." He used his marker to add two dashes to the figure and grinned. "Does this guy look like he's fixing for a fight or what?"

The kids laughed, which only fired Ian up more. "There's hundreds where that came from—goofy and naughty and sleep—" And then he looked up and saw me. I got one of the best smiles I've ever seen.

He turned back to the kids. "And sometimes when you're in the middle of drawing, you might change your mind," he said. "Like maybe you're drawing Mr. Angry Guy and then you decide you want him to be happy. What do you do?"

"Give him Prozac!" yelled out one of the students.

Ian seemed taken aback. "Okay . . . any other ideas?"

"Tell him something to cheer him up!" I creaked from my spot by the Calvin and Hobbes display. "Like . . . his friend is sorry she temporarily erased herself. She's ready to commit to ink."

Ian grinned, then turned around and started scribbling furiously over the stick figure's hands. "You can also build on the picture to add feelings." And when he stepped away, I saw what he'd done: he'd added two bouquets of daisies. "You see?" He was focusing on the kids, but he wasn't fooling anyone—the flowers were all mine.

• • •

When Sig called me with her report that night, her words chilled me to the core. It's not that I was entirely surprised to hear that Sink Landon was the mysterious cigar box collector. Who else stood to benefit from holding up the platinum bridge fortification?

Still, there was something irreversible about hearing her say his name out loud. This wasn't just a competition between a couple of girls' clubs. Sink was a dangerous guy, and not just because of his plan to diminish the prettiest city on earth. I was scared. Andy had hinted that Sink wasn't above downright thuggery, and I had no reason to believe he had a policy of sparing half-French girl detectives.

Anxiety coursed through me, but I tried to keep my tone even. "Does it say anything else about him?"

"Just that his account at the auction house has been frozen," Sig said. "Looks like somebody had a little case of bouncing checks. But that was after he bought the cigar box."

That got a chuckle out of me, though I was too scared to laugh heartily. Plus, there was still a major piece that didn't compute: why was a member of Helle House talking on the phone to Sink? Unless . . .

"Say, Sig." I was feeling pretty crafty by this point. "Any chance I can convince you to check out one more thing?"

"You kidding? I live for this stuff."

"Well, we still need to figure out—"

"What a girl at Helle House was doing talking to Sink?"

"Exactly." I sat there breathing hotly into the phone while Sig surfed around and accessed a few more protected files. "Got your answer," she said a few minutes later. "Check your e-mail. It's all there."

I tapped my fingers and smiled into the phone while I waited for my in-box to refresh.

• • •

There was only one thing to do: share our findings with the other Moons, who were all at the Wiley Martins record party. Sig and I met up forty-five minutes later outside the Pickle Factory, the latest in a string of struggling old New York concerns to be appropriated by well-meaning hipsters. Like the old piano and hat-blocking stores that had recently been converted into nightclubs trafficking in nostalgia, the Pickle Factory relied on its old-world accoutrements for ambience: the black-and-white photographs of Frank the pickle man hung over the newly painted walls, and the original pickle barrels had been turned upside down and converted into bar stools.

My Secret Girlfriend, Wiley Martins's unfortunately named new album, was blasting on the speakers, but nobody seemed to be paying much attention to it. There was something far more interesting to talk about.

Sills and Wiley were seated at a roped-off table, ignoring the masses that surrounded them and confirming the Moonwatcher.net rumors. They couldn't have looked more ill-matched—Wiley was a big scruffy mess, and Sills was the epitome of old Hollywood glamour, with her long dress and her hair set in huge waves. And yet, they were also the picture of young love, stroking hands and nuzzling sweetly.

"You know what this means, right?" Becca appeared at my side.

"That the Helle Housers had it right about Sills and Wiley being a couple?" I asked.

"Of course they did. Rumors are always true—except when they're about girls and their effeminate opera coaches." She cleared her throat. "But I'm talking about something different."

The answer hit me with a start.

"Nuh-uh!" I cried, remembering the Moons' house rule against cavorting with celebrities. "Sills is out of the Moons?"

Becca nodded crisply. "Handed in her boat today. I guess she didn't see much point in keeping her affair with Wiley on the D.L. when the Moons are falling apart at the seams."

"But I came—" Just then Reagan interrupted us from behind. She was wearing a transparent white button-down shirt over a long black dress. "You guys must be talking about Wiley and Sills. Isn't it romantic?"

"Sure," Becca drawled. "For Sills it is."

She sounded uncharacteristically uncharitable.

"What's the deal?" Reagan said. "You could have any guy you wanted."

"Is that what you think is bothering me?" Becca was losing her patience by the second. "Earth to Reagan: we've lost one of our best members, and I just heard Diana's thinking about dropping out too."

Reagan's eyes widened. "Who's her mystery celebrity boyfriend? Some horse?"

"Marc Jacobs," Becca whispered.

"Isn't he gay?" I butted in.

Becca rolled her eyes at me. "It's not like that. He wants her to be the poster girl for his new cruelty-free clothing line."

"Too bad clothes aren't her thing," I muttered.

"Meanwhile, I know what the, like, two remaining Moons can do," Becca said. "Write up an obituary for *Vertigo Girl*. And for New York as we know it."

Reagan tried to comfort Becca with a halfhearted back rub. "It's not the end of the world. We'll come up with something good."

I could barely speak and Sig elbowed me in the side, reminding me of my mission. "Guys," I said. "We might not have to come up with something else after all. I have some good news about the Al Capone mystery."

Reagan looked at me like I was crazy.

"What is it?" Becca asked.

"Let's go somewhere quiet," I suggested, scanning the room. My eyes stopped at a STORAGE door in the back of the club. "Follow me," I told them, weaving my way through the crowd.

"You can't just barge into restricted areas," Reagan said from behind. "When I got the publicist to put our names on the list I promised we'd lay low." Contempt colored her voice, and I knew she hadn't forgiven me yet.

"Don't worry," I told her as I lifted the velvet divider. "I won't light anything on fire."

We found ourselves in a storage room crammed with boxes of paper napkins and beer. Everything was new, but the smell of dill and brine still lingered.

"It's like a sauna in here," Reagan moaned. She removed her jacket and set it on top of a pile of boxes.

We heard the creaky sound of a door opening and Reagan put the heels of her hands to her eyes. "What did I tell you?"

But it was just the other Moons. I was surprised to see them there.

"Get over here and close the door," Becca instructed them. "Claire has something to share with us. She knows where the iPod is."

"Well, not precisely, but we're getting warmer." Careful to keep my voice low, I told them all what Sig and I had discovered. "The only thing left from Christie's Al Capone auction is his cigar box. And it sold for a hundred grand to Sink Landon."

Becca paled. "You've got to be kidding me."

"That's only the half of it," I said. "Ever heard of Violet Gore Landon?" My mouth curled into a smile. "She's Sink's fourteen-year-old daughter. Once I realized the box was his, I had to place the girl from Helle House he'd been talking to on the phone. And I figured it was either his daughter or his girl-friend. And since he's, like, fifty . . . Sig went through all the private school directories until we found her. She's a fresh-man at Regents Academy and her yearbook picture matches the face of the girl I saw that night."

"And that's not all," Sig added. "She's also an awesome web designer. Regents Academy's site was made by VGL Designs."

I looked around the circle and waited for it to sink in. "If you add it all up, it looks like we got played. Violet must've been talking to her father that night. And she must've been the one to post all those taunting clues on the Helle House Web site, like the one about the 'bridge to paradise' and making 'movie night' vague enough to throw us off. She wanted us to believe it was a Helle House project."

"You don't think she told her fellow club members?" asked Becca.

"No way," I said. "Those girls are as unsubtle as bad body spray. She had to be tight-lipped. There's too much at stake."

"Nice work, Voyante!" Reagan clasped my shoulder. "I thought your skill was curtseying and minding your p's and q's. I had no idea you were also a little conspiracy theorist." She let out a weird guffaw and it suddenly dawned on me she wasn't so nice after all.

My palms were getting wet. "There's no conspiracy," I told her. "It's just facts. Can't you see? Sink owns the Al Capone cigar box and he's been using his daughter to keep us distracted by try-ing to make it seem like the Helle Housers are the ones out to get us. The only thing we don't know is how he knew there was an iPod in the first place. The only people who were clued in to any of this were Mayor Irving's people and the club members, right?"

I could tell something was clicking inside Becca's head. "Sink's the biggest developer since Donald Trump. He probably knows somebody in City Hall. We have to trip him up."

"Don't you think we're getting ahead of ourselves?" Reagan said. "You have a link between some developer with a lisp and an overpriced piece of gangster memorabilia. But where's the smoking gun?"

"What else do you want?" Becca came to my defense. "A videotaped confession? There are too many clues pointing to Sink. It has to be him."

"Then tell me this," Reagan said to me. "Have you actually *seen* him with the pink iPod?"

"Not exactly, but—"

"And you hacked into all these private networks?"

My head bobbed up and down.

"You *are* naive, aren't you," Reagan muttered. "Sneaking into some girls' clubhouse is one thing, but Christie's is a multinational company. They probably have ways of tracking this stuff down. If there's one thing my dad has taught me, it's don't do anything incriminating on a computer. It'll come back to bite you in the ass."

"All we did was—" Sig started.

"I don't want to have to give up my spot at Dartmouth because some new blood got it in her head to do something this stupid."

Speaking of blood, mine was boiling. Becca and I exchanged confused glances.

"You don't get it, do you?" Reagan narrowed her eyes at me. "Hacking is illegal. It's larceny."

"Burglary," Sig corrected her.

"Whatever." She grabbed an industrial-sized jar of maraschino cherries from a shelf and pried off the lid. After downing a dozen or so cherries, Reagan licked her fingers clean. "As much fun as hanging out in this old pickle barrel is, I have a party to return to."

I could hardly comprehend what I was seeing. Reagan, who

was usually the picture of composure, was going bananas. "I'll see you back out there," she said, and stormed off without even remembering to take her jacket.

"Dude," Poppy said after Reagan had left the scene. "That was some freaky stuff."

Sig said something about filling an IV drip with maple or strawberry syrup—I'm not quite sure. My mind was stuck on something far more disturbing to follow anything else closely. I remembered an image from that dream I'd had about trying to find a bathroom in that long corridor. Not only had the girl been wearing a long black dress, like Reagan, but she'd been washing her hands in a *sink*.

And then I replayed Reagan's words. *Some developer with a lisp.*

"Guys, how many of you knew that Sink Landon had a lisp?" My question earned a ring of shell-shocked expressions.

Becca's lips were shaking. "Wait—how'd *she* know?"

"I'm no expert on speech impediments," I said after a loaded moment, "but it would follow . . ."

"That the two of them have been talking," Sig completed my thought.

Hallie was incredulous. "That doesn't make any sense. Why would she do that?"

"Maybe it's something to do with her daddy issues?" This was Diana.

Poppy cast her a dark look. "Maybe we can save the psycho-analyzing for later? We need to stop her." She started for the door then turned back to make sure we were following her. "Let's get Reagan. Now!"

Like I needed any encouragement. I'd only been waiting for this moment since the beginning of time.

{ 23 }

Hook, Line, and Sink Her

We ran through the party and burst onto the street. It was empty except for a pack of smokers milling around outside of some bar called the Mermaid's Foot. My pulse quickening, I looked both ways, then up at the fancy apartment building across the street. Nothing helpful there, just a whole lot of televisions tuned to the same cheesy dance competition. Exhaling in desperation, I looked higher up. The moon seemed to be taunting me from its perch five million miles away. I didn't know if I'd ever felt smaller or the world had ever felt bigger, but this much was sure: my chances of finding Reagan were shrinking by the second.

Sig was spinning around in circles. "Now what?"

"She's got to be calling him now," said Diana. "Sink gets the heads-up, he hides the iPod somewhere safe, and just like that, we're toast."

Becca dialed a number on her cell phone and frowned a moment later. "No answer."

"She left her jacket at the party," Sig remembered. "Her phone must be in it."

"She must have gone to find him in person," I reasoned.

"If you want to call him a person." Poppy played around on her PDA's Web browser, and came up with the addresses for Sink's home and office.

"And don't forget about that steakhouse that he was bragging about being his second office in that *Post* article," I said.

"Silty's," Becca remembered. "Definitely worth a shot. You and Hallie can go there. I'll go to his real office. Poppy, you take his apartment. Sig, you can check out Reagan's place. If all else fails, she'll go home at some point."

Our plan settled, everyone set off. Well, with one exception.

"You coming or what?" Hallie asked me.

I hesitated. My throat was burning up. Great. I'd developed a lethal case of tonsillitis at the very moment I was most needed. But then I swallowed and realized I was perfectly fine. It was the gold around my neck that was on fire.

My necklace was trying to tell me something.

"Okay, okay," I said more to myself than Hallie, surveying the scene one last time and looking for a glimmer of hope. All my black-and-white dreams were pinwheeling through my head.

C'mon, c'mon, will something please fall into place?

"Dude, she's not coming back here to find *us*." Hallie reached out and started to pull me down the block. I shook free of Hallie and took a step backward. The throat stinging let up— and no prescription painkillers were involved!

And then it clicked.

The problem with the plastic mermaid outside the Mermaid's Foot was that it was so big I'd nearly ignored it. Of course—it was related to my mermaid dream. The connection snapped through me like a rubber band and I bolted across the street.

I spotted Reagan through the window, leaning over the bar and playing with her hair.

"What the hell is—" Hallie stopped speaking when she caught up to me. She saw what I was looking at.

"Take that and stay out here." I pointed to a cracked hockey stick that somebody had put out with the trash. "If she tries to make a run for it, it'll come in handy."

"Huh?" She stared at me. "Can I fly with it?"

"No, but if you trip her, *she'll* fly."

I opened the door and approached the bar just in time to see Reagan and the bartender exchange a one-dollar bill for quarters. "Phone's in the back." He pressed the change into the palm of her hand. "It's a little glitchy!" he added a moment later. "If the service goes out, just knock 'er around a little."

The back corridor smelled like old lettuce and vinegar. I leaned against a dark velvet curtain and watched her punch in a number. Her eyes darted over to the main room, then she turned away.

Excited beyond belief, I stuffed my fingers in my mouth.

"Sink?" she said after a tense silence. "It's me."

And even if I'd misheard it, I would've known I was nearing my victory lap. My necklace shifted by a millimeter and snuggled perfectly against my collarbone.

I could take a hint.

I sprang out of my hiding spot and reached out to press down the phone's receiver.

"Hello?" Reagan must not have seen me come up from be-hind. "You there?" she hissed into the phone.

"Sink isn't, but I am," I rasped.

She pivoted around to see my stubby little hands cutting off the connection.

"I hear this phone's a little glitchy," I murmured and waited for her to come up with a response.

"It's not what you think." She could hardly get the words out.

"It doesn't matter what I think. I heard you say his name."

A look of panic crossed her face and she glanced at the door.

"Don't even try it." I grabbed her elbow. "I'm not flying solo here. The outside's covered."

I was feeling surer of myself by the second.

Her face twitched and she tottered back to lean against the wall. "Fine. I'm the bad guy and you're the little miss perfect who saves the day. Happy?"

"I've had worse days." I smirked.

My euphoric victory was undercut by the tear that came rolling down her cheek. And then she started with the full-fledged crying. I looked away in disappointment. I wanted things to be cut-and-dry.

"If you want to paint me as the villain, go ahead," she spluttered through a torrent of tears. "But you have no idea what a madman he is. He's totally sick. He found out all this stuff about me and he threatened to—"

"Save it, Ray." I could feel my resolve starting to go soft and I didn't trust myself. "I wouldn't waste your breath on just me. Let me see the rest of those quarters you've got. There are a few people we need to call."

She bit down on her bottom lip and relented.

After I'd made the necessary phone calls, I brought Reagan out to the front of the bar and we joined Hallie at a table. While we waited for the gang to show up, our silence was palpably uncomfortable.

Becca was the first to arrive. Without saying a word, she took a seat directly across from Reagan. She had a look in her eyes that I'd seen a few times before—Becca isn't good at angry. Instead, she gets hurt.

Finally, Poppy entered, holding Reagan's jacket. "You forgot this," she said, pushing it across the table. Reagan dug around the pockets and made a face when she couldn't find her cell phone. "It slipped out," Poppy said curtly. "I put it in my bag." She slowly retrieved Reagan's phone and handed it to her.

"Thanks," Reagan sniffled.

"This isn't a bus stop, girls," the bartender reminded us, and Becca got up to fetch us a round of Cokes. She carried the glasses over in batches, and by her third trip, all the other girls were at the table. Everyone was brimming with questions, but I wouldn't let Reagan start until Becca was seated.

Becca pushed a glass with a lime wedge Reagan's way. "Yours is diet."

"My favorite." The sugar fiend's tone was laced with sarcasm, but she must have been parched—she drained it in one sip. "Okay," Reagan said. "I'm ready. Go ahead, throw your stones."

"Enough of this victim stuff," I said. "Just tell us what happened, will you?"

Reagan's shoulders shot up to her ears. "Sink had me cornered. He knew my weak spot better than I did. By the time he came to me I was so freaked out I couldn't think straight."

"You can't tell a story straight either." Poppy squeezed

her lemon wedge into her drink. "Start from the beginning, will you?"

Reagan rested her elbows on the table and balanced her head on her hands. She must have been perspiring pretty heavily—the roots of her hair were rising up into a snow-white halo. "First off, Sink knew that the Blue Moons were up to something."

Now we were getting somewhere.

"Who told him?" I asked.

"He figured it out on his own. His projects were getting bungled because of last-minute donations that were coming from a trust fund called Pookie Holdings."

"And he was able to link it to us?" Becca said.

Reagan nodded. "To Gummy Salzman. The *New York Sun* obit mentioned her nickname. And he knew Gummy was a big Moon supporter."

Diana groaned. "Why didn't we think of that?"

"Believe me, I wish you had," said Reagan. "He was prepared to get flack for the Bridge Towers plan, and he's smarter than he looks. He'd had his eye on us and he had a feeling we were going to throw a wrench in his plan somehow, so he did research on all of us. And"—her eyes darted away—"he discovered that one of us had a serious problem."

One of us had a problem? As far as I was concerned, we were *all* up crap's creek.

"What problem?" Poppy was speeding her along.

Reagan's eyes darted away shamefully. "I'd rather not say."

But she didn't need to. My thoughts cast back to the new goodies that always seemed to be at the top of Reagan's bag—random lipsticks and candies and souvenir pens that nobody in her right mind would actually pay for. And then there was the Whole Foods chocolate-taking incident, and the time she grabbed all the magazines at the hair salon. Reagan made off with pretty much anything that wasn't superglued in place. And then how could I forget the dream that had started all this? The night I was having my predate wardrobe meltdown at H&M, I'd seen the ship that had led me right to the original girl with the pale hair and sticky fingers: Reagan.

"Allow me," I whispered. "You're a kleptomaniac."

Reagan tried to glare at me but her expression didn't completely harden. "How did you know?"

"Just a hunch," I tossed out as nonchalantly as my bad acting gene would allow.

Reagan looked around the table, as if expecting one of us to arrest her. But the faces that met her carried expressions of concern.

"I have a little record," she peeped. "And college admissions committees don't take kindly to these sorts of things."

"So that's why you were wait-listed everywhere?" Poppy asked.

"I wasn't even wait-listed." Reagan grabbed the nearest full-sugar Coke and drained it. "I just couldn't face the truth."

"So you lied about getting into Dartmouth?" Becca said.

I thought back to all the times I'd heard Reagan drop Dartmouth into conversation. She had more than one problem.

"No, that was true." She grinned joylessly. "Sink's alma mater. He's, like, their biggest donor."

I couldn't believe it. "So he came to you and said 'I'll get you into college if you'll rat out the Moons'?"

Reagan breathed in hard. "You have no idea how sorry I am." Tears gushed down her face.

Poppy tilted her head. "Sorry doesn't cut it."

I know I should have been basking in post-gotcha victory, but the whole thing just made me feel blue. What did it matter if I'd fingered Reagan? Sink had beat us at our game.

I tugged on my necklace without really thinking about it.

The cameo was the best kind of warm, like freshly drawn bathwater or April sunshine.

Call me crazy, but it was trying to tell me something. And then lightning struck.

"Ray," I said. "Sink has no idea that we're on to you, right?"

She shrugged. "Not unless he's got this bar wiretapped."

Even though she was joking, I ran my hands along the underside of the table just to make sure. Never had a wad of a stranger's chewed-up gum felt so beautiful.

"So it's actually the best thing on earth that it's you who's collaborating with Sink and not some random stranger," I said.

Everyone looked at me like I was off my rocker.

"We can get the iPod back," I said. "Ray, where does he keep the cigar box?"

Reagan fixed a hard stare on me that was meant to freeze me out but instead just gave away how scared she was feeling.

For a second there, I felt a twinge of compassion. I needed to remind myself of my priorities.

"Reagan," I said, shifting to sotto voce. "If you don't fix this, it's going to get a whole lot worse than your not being able to go to Dartmouth."

She flicked her hair over her shoulder. "How's that?"

"How do you think all of this would go over with your dad?" I asked. "You think he'd be happier to hear about your run-ins with the law from you or from us?"

Reagan's skin drained of the little color it had.

"And what about the fact the only way you got into a decent college was by aligning yourself with one of the city's most notorious scumbags?" Becca threw in. "Not exactly a surefire recipe for improved father-daughter relations."

Reagan blinked hard and slumped deep into her seat. "I hope you guys are enjoying yourselves."

"Not really," I said. "I can think of a whole lot more enjoyable ways to be spending my time. I know your problems with your father make it hard for you to see any of this clearly. But try to take a step outside yourself and your college admissions troubles. Imagine yourself in ten years, looking out of the window of your Midtown office."

"N-not gonna happen," Reagan stammered. "I want to live in London when I'm older."

"Whatever." I ignored her. "Imagine you're on a high enough floor to see that Bridge Towers, the biggest blight on the city, is out there, and the Brooklyn Bridge is all but invisible. And you think to yourself, *Ahh, I did this*." Reagan squirmed. "Is that really the mark you want to leave on the world?"

"Ray," Becca picked up for me. "This is your chance to dig yourself out of this mess. So what if your dad is mad at you for a little while and you don't go to college next year? You're crazy smart and great schools will take you after you've come clean and gone into whatever reform program you need to."

"That's easy for you to say," Reagan replied at last. "Nobody's going to want to go near me. I'm a walking liability."

"You're making it sound like you're a mass murderer," Poppy interjected. "You've had a few bouts with in-store security guards. Big deal. My cousin Justine got kicked out of Andover for selling booze to freshmen, and she's at Cornell."

"I don't believe you," murmured Reagan, fiddling with the buttons on her shirt.

"Has it ever occurred to you that your dad isn't the only one who's too hard on you?" asked Becca.

Reagan fixed her a confused look. "You're just saying that because you need my help. What's it to you if I get my butt into college?"

"Honestly," Diana said, "not much anymore. Are you going to get us out of this mess or do you want us making more trouble for you and your dad?"

Reagan was silent, but her body language spoke volumes. Her slumped shoulders and extended belly could only mean one thing: defeat.

"Fine," she whispered. "Happy?"

Becca looked satisfied, and I felt a wave of pleasure roll over me too.

I cleared my throat "Okay, Reagan. Now where is the cigar box?"

It took Reagan a moment to speak. "His office," she said. "Under his signed *Godfather* poster. He loves anything to do with gangsters."

Takes one to love one.

"So you can visit him at his office," I said. "Pretend you're there to talk about Dartmouth's freshman orientation and replace the iPod with another one."

Becca didn't even wait for Reagan to agree. "We'll go to the twenty-four-hour Apple store right now and pick up a decoy."

"But—but—it's not like I'm good friends with him," Reagan protested. "We're not on dropping-by terms. And if he finds out that I'm going back on my word, he'll, like, kill me."

"Then we'll have to make sure he doesn't find out," I said. "While you're in there, we'll send in something big to distract him . . . I know what. How about one of your dad's news crews? I'm sure they won't say no when the boss's daughter asks them to bum-rush Sink about some new controversy. Don't let them waste any time. Tell them it's something urgent."

"Like what?" Reagan said.

"Those are easy to make up," Becca said. "It can be about how a bunch of soul stars are protesting Sink's Showtime Lofts.

We'll just tell Sink there are cries of protest coming from Aretha Franklin and James Brown."

"Maybe not him." I coughed. "He's dead."

"Really?" Diana looked at me. "Wasn't he just at the Apollo?"

"Yeah, for the public viewing of his body." I smiled. "I'd stick with Aretha."

"Perfect." Poppy smiled and slid her unfinished Coke Reagan's way. "Drink up, sister."

{ 24 }

Day of the Dog

The next week, I could do nothing but fret over the myriad ways the great iPod switcheroo could go wrong. Reagan had promised us she had a tea with Sink scheduled for Thursday afternoon, and I was terrified that in those intervening days he'd move the iPod or Reagan would chicken out.

Thursday evening, my hands were shaking when I turned on the local news. When a segment on hidden fat in Ogo-Yogo frozen yogurt gave way to an image of Sink Landon, I nearly jumped out of my seat. "The reports are completely un-thub-thantiated," he was saying. "Zeta Equitieth ith nothing if not rethpectful of the thurrounding community."

Mom cringed from behind. "He's so slimy. He doesn't care at all about the community."

"Capitalists can't be trusted," Dad threw in. "They just take and take."

I shushed them and watched in glee as a platinum-blond girl flashed by in the background. She was going to replace the Moons' sacred iPod with an empty one.

Go, Reagan, go!

Happiness spread through me like wildfire, and I went into my room to call Louis. He'd been trying to get ahold of me for days, but I hadn't been able to concentrate on anything that didn't have to do with sinking Sink.

I picked up the phone and it took me a moment to remember his number. I was riddled with guilty nerves as I waited for him to pick up.

"Who's this again?" He was pouting.

"Now you know how it feels," I said. "It's been a rough week, Lou."

"And I'm supposed to be sympathetic?"

"Can we just skip over the guilt trip and make a plan to hang out?"

"What do you have in mind?" he asked.

A bike ride through Central Park wasn't going to cut it. I had to think of something good.

"I know!" I said after a couple of seconds. "An early-morning bike ride and Gray's Papaya for breakfast. We've always wondered about breakfast there."

Louis didn't answer immediately. "I'll think it over."

I smiled into the phone. "Saturday at eight?"

"Eight in the morning? You're joking."

"Is that a no?"

Louis sighed and we made a plan. "The breakfast had better be good."

• • •

On Saturday morning, when I showed up at the hot-dog joint at the appointed hour, the place was dead, and the white-hot fluorescent lighting only heightened the feeling of empti-ness. "Hello, Lemonhead." Louis smiled from his spot against the counter. "Or should I say sleepyhead?"

I wasn't feeling sleepy—more like discombobulated. The night before, all the Moons but Reagan had hit a shoebox-sized nightclub in the Little Brazil section of Queens. It had been a good call—not a single fake tan in the room—but the band was louder than a fleet of ocean liners, and the thump-thump of it all was still reverberating in my head.

I gave Louis a floppy wave and helped myself to a bite of his early-bird hot dog. "It doesn't taste like meat."

"Whoever said it *was* meat?" A smile played out on Louis's face. "Nice eye makeup. Very asymmetrical."

I smiled. Only Louis could say something so critical and have it come out sounding sweet.

"Like you're camera-ready?" I stared at his SAFE SEX T-shirt that showed two safe deposit boxes smooching.

He grimaced. "I was running low on laundry. I got it for free at a tennis tournament, one of the sponsors is a . . ."

"Padlock manufacturer?"

"How'd you know?" He popped the remainder of his breakfast dog in his mouth and pulled his coat tight. "Ready?"

That was an understatement. Seeing Louis made me realize how badly I was dying to hang out again, just the two of us.

When we stepped outside, the sky was brightening. The unmistakably optimistic smell of spring hung in the air.

Our agenda involved hanging out in Washington Square Park until the Film Forum's noon screening of *Evil Under the Sun*, one of the few Agatha Christie classics I hadn't already seen. Our senior-screening Saturdays were a time-honored tradition that I was happy to revive. I was a little nervous he'd want to share war stories about how we were both dating Shuttleworths, but the conversation never took off in that direction. As we threaded down East Eighth Street, passing all the discount shoe stores, it was like old times. Straightforward. Mellow.

"Guess what?" I said as we turned onto Fifth Avenue. The park's arch was just a couple of blocks away, pulling us in like a big white magnet. "Dad finally delivered his book."

"The whole enchilada?" He sounded incredulous.

"No, just the first two chapters. Of course the whole thing!" I felt a surge of protectiveness toward my father and changed the subject. "How's things chez Ibbits?"

"The usual . . . lots of takeout and expensive bathroom tiles you're not allowed to get wet. Ulrika just went on a two-week career reassessment retreat in the Turks and Caicos."

"But what's there to—"

"Reassess? You mean because she doesn't have a career?" He shook his head. "Good question, my friend."

We both started laughing, and by the time we reached the park I was feeling good—so what if Louis and I had complicated things by hooking up with two people who happened to be brother and sister? We were friends to the core, and nothing was going to change that.

We found a bench in the northeast corner that faced away from the park. Hardly ideal for people-watching purposes, but there was one small consolation prize: somebody had left a folded-up copy of the Post on the seat.

I leaned back and closed my eyes while Louis read out loud from our favorite gossip column. " 'Which aging Oscar winner was spotted at the Time Warner Center's anniversary party trying to talk about geopolitics to a Tibetan supermodel? Only in New York.' " I thought he was reciting the columnist's catchphrase, but then I heard a third party chime in: "It's a smaller town than you'd think."

That familiar voice leached the moment of all its comfort. I opened my eyes and saw Becca and Andy standing over us. Becca wasn't wearing any makeup, which made her look paler than usual, and Andy was holding on to one of those tank-sized cups from Starbucks.

My eyes slid over to Louis. "Did you guys plan this?"

He made an are-you-crazy face and cut his eyes quickly at his T-shirt. Okay, I believed him.

"What are you doing here?" I asked them.

"We just picked up Mom's birthday present at this apartment on MacDougal Street." Becca gestured to the leather Louis Vuitton duffel bag slung over her shoulder. "It's so tiny, we had no idea."

"*That* bag is tiny?" I asked.

Becca rolled her eyes and put the bag on my lap. Something inside it was moving.

"Open it," Andy instructed me, and I studied the hazel flecks in his green eyes.

I'd pulled the zipper a little farther down the line of teeth to find the cutest black-and-white puppy poking its wet nose at me.

"It was the only thing we could think of that our mom doesn't already have," Becca said.

"It's polka-dotted!" I exclaimed moronically.

"She," Andy corrected me. "Her name is Bella Abzug."

"Bella Abzug was a famous New Yorker who wore huge hats," Becca explained.

Andy rolled his eyes at his sister. "She was also this very cool activist."

"Whatever," she said. "I'm going along with the name because you can also call her Bug."

Andy sat down next to me and slung his arm over my shoulder. My heart was about to explode—I couldn't believe he was acting all lovey-dovey with me in front of the other two. It appeared I wasn't the only one who felt uncomfortable; Becca was clicking her studded ankle boots together and studying the dust patterns underfoot.

"C'mere, little monster." It took me a second to realize Louis wasn't talking to the dog. He'd reached up for Becca's ivory hands and pulled her down next to him.

I bit down on my lip and kept petting Bella's cashmere-soft coat, trying not to think about how weird it was that Louis had nicknames for Becca that I'd never heard of.

Becca started talking about how absentminded the dog breeder had been. "She had wads of tissue between her toes and she kept saying 'Bingo' to everything."

"That was the least of it," her brother added. "She tried to give us somebody else's puppy. Total nut job."

"They're probably hard to tell apart when they're this young," I said.

"Um, I'm no vet," Becca said, "but I can tell the difference between a Dalmatian and a standard poodle."

"I always knew you were smart," Louis said in fake admiration.

"She does go to Henry Hudson," I threw in. "Home of New York's best—"

"And brightest," Becca finished for me, her voice shot through with mock pride.

We deserved a gold medal for the way we were hanging out as a foursome, as if it were something we did all the time.

Suddenly Bella let off a yelp.

"I think you scared her." Andy pulled the puppy out of the bag and held her tight against his chest. "Nobody's going to eat you, little munchkin," he cooed, then launched into a story about the original Nathan's Famous hot dog stand in Coney Island. "There was a rumor that they were serving actual dogs, so Nathan got doctors to stand on line outside in their white coats. He paid them off with free hot dogs, and sure enough, customers assumed they must be healthy and started lining up." Andy peered into his new love's sleepy eyes. "I bet you'd like a wiener, little bug."

Bella let out a whimper of agreement.

Louis looked at his watch. "The movie starts in twenty minutes."

"You guys are leaving?" Andy made a pleading face.

I looked over to make sure Louis would be okay with Andy's implication. Our eyes connected, and in that instant we both silently consented. What choice did we have? If we tried to hold our friendship in a cocoon for two it was going to get left behind.

"You guys are welcome to come," I said. "Seriously, the more popcorn the merrier."

"Awesome." Becca leaped to her feet and mussed my hair. "And don't forget, we have doggie snacks too."

{ 25 }

Vertigo Girl to the Rescue!

Back at school on Monday, I was sitting in the cafeteria, going over the night's plan in my head again and again. After school, I had to pick up the Vertigo Girl mask that Ian was making for the production. And at nine o'clock, the bridge would be closed to traffic and we'd set up the film shoot. At 11:18, when the power went out, workers disguised as actors would scramble up the bridge's weak cable and reinforce it with platinum. Nearly ten minutes later, the bridge would be in perfect shape and Sink's plan to take over the waterfront would be nothing but a pipe dream. It was a plan worthy of an Academy Award, and yet I had an eerie sense the other shoe was going to drop. The Directors Guild would go on strike or compromising documents were going to surface on Moonwatcher.net or Sink was going to clue in to what had happened and send a ninja after Reagan and the rest of us.

I had to stop thinking about all the ways things could go wrong, so I tried to concentrate on how smoothly my life was going—for once. Dad had finished his book. I'd made up with Louis and Ian. As for Andy, even though he had one last test to study for, he was being as attentive as could be—during Kiki's Sunday night Starlight Roof Scrabble party, he called Clem's cell phone to check up on me. Twice.

And there were no hiccups on the school front, either. Classes were easy. Somehow I was on "hey" terms with more kids than I could count on two hands. And dear old Sheila was too busy carrying around fifty-pound film theory books Alex had lent her and posing as a budding intellectual to hate on me.

As I started to unwrap my ham baguette, someone nudged me from behind.

"Hey, stranger," came a voice. It was Alex, who lowered himself into the seat across from me.

"Hey yourself," I said, unable to look him in the eye. He pulled a school paper out of his back pocket and studied the front page. "Anything good there?" I asked, still studying my lap.

"Typical mediocrity," he said, "but there's some funny stuff on the plagiarism fallout."

I looked up. My blank expression must have said it all.

"You didn't hear? Like, three kids in Bunting's freshman English class handed in the exact same essay, on the inner self and the outside world in *Wuthering Heights*."

"And the lazy bastard noticed? I didn't think Hudson teachers bothered to read papers—mine just get graded on length."

Alex dismissed my question with a flick of the wrist. "Of

course he didn't notice. But he gave some of them different grades, and one of the girls made a stink about the injustice of it all."

I shook my head and laughed. Sometimes you just had to love Henry Hudson.

"Hey, Claire." Alex gave me a crooked smile. "I think I owe you an apology. I guess I just went after what I wanted without thinking of you. I'm sorry."

"No worries." I looked down at my stack of Bakelite bracelets and I wondered how I'd ever thought he was anything more than a goofy kid who had some growing up to do. "You gave business cards out at Kiki's party. It's not a biggie."

"What?" he said. "I'm talking about going after Sheila." He looked at me sheepishly. "I know you guys aren't exactly tight these days."

"Alex," I said, holding back a smile, "I'm not mad at you at all."

"Really?" He was squinting. "You're way cooler than I'd given you credit for." In the moment of silence that followed, I marveled at the ridiculousness of the way things had turned out. "You know what? Maybe the three of us can hang out sometime, unless it would be too strange."

"Maybe." I ran my finger along the chain around my neck. "Stranger things have happened."

It was a cool, misty night, and my heart was beating fast as I approached the foot of the Brooklyn Bridge. A huge orange sign said: CLOSED THRU 12:00 A.M. USE ALTERNATE ROUTE.

A megaphone-happy woman greeted me with: "Nobody beyond this point! Film shoot in progress!" The scene playing out over her shoulder was unbelievable. Whenever the girls had talked about staging a shoot, I'd pictured something along the lines of the handful of low-budget music video productions that I'd pedaled past on my bike rides over the bridge. Those crews always seemed to consist of nothing more than a kid holding on to a video camera while a friend steadied him on his skateboard. Tonight, though, the bridge was a hive of activity, the walkway clogged with hundreds of crew members who were fiddling with equipment and muttering important-looking messages into their headsets.

When I walked up to the woman with the megaphone, her nostrils flared at me. "This is a closed set."

"I'm—I'm here for the movie," I blurted. "I have a delivery for Becca Shuttleworth. She's one of the Blue Mo—" I caught myself just in time. "Producers?"

The woman did little to conceal her skepticism. "I'll see if there's anyone here by that name. Stand back." My hands went clammy while I waited. Finally my friend's voice came through the walkie-talkie. "It's Claire? Tell her we're under the Manhattan-side arch."

"Be right up!" I hollered, hoping the walkie-talkie would pick up my words.

I found Becca standing in front of a Porta Potti, arms akimbo. A flash of pink was visible in her down-jacket pocket—looked like the iPod was safe and sound. My chest heaved in relief.

Poppy and Sig were off to the side, conferring with a goa-teed guy wearing head-to-toe black fleece. Becca's eyes warmed up when she saw me. "Did you bring the mask?"

"No, I forgot my one and only task."

"Are you kid—" She stopped short when she saw I was rolling my eyes. "Don't mess with me. My nerves are a little frayed here. My sleep was all messed up last night."

"I know the feeling," I told her, and handed over the brown

paper bag I'd picked up at Propeller Comics. Without bothering to check out the mask Ian had made, she cracked open the white structure's door and shoved it through. A TALENT sign came into focus, and I realized Becca was guarding a tiny little trailer. It beat me how anybody would find it soothing to hide out in a box that was the size of a phone booth, but status and comfort didn't always stand shoulder to shoulder.

"How is it?" A girl came flying out the door. She was wearing a black cat suit and the Vertigo Girl mask that Ian had made out of origami paper and tiny fake diamonds he'd removed from a kid-sized tiara he'd found on the street. When Ian had shown it to me at the comic-book store, it had seemed like a fantastic piece of art that might call to you from a museum wall—but set against those unmistakable waves and the mist-coated New York skyline, it sprang to life far beyond that. Vertigo Girl was mythical goddess and dream girl all wrapped up in one.

"Sills," I whispered, "you have no idea how fierce you look."

"I don't know what you're talking about," she said in a low voice before floating away.

"Don't let the cat out of the bag," Becca ordered. "Sills isn't supposed to be here, given her celebrity-girlfriend status, but we couldn't keep her out. She did write the damn thing, after all, and she really wanted to play the role."

Seemed fair.

"All clear!" somebody shouted in the background.

"Watch out!" Becca pulled me aside to keep me from getting mauled by a crane that was tearing through the air. "Let's get you parked somewhere a little more comfortable. I'll show you to the holding area."

I knew this trick—Kiki is the master of saying "Now, there's a spot on the davenport!" to guests she doesn't find worthy of more than two minutes of her time. Becca's desire to unload me stung, but when we got to the holding area and I saw it was less of the jail cell its name implied and more of an upscale banquet, with endless tables stocked with cookies and fried zucchini sticks and roast beef wraps, my sense of injury evaporated.

Vertigo Girl and Samurai Sam, the movie's stars, were now standing on their marks about twenty feet away. A wardrobe assistant was down on her knees, running a lint roller along every square inch of their costumes. Then a makeup artist came in for one final coat of powder (Vertigo Girl's mask didn't cover her neck) and the continuity girl homed in to snap Polaroids.

Just when it was beginning to feel like they'd never actually start filming, the man in black fleece boomed: "Quiet on the set! Rolling! And action!"

This was beginning to be fun.

After watching Vertigo Girl deliver her line where she tells Samurai Sam that she's afraid of heights for the fourteenth time, I began to get twitchy. I got up to grab a Coke, but one of the wardrobe girls clawed my arm. "Don't move," she hissed. "Visitors always distract the talent." I wanted to pull rank and let her know I was hardly a mere visitor—if it weren't for me, there would be no shoot. And when she and a couple of cohorts started talking about how sick they were of working on rich kids' vanity projects, I had to count to ten to hold back from explaining what this whole circus was really about.

"You ready?" a familiar voice whispered from behind, and I turned around to see Diana smiling devilishly, her chin jutting toward the huge digital clock over the Watchtower building. It was 11:15, three minutes before blackout time. My chest clenched in fear—what if the plan didn't work? But a minute later the clock went dead and blackness settled over the city. Chaos broke out among the crew members and I felt a surge of nervousness.

Across the river, without their lights on, the skyscrapers and buildings staggered along the waterfront looked like thick cardboard cutouts. I held my breath and prayed for the team of acrobatic engineers that was scurrying up the cables and doing their magic.

When the lights came back on, I tried to deep-breathe my residual nervousness away. Becca appeared by my side, wearing an ear-to-ear smile. "It's done! It's done!"

There was a lot of commotion on the set, and an amplified voice said: "Back to your places, everyone."

Becca leaned in closer and lowered her voice to a whisper. "Save next Saturday night. There's a little initiation ceremony."

I nearly fell out of my director's chair. I'd gotten so preoccupied with saving the Brooklyn Bridge, I'd forgotten all about becoming a Full Moon. I glanced around to see if any of the crew members had caught wind of our little tête-à-tête. No worries on that front. Everyone was whizzing about, far too stressed about making up for lost time to pay the annoying blond visitor any mind.

As far as they were concerned, it was back to making a lousy movie. Little did they know they were also making history.

{ 26 }

Tit for Tat

And you must be Claire's parents," Becca's mom said by way of greeting at the doorway. True to form, her plain navy dress was set off with to-die-for accessories, including the chunky jade and ruby necklace that I could have sworn I'd just seen on the back page of *Vogue*. The pièce de résistance, though, was the tiny polka-dotted dog draped over her shoulder. "I'm Deirdre," she said. "I wish I could shake your hand but I'm covered in doggy drool." As if on cue, Bella snarfed.

"Then you will have to settle for a French introduction." Dad moved in to plant a kiss on each of the hostess's cheeks. "Gustave Voyante. *Enchanté*."

I felt my face burn but Becca's mom thrilled to the double

kiss. "*Enchantée!*" she replied in a girlish squeal, repeating the exercise with my mother. "I'm so glad you could come to my birthday party." She winked at me to convey that we were both in on the secret—all the Half Moons' parents had been told that we were here to celebrate Deirdre Shuttleworth's birthday and not Sink Landon's downfall.

Once she'd closed the door behind us, she guided my parents over to Becca's dad, who was presiding over the party from a spot by the staircase.

I hung back in the entryway and scanned the living room. A string quartet played in the corner and late-afternoon light poured through the windows. All the girls were decked out in their parent-approved best, and I was glad I'd worn my Kiki-donated aqua blue Oleg Cassini cocktail dress instead of the purple Diana Ross–esque mini I'd nearly opted for.

"There you are." Becca was looking like a prim schoolgirl in her red pleated skirt and white button-down shirt. "I need your social know-how like never before." Her brown eyes gleamed with eagerness in the semi-darkness of the corridor.

"Don't tell me the Helle Housers are crashing another party," I said.

"I wish." She turned and indicated our own traitor's spot by the bay window with her chin.

Reagan looked gloomier than I'd ever seen. My stomach drew into a knot. "What's she doing here?" I asked.

"I invited her," Becca said. "I didn't want to have to explain to my parents why she couldn't come. Plus, better to keep an eye on her, don't you think? But the way she's standing there looking like the queen of death is creeping me out."

"And you want *me* to keep her company?"

"Becca!" My friend's mom was making an indecipherable hand signal and her little friend growled.

"Just go and talk to her, will you, C? Wait—" She wiped at my ear and smiled placidly. "Attack of the random glitter."

"Henry was having a creative morning," I told her. "Thanks." As I tried to cross the room, I kept getting wrangled into parental meet-and-greets, but I finally made my way over to Reagan. "Having fun?" I asked when I finally arrived at her side.

"Oodles," she said sarcastically, and kept staring out the window.

She wasn't going to make this easy on me.

"Your parents coming?" I asked.

"They had other plans."

"What could trump a Shuttleworth soiree?" I asked lamely.

"They're busy having nothing to do with their daughter." She glared at me and she pulled a letter out of her bag.

I saw the Dartmouth letterhead and the words "regret" and "admission" and "withdrawal." The movie shoot had been only three days ago. When you double-cross Sink Landon, he sure works fast.

I felt a lump in my throat and looked back up at her. "Maybe if you talk to your parents they can help you. Come clean."

"I already did." Her smile was bitter. "They said I have to figure it out on my own. So here I am, with nothing to show for myself but an unacceptance letter and a dad who wishes I'd never been born."

I gazed out the window. Golden light was flooding the street and a young father and pair of little boys hopped out of a yellow cab.

"You know, Ray, it was worth it." A picture of the foiled Bridge Towers project leaped to my mind's eye. "And college can wait. I'm sure you'll work something out."

"Or not." Her tone was fake-chirpy. "Lots of highly successful people don't go to college. Like, um . . . well, I'll let you know if I think of any."

I felt sad and breathed in deep as I looked around the room. When I turned back to Reagan, the spot where she'd been standing was empty.

Kiki's "circulate, circulate" maxim popped into my head and I drifted over to Diana and a white-haired man who must have been her grandfather.

"Claire, meet my dad," Diana said, and I had to stop myself from doing a double take.

Mr. Stoeffels took a sip from his amber-colored drink and stooped down to extend a liver-spotted hand. "I hear I have you to thank for saving the day."

"My pleasure," I said. "It's not every day you get to save the Brooklyn Bridge."

"Not to mention our businesses." He took a swig from his drink and laughed in the charmed, nothing-can-touch-me way they do in old movies. "You gals are terrific."

I could feel creases stretching across my forehead. "Becca said the exact opposite—she said that the bridge needed to be fixed anonymously so people didn't get the wrong idea and assume that—"

"It's a general rule that when people say that, what they mean is they don't want people to get the 'right' idea." He let off a chuckle and took another sip.

Diana's drained expression told me her father was speaking out of line. "Dad," she said quickly. "Let's go find those spring rolls."

"Don't interrupt me, Diana." He sounded stern.

"Agreed." I glared at Diana. "Go on, Mr. Stoeffels."

"In case you haven't heard," he continued, "your work paid

off quite handsomely. The city just approved a land use application the Stoeffels Realty Company submitted over two years ago. Now our plan for the Liberty Building is good to go." He raised his glass at me.

And suddenly, like the meaning of a song you've already heard a thousand times but never really listened to, it all crystallized.

Mayor Irving wasn't just accepting favors—he was granting them too. Operation Vertigo Girl wasn't just a good-for-the-sake-of-good project—it was a means to another end. Or, looking around at the happy parental faces in the room, four other ends. It must be convenient to have a daughter whose secret club is doing favors for the city when your business stands to make millions off of it. And, I realized with a shudder, it was no coincidence that the Shuttleworths' new ketchup factory was going up without a single problem.

Diana was pulling at her hair and wouldn't meet my eye.

"Funny how things work around here," Diana's dad said.

"A laugh a minute," I muttered, and tore away.

I was too hurt by Becca's duplicity to even consider saying good-bye to her. I approached a friendly looking caterer and asked if she could do me a favor.

"Let me guess. You want me to see if we have more mini lobster rolls in the back?"

"No, I have to go." I pointed my parents out to her. "Can you wait ten minutes and tell them their daughter left? I'd say good-bye myself but—"

"They won't let you," she finished off my thought.

"Well done." I looked up and glimpsed Becca across the room. She was swanning around, looking happy and effortless. And then she caught my eye and raised her glass at me.

Something inside me went dead and I fake-smiled back at her.

"I understand, I get bored at parties, too," came the caterer's voice.

I forced a grin. "I'm having fun, but I just have something else to take care of."

"Sure you do. Get out of here." She shooed me away.

The Waldorf isn't too far away from Becca's place, and when the hotel came into view, my walking went from fast to hyperactive. I flew into the lobby fast as a whippet and the elevator ride up to Kiki's thirty-seventh floor apartment felt like the longest journey of my life.

Clem let me in and Kiki squinted at me from her spot by the coffee table. She gave the Oleg Cassini dress a nod of approval.

"Something about your face says 'code red,'" Clem said. His pants were rolled up to his knees, a habit he'd taken to ever since concluding that his shins were his best-looking feature.

"Can you excuse us for a second, Clem?" I asked.

Kiki gave me a not-this-again look and started tottering toward her bedroom.

"I just went to the Blue Moons' celebration at the Shuttleworths', and there's more to the club than I'd realized," I said after she'd shut the door behind us.

"Go on," Kiki said from her perch on the cranberry ottoman.

"You're never going to believe this." I was pacing so hard I thought I'd make permanent dents in the carpet. "The Blue Moons aren't just doing good works for the city out of the kindness of their hearts. All of their parents are reaping benefits."

"Is that so?" She chuckled lightly.

I was outraged. She knew!

"How could you not tell me there was a dirty conspiracy all along?"

"I compliment you on your innocent worldview, but there's no conspiracy. I believe the term you're looking for is 'quid pro quo.'" She must have read my confused expression. "It's a Latin way of saying 'I'll scratch your back if you scratch mine.'"

"You make it sound like it's something cute." I was so flustered my voice was violently bouncing off the silk wallpaper. "These people are buying their way through life. And they had me helping them without bothering to tell me what I was getting into. And—" I paused, feeling my throat clench the way it does when I'm about to cry. "Becca didn't say anything about it all this time."

"You can't mean to tell me you've never repaid a favor."

"Sure, I burned Louis a Ronettes CD when he fed my fish one weekend. That's not exactly the same thing."

"Ah, but that's where you're wrong. Same thing, different scale. People are bound to be selfish. It's human nature."

"That's highly debatable." I looked up at the ceiling.

"We can debate it if that's what you want. And I'd win." Kiki stretched out her arms and cracked her knuckles. "Maybe you're just feeling left out."

"I don't think so." My tone was defensive.

"I'm sure there are some favors you wouldn't be above accepting."

"That's not the point." I was swatting away the ideas that were springing to mind. My inner wishes had nothing to do with multimillion-dollar deals or ketchup factories.

"Now why don't you stop being so coy and tell me what strings need to be pulled to make you happy."

I turned away and caught my reflection in the windowpane.

With my blond bob and puckered expression, I looked more than a little like Kiki circa 1959.

"Don't be a Stubborn Susie. Tell me. If you don't I'll figure it out." She whistled.

I inhaled deeply. "Fine. I know that what Reagan did was terrible, but I think she deserves another shot. She risked everything to undo her bad behavior and all she got was kicked out of the Moons and a Dartmouth rejection letter. Her future is totally ruined."

"Enough of the negative. What would you like to happen?"

"A lot," I said, thinking it through. "I want Reagan to get into college. At this point she's suffered enough."

"What else?"

"I want Ian to get to correct the Toro Boy movie."

"And? I feel there's something else."

A moment passed before an idea hit me. I checked to make sure she was ready for it. "And I'd like you and Mom to make up."

Kiki brushed her hands together. "That all seems eminently within reach."

"Even the last part?" I could feel my guard slipping down.

"I'm not the queen of warm and fuzzy, but I can ask your mother to lunch. So long as it isn't one of those French places." She sniffed disapprovingly. "Now let me ask you one thing about this Reagan girl. Do you think she'd be willing to attend therapy sessions? There's the Trilling Institute on the Upper West Side that Mamie Swinson went to when she kept getting caught nicking dresses at Saks."

"She's a shoplifter too?" I repeated, my jaw dropping. Mamie Swinson, who had been married to an Austrian prince as well as the CEO of some huge French bank, was one of Kiki's wealthiest friends.

"She *was*. There's no accounting for these complexes," Kiki said. "Mamie's all cured, and serves on the board. I'd be happy to ring her up and see if she could get your friend into the program."

"That would be great," I gushed.

"And you're sure that Reagan can get by as a student?"

"What do you mean?"

"She wouldn't be using her scrapes with the law as an excuse for her unpopularity with the admission committees, would she?"

"She's at the top of her class," I assured my grandmother.

"Good. As it happens, Dean Rabinowitz and I are overdue for a dinner. Tell that poor friend of yours if she gets me her transcript before then, we'll get her straightened out." A pause followed. "So long as she straightens out the rest."

She was losing me. "What rest?"

Kiki looked at me like I had a one-digit IQ. "With the culinary boy. Her father does run the movie studio, does he not?"

"He won't even talk to her."

"I have a feeling that will change if she promises to give the Trilling Institute a fair shake. It's highly respected. Seems like a fair deal, does it not?"

My eyes darted away and I mulled it over for a moment. Doing nice things for people was one thing, but I didn't like to think of people trading life-changing favors like Pokémon cards. And wasn't it slightly hypocritical of me to be having this vaguely sleazy conversation if it was exactly the kind of thing I was mad at Becca for participating in?

"Don't let your thoughts wander there," Kiki said, reading my mind. "I'm one hundred percent sure your friend had your best intentions at heart."

I rolled my eyes. "She totally used me."

"Is that right? And you're telling me you would have been happy if she'd kept sliding out of sight and leaving you to your own devices this semester?"

I felt stumped. The way Kiki was spinning it, Becca's inviting me into the club didn't sound so bad.

"You two are due for a chat. And now that you've learned your big lesson, are you going to put it to use or sit there like a lemon?" Kiki came closer and rubbed my shoulder. "Your friends need you."

"Fine," I said at last. I felt twin pangs of helplessness and relief.

"Tremendous," Kiki boomed as she rose to her feet. "I'd tell your friend to go ahead and order one of those Columbia sweatshirts. Not to wear, of course." She wrinkled her nose like a rabbit. "Hooded garments are for stick-up artists, not pretty girls."

{ 27 }

The Heart of the Matter

Half an hour later, I pulled my bike up outside the Shuttle-worths' house. I could see through the windows that the party was still going strong. A caterer opened the door for me, and I tiptoed in, hoping my reentry wouldn't rate a second glance from any of the guests.

Looked like today was my lucky day. My parents were still chatting with Diana's family and Becca was at the back of the living room, talking to Poppy's parents under an oil painting of a devilish-looking cherub. She looked up and smiled but my determination must have showed. Becca's face had morphed into a dark cloud by the time I reached her side.

"Everything okay?" she asked, giggling nervously.

"Sure," I said unconvincingly. "I just need to show you something upstairs."

It took Becca a second to get the hint.

"Of course." Becca turned to face Mr. and Mrs. Williamson and plastered on a fake smile. "If you'll excuse me."

I barely glanced at the grown-ups before leading Becca up the stairs and into her room. It was messier than usual, with piles of dresses on the bed and colorful shoes scattered around the floor like confetti.

She cleared a spot on her comforter and sat down, crushing a sweater sleeve in the process. "What's the matter? Did something happen?"

"You could say that." I was having trouble figuring out where to start and turned to stare out the window. I let myself go with the bull's-eye. "I'm not coming to the initiation ceremony."

"Did you get a better invitation?" Her tone was uncertain.

I pivoted to look her in the eye. "Stop messing with me, B. I finally get it."

"Get what?" She sounded genuinely exasperated.

"The Moons. They're not just a bunch of girls doing good stuff because they're so great. It's all a scheme to get the city to do favors for their families." I stopped. "For *your* families."

She shifted in place, momentarily speechless.

"That's not fair," she said at last. "We *do* care about the city."

"Well, whatever. That's not even the worst of it," I said.

Just at that moment, the door creaked and we both looked up, expecting to see a person. It took me a second to realize that Bella had butted her way into the room. She scurried over to the bed and jumped into Becca's lap.

"Sorry for that," Becca said. "For the dog, I mean." Bella wheezed and we both had to contain our smiles. "Go on."

"Becca, you and your families are free to do whatever you want. But why would you let me get so obsessed with helping you out and not tell me the truth? This whole project was about a sweet real estate deal for Diana's father. And that ketchup factory your parents are building. And, for all I know, all the other Moons' parents are benefiting too." Tears were filling my eyes as I waited for her to speak, but she was just playing with the dog's paws. "Aren't you going to say anything?" I had to swallow hard to keep from crying. "For God's sake, you totally used me."

When Becca finally looked up at me, tears were streaming down her face. "Claire, I'm so sorry. But for the record, I didn't bring you in so you could do anything for my family." She wiped her face with the back of her hand. "I only invited you because I missed having you around. So I convinced the rest of the girls to let in a few new members. That's the only way I got to tell you about the club."

"But not the important part," I reminded her, still smarting from it all.

"It didn't seem relevant," she protested.

"What about it wasn't relevant?" I challenged.

Becca sniffed. "Not the way I see it. In my view, what Mayor Irving does at the end of the day isn't even my business. I just like the stuff that comes before it." She breathed deeply. "I'm so sorry it had to play out like this. I just wanted my best friend around, that's it."

I wanted to be furious with her, but her sincerity was melting my resolve.

"I should have told you." Her words were breaking up. "I'm sorry. It was a big fat mistake. But my heart was in the right place. And you still saved the city from more Sink Landon eyesores. Will you forgive me?"

I took a deep breath. "Okay," I said after a moment's thought. "But I'm still not becoming a Full Moon."

"You have to stay in," Becca pleaded. "I'll level with you next time. I'll tell you more ugly details than you could ever want to know."

"No," I said. "I'm serious."

Becca's eyes glistened with tears.

"I'm still your friend. I'm just saying no to the Moon part. The whole payment scheme, it icks me out."

She sighed and cracked her knuckles. "I wish I had the same reaction to it all, but I guess I'm used to that sort of thing. It's been going on around me ever since I can remember."

I glanced around the room, my gaze sweeping past the jewelry boxes on the vanity up to the outrageously high ceilings. "I'll bet."

A bittersweet smile passed Becca's lips.

"We still have to clean up this mess," I told her.

She chuckled. "I know, it's a pigsty in here. It was actually pin-neat this morning, but then I had to go and have a preparty wardrobe meltdown." She gave Bella a hearty pat before lifting her off her lap. Then she crouched in front of a pile of shoes, reaching for a pair of canary-yellow pumps. "Lemme just toss these in the closet."

"B, hold up." I was shaking my head. "I wasn't talking about your room. I meant a really important mess."

She scrunched up her nose in confusion.

"Reagan," I said. "Not to be little miss bleeding heart, but I think she deserves a second chance."

Becca looked mortified. "At being in the Moons? No way."

"No, that's not what I'm talking about," I said. "College. She came through for us, and now she's royally screwed."

"Isn't that what we wanted?" Becca checked. "She totally went behind our backs and was helping Sink Landon."

"There are degrees of screwed," I said. "I'm not saying we should be friends with her. But I think a thank-you for coming through for us wouldn't be the worst thing in the world. Besides, there's something she can help me with that would mean a lot to me."

"Well, what do you propose? It's not like we can magically fix her life."

"We don't need magic," I said. "Just a kernel of kindness."

She rolled her eyes and let go of one pump. Smiling, I waited for the other shoe to drop.

{ 28 }

The Sweet Spot

I chose Serendipity 3, a Candy Land–pink Upper East Side institution known for its extravagant dessert menu. According to Kiki, it used to be popular with people like Andy Warhol and Jackie Kennedy, though now it caters nearly exclusively to little-girl-and-grandmother pairings. It didn't seem like the most obvious place for a transaction like the one we were about to conduct, though you never knew. Ever since Thursday's bombshell, the world had seemed a whole lot harder to read.

Right after the party at the Shuttleworths', I'd called Reagan and told her that Kiki had an ingenious plan to get her into Columbia. I instructed her to meet me at Serendipity on Saturday. All she needed was to bring her academic records and have a little conversation with her father regarding my favorite male classmate.

Becca licked a globule of chocolate fudge off the back of a long wooden spoon. "Their sundaes used to be way bigger," she recalled. "You could hardly see over them."

"They're still huge for some." I pointed to a little girl who was devouring a sundae at a nearby table. "I think it's you who's changed size," I said, and Becca laughed.

With the Moon initiation only a few hours away, Becca probably should have been at the Moonery strewing rose petals around Gummy's skeleton or whatever the mysterious-sounding ceremony required, but she'd agreed to tag along at my Saturday rendezvous.

I looked back at the door—still no sign of Reagan.

"Do you think she changed her mind?" I asked.

"Will you relax?" Becca said. "You came to her with a win-win situation. And on top of that, Serendipity Three is a sugar fiend's skid row." She tugged at the green and white shoelace she'd double-wrapped around her wrist. Only Becca could make one of Louis's tennis doodads look like a fashion accessory worth going on a two-year waiting list for. I smiled at her and brought a spoonful of frozen hot chocolate to my lips.

A soft rain had been falling ever since the morning, lending the day a fuzzy quality. We settled into a lazy silence and I snapped to attention when Reagan breezed in. She was wearing a short gray trench coat, and her normally straight hair was starting to curl.

"Sorry I'm late." She lowered herself into a chair and shimmied out of her coat. "No matter how many times I come here, I always forget how far east it is and tell the cab to let me off a hundred blocks away. I mean, not a hundred, but a lot."

She was on edge, and her nervousness was contagious.

Becca was still furious with her, but had the heart to nod understandingly. "I have weird brain freezes too. It took me until, like, last year to get ahold of left and right. I had to keep going like this." She made two Ls with her thumbs and index fingers.

I smiled. It was sweet, the way she was trying to lighten the situation.

"I saw this thing on the Internet about a guy who got the words 'left' and 'right' tattooed on his hands, but the tattoo artist did it the wrong way," Reagan said.

Now we were all looking around the table, and it was obvious somebody needed to kill the small talk.

"Is it true what you said about Kiki being able to get me into Columbia?" Reagan asked me.

"It's looking good. She and Dean Rabinowitz are like this." I crossed my middle and index fingers.

"Wow. This is unbelievable. Oh—I almost forgot. As requested." Reagan produced an enormous green leather satchel and handed it to me. "You don't know how much this means to me. Thank you." She was so emotional her words came out as whispers.

"And you held up your end of the deal?"

She nodded tentatively. "Dad thawed out when I told him I'd go to that clinic. He'd heard of it—apparently a lot of Global actors have gone there."

"Sounds good," I said. "And speaking of Global Media, anything else to report?"

"Yeah, of course." Reagan pulled her frizzing hair back into a ponytail. "Dad and Ian had a little chat about Ian coming on to work as the Toro Boy consultant."

"It worked!" I exclaimed, and felt pride flash through me. I glimpsed Becca biting down a smile.

"Dad promised me your buddy's opinions will be heard

loud and clear, and he seems pretty serious about it," Reagan assured me. "Of course, Ian's employment is contingent on my continued welcome at a certain institution of higher learning." My cheeks went hot and I looked around the room, half expecting her father's local news team to bear down on us and expose us for the slimy wheel greasers we were. But everybody else in the restaurant was carrying on as if it were just another Saturday afternoon—little kids pigging out on junk food while their guardians smiled vacantly.

"And you didn't tell Ian that I was behind any of it, did you?" I asked.

"Give me some credit." Her eyes sparkled. "It was funny. Dad got the name of the store wrong and said they knew him from Powder Keg Comics. But Ian didn't correct him."

Becca raised an eyebrow. "Or maybe he didn't catch the mistake. It's amazing how far people will go to hear what they want to hear."

Becca's phone rang and at the same time a waiter appeared at our table. "Name your pleasure," he said to Reagan.

Talk about hearing what you want to hear.

"No way!" Becca was saying to someone on the phone, her eyes growing like balloons. "Are you serious? . . . Actually, she's right here. . . . No, you tell her." She smiled at me in a way that could only mean one thing.

"Hello?" I said into the phone.

"What are you doing hanging out with my sister when you could be here with me?" Only Andy's voice could make my stomach cartwheel. "I have something to tell you."

"Is it bad?" My voice croaked.

"Why would I want to say something bad to you? How fast can you get up to the Columbia gates? One Sixteenth and Broadway."

"You mean now?"

"No, *next* April. Yes, now."

I fought back a grin and glanced around the table. "I'm sort of in the mid—"

"No you're not. The meeting's adjourned." Becca grabbed the phone back from me. "She'll be there soon. Just be nice to her or I kill you."

Reagan's lips started to wobble as I rose to my feet.

"Don't worry." I tucked the folder into my bag. "When Kiki says she's got you covered, she means it. See you around."

Reagan smiled. "Yeah, I hope so."

When I got out of the cab, Andy was leaning against the black iron gate, holding up an oversized umbrella and talking to a guy and a girl. He waved me over when he saw me.

"Hey," I said, careful not to step too close. We'd never hung out on Columbia turf, and I didn't know how he wanted to play it. Could be embarrassing to have an almost-girlfriend who was only in tenth grade. My Kewpie doll height and flimsy tote bag instead of laptop carrier didn't exactly help my case.

But he just gave me that we're-the-only-two-people-in-the-world look he does so well and pulled me in tight, resting his chin on top of my head.

"Everyone, this is Claire." Andy was so close I could feel his chest moving with every syllable. "And Claire, these are my roommates for next year, James and Anna."

And that was when it clicked. Andy had aced all his midterms. He was back in at Columbia. And, more important, back in my life.

"Are you serious?" I craned my neck his way. "You're all living together?"

"Unless there's something you want to tell me about them. Oh, while you guys are all here, I should warn you that Claire has an uncanny ability to sniff out people's dirty secrets."

Anna eyed me appraisingly. "You're a mind reader?"

"I'm just good at paying attention," I said, blushing.

"Lucky you," she said. "If I could pay attention long enough to finish my Russian lit essay, I could have a normal weekend."

Two bells clanged in the background and James made a fist and knocked it against Andy's. "I gotta go."

"Me too," Anna said. "And Claire, I look forward to learning about everybody's dirty secrets." Her eyes lit up in a way that made me feel safe and I turned to look at Andy.

"I've known them both since we were little kids. They seem pretty okay, right?" Andy checked after the two had started down the path.

Maybe even more than just okay, I thought.

I hummed in assent and watched as he removed a letter from his coat pocket. "I wanted to show you—actually, let's wait until we're indoors. If the rain smudges it, I'm screwed."

"What is it?" I reached out for it and he jumped back.

"Trust me, it's worth the wait." He grabbed my wrist. "There's a place just around the corner I've been meaning to bring you anyway."

A couple minutes later we were propped up on two adjoining barstools at the Old Town Saloon. It was middle-of-the-evening crowded, thanks to the lousy weather, and more than a couple of customers were offering beery commentary on the basketball game playing on the television set overhead.

Andy ordered a seltzer and a grilled chicken sandwich. I asked for a Coke. "You sure you don't want anything else?" Andy double-checked.

"I'm good," I said.

Just then I noticed the huge framed map of New York City on the wall. It was old and faded, with a rash of age spots eating away at the far end of the Brooklyn Bridge. It made me think of Sink Landon and everything the Moons and I had been through to stop him. And for the first time since finding out about the extent of the Moons' deal with the city, I felt a pang of warmth, like I was thinking about an old friend.

"Here's what I wanted to show you." Andy plunked the note on City College letterhead in the spot between my two elbows and ran his palm over his fuzzy head while he waited.

"Three deans' signatures and four A-minuses," I said. "Impressive."

"I'm back in . . . completely." Hearing this gave me such a rush I thought I might hiccup. "So now you and I can be sitting here."

"No offense," I said, watching a potbellied man run up and down the bar giving high-fives to anyone who would let him. "I don't think they're that discriminating around these parts."

He play-punched me in the arm. "You know what I mean. You and I can be together. And I don't have to look over my shoulder every other second to make sure that someone I know isn't going to embarrass me by coming over and blowing my cover."

"How many times do I have to tell you I wouldn't have minded?"

He smiled. "How many times have I told you I'm a slow learner?"

My necklace was heating up like a glowworm and I suddenly got the feeling I was about to cry. I had to look away.

"You okay?"

"Yeah." I turned to face him, then found the sports enthusiast's palm within an inch of my face.

"What are you waiting for, Shorty?" Andy said. "Show him some love."

Laughing, I gave the guy his high-five. It actually felt good, coming undone like this, and when I pulled myself back together, I blurted, "What would you say if I told you I wasn't going to tonight's initiation?"

Andy looked confused. "Why not?"

I tapped at the leg of his stool with the tip of my shoe. "I don't think it's for me."

He pursed his lips. "But I thought you were having fun hanging out with Becca and all her friends."

"I was," I told him. "A lot of fun."

"And I thought you wanted in."

"I did." My cheeks were burning. "So much."

"Until?" He paused. "You found out they were a bunch of bloodsucking vampires?"

I willed a smile and glanced back over at the map. New York looked so vast, and the Moonery barely merited a speck. "It's just . . ." My gaze traveled back to him. "Maybe it's time I find a spot of my own, you know? Something where I don't always feel like I have my nose pressed up against a window looking into someone else's world."

"That's not how Becca sees it."

"Trust me. It's the right thing to do."

He puckered his lips. "You sure you've thought this all the way through?"

I looked down and tapped my toes together. "Of course not. But I have a strong feeling. And my strong feelings don't get any less strong."

At all.

He mulled it over for a moment, then cocked his head, a sign of reluctant acceptance. "Does Becca know?"

322

I nodded.

"Did she flip out?"

"Initially, but she gets it."

He made a slow nod. "I'm impressed you were able to calm her down. Say what you will about tenth-grade girls, they're a force to be reckoned with. Criminally underrated."

When I saw the way he was looking at me, I had a hunch he wasn't just talking about his sister. And then he scooted his stool a little closer, and closer, and closer still.

No, he definitely wasn't.

This book would not have been possible without my unfailingly excellent editor, Krista Marino.

And futhermore, thanks to the Fall Café Mafia, Christy Fletcher, Ben Greenman, Errol Louis, Barbara Pym, Tim Rostron, Seth Lipsky, Ben Schrank, Eben Shapiro, the 111 State Society, and, most of all, to MHxx.

Tobias Everke

LAUREN MECHLING is the coauthor of all three 10th-Grade Social Climber books as well as the author of the first book about Claire Voyante, *Dream Girl*. She is an editor at the *Wall Street Journal* and lives and writes in New York City. You can visit her at www.laurenmechling.com.